Helen MacInnes' suspense novels are bestsellers throughout the world. Millions of copies of her books have been sold and readers everywhere wait eagerly for her new masterpieces. "In her field she is a master. In fact she may well be *the* master."

—CLIFTON FADIMAN

Fawcett Crest Books
by Helen MacInnes:

TO GILBERT

June 22, 1954

Pray for a brave heart, which does not fear death,
which places a long life last among the gifts
of nature, which has the power to endure any trials,
rejects anger, discards desire. . . .
If we have common sense, Chance, you are not divine:
it is we who make you a goddess, yes, and place you in
    heaven.

—JUVENAL 10. 357-360, 365-366.

HELEN MacINNES

Pray for a Brave Heart

FAWCETT CREST • NEW YORK

"Just foot-loose as usual," Max Meyer said, pulling off his black coat and then looking round for a free chair. "Charming bit of chaos you've got here, Bill. Taking an inventory?"

"Don't let it bother you. I'm almost packed."

"So I see. Now, don't start clearing a space for me—you'd better keep your system intact. Here's a free spot, anyway." He dropped his hat and coat on the floor. "Good to see you, Bill."

"Good to see you."

They clasped hands.

"Two years, almost, since I was last here," Meyer said, wandering across the room. "June, 1951, to be precise. What happens to time these days?" He picked up Denning's empty glass and sniffed it. "Any more where this came from? I've a thirst I wouldn't sell for twenty dollars."

"The price used to be ten," Bill Denning said with a grin. He went to the cupboard and brought out all the remaining bottles of beer.

"Cost of living is rising." Meyer sat down in the armchair with a sigh of relief and studied his flimsy shoes. "Can you imagine it, Bill?—Some people actually choose this kind of clothes, of their own free will." He gestured with distaste to his sharp-shouldered, waist-nipped jacket, its gray color too silvered, its pin-stripe black and emphatic. His blue shirt had horizontal stripes of white, cuffs too long, a deeply peaked collar stiffly angled around the tight knot of his black artificial satin tie. His chin was blue-shadowed. His dark hair needed cutting, but he kept it plastered back with plenty of brilliantine. Only the hawklike, inquiring nose and the fine brown eyes, now watching Denning with amusement, were recognizably Max Meyer. "Go on," he said encouragingly.

"I didn't say anything."

"You didn't have to." Meyer took the offered glass of beer and propped his feet wearily on a pile of magazines. "Now stop jeering, and sympathize."

"You look like a man who'd have a stolen car to help him get around." Denning was studying Meyer's clothes with interest.

"I have, actually. But tonight was definitely pedestrian. To you, Bill!" Meyer drank thankfully. "And continue packing. I like seeing other people work."

"That's part of your new character?" Denning brought over some more bottles of beer and stacked them near the armchair. "Interesting company you must be keeping these days, Major."

"A half-colonel, my boy, and don't forget it."

"A half-intelligent colonel? Congratulations. But be careful. Or you'll end up as one of those damn-fool colonels we used to curse." He enlarged a space on the floor with his foot—that was easier than clearing a chair piled with clean shirts—and sat down with his back against a wall.

Meyer studied his friend. *"You* look fine, anyhow. And you stayed with Restitution of Property up to the last?"

"We recovered most of the Nazi loot. There are still a few outstanding items, though. I guess we'll have to file them under *Failures."*

"Will we?" There was a sudden gleam in Meyer's eyes. Then he began examining the white embroidered arrows on his black artificial silk socks, and was very silent.

"Recently, I've been doing some interrogation of displaced persons," Denning went on. "I thought we might get some leads from them, but—" He watched Meyer, who seemed scarcely to be listening. I remember that look, Denning thought: Max is getting ready to tell me something important, in his own way, in his own time.

"But no dice?"

"I got more interested in people than in property," Denning admitted. "What we need now is a new department— the Restitution of Lives."

"And you've started restituting your own?" Meyer waved his hand vaguely toward the trunk.

"What's wrong with that?"

"Nothing. Not a bad idea, not bad at all. And yet, you know, I've often wondered why you did stick with the old Restitution of Property when it became practically moribund."

"Just naturally stubborn, I suppose."

"Or you don't like seeing crooks getting away with their crookery?"

Denning looked up in surprise. There had been an edge to Meyer's usually soft, almost lazy voice.

Meyer said, his tone normal again, "I've always thought it was a pity you didn't come into counter-intelligence with me a couple of years ago. We'd have made a damned good team. As we always did."

Denning lit a cigarette. His cool gray eyes watched his friend with some amusement over the flame of his lighter.

1: Meeting in Berlin

ON THE NARROW BED LAY TWO UNIFORMS, AN army greatcoat, a stack of khaki shirts and socks. The table, holding a neat small pile of civilian clothes, was jammed against one wall to give more space for an open trunk and a clutter of books on the floor. Letters and pencils and odd sheets of paper, stamps, bits and pieces of old erasers, pens broken and pens usable, had been emptied from the desk drawer on top of the blotter. The traveling clock, pushing its face through a tangle of ties and handkerchiefs, gave quiet warning that the evening was slipping away. But William Denning, sleeves rolled up, a smudge of dust streaking his brow, stood at the window and watched the street lights go on, bringing his last night in Berlin.

He was a quiet-faced man, with watchful gray eyes, even features, and brown hair trimmed close. His height was average, his body thin; but his shoulders were good and his tight army shirt (with captain's insignia on its collar) stretched across firm muscles. He looked like a capable man, self-disciplined, serious, older than his thirty-three years. At this moment, by himself, his face was relaxed. His eyes were amused. The usual firm line of his mouth had eased into a smile.

The hurrying people down in the street had hurried along there yesterday, would hurry tomorrow. They always seemed the same, as anonymous as the row of buildings opposite him. Buildings? Someone called them apartments, even called them home. "All right, all right," he told the street, "I'm a stranger here, a stranger who lived four years with you. Go on, give me one kind word, one first and last kind word." But the street was too busy. At least, he thought, it would be easy to say good-by. He had been neither happy nor unhappy in this room: he had no deep memories of this place. Was this the best he could hope for, now?

He drew the curtains, switched on the reading lamp by his armchair, and poured himself some beer. Then he sat down, studying the art magazines. What about this lot on sculpture and architecture? Good illustrations, they'd probably come in useful, back numbers were always difficult to get; better pack them for New York. Now what about these others? Leave them, he decided, and tossed them lightly onto a growing pyramid of books and magazines in front of his chair.

Next, he reached for the books piled on the small table at his elbow. Those three were just surplus weight: he threw them onto the pyramid. But these—no doubt about these, they'd go back home to America along with the magazines. He finished his beer, and began carrying his selection toward the trunk. He frowned down at the layer of shoes and books, already tightly packed. It was then that the doorbell rang, briefly, gently.

Denning's frown deepened and he glanced impatiently at his watch. But he dropped his load into the trunk, and opened the door. Outside, the landing was in darkness. What had happened to the lights? he wondered, and then stared at the figure which took a quick step from the darkness toward the open door. As Denning's shoulders straightened, the stranger smiled, made a gesture of caution, and flicked his thumb against the drooping brim of his hat so that it snapped back to show his deep-set eyes and prominent brow. Just as quickly, he glanced back over the well of the staircase, seemed satisfied with the silent hallway beneath him, and slipped into the room.

Denning closed and locked the door. "Max! What are you doing in Berlin?"

Contents

"All right, all right," Meyer said, sharing the amusement. "So you're going to Switzerland for your terminal leave?" He pointed to the table which held civilian clothes. "Right?"

"Frankfurt knows a damn sight more about Berlin than Berlin knows about Frankfurt," Denning remarked dryly.

But Meyer kept right on. "What's your first stop in Switzerland?"

"Basel."

"Are you serious? Basel? Why on earth Basel?"

"Holbein."

"Yes, of course. Hans Holbein. Renaissance art was your field, wasn't it?"

Denning said nothing at all. He was enjoying himself, watching Max and his maneuvers. Max ought to have been a diplomat, he thought: that was certainly Max's field, handling light remarks and delicate tangents with equal skill while he steadily pursued his own purpose.

Max Meyer cleared his throat. "Why don't you go on packing while we talk? You've made me feel guilty, using up your last hours in Germany. You didn't have a party all arranged for tonight, by any chance?"

Denning shook his head. "Don't worry, I'm practically ready." Then, suddenly, he found himself looking at Peggy's photograph on the bureau. For a moment, he was no longer in this room. He was four years back. In Princeton, working for a Fine Arts degree on the GI Bill. Living in the cramped little apartment that seemed a pretty fine place to him. And Peggy—Peggy getting ready for a special party while he waited, all dressed, nervous about the evening ahead at the Dean's house, glancing at his watch, fifteen minutes to go and they were supposed to be sitting down to dinner. And Peggy coming out of the bathroom, her face powdered, her hair arranged, but without a stitch of clothing on. Peggy saying earnestly, "Now, Bill, darling, don't look so worried. I'm practically ready!"

"I'm practically ready," he repeated to Meyer; and he looked away from the photograph. Yes, he thought, I can now remember Peggy: once, I couldn't even trust myself to do that. He became aware that Max was watching him. "What is it, Max?" he asked defensively. "What is it you want me to do?"

Max Meyer looked at him blankly.

"You didn't come here tonight to talk me again into another hitch in the army, did you? It's too late, anyway. I'm going back to pick up my own work where it was all broken off."

"Take it easy, Bill, take it easy." Meyer poured himself some more beer. "I think you're right, perfectly right in what you're doing. I only hope you don't regret listening to my advice in 1949 when I persuaded you back into Germany."

"No. That was the right idea then. It worked out."

"I've often wondered." And worried, too, Meyer thought.

"It worked out." Denning looked again at Peggy's photograph, then he searched in his pocket for his cigarettes. "You don't, do you?" He offered the crumpled pack politely.

"Still don't use them. You've a good memory, Bill."

"That has its drawbacks." Denning's face was a quiet mask.

"Look," Meyer said suddenly, "when do you leave for Switzerland? Tomorrow, isn't it?"

"Tomorrow." Denning's smile came back. "And you probably know the train I'm taking, too."

"You'll enter Switzerland by Basel."

"That's the general idea."

"Couldn't I interest you in Bern instead? It's less than two hours further south. Surely, there's *some* Renaissance art in Bern too. Wasn't there a fellow called Nicolas Manuel who did a good altarpiece there?"

Denning's smile broadened. "1515 is the date. I see you've been doing your homework. But I hate to spoil it—Manuel's best paintings are in Basel."

Meyer ignored that, and pointed to the bag of golf clubs leaning against the table. "And if you want to balance museums with the great outdoors, there's a golf course near Bern. Now, Basel has only—"

"Come on, Max. You've baited the hook. What are you fishing for? You want me in Bern. Why?"

"For the last six weeks, you've been tidying up your office, clearing the IN trays, briefing your replacement, answering friendly questions about your future plans. All routine. All perfectly normal. Everyone expects you to be doing just what you're doing. Right?"

"Right." So that's my cover, Denning thought.

"You and I have worked together, before, tracking down Nazi loot. How many of our original team do you think are still around?"

"You, and I, and a couple of others." So that's my necessary experience, Denning thought now.

"That's just about it. Eight years ago, there were hundreds of us. Today? They're back home, being lawyers or teachers or art critics or insurance brokers."

"Smart fellows."

"Even you and I haven't been working together for some years, now," Meyer went on smoothly.

"That's right," Denning said with mock cheerfulness. "That makes me contact-pure."

Meyer studied his face. "What I like most about you, Bill, is that I just tell you—I don't have to explain."

"Well, before you tell me any more, I think you should get one thing straight. I'm a civilian now. Practically."

Meyer could have said, "You're still under orders until you're finally separated from the army." But he didn't. He studied the back of his hands. "Don't worry, Bill. I didn't go to your command and plead special emergency and get your leave postponed. I've come to you, yourself, as the almost-civilian. The choice is yours. You're free to refuse. Besides, I wouldn't want your help unless you were really interested."

"Interested in what?"

"Think back to 1946 . . . just before you left the army—"

"Twice in the army and twice out. Don't I get a medal or something?"

"Think back," Meyer said, refusing to be humorous about it, "think back to the Nazi loot we were tracking down."

"I'm thinking." But Denning's actual thoughts were more sober than his words. Nazi loot. Mass plunder. Everything from museum pieces to gold teeth. Church bells, acres of church bells stolen from Belgium and Poland. Medical instruments from Dutch hospitals. Silk-mill machinery from Lyons. Prize cows. Libraries. Furs. Everything, anything, that could be sneaked or ripped out. Even that truckload of baby clothes which the British discovered, emptied out of Amsterdam stores and shipped eastward with the retreating Nazis. "It all seems incredible now," Denning said grimly. "But it's still more incredible that we did find so much to hand back to the right owners." He was thinking of the hiding places: deserted quarries, salt mines, warehouses, factory yards, railway sidings, pleasant gardens, quiet fields, peaceful cottages. His lip curled with distaste as he remembered the protests and outraged indignation when the stolen property had been recovered: the honest-faced farmer who swore the collection of rare sixteenth-century books belonged in his barn, no matter what the bookplates said about a Danish doctor; the factory girl, denying anything unusual in possessing three silver-fox capes from Norway, a gold Cellini snuffbox from Czechoslovakia, and twenty-four dozen pairs of silk stockings from France; the placid housewife, aroused to fury over the lies that the Luxembourgers were telling—why, those paintings had been in her grandmother's parlor.

Meyer nodded. "But we didn't find everything. Such as nice portable pieces of property, easily hidden, intensely valuable. Do you remember the Herz diamonds, the Delval emeralds, the Dyckman jade collection? Considerable fortunes, all of them."

"Three for the file marked *Failures*." Something stirred in Denning's memory. "Gentleman Goering lifted them, didn't he?"

"Yes. But once the war was over, we couldn't find them. They vanished, into air, into thin air."

"Or into neat leather bags buried under some potato patch."

"The British searched their Zone. We searched. The French searched—but madly."

"Oh yes, I remember now. . . . The Herz collection belongs to France."

"The owner having died at Dachau, his daughter in Ravensbrück, and every known relative in Auschwitz. The Nazis were thorough."

"I suppose the Russians searched, too?"

"They assured us there was no sign of Goering's precious stones. They assured us three times, and then even I ran out of ideas how to ask them again, politely.

"You didn't risk sending any of your own men into East Germany?"

"We've had all kinds of fun and games," Max said soberly. "Some of them weren't very amusing, either. Then," he studied his over-decorated shoes with distate, "I was taken off the job in 1948. Someone higher up was persuaded it was all a waste of time."

"Was persuaded?" Denning echoed. "You mean that literally?"

Meyer shrugged his shoulders.

Denning said, "And who put you back on the job?"

Meyer stared. Then he smiled. "I like you, Bill. I like you very much."

"But you've moved out of Restitution of Property. I don't see why—" He hesitated.

"Why I've started being interested again?"

Denning said, "I don't suppose you ever stopped being interested. But—" he hesitated again—"why not let it all rest, Max? Especially," he added, "especially when diamonds and emeralds are just a lot of decorative glitter." He rose, stretching his back muscles stiffly, and started hunting for more cigarettes.

Meyer watched him as he searched under the ties on the bureau. He said quietly, "I don't suppose anyone who has been working with displaced persons, as you've been doing recently, feels much interest in glitter. Not even in three million dollars' worth of Herz diamonds."

"You're damn well right," Denning said. He found the cigarettes and tore open the pack roughly.

"But what will the glitter buy? That's something else again."

Denning lit a cigarette and walked over to the window.

"There are people, you know, who will pay a fortune willingly for the Herz collection." Meyer's low voice came softly across the room. "No questions asked about how the money will be used. But that's what interests us, Bill: just how will the money be used?"

"How?" Denning pulled back the folds of the heavy curtain, and looked down into the prim street with its row of placid gray buildings now retreating into black shadows, remote and cold under the sparse street lights. People still walked down there, fewer in number, more slowly, but with the same preoccupation in their own lives.

"If someone wanted to finance a secret project, then the possession of the Herz collection would be doubly valuable. No one suspects its existence: everyone agrees it was a casualty of the war, buried too well, forgotten, probably to be discovered by some astounded farmer a hundred years from now. So the secret sale of the Herz diamonds could start a huge hidden fund. The Dyckman jade would add to it. So would the Delval emeralds. Yes: it would grow into a sizable fund."

Denning let the curtain fall back into place before he answered. "For what?"

"For the buying of men's minds. It costs money to finance treachery."

For a moment Denning said nothing. "Then I'd double my advice about giving up your search. Leave the glitter buried safely under the potato patch."

"I wish we could."

Denning came back into the center of the room, and stood there, watching Meyer.

"The Herz diamonds are moving out of Europe," Meyer said.

"What?"

"Moving, secretly. Much too secretly."

"But where?"

"Destination ultimately America, we are told. They will be smuggled skillfully. Sold discreetly. And the secret fund will be established. Or reinforced. To be used—" Meyer shrugged his shoulders.

"Against us?"

"It certainly won't be used to aid and comfort us."

Denning reached for a chair, emptied its contents onto the floor, and then bestrode it. He said thoughtfully, "And who's behind all this?"

"Whoever was in a position to find the diamonds."

"Is that all you can tell me?"

"For the moment, yes. Except that it's a major operation, obviously."

"How did you find out about the Herz collection?"

"That's one of the ironies of our jobs, Bill. For years I've worked on this problem. Results: zero. Then, three days ago, suddenly, a man came to see me in Frankfurt. Quietly. A frightened little man."

"An informer?" Denning spoke the word without enthusiasm.

"If it weren't for informers, the jails would be half-empty, and murderers would walk free," Meyer replied calmly. "Ask any policeman, Bill."

"I know, I know." Denning was impatient. "But can you trust this man?"

"I wouldn't exactly throw my arms around him and kiss him on the brow, but I'd listen to what he has to tell. An informer and his information are two quite separate things. You don't have to stroke the bee to get the honey."

"He isn't just one of those types who want a little publicity?"

Meyer was suddenly amused. "Hardly. He's a jewel thief, Bill."

Denning looked startled.

"He's one of a syndicate, a very minor member," Meyer continued, enjoying the moment thoroughly. "Actually, it was his boss who sent him to tell me what *their* intelligence service had discovered. Amusing, isn't it?"

"In a sour kind of way." Then, thoughtfully, Denning said, "How do you rate their intelligence?"

"Judge for yourself. Here's their information. First, the diamonds have moved out of East Germany. Second, they have already reached as far south as Switzerland. Third, they are to be smuggled out of Europe, probably by way of Genoa. Fourth, the flat price is three million American dollars, cash on the barrelhead."

Denning considered all that. "If this syndicate is any good at its own specialty, why don't they steal the diamonds before they leave Europe?"

"Because they've discovered that the organization which is moving the diamonds is more powerful than they are. Much more powerful."

"And I suppose we are to take action—"

"We haven't much choice, have we? Genoa worries us. Naturally. Next stop, New York."

"—and once we've controlled the situation, they will take the diamonds before the French can get them. Is that the idea?"

"I shouldn't be surprised. We're the simple-minded Americans. Once we stop the diamonds from reaching New York, we lose interest. That's what the jewel thieves expect, anyhow. Naïve characters, in their own way."

"So that's why they came to you, and not to the French?"

"They refuse to give any information to the French."

"Somehow, I don't feel this is very complimentary to us. Who is the head of the syndicate?"

"Nikolaides, a Bulgarian possibly, or probably Greek descent, now a French citizen." Meyer gave a wave of his hand, dispensing with Nikolaides. "He isn't important to us, except that he sent Charles-Auguste with that startling information."

"Charles-Auguste who?"

"Maartens. Charles-Auguste Maartens. Let's call him

Charlie for short. I'm meeting him in Bern. Thursday night. Eleven o'clock."

"And he's scared?" A frightened little man, Denning remembered.

"He's scared stiff."

"I don't like it, Max," Denning said slowly. "I don't like it one bit. You're meeting this man, yourself?"

"That's the arrangement he made. I wasn't in any position to argue with him." Meyer grinned suddenly. "That's my general excuse. Between us, I just want to close the file on the Herz collection—personally."

"What do you expect to find out from him?"

"The sailing date from Genoa. That, at the very least." Meyer didn't elaborate. He went on, "We're meeting at the Café Henzi."

Denning frowned, trying to place the café. "Where is it?" he had to ask.

"It's just off the Kramgasse, north of the cheese market. It's popular with tourists. Strange how they always like to eat and drink near an open market place: makes them feel the food must be good, I suppose."

"I could reach Bern by Thursday morning," Denning said. That would give him the day to wander around the Lower Town, time to make sure of the Café Henzi.

Meyer's face relaxed. He said quietly, "That would be fine, Bill." Then, watching Denning's thoughtful eyes, he added, "Don't start worrying about the details. You won't be in the Café Henzi, anyway."

Denning looked up swiftly. "You're meeting Charlie by yourself? Alone?" He shook his head. "That's really tricky, Max. Very tricky."

"It will be easy," Meyer assured him, "compared with these last three days. God!" He sighed wearily. "I've been checking on Charlie-for-Short,"—he pointed to his clothes— "I've started some of our people doing research on Boss Nikolaides and his syndicate. I got one of our men, Taylor, to make a journey to Munich and contact Le Brun of the French Intelligence. I got another to meet Johann Keppler who's in Swiss Security. And neither Boss Nikolaides, nor the group that is moving the diamonds, had to have the least suspicion that we were doing any of that."

"I must say you're a fair example of the simple-minded American. Nikolaides *will* be disappointed with you."

Meyer grinned cheerfully. "To hell with men like Niko-laides. He uses me, so all right, I'll use him."

"I can imagine the feelings of the French if you had hidden this news from them," Denning said dryly. "Or of the Swiss, who must be pretty tired of having their peaceful country used by other people for their secret skirmishes."

Meyer nodded, and rose. He smoothed down his trousers, pulled at his coat. "Too damned tight," he observed critically.

"Très chic, très snob, presque cad," Denning consoled him. "But I still feel the overcoat is a mistake."

Meyer said, "Black and shapeless as the shadows. It has its merits. I take it off before I enter the cellar café. In the streets—I prefer to be undistinguished. Sometimes not even a friend of Charlie's." He moved over to pick up his criticized coat. "I hope I look just one of the little men—sporad-ically affluent. Now, if I were mixing with the upper echelons, such as Boss Nikolaides, I'd have monograms and caviar all over my shirt front."

"Real *black* caviar, daddy? The kind whose dye doesn't come off?"

"One more crack out of you, son, and I'll promote you to carrying my gold toothpick."

Denning said, in a thick accent, "Enoff of thiss foolish laugh-making. Where do I stay in Bern, blast you?"

"Try the Aarhof. Reasonable. Respectable. Not too far from the station."

"That may be useful, for a quick exit."

"I hope you won't need that kind of usefulness," Meyer said, his voice now completely serious. "Take it easy, won't you, Bill? Just travel as you planned, and enjoy yourself. Have fun."

"Sure. Almost," Denning reminded him.

"Golf clubs, camera, and all. Don't pretend anything. You still know me, in case anyone should inquire. But you just haven't seen me for a couple of years."

"You're desk-bound in Frankfurt," Denning agreed; "and how shall I get in touch with you?"

"I'll let Keppler, the Swiss Security man, arrange that. He knows Bern's possibilities. Once I've met Charlie at the Café Henzi, we'd all better get together—you and Le Brun and Keppler and I. And then, you can deliver my report, word for word, in case I have to go jet-propelled off to Genoa."

"I hope you aren't relying on me alone—" Denning began quickly.

"Oh, I'll have other reinforcements," Meyer said quickly. "I hope," he added. Then he smiled grimly. "Perhaps I'll be busted right down to a lieutenant without either hyphen or colonel, next time we meet." He studied the floor at his feet for a long moment. "I'm too vague for you, Bill?" he asked suddenly.

"I don't suppose it's wise to be more specific."

"Actually," Meyer struggled into his coat, "I've told you more than I've told any one man. I've turned in a full report, of course, so that I'll get some backing and proper action. But a report is a report." He faced Denning suddenly. "Remember my regrettably emotional outburst earlier this evening? 'For the buying of men's minds,' I think I said. How would that look in a report? Yet I meant it. I know I'm right. But how would it look?"

"Regrettably emotional."

"You can imagine some poor guy, just below the policy-making level, scratching it out and substituting 'presumably for propaganda purposes.' Then the next man to read it murmurs, 'Oh, not those dreary peace-front meetings; not those mimeographed appeals, all over again.' "

Denning's face showed the shadow of embarrassment. He had translated Meyer's phrase about buying men's minds on that same pedestrian level.

But if Meyer noticed he had scored sharply, he didn't say. He went on, quietly, "By the time the report reached the policy makers, it would be as weak as China tea, watered down until a three-day-old baby could drink it."

Denning dusted off Meyer's hat and held it out. "I'll be your report. And I don't water down easily."

"That's what I want, Bill." Meyer smiled suddenly. "When we meet in Bern, I'll be able to fill in a lot of gaps for you." He frowned at the floor again.

"Forgotten something?" Denning asked. He knew Meyer's difficulty: to tell enough, without telling too much. Only the complete necessary facts had been given, and now Max was reviewing them, worried in case he had left out something small but vital.

"Recently, in my own job," Meyer said slowly, "I've—" Then he stopped short. What he had discovered during the last three weeks wasn't proved yet. Perhaps there was no connection after all with the money which the diamonds would bring. He looked at Denning. "Never mind about that—it's just something I'm going to work on, once I finish this business with Charlie. It may all connect." He gripped Denning's arm and moved to the door. "One thing I did forget," he said lightly. "About Keppler. Don't be alarmed if he sends you messages signed Elizabeth. He's definitely well-adjusted."

And with that, he was at the door, pausing, listening, and then opening it. Just as quickly, as silently, it closed behind him.

For a long moment, Denning stood quite motionless. He could hear nothing at all. He resisted a foolish impulse to switch off the lights and go over to the window. In the quiet street below, two cars passed.

Then he moved slowly over to the bureau. He straightened Peggy's photograph. He stayed there with it, his hand on the leather frame, his eyes thoughtful. There was something more to all this than Max had been able to tell him. He remembered the grim look on Meyer's face—*just something I'm going to work on, once I finish this business with Charlie. It may all connect.* And he remembered, too, that Max Meyer's instinct for connecting odd facts had never yet failed him. He wished, suddenly, that Meyer's instinct for self-preservation was as keenly developed. His eyes looked at Peggy for a moment. He thought, what have I to lose now, anyway?

The clock said it was almost midnight. Briskly, he turned to face the room, saw confusion worse than he had imagined, cursed crisply, and began jamming his gear into his trunk. The time for decisions was over.

2: *Arrival in Bern*

THERE HAD BEEN AN EARLY SHOWER OF RAIN, just enough to add a polish to the clean streets, but now the sky was blue with white friendly clouds chasing each other high above the pointed roofs and sharp steeples of Bern.

The Aarhof on the Spitalgasse was a medium-sized hotel, efficient and comfortable even from the outside. Like the other buildings in the street, with which it formed a continuous row, its first floor consisted of arches (the Aarhof had five) leading from the curb into the arcade that covered the whole stretch of sidewalk. Above the arches were four floors of ten tall windows, slightly shortening as they reached the broad overhang from the red-tiled roof. And every window, like all the other windows in this street, like most windows in all the streets, had its green box of bright red geraniums.

Eminently respectable, Bill Denning decided as he stepped out of the Aarhof's small bus which had brought him in solitary magnificence from the station. And he recalled, with some nostalgia, the little hotel in the Lower Town where he had once spent a couple of nights. Switzerland was one of the few countries where you could have a cheap room under the eaves, overlooking a seventeenth-century courtyard, without forcing yourself to ignore a delicate smell of sewage or a welcoming bedbug between the sheets. But it seemed ungrateful in a way to regret his promotion to a five-arch hotel. It could have been much more painful: he could have drawn one of those three-hundred-bed affairs where the feeling of afternoon tea under the potted palms still hung over the lobby at breakfast time, and it would only take a mild swaying of the floor to make you think you were trapped in the lounge of an Atlantic liner. And he took some comfort, before he stepped into the cool shadow of the arcade, that in the middle of the street behind him there stood, on top of a geranium-ringed fountain, a figure out of Breughel, a red-smocked bagpiper with cheeks puffed out and a goose for his audience.

The clerk behind the reception desk in the highly polished lobby, stirring into life even at this early hour, was polite and discreet. Certainly, a room for Mr. William Denning. With bath. And a view of the fountain?

Denning nodded and went on filling up the necessary forms. For a moment he wondered if the clerk had expected his arrival; then he decided that the hushed voice was only the man's well-practiced manner. He signed his name and glanced round the lobby. Beside him there was the hotel porter's desk with a busy clerk handing out mail and information, keys and theater tickets. The voices, some speaking French and Italian as well as German, reminded him that Bern was the capital where Parliament met and the three languages were all equally used. And over there stood four American soldiers, on furlough, studying a map. Near them was an English businessman who had brought along his wife—probably smuggling her out with the help of his expense account, and now wondering why he hadn't had the good sense to leave her at home. Beside the dining-room door stood another group of foreigners, three pink-cheeked round-faced clergymen in tweed jackets and dog collars. And that French couple were on their honeymoon. And the cluster of bored schoolgirls were pretending they didn't belong to the severely tailored, slightly flustered teacher who was trying to organize an excursion. Yes, this was an ideally normal hotel. Respectable, to the point of being soporific.

"Of course," said the reception clerk, noticing Denning's brief inspection, "the season has not quite begun as yet." He was a young man, with intense eyes and an expression of automatic attentiveness.

Denning said, with a smile, "Tell me, where does Bern grow all its geraniums?" He looked at a mass of flowers on the central table of the lobby, as he took a step away from the desk.

"Ah," said the clerk, and relaxed. Mr. Denning had only been admiring the decorations. He plunged into a detailed explanation about the geraniums, and Mr. Denning was most gratifyingly surprised, perhaps a little overwhelmed, for he halted, and stood quite silent, and didn't ask any more questions, not even after the final details were given. Then another new guest arrived, and Mr. Denning moved away very quickly.

With a feeling of delightful well-being, the clerk turned to deal with the latest customer—a middle-aged gentleman, small, plump, dressed in very smart new clothes. Almost too new, the clerk thought, but definitely expensive: where could he find a suiting like that, at a reasonable price, of course?

"Certainly," he said, giving his full attention now to the sprawling signature, quickly scribbled. Certainly. A room for Mr. Charles A. Maartens. With bath. And a view of the fountain?

One thing I've learned, Denning decided as he followed the installation clerk along the corridor to his room, one thing: next time I make a small joke, I'll avoid putting it in the form of a question. And another thing to remember is that the clerk has quick eyes. Perhaps I was too obvious; or was I? Any stranger looks round a hotel lobby to see what kind of place he has chosen.

And yet, even as he reassured himself, he was left with a small doubt. Now you are being overanxious, he told himself, just as your pride was too quick down there in the lobby. You were too eager to see how Max Meyer imagined you: this was the kind of hotel where you'd merge into the general background. Do you? Sweet, suffering—and then he began to smile at himself, and his quick irritation with Max was over. What we think we are, how our friends see us—that contrast was always a slight shock. Like suddenly catching a glimpse of yourself in an unexpected mirror in a frank light.

He stared at himself in the looking glass over the white-covered dressing table. He needed a shave, a shower, some rest to chase away the grime and discomfort of an overnight train journey. He needed a lot more than that, he thought grimly, to look like a human being again. Then he noticed the clerk had gone and the green-aproned boy who had brought his luggage was waiting politely.

"Ever look in a mirror and think what an ugly—" Denning began, and then choked his question abruptly off. No more jokes in the form of questions.

The boy, dark-haired, with a long thin face and anxious eyes, said, "Please?"

"Can I have some rolls and coffee?"

"Here, sir?"

No, in the elevator. "Yes, here, if it can be managed," Denning said with considerable restraint. He reached into his pocket and counted out a tip, nervous a little with the unaccustomed money. He added an extra ten per cent to take care of the probable increase in the cost of living since his last visit. Damn the man who had invented tips. Or was it damn the first employer who had skimped on wages? "Is this all right?" he asked frankly.

"Sure," said the boy in impeccable American, breaking away from the German they had both been using.

"You have a lot of Americans staying here?"

"Plenty."

"So it sounds. Well, I'll be taking a shower, so just leave the coffee—" Then Denning's eyes counted the pieces of luggage: a suitcase, golf clubs. "Where's my small bag?" He gestured with his hands to show the size of his grip.

The boy looked startled, then crestfallen. "It must have been left downstairs, sir," he said in German. "I'll get it immediately."

"You'd better," Denning told him with a grin. "It holds my razor and my clean shirts."

"I'll get it," said the boy reassuringly. "Don't worry, sir."

"And hurry up that coffee, will you?"

"Yes, sir," the boy said, smiling too, breaking into English again. He paused at the door to say, "My name is Gustav. I'm in charge of this floor. Anything you need—"

"—I'll call on you." Denning began sliding out the knot of his tie. "Meanwhile, coffee, coffee, for the love of Allah."

Gustav gave a startled look at Denning, and then closed the door. Or rather, both doors. For there were two, as in most Swiss hotels: one shutting in the room, one shutting out the corridor, with a brief threshold between them. I'll have some privacy here, thought Denning with considerable satisfaction.

Denning had his shirt off, when a quiet knock sounded on his room door. That's Gustav with my bag, he thought, and called, "Come in, come in." But a round-faced woman, crisply dressed in blue, with towels over her arm, entered.

"Excuse me, sir." She didn't retreat, but left both doors tactfully open as she hurried over to the bathroom. "Would you like me to run your bath?"

"Don't bother," Denning said. "I think I've still got strength enough left for that."

"Please?"

But just then, he heard an angry voice outside his room. A small procession passed along the corridor. First, a dapper little figure in a silver-gray suit, who was talking peremptorily over his shoulder to two boys laden with luggage, followed by a polite, persevering, but breathless Gustav. "It's all mine, I tell you, such stupidity, it's all mine," the man's precise voice was saying with increasing annoyance as he hurried his short steps.

Denning moved swiftly into the corridor. "Just a minute," he told one of the green-aproned boys, "I think you've got my bag mixed up with that stuff."

The procession halted.

Gustav, red-faced and still breathing heavily from all the running he had done, said, "The hall porter told me it must be—"

But the little man broke in with "What's this? What's this?" He gave Denning's naked chest a withering glance.

"I think," said Denning, his face expressionless, "I think this is my bag." He pointed to one of the smaller grips.

"Are you sure?" The man had realized Denning was right, but he wouldn't admit his mistake too quickly. He looked at the label on Denning's bag. "Let me see. . . ."

"Yes, let us see," Denning said shortly and flipped over a label on one of the other small bags. *Charles A. Maartens,* he read. The man looked at him angrily.

Denning could only hope that neither surprise nor confusion had shown in his face. He glanced along the corridor where two stray schoolgirls had halted, wide-eyed, surprised into a giggling match. He stepped quickly back into the shelter of his room. From there, he heard Mr. Charles A.

Maartens' high-pitched voice say, "Idiot! Take this bag away. Why don't you pay attention?"

Gustav, his face red once more—but this time not from running—brought the offending bag into Denning's room.

"That's fine," Denning said, "and don't worry, Gustav. It wasn't your mistake."

The boy wasn't much comforted. "He doesn't know German very well." Gustav was trying to excuse his hotel's new guest. "That's why the gentleman did not understand me at first."

"I've run the bath, sir," the chambermaid said with conscious virtue, coming out of the bathroom. "If there's anything you need—" She frowned at Gustav and fluttered her hand, which had been pointing to the bell, angrily toward the corridor. They both left, and the woman—now speaking in a quick rush of Bernese German—was asking Gustav if he didn't know everyone was arriving today, everyone, and there was so much to do, if he had time to waste then he'd better help her count pillowcases and hand towels.

Denning looked at his bag. That possessive little character in the pearl-gray suit had almost set him doubting. But it was his bag, all right. It wasn't locked, though. He searched quickly through it. The contents were all in order. Seemingly. Except that Peggy's photograph had shifted, and now lay under, instead of over, his handkerchiefs. Someone had been checking on him. A friend?

He looked round the room, thinking of Meyer again. It was an efficient, comfortable, and antiseptic box. Quiet, restrained to the point of anonymity. That polished brass bed with its white starched cover had welcomed more schoolteachers, businessmen, curious tourists, nervous honeymooners, than jewel thieves and crooks. This hotel was hardly promising territory for Maartens. Or perhaps that was what he wanted at the moment—an unobtrusive place to hang his pearl-gray suit until this evening. But why—if it was complete anonymity he wanted—why use his name so openly? That, of course, could be part of his present stage setting: the innocent visitor with a few days to spend in Bern. Denning, too, was concealing nothing about himself, beyond the fact that Max Meyer had enlisted his sympathies and brought him into the game. And yet—and yet—Denning wasn't *in* this game, the way Charlie-for-Short was involved. Charlie-for-Short. . . . Not a particularly happy nickname. Charles-the-

Bold would have been better. Perhaps, he thought as he half-opened the long narrow windows and looked down into the street over two green window boxes with red geraniums, perhaps Max is slipping a little. Once, when Max labeled anyone, the name stuck just because its aptness had a glue that didn't flake off.

There was a good deal of bustle, now, down in the street. Low gears, sudden brakings of cars; footsteps echoing because of the arcades; a trolley with its high-powered purr; a mixture of creaks and screeches and voices and hard heels mingled together and rose to his window in an ebb and flow as constant as the rhythm of a restless sea. Remember that image, he told himself, and perhaps you'll get some sleep tonight. Then he shivered. Chilly out there, even if it was the end of May. He shut the windows, ending the cold draft, and brought some peace back into the room.

He picked up his shaving kit from his bag and went into the bathroom. The outsize bath on its elaborate dais was nicely full of water turned cold. He cursed all overhelpful women, and let the bath run out. Majestically slow, he noted. He'd have plenty of time to shave. But then he heard his bedroom door being opened, and Gustav's voice was saying, "Breakfast, Herr Denning." So it would be a choice of either a hot bath or hot coffee. He took the bath cold, shallow, and quick. This is one hell of a way to begin a vacation, he thought savagely. And when there was a knock at his door, he wasn't surprised to see it open before he even could swallow a mouthful of roll and clear his throat to yell "Stay out!"

The man who entered probably wouldn't have stayed out in any case. He went straight to the window, carrying two pots of geraniums and a gardening trowel, and wearing an air of dedication.

"Look here," said Denning, "whatever you are about to do, don't! Just leave me in peace with my second cup of coffee. What's the idea anyway?" He drew the bath towel closely around him as the man opened the windows wide. I like fresh air, Denning thought, but this isn't air, it's a howling tornado.

"The geraniums," the man said, a solid-looking type who would make sure of enjoying his own breakfast.

"What about them?"

The man examined the window boxes with an expert eye. He shook his head sadly and muttered to himself in disapproval.

"Couldn't you do them later in the day?" Then Denning looked at the bed where he had thought he might catch up on some sleep. Later in the day might not be such a good idea, after all.

"Excuse me, sir," said the man, paying no attention to him as he neatly troweled the offending plants out of the box and replaced them with the geraniums he had brought. He was a good workman, Denning had to admit, neat and quick; but he had a tuneless way of quietly whistling between his teeth. Denning, drinking his coffee with more determination now than enjoyment, wondered what the man was whistling—just the same eight bars or so, over and over and over again. His musical range was limited. The whistling stopped suddenly, so suddenly that Denning found himself mentally completing the last bars. "Yankee Doodle Dandy," that was all it had been. Another sample of insidious American imperialism like the boy Gustav's "Sure" and "Plenty." Denning almost smiled.

The man closed the windows, and passed near the table to reach the door. He held out the two discarded plants for inspection, as if to justify himself.

To Denning, they looked as fresh as the geraniums which had been carried in. "Yes," he said gravely, "they certainly would have ruined the hotel."

The man nodded, and continued quietly on his way. He opened the door with surprising swiftness. The second door lay wide open, and the maid who liked to run baths ahead of time was just outside. The bedroom door closed firmly.

Denning stared at it, frowning. There had been nothing wrong with the geraniums. He was suddenly sure of that. Warned, he looked down at the table where the man had halted. A neatly folded note lay beside his pack of cigarettes. He laid his hand over them both as the door opened once again.

"Didn't you learn to knock before entering?" he asked the maid sharply. "What is it now?"

"I did knock, sir," the maid said most politely. "I was just checking up. Michel makes such a mess." She bustled to the window.

"Then clear it up later," Denning said. He jammed the small note inside the half-empty pack of cigarettes.

"Yes, sir." But she had checked on the window boxes and the signs of planting. She glanced at the table as she turned back to face the room. Denning was lighting a cigarette. He didn't look at her. He said angrily, "Shut that door. And keep it shut. Both doors. Can you remember that?"

"Yes, sir." She was nervous now, and impressed: he was not only angry, but honestly indignant. "Shall I remove the table now, sir, so that Gustav won't bother you with that?"

Denning nodded and rose, throwing one edge of the bath towel carelessly over his shoulder. "What did the Romans use for pockets?" he wondered aloud.

"Please?" But she had noted his hands were as empty as the slipping folds of his towel. He lifted cigarettes and lighter as she wheeled the table away, and tossed them carelessly on top of the dressing table. He was opening his suitcase, shaking out a tweed jacket and flannels with one hand, holding the towel in place with the other, as the door closed. There was no key in the lock, he noticed. He went on unpacking, letting the towel have its own way now, and there was a good deal of opening of drawers, of moving around, of snatches of whistling. Dressed at last, he found the missing key lying inconspicuously beside the lamp on the bed table. It turned in the lock with a most reassuring click.

At least, now, he had some peace. And he could open the windows without inviting pleurisy.

He picked up the half-empty pack of cigarettes, and extracted the small note from its emergency hiding place. For a moment all this excessive caution embarrassed him. And yet, whoever had sent the note hadn't shown marked trust in either mail clerk or chambermaid.

He smoothed out the many folds of the thin sheet of paper. The handwriting was excited, but the invitation was clear, and the signature, Elizabeth, was ended with rather a schoolgirl flourish. Johann Keppler had enjoyed his invention.

Bill dearest,

I can hardly wait to see you again. As *soon* as *possible*. Tonight? I've found a new room—you'll like it much better than the one we had last time. It's on the little Henziplatz, quiet, very romantic, No. 10, one flight up. I've got to have dinner with the family this evening (groan!) but I can slip away about ten thirty. Darling, darling. Isn't it lovely that spring is here?

Ever,
Elizabeth

First, Denning thought, Keppler isn't wasting much time

in getting us together. Are we to assemble there—Keppler, Le Brun, and myself—right on the Henziplatz, while Max is meeting Charlie-for-Short over at the Café Henzi itself?

Next, Denning thought, Max makes a few detours and then doubles back to join us once the café meeting is over. Audacious but unexpected. I'd vote Keppler as the man most likely to succeed, this or any year.

And then, as he struck his lighter and watched the orange flame curl over the note toward his thumb and forefinger, Denning thought, too bad that the note isn't real. It must be kind of nice to get a hurried letter like that. In the spring. He dropped the burned note into the ash tray.

Then he glanced over at Peggy's photograph on the dressing table. "The thought only slipped out," he told her, smiling broadly.

He was still amused by himself as he carried the ash tray into the bathroom and flushed the black ashes of the little love note down the toilet.

He was excited. He was restless. I'll get some exercise, he decided. A walk through the old streets of the Lower Town, a quiet inspection of the Henziplatz, a visit to the neighboring cheese market or the Minster nearby would combine business with—this feeling of spring. He picked up his brown felt hat; but, after years of wearing an army cap, he looked all wrong. He threw the hat on a chair and went out bareheaded.

The bagpiper on top of his fountain was blowing his silent tune. The large round clock, high on the square tower at the end of the street, was red-faced too. Who wants sleep? Denning asked himself, and began looking at the gay shop windows and the pretty girls.

3: Reconnaissance

THE COBBLED STREET WIDENED SUDDENLY FOR about fifty yards, and then contracted again into an alley. That bit of extra breadth was the Henziplatz, edged by narrow-faced houses in an endless row, with their jutting eaves shadowing the top floors, their sharply pointed roofs broken by dormer windows and covered chimneys. The sun found its way into the Square, but the arcades were shadowed and cool. No shops here. A few cafés and small restaurants, many of them climbing upstairs to invade the second floors. A swinging sign or two, carefully lettered. A window box here and there. A good deal of foot traffic flowing from the busy Kramgasse which bounded the north of the little street. And above the steep red-tiled roofs rose the tall spire of the Minster, a massive background in the sky.

The Café Henzi was no more remarkable than any of the other eating places in the Square. The only remarkable thing, amusing perhaps, was the fact that the house marked No. 10 lay almost opposite. For tonight's performance, Denning thought as he walked through the Henziplatz, we shall practically have box seats.

His pace was steady, unhurried; he resisted the temptation to enter the Café Henzi and have lunch there. This leisurely tour of inspection was enough. Tonight, he'd reach the Square easily. And these arcades would be useful to shelter his approach. His confidence grew. But so did his sense of trouble ahead. Why had Johann Keppler chosen a room almost opposite the café? Did he expect the need for immediate action? Or was that the only room for rent on the Square? Or had Keppler—

"Bill!" It was a woman's voice. "Bill!—Bill Denning!"

He felt his arm grasped lightly. He turned sharply round. And there was Paula Waysmith with a wide smile and astounded blue eyes looking out from her round merry face. A step beyond her, there hesitated a young woman, a little embarrassed, deciding perhaps that she ought to walk on, except that Paula's other hand was holding her arm.

"Why, you passed me by!" said Paula. "Didn't even recognize your name. Is this the way you treat old friends? And what are you doing here, anyway?"

"Heading south by southwest for the cheese market."

"I mean, what—" Then Paula laughed and shook her head. "You know what I meant perfectly well, Bill Denning." She suddenly gave him a hug, and a kiss on the side of his cheek. Then, to her friend, "Francesca—don't move away! I want Bill to meet you." She pulled the girl forward. "Bill, this is Francesca Vivenzio: we used to go to school together near here, so we're having a celebration. Francesca, this is Bill Denning, who's one of our oldest friends."

"Yes, we came out of the Ark together," Denning said, and took the strange girl's politely outstretched hand. She was younger than he had thought at first, a pale blonde, too thin, with hair brushed severely back from a well-shaped forehead. The straight eyebrows looked puzzled for a moment, and then she smiled. The slender hand closed round his, and he started with surprise. Her grip was as strong as a man's. She let his hand go just as suddenly, saying in careful English, "How nice to meet you, Mr. Denning." Her voice was soft and charming. Then she looked away, shyly, and studied the traffic on the street. A straight nose, a determined chin, and dark eyelashes, he noted.

"Well, why don't we stop obstructing traffic? Come and have lunch with us. Francesca is taking me to her favorite little place along here—the Café Henzi."

"And spoil your class reunion?"

Paula ignored that. "It serves the most wonderful cheese fondue."

"I'd spend the afternoon sleeping it off. Actually, at the moment, I'm making up my mind between a ham and a chicken sandwich."

The girl with the Italian name looked at him sharply.

"Andy will be here tomorrow," said Paula.

"How is he?"

"Couldn't be better."

"Give him my regards, won't you?" He took a step away.

But Paula was not ready to say good-by. "He's in Bonn at the moment. I came on ahead of him to look for an apartment. We'll probably be here only a couple of months, but you know how Andy loathes hotels." And then as she noted Denning's surprise, "Didn't you hear? Andy's been made European editor for *Policy*, and we're doing a study of the capitals of Europe." Her delight was infectious.

Denning smiled in spite of his worry. "Now, that's what I like to see. Wifely pride bursting out all over."

Paula glanced at him quickly, almost nervously. "Where are you staying, Bill?"

"At the Aarhof."

"We're at the Victoria, meanwhile."

"Congratulations." He had meant it well, but Paula's frown deepened.

The blonde girl stirred restlessly. "Paula, I'm afraid Mr. Denning's ham sandwich will get cold."

Paula's smile was determined. "I'll call you," she told him. "We must all get together. Andy will want to see you."

"That would be fine," Denning said. But did he want to see Andy Waysmith? Not for the next few days, certainly. He took two more steps away. He bowed to the cold, calm blonde. "Good-by," he said to both of them. Then to Paula, "And I like your hat." He gave his very best smile. He was fond of Paula. For one thing, she made Andy the happiest friend he had.

"*Not* good-by," Paula called after him. "We'll see you soon."

"Fine," he said again, and walked away.

But it wasn't fine.

"Didn't you like him?" Paula asked.

Francesca said, "Not particularly."

"Why not?"

Francesca studied her American friend's worried face. "Is there any need for me to like him? You like him, and I like you, but that's no reason why I should like him. Is it?"

"I suppose not," Paula agreed. But she was disappointed. "Do you think I can risk any more of this fondue?"

"It has never killed anyone yet."

Paula giggled. "I know why you don't like Bill."

Francesca shrugged her shoulders and looked round the oak-paneled room of the Café Henzi. It was crowded now, cheerful and warm and bustling. "It's still better here in the evening," she said. "People sing. When they feel like it. That's the best way to sing."

"You don't like him because you both talk the same way," said Paula. "Almost."

Francesca stared at her.

"Of course your phrases are different and your accents are different," Paula went on. "But there's the same—the same bite. Every now and again. Look, do you think this fondue is making me just a little bit, a little bit drunk?"

"Impossible."

"Well, they say here," Paula picked up the menu, "they say here it's made from vintage cheeses."

Francesca began to laugh. Her face softened and became warm. "Dear Paula," she said affectionately. "It's so very good to hear you again."

"I think," Paula helped herself to some more fondue, "I think I was just empty with hunger, and so the blood is now coping with all the calories in my stomach, leaving me slightly lightheaded. Could that be my trouble?" She looked at her fork, and frowned. "Or perhaps I'm just so sorry for Bill," she said gravely.

"For *him?* Why, he's the most composed, cool, and self-sufficient individual I've met in a long, long time."

"You know, Francesca, your English is amazing."

"I've been having a lot of practice."

"Are you thinking of coming to America?"

Francesca shook her head. "I've merely been teaching those who are going to America," she said very quietly.

"Oh, you mean those—"

"Yes," Francesca said quickly. "But not here, Paula. Later, we'll talk about it. When we're out in the open air."

"But this looks like a most respectable place." Paula looked round it, now with added interest.

"Of course it is," Francesca assured her. She smiled at Paula's sudden disappointment. "Nothing but students, and representatives from the Cantons when Parliament is in session, and a few businessmen, and some scholars, and a poet or two, and the usual painters."

"And tourists."

"I'm afraid so. In Switzerland, they take the place of the poor. They are always with us."

"I wonder what Bill is doing in Bern?"

"What does anyone do? He is on holiday, perhaps."

"On furlough, darling. He's in the army."

"On furlough," Francesca repeated carefully, memorizing it. "But why must we talk about this Bill Denning? Because you're sorry for him?"

"I hurt him. Didn't you see?"

"Hurt *him?* Why, he didn't even want to talk to us. He was thinking of something else all the time. That I did see."

"You don't understand, Francesca."

"I hate people who tell me I don't understand."

Paula said, "But you *don't,* darling, not at this minute. You see, every time I meet Bill I have a mad genius for being tactless. I talk so enthusiastically about Andy, I kind of show off—without meaning to—all the fun we have together, and how well we've done, and what a happy marriage I have."

Francesca had a strange smile on her face. "Your friends forgive you that," she said. There was pleasure, however painful, in being reminded that personal happiness still existed.

"But Bill—well, once he was as happily married as Andy and I."

"*Was* married?"

"Now, don't look like that. Not all Americans get divorced, you know."

Francesca's pale cheeks colored. "I'm sorry," she said.

"You know, Francesca, I don't think you're looking after yourself properly. You're much too pale. Where's the color you used to have?"

"I'm all right. I've just had two weeks of flu."

"You are working too hard."

"Stop it, Paula." Francesca tried to smile. "I know I couldn't look worse, but don't keep telling me. You're as bad as Aunt Louisa."

"Perhaps you ought to go back to live in Italy."

"With whom? My family is dead. All of them."

"If they had been alive, would you have lived with them anyway?"

"Probably not. I'd have had my own life. But—" Francesca hesitated. How could she explain all this to someone as secure as Paula? "But then I'd have had my friends too."

"You could make new friends now."

"Not until I learn to trust people again," Francesca said bitterly. "I've still too much hate in my heart. Let me get that under control, first. I've shocked you?"

"No, no." But Paula was startled.

"It's better for me to stay here. Meanwhile. Switzerland is a good place for a cure, isn't it?"

Paula, for once, had nothing to say. She looked at the long table at the end of the room, where a dozen girls in Panama hats and navy dresses were chattering in peculiar French to an exhausted schoolmistress. It was only twelve years ago, she thought in distress, twelve years since Francesca and I were two of those schoolgirls over there.

"For here," Francesca was saying, "I have Aunt Louisa to worry over me and that is always a comforting thing, even if sometimes it's irritating. And I have friends here, people who have not deceived me and betrayed my family and helped to kill them. And I have my work."

"Francesca," Paula lowered her voice, "will you tell Andy about this work?"

Francesca said slowly, "But I don't want any publicity."

"You're wrong there," Paula said. "The more people know what your Committee is doing, the safer you will all be. Don't you see?"

"Put your trust in the people?" Francesca asked, and her sad smile was back again.

"Yes," Paula said stubbornly. "Some don't listen. Some will be against you. But plenty will be on your side. And when you're fighting something like—"

Francesca said quickly, "Shouldn't we start looking for your apartment? Or do you want dessert?"

"No," Paula said, gathering up her gloves and bag hastily. "No dessert, thank you. I've had enough calories to last me for a week." She fixed her small white hat more firmly on top of her short dark curls. Almost in the same breath she added, "When you're fighting, you need all the help you can get. That's all." She looked for their waitress, but without success, so she signaled to a white-coated waiter who had been hovering vaguely in the background. Protocol, she thought with amusement as she watched the man, embarrassed, hurry to find the waitress for them. "This is my lunch," she told Francesca firmly. "We won't argue about that, at least. Now, here's my list of furnished apartments. Where shall we start? What district do you think Andy would like?"

Francesca said, as they reached the street, "We'll walk up to the Clock Tower and take a tramcar there over to Kirchenfeld. It's a pleasant district. Or would Andy prefer a view? Then we ought to try the northwest, perhaps. . . . Let me see your list."

Paula handed it over in an abstracted way. "Tell me," she asked suddenly, "did you know that waiter in the Café Henzi?"

Francesca looked at the list. "Was it so obvious?" she asked very quietly.

"Not to most people. But I *do* know you very well."

"You must, indeed." Francesca bit her lip.

Paula looked over her shoulder, but the street was quiet now. Bern was a place which took its noonday meal seriously. "Is he one of your pupils in English?" she asked in a low voice.

Francesca hesitated. Then she nodded.

"He escaped?"

"Yes." Francesca looked around her nervously. But no one was near.

"Where did he escape from?"

"Hungary. He's quite a famous man."

"And he's a *waiter* now?"

"He has to eat, as you say. But soon his papers will all be in order. And then—"

"America?"

Francesca glanced over her shoulder once again, but there was still no one near enough to hear. She suddenly smiled. "Remember when I wrote you at Christmas and asked if you could find some school of music interested in Peter Andrássy? And you got a friend of yours to invite him to that college in California? Well—"

"*That* was Andrássy?"

"Yes. That was why I took you to the restaurant. He did

want to see you. Just to see you, and say thank you by seeing you. That was all."

"That was Peter Andrássy," Paula said almost to herself, "and I never guessed."

"We've dyed his hair. He calls himself Schmid. And who would expect to see one of Europe's best composers hurrying around with a tray?"

"I wish, somehow, he was already on the other side of the Atlantic."

"Soon he will be. Next week he sails from Genoa."

"Francesca," Paula said excitedly, "you've simply got to tell Andy all about this."

"We'll see."

They turned westward on the Kramgasse.

"How many have you helped in this way?" Paula asked.

But this street was more crowded, and Francesca only shook her head, smiling.

Paula was contented with the smile. There must have been several men and women, all first-rate in their own highly specialized fields. She looked at Francesca with pride, and pressed her arm gratefully. "You just make me feel good. You make me feel very good. But how mad you must make some other people feel!"

"We don't entice anyone. All the men and women we have helped have come here by their own choice. They have the courage. We just give them hope, and some help." Francesca laughed suddenly. It was the kind of happy laugh she used to have: it hasn't gone, Paula thought, it has just been buried.

"If we run," said Paula, "if we run, do you think we'll make that trolley car?"

Bill Denning, coming out of the restaurant where he had eaten, not a sandwich, but at least an undisturbed meal, saw them climbing aboard. They were back to their schooldays, he thought with amazement. Women were fantastic. Paula was crazy, of course, you could expect anything from Paula. But that tragedy queen—he stared, unbelieving, at the blonde Italian—she not only could run, she could laugh.

Then he turned away before they could see him. He would go and shut himself up in his hotel room. That was one way to avoid these two lunatics, one way to keep them clear of him. In a town like Bern, so closely centered—for visitors, at least—on the tight peninsula circled by the river Aare, he could meet Paula too easily again. Today he didn't want to meet anyone, least of all a friend. For it was possible that he was being followed, that his movements were being checked, that all his contacts were being noted. Better keep Paula and her blue-eyed friend out of all this. Danger was like cholera: it had an unguessable way of spreading.

4: The Waiting Hours

THAT AFTERNOON WAS QUIET ENOUGH IN DEN-
ning's room. There were no more interruptions from the
inquisitive chambermaid. There were no more gardening operations. But Denning, in spite of stretching himself out on
his bed, didn't sleep. He couldn't read, either: Malraux' *Les
Voix du Silence* lay beside him unopened. He couldn't plan
for tomorrow. He was a man caught by the moment and
held there captive.

An unpleasant afternoon.

Waiting. Waiting while the sunshine slipped across the
room, and then abandoned it to gray shadow.

Six o'clock at last. Better start choosing a restaurant, some
place with its quota of early tourists, some place with leisurely
service and good food and decent wine, some place within
casual walking distance of Henziplatz, No. 10.

Or was six too early? Perhaps. But this room was getting
on his nerves. He picked up the guidebook he had bought
that morning, and turned to its index of restaurants.

"Looks very much like a shower of rain, sir," the desk clerk told him cheerfully.

Denning glanced at the downpour on the pavement, and then at the heavy gray clouds overhead. How long would the desk clerk's shower last? Can't risk it, he thought: this is a walking kind of night. He went back to his room.

The inner door was closed, but unlocked. The chambermaid looked round in surprise. Then she smiled. "Towels," she said, pointing to the bathroom.

"Towels, to be sure."

"I'll turn down your bed, sir." She moved away from his suitcase. Or perhaps she had just been standing there, admiring the pretty rain.

"Don't you ever stop working?" he asked, and reached into the wardrobe for his raincoat.

"Please?" She was as plump as a pincushion, except for her thin muscular legs. Her hair was dully fair, straight, heavily braided over her ears. Her round face and slightly protuberant eyes were disarming. At this moment she even looked most comfortingly stupid, her pale lips parted, her thin eyebrows raised.

"Rain," he said, and held up his coat for her to see. No white rabbits, no mirrors, positively no deception.

She nodded sympathetically, and watched him find his hat.

"What's your name?" he asked suddenly.

"Eva," she answered, startled.

With a smile, he said "Good night, Eva." He closed the doors firmly. "And it's all yours," he added softly.

Then, as he walked toward the gilded cage of an elevator, he decided that he was imagining either too much or not enough. That was the trouble with the amateur in this kind of work: the hard-shell professional like Max Meyer would already have summed up the situation and would now be taking appropriate action. It had been a long time since Denning had parachuted into occupied France. Nine years ago was a long time. Then, he had been one of the hunted. And now—after some years in Germany of being the hunter —he was beginning to feel he was one of the hunted again. It was a difficult mental switch to make, but it might have to be made all the same. Might have to be made. Why did he feel that? Why, as he had faced that woman and asked her name, why could he only think that this had happened long ago? He had even been able to guess the startled look he would see in the protruding eyes, before she reacted to his sudden question. He had known that look—not one of innocence surprised, or stupidity suddenly challenged—that look of control, abruptly jolted by a moment's alarm into fear and suspicion, then just as rapidly recaptured.

The elevator was long in coming, slow in rising. Impatiently, he started toward the carpeted staircase which circled round the elevator shaft. Halfway down, he stopped. That was it, that was it, he'd got it—the woman who had stood in a Norman kitchen and watched him as he had been watched only five minutes ago. The woman whose husband was a prisoner of war in Germany, the woman who was trusted because she was pitied, the woman who was the Gestapo informer. Marthe Boisseau, he'd even got her name now.

He drew a deep breath. That had been quite an effort. Then he realized he had company.

Round the curve of the staircase had come a plodding figure dressed in navy blue, with long black stockings and flat-heeled shoes. A white Panama hat was swinging from one hand, while the other counted the railings with a trailing forefinger. The girl, fourteen perhaps, was standing there watching him.

"Oh!" she said, as if she had only just arrived and must register surprise. Impatiently she pushed a short pigtail of straight red hair back from her shoulder. "Have you lost something?" she asked with excessive politeness, and gave Denning a dazzling smile somewhat dimmed by silver bands over her teeth. "Oh," she said again, as if she remembered them, and she stopped smiling.

"No, I haven't lost anything," Denning said. He stood aside to let her pass, although there was more than enough room.

"I thought I might help you find it," she said. She didn't move. Her high flute-like voice had become more grown-up, emphasizing its Englishness.

"I've found what I wanted," he assured her. "Thank you."

She looked at the toe of her shoe, and then off into the middle distance. "You're an American," she told him.

"How could you guess?" He had to smile at her serious face, searching so earnestly for the right thing to say.

"I know them *extremely* well. My sister married an American. He was a general."

"That's above my level, I'm afraid."

"Oh," she said comfortingly, using that long-drawn-out

narrow vowel again, "but I *don't* think he was a particularly good general." She gave him a quick side glance to see if she had been tactful enough. Then she looked at the narrow elastic which formed the chin strap to her hat. She twisted it nervously, but her voice still held valiantly to her upper level of conversation. "Frightful weather, isn't it?"

He nodded. He took a step downward. Yet it was impossible, he found, to slip past those young anxious-to-be-old eyes—deep dark eyes which made the plain little face, with its snub nose and freckles, its pale lips and light eyebrows, somehow pathetic. Whom was she imitating, anyway—the sister who had married a general, or her mother, or some character from a nineteenth-century novel?

"I'm English, you know," she told him gravely.

"No!" he said. "I thought you were French."

"Really?" She tasted that idea twice. She smiled with delight, forgetting about the hideous bands on her teeth, a wide innocent smile as beautiful as it was ugly. "Of course," she said, giving him the tilted profile again, "of course I have lived in the south of France. For the Easter holidays, at least. Mother has a friend who has a house there." And then suddenly she turned sparkling eyes on him. "We saw you today. You were really *smashing* with the monster."

He hadn't kept up with her. He tried not to look puzzled.

"Marie and I," she said, "we saw you. This morning. Was he trying to *steal* your bag? He is an absolute horror, isn't he?"

He remembered the two startled schoolgirls that morning who had watched his encounter with Charles-Auguste Maartens. "Not my brew of beer," he agreed.

She giggled, then. "We always call him the monster. He's so hairy when he goes bathing."

"The King Kong type," Denning suggested, but he still stared at her in bewilderment. It was all so clear to her.

She sighed. "Well, I suppose I must really go. My friends will all be wondering—" She looked delighted at that idea. "They're so lazy. They won't walk upstairs. But I hate lifts, don't you?"

He admitted he often was lazy, too.

"But climbing stairs is so *good* for your ankles," she told him.

"I'll remember that."

"All the girls are foreigners, of course, except for me."

"Hey, there—this is Switzerland," he reminded her.

"But I *know* that." She moved one foot at last onto the next step. Politely, she arched the invisible eyebrows. "I don't think I quite caught your name?"

"Bill. I agree—it's a very difficult name."

"Bill." She considered that and found it wanting. "Doesn't anyone ever call you William?"

"Not since I left school."

"How very odd. It's all so upside-down, isn't it?"

"Completely."

"I'm called Emily," she said, thrusting her hand out in good tennis-playing style, and then remembering to let it go limp. "Hideous, isn't it? But it's Mother's name. I suppose Daddy hoped I was going to be like her." She sighed wearily.

"And aren't you?" he asked, letting her helpless hand drop free.

"Oh, no!" She relaxed for a moment and giggled. "I'm Mother's despair."

"What about your sister who married an American?"

She looked down at him, now three steps below her. "Is that a joke?" she asked gravely.

"Good for you," he said encouragingly. He gave a wave of his hand and started downstairs. Then he halted. "About the monster—do you know him?"

She froze with disdain. "Certainly *not*. I shouldn't dream of speaking to him. Mother says he's totally impossible."

"Your mother knows—I mean, your mother has seen the monster?"

"Only in the distance. But that's quite enough, isn't it?"

"Quite," Denning said thoughtfully. He added, "Perhaps some time before you leave here, you'll do me the honor of having an ice-cream soda with me?"

She beamed with delight. "If I can get permiss— I mean, if I can arrange it."

"Tell your teacher I need some lessons in English, will you?"

"I don't think Mademoiselle Dupré would listen to *that*—" She looked at him quickly. "I wish you'd smile when you make a joke," she said sharply. Then she relented. "And I think your voice is really very nice, considering." She gave him an encouraging nod and began walking upstairs sedately, but once she was hidden from sight she started to run, two steps at one stride, judging by the series of spaced-out thuds.

Emily . . . Emily and her mother and the totally impossible

monster who was so hairy when he went bathing. I guess I do need some lessons in English, Denning thought as he went on downstairs. Translate "bathing" into "swimming." Then you'd have a beach. Or, as Mother's Despair would say, the seaside. And "the south of France" could be translated to mean "the Riviera." And the Riviera had a seaside, where one could go bathing during the Easter holidays.

You're catching on, Denning told himself half-humorously. Then his amusement ended abruptly. His steps halted, too. The monster . . . He had been handed Mr. Charles-Auguste Maartens on a conversational platter, and he had only picked at the dish. Now, he had two more questions to ask. Could Emily answer them? He half-turned, ready to run back upstairs. But there was only silence overhead. Emily was already with her friends, relating her adventures, or trying to convince the unfortunate Mademoiselle Dupré that the more slowly one walked upstairs the better it was for one's ankles. She was probably Mademoiselle's despair, too.

Or perhaps, he thought as he at last reached the lobby, I'm too much on edge. I'm adding up everything, chambermaids and monsters, into a fantastic kind of sum. Better calm down and leave all this to Max Meyer or Johann Keppler. They could evaluate it. Evaluate? Emily wouldn't care much for that word, he guessed.

He handed in his key at the porter's desk. The reception clerk, with the intense eyes and horticultural knowledge, noticed his hat and raincoat, and called over, "I think you are wise, Mr. Denning. It seems to be a prolonged shower. Most unseasonable weather."

"It always is. But it's good for the crops."

"Please?"

"Good for the geraniums."

"On the contrary, I'm afraid." The clerk shook his head sadly. "Precipitation such as this—"

Fortunately, there was an interruption.

"Mr. Denning?" asked the clerk on duty at the porter's desk, leafing through a pile of letters. "I believe there's a message here for you, sir. Yes, a telephone call. It came this afternoon when you were out." The man picked up a slip of paper.

The reception clerk, who knew all about geraniums and rain, looked annoyed. He moved along his counter to the adjoining desk. "I'm sorry for the delay, sir," he told Denning, and then turned on the other clerk. "Mr. Denning ought to have had that message at once," he said, trying to conceal his irritation from the guest. But the man with the slip of paper —he was a small thin man, dark-haired, weak-chinned—ignored that except to say, "Sorry, Mr. Denning." And instead of handing over the piece of paper, he chose to read it aloud. "It was a Mr. Meyer who called."

Denning looked as blank-faced as possible. Careful, he told himself, careful now. . . . "Meyer?" he repeated questioningly. "Meyer . . ." He held out his hand for the note.

"There's no message, sir," said the clerk. "Just the name, and the fact that he called. Mr. Max Meyer."

Denning had to make a quick decision. He hoped it was the correct one. "Colonel Meyer, you mean," he said, suddenly recognizing the name. "Then that must have been a long-distance call from Frankfurt. And you didn't let me know about it until *now?*"

The geranium expert was completely horrified. He looked as angrily as Denning at the sorting clerk, who handed over the slip of paper without another word.

Denning frowned. "If he took the trouble to call me from Frankfurt, surely there must be some message about calling him back?"

"There was no message," the little dark-haired man said. His eyes were nervous. "I think it was a local call, sir."

"We can verify that," said the reception clerk crisply. "Find out from the operator. At once!"

"It couldn't have been a local call," Denning said.

"It was, sir, I verified that at the time." The nervous eyes flickered over Denning's amazed face.

"I give up," Denning said in exasperation, as if the whole matter was quite beyond his powers of guessing, and turned away from the desk.

The reception clerk said quickly in his polite, discreet voice, "I assure you this is most unusual." But the look he threw at the other clerk was enough to shrivel the man's flesh from his bones.

Indeed it was unusual, much too unusual. Denning pulled on his raincoat, jammed his hat into better shape, and stood at the doorway for a moment looking through the arch of the arcade at the pouring rain. There was one thing of which he could be certain: Max Meyer had not left his name at any hotel desk.

He searched his pockets for his cigarettes.

The doorman said, "Taxi, sir?"

"If you can find one." He lit a cigarette carefully and waited patiently, a man who had no appointment to keep, whose time was his own, whose evening had to be enjoyed in spite of weather, a simple, harmless visitor whose business was pleasure.

And, waiting, he became convinced of one more thing. They weren't sure about him. The note had been a test, that was all. They had found some connection between Meyer and himself, but they weren't quite sure why he was in Bern. The note had been a test, but he was taking it as a warning. Go carefully, he told himself, go carefully. They may not be sure, but they're interested. They . . . Who were *they,* anyway?

"Heavy traffic, tonight," the doorman said, as a free cab drew up at last. "Everyone wants a taxi."

Three women came out of the hotel, waved to the cab, cried, "There's one!" with remarkable powers of observation, and then wheeled in a tight phalanx toward its opened door.

"I beg your pardon," Denning said overpolitely. "You know what?" he asked the open-mouthed doorman, as the women shut the cab door behind them, "I believe they thought I was trying to steal their taxi." He slipped a coin into the man's empty hand, won a sympathetic if startled look, and began walking.

5: The Café Henzi

THAT EVENING, PAULA WAYSMITH SAID, "LOOK here, Francesca, you can't possibly go back to Falken to-night."

"Why not? It isn't so far—it's less than an hour away by motor coach."

"By bus, darling. Just simple everyday bus. Your pupils will find American travel peculiar if you teach them things like motor coach and tramcar."

"Bus," Francesca agreed. The afternoon had been exhausting: Paula, trying to make up Andy's mind by remote thought-control, hadn't found an apartment or a house. At five o'clock she had said, "My decider is all worn out. Let's get back to the hotel and rest, and finish all the rest of our news." So here they were, back in the Waysmiths' room at the Victoria, an elegant room of cream and gold, warmly comforting. Francesca was stretched out on one of the beds, Paula lay on the other. They each had a cigarette, their shoes off, a cocktail which Paula had ordered (Americans were even businesslike in arranging their comforts, Francesca decided), and the wonderful feeling of having earned it. "Bliss!" Francesca

51

said, straightening her spine and stretching her feet. "The life of the Duchess of Parma."

"I suppose it isn't so far," said Paula, thinking of Falken, a small village with pretty little houses scattered over green slopes. It was definitely pure country, not a touch of suburb: just unpaved roads leading from a wandering street, an inn for skiers in winter and walkers in summer, two slopes, historical assets (a seventeenth-century church and an eighteenth-century bridge over the Falkenbach which chattered through the village), cowbells, cockcrows, the smell of hay and farm mud and sawed wood and barns, the smell of the hilly meadows which stretched out between the houses, the smell of the woods circling around. "Strange how quickly the country begins outside of a Swiss city," she said. She was perpetually surprised by the shortness of distances in Switzerland.

She frowned, thinking up another reason to keep Francesca in Bern. "Still, I wish you'd call up your aunt and tell her there's a spare bed here for you tonight. Listen to that rain!"

"I'm a country girl nowadays," Francesca reminded her. "What's rain?"

"You'll come down with another attack of grippe. Besides, if you go back to Falken, I'll have to spend a wet Thursday night all by myself in Bern."

Francesca smiled. "Yes, Thursday makes a wet night particularly bad."

"Then you'll stay?" Paula asked quickly, pressing her advantage. "Wonderful. Where shall we eat?"

But Francesca was having a mild attack of afterthought. "I really ought to go back tonight." There was a Committee meeting tomorrow morning, for one thing. But there wasn't too much self-persuasion in her voice.

Paula, sighing, said, "It's funny, isn't it, how a woman can't enjoy an evening alone—unless she stays inside her hotel and then finds a good book for bed."

"Which only proves you're virtuous, darling."

"Aren't most of us? And it isn't virtue so much either as— as just hating to be annoyed, or to be judged for something you aren't. Now, if Andy were alone in Bern, he'd drop into a bar for a cocktail, then have a decent little dinner anywhere, but *anywhere*, he liked. Then he'd take in a theater, or a movie, or go for a walk through the streets. And then he'd

end with a nightcap at a place like the Café Henzi. But could
I do that by myself?"

"Not for very long."

"I couldn't stay myself for very long, either. I couldn't be
natural."

"Not honestly natural," Francesca said. "I hate innocence
when it starts pretending it doesn't know. Either it becomes
aggressive. Or artful. Which is the worse?"

"The question that's occupying my stomach at the moment
is—where shall we find that decent little dinner Andy would
go out and have?"

Francesca glanced down at her clothes.

Paula said, "If I looked as well in a blouse and skirt as you
do, I'd wear it dining at the Ritz. Look, why don't I call
your aunt while you think of food? You know, if inspiration
fails you, I shouldn't mind going back to the Café Henzi
again. I liked it.

"Did you?" There was a half-smile round Francesca's lips.

"I'd like to hear that singing."

"That happens much later in the evening."

"Then what about going on there, after dinner?"

"What about that telephone call?" Francesca closed her
eyes, thinking how delightful it was to allow yourself to be
completely lackadaisical. And if Aunt Louisa raised any ob-
jections to this overnight stay in town, then Paula would be
able to deal more firmly with them. It was strange: there was
Aunt Louisa, Swiss born and bred, still living in her grand-
father's house where she and Francesca's mother had grown
up together, a placid calm woman in a placid quiet village,
and she did nothing but worry secretly. And there, on the
other hand, had been Francesca's father, an Italian, a pro-
fessor of music, living in a voluble excitable little Italian town
—and had he ever worried at all? Perhaps emotion, when it
is tightly disciplined, turns into worry. Perhaps her father,
with his laughter and passion and arguments and music, perhaps he had had no emotion left over to be turned into any
of the negative fears. And perhaps, she thought (as her Swiss
mother might have thought), perhaps it might have been
better for us all if he had known worry, been less confident
about people, been more wary of treachery. And that was
another strange thing: after an injury had been done to him,
the Italian would remember it. He rarely foresaw it, but he
would remember it. While Aunt Louisa would foresee every

possible danger, probably avoid most of them, and blame herself if there was one she had underestimated.

That was the way it had been. Her father betrayed by a Fascist into German hands. Her brother betrayed by a Communist, murdered, his war record covered with lies and calumny to win a propaganda victory. And her mother dead with the pain of it, blaming herself for not having foreseen the treachery.

And I'm left alone, Francesca thought. And for what? I can't even warn people: they won't listen. I am only heard by the ones who are already convinced. What good is that?

She swung her body off the bed. She was tense and cold again. "Well?" she asked Paula, who had just turned away from the phone. "Was Aunt Louisa worried in case I caught pneumonia?"

Paula said, smiling, "She did say you were to go to bed *early* tonight, with a good hot drink."

Francesca searched for her shoes.

"She really is very kind," Paula said, half-worried as she watched Francesca's drawn face. "She's asked Andy and me out to Falken for the week end. I do hope Andy will be free."

"I hope so." Francesca was combing her hair, her long fair silken hair. Then swiftly she twisted it into a loose knot, low on the back of her neck, and pinned it quickly, skillfully, into exact place.

"She said that Gregor came to see you this afternoon."

"Gregor?"

"That was the name, I think. Sounds Russian."

"He is." Francesca studied her pale cheeks in the looking glass. "You wouldn't think I lived in one of the healthiest villages in Switzerland, would you? Remember that old castle just over a mile away from Falken? They've discovered water there with lime and sulphur and horrible tastes, so it's now called Schlossfalken-Bad, and people go there to take the cure. Perhaps I ought to walk in that direction more regularly." She tried to smile.

But Paula was not sidetracked. "What kind of life do you have in Falken, anyway?"

"Oh—fresh air and mountains."

"What about friends?"

"Difficult. Swiss air seems to bring out my Italian blood. Everyone is kind, but they think I'm a little bit of a freak.

I read books, I like music, I enjoy arguing about politics. Man's work, darling."

"But there must be women your age."

"Plenty. They're round and pretty and red-cheeked, and they're all married with at least three children."

"Why don't you get married?"

Francesca smiled.

"Who's this Gregor?"

"A friend. A very good friend," Francesca said gently. Then she looked quickly up at Paula, "And that's all. We're both too crazy to be able to live together peacefully. But Gregor *is* my friend."

Paula looked worriedly at Francesca. "Well, if there is no one in the village who interests you, aren't there ever any visitors to Falken?"

Francesca said, "Oh, they come. And they go." She half-paused. "There's one who has just bought a house. An American. He says he means to stay."

"Do you like him?"

Francesca's cheeks colored for a moment. "I don't like or dislike him," she said too quickly. "But he *is* different. . . . He's so anxious to make friends, to be happy, and yet—he can't, somehow. He's incredibly shy, perhaps unsure of himself." And that's something I do understand, she thought sadly.

"But he keeps looking at you?" Paula asked with a smile.

Francesca glanced at her. "Really—" she began coldly.

"Very flattering," Paula conceded. "But if he starts making you feel sorry for him, then that's a type I'd discourage most heartily. Pale knights lonely loitering are much more devastating than any *belle dame sans merci*. See, I do remember some of the poetry that was pumped into us at school." And Francesca had begun to smile, too. "But I'm sorry, if I spoiled Gregor's evening. Perhaps he wanted to give you a party."

"Probably he just called to discuss some things before the Committee meeting tomorrow. Gregor loves discussions."

"Gregor's on the Committee?" Paula couldn't hide her surprise.

"He began it, actually. But then, he knew what it was like to be a prisoner. He's thirty-four, and he has spent nine of those years in concentration camps. Russian and German. He was a music student, before that."

"How does he live now?" asked the practical Paula.

"Gregor would say he existed by cutting down trees, and lived by composing music. But mostly he thinks about the Committee. It's his hope and joy."

"Haven't you given it a name, yet?"

"Oh, we've had such arguments about that! We usually end by simply calling it the Falken Committee. After all, it is composed of people who live in Falken, or who have houses there. One is a doctor at Schlossfalken-Bad, for instance; a nice elderly Frenchman. Then there's a retired Englishman who has lived in Falken for thirty years. And we've a lawyer from Bern—and so on."

"You don't keep it secret?" It almost scares me, Paula thought, the calm way she takes all this.

"Secret enough. We had to let the government know what we planned—we didn't want them to come asking, 'Now what kind of conspiracy is going on here?' But we do work discreetly. The people we help remain anonymous even to Falken —and that's easy enough to arrange. Why, Switzerland always did have so many committees and clubs and associations and sanitariums and children's homes and lunatic asylums and metaphysical societies, that one more group of people getting together to try to help others—well—" Francesca shrugged her shoulders. "What about dinner? The Café du Théâtre is good. Then we can go on to the Kursaal, up on the Schänzli. There's music there, if you want that."

"You ought to give the Committee a name, though," Paula said, trying to think of one. Committees always had names.

"Gregor wants it to be called 'The Committee for Freedom of Choice.' He says that's the basic freedom, and he ought to know. But then our retired Englishman wants us called 'The Iron-Smelters' or 'The Curtain-Raisers.' That shocks Gregor."

"It startles me, too. But tell him Englishmen always make a joke about anything over which they're deadly serious."

"None of us think we are playing a game," Francesca said slowly.

Paula looked at her. I ought not to have suggested revisiting the Café Henzi, she realized. That was silly; cheap. Peter Andrássy may be one of the great composers in this world, but I was foolish in wanting to see him again. More than foolish in being excited about the small part I had in getting him a job in America. What is danger to the Committee is only excitement to me.

She was very silent, for Paula, all through an excellent dinner.

But later that evening when the Kursaal's concert was over and dancing was about to begin, it was Francesca who said, "Well, if you still want to go to the Café Henzi, why don't we go now?"

"Wouldn't you object?" Paula was startled. "I mean—oh, you know!"

Francesca smiled at Paula's new caution. "Thursday is his half-day. He will be out in Falken, playing chess and talking music with Gregor. He always does that."

"He won't be at the Henzi, then?" Paula was half-disappointed in spite of her resolutions.

"No. Do you still want to go?" Francesca's amusement grew.

"Of course," said Paula swiftly. "You see, I've been thinking about the houses for rent which we saw today. And I've begun to wonder if Andy wouldn't prefer something more in town, and the older the town the better. You know how men always rush for the Île St. Louis in Paris? So I'd like to see the old town—"

"The Lower Town?"

"—the Lower Town, by night."

"Now, we aren't house-hunting at this hour!"

"No, no, no. I just like getting the feel of a place, that's all." Paula glanced at a table nearby, and then casually across the room at its curve of giant windows, at its sedate groups of families out together for an evening's relaxation, at the clusters of couples who were engrossed in each other. "There's a man over there," she said with amusement, "who's much too interested. He pretends he's only studying this huge room, but you know how it is—the more he avoids being found watching us, the more he actually gives himself away. Is he a friend of yours?"

Francesca let her eyes wander slowly round the tables. "That creature in the silver-gray suit?" she asked.

"No," Paula said. "That's only a landmark."

"He certainly is."

"Beyond him to the left. I mean to the right. Your right, his left. It's always so mixing."

"I see," Francesca said slowly, and looked at the man, and then quickly at another table where three girls expanded in pink blushes, pure Renoir color, under the proud eyes of their parents. "No, he is no friend of mine." She looked back at the man. He was hunched, now, as if he were trying to contract into nothingness. Thin face, weak chin, nondescript clothes. He wasn't even the kind of man who would seem likely to be interested in anything except his own dull life. "You're joking, Paula," she said.

"Oh, he's just some little clerk putting in a lonely evening," Paula said. "But why come here if he enjoys himself so little? Perhaps he's going straight back to his attic room to start Chapter Three of his autobiographical novel—*How I Suffer among the Bourgeoisie*. You'll be the heroine with the sensitive face who is being led astray by Swiss comfort and American materialism. Now, wouldn't he be delighted if that dark-haired gigolo in the fancy suit came over here to join us? It would fit all theories perfectly."

"I'm afraid the pearl-gray suit is too interested in his brandy and cigar," Francesca said, "and thank heaven for that."

"He's leaving, trailing clouds of richness," Paula reported.

"Some men would do better to stay poor," Francesca said. "Money only exaggerates their vulgarities."

Paula laughed. But her eyes were thoughtful as she noticed that the thin-faced man paid no attention at all to the departure of the pearl-gray suit, so that when he had been looking in this direction he must indeed have been watching Francesca and herself. Paula didn't need to glance over her shoulder to see what table lay behind theirs: there was none—Francesca and she had chosen a corner.

Francesca said, "Shall we leave, too? Then let's do it quickly." Paula looked at her grave face and nodded. Within three minutes they were standing at street level far below the high terraces of the Kursaal, deposited there by an outsize elevator which had descended through the solid rock of the Schänzli. Their luck continued. Even as Paula looked with dismay through the drizzling darkness at the long, lonely expanse of bridge back into town, a solitary taxi passed them, hesitated, halted. "Quick, quick!" said Francesca, and ran for it. But once they were over the Kornhaus Bridge, it was Francesca who suggested they might drive slowly around the Lower Town following the loop of the River Aare which semicircled this tongue of land with its eighteenth-century houses and twisting streets. "To let you see how it looks on a rainy night,"

Francesca said. "Houses are like husbands: you should see them at their worst before you decide which to choose."

The rain was easing, but the weather had kept many people indoors. Most of the restaurants were closing. The streets were bleak, the fountains lonely, chattering shadows robbed of color and design by the blackness around them. It might have been three o'clock in the morning instead of eleven at night. It could have been almost a medieval city, except that the gutters held only rain, the streets were not buried in mud and garbage, the lights were steady and methodically spaced, the smells were unnoticeable, the few pedestrians did not need a torchbearer or an armed retainer to get them safely home.

"The twentieth century adds a little something, after all," Paula said as she got out of the taxi. "The Middle Ages were probably only romantic when seen from this distance. Yet I used to think I'd have been happier in another era."

"You couldn't take penicillin with you," Francesca reminded her.

"I'd just have to cover the pockmarks on my face with black patches. If I lived through the plague."

But Francesca had stopped listening. She glanced along the arcade, and then back over her shoulder at the quiet Henzi-platz.

"It's peaceful enough," Paula said reassuringly, and they crossed the bright threshold of the Café Henzi.

Madame at the cash desk gave them a cheerful greeting. There were a few tables left downstairs, but tonight the Convention of Econophilosophists had taken all upstairs for its annual social dinner.

"Of *what?*" Paula asked, as Francesca led her past a telephone booth into the downstairs room, wood-paneled, dimly lighted. It was fairly crowded, gently noisy, with groups of men talking over smoke-circled tables, some women sprinkled here and there among them, students arguing, one or two solitary guests enjoying a glass of wine within the friendliness of the room.

"I told you we had our share of conventions and committees," Francesca said with a smile. "Is this all right?" She had chosen a quiet corner. "We can hear the singing when it begins, just as well down here. More comfortably, perhaps." In spite of her light voice, she had glanced quickly round the room. Seemingly she felt reassured, for she sighed now and relaxed. Paula was suddenly aware that the tension which had followed them down from the high terraces of the Kursaal was over.

"Perhaps we ought to have gone straight back to the hotel," she said. The enjoyment of the evening was diluted somehow. She was vaguely disturbed, worried. To her, the dim lights, swinging from the cart wheels which hung from the ceiling, made everyone seem a Pirandello character. But Francesca was more at ease, as if she welcomed the shaded anonymity of the room. And then Paula wondered if the long roundabout drive through the Lower Town hadn't been partly inspired by the chinless little man's interest in them at the Kursaal. "Anyway, he didn't follow us," she said, dropping her voice, keeping her eyes on the doorway. I'm going to watch that entrance as long as we sit here, she promised herself. I wish I had never joked about him, never drawn Francesca's attention to him. He was just a harmless little man, lonely and bored, with a wandering eye.

Francesca ordered the wine, something called Fendant de Sion, and Paula began talking about Paris where Andy and she had spent part of the winter. But Francesca's listening was broken by her own thoughts. It was only to be expected, she told herself, that someone had started being interested in the Falken Committee. It was amazingly good luck that they had been left so long in peace. Or was it possible that they had been watched for some time, and that only this week the watchers had grown careless? Last Tuesday, when she had visited Bern, there had been that woman with the braids heavy over her ears making her round face rounder, the woman with the thick heavy body and the thin legs. And now, tonight at the Kursaal, there had been that haggard-faced man with the shifting eyes. And yet how did the fat woman or the thin man know she was in Bern, know where to look for her? Who had told them where to look for her? Who had told them where to find her—or to let themselves be noticed once they had found her?

They are trying to scare me, she thought suddenly. That was an old trick: frightening people into making a false move. She smiled suddenly, feeling the excitement coming back into her blood. An old hand didn't scare so easily at old tricks. Why, she had known that one when she was sixteen. She and her brother had used it to frighten a Nazi informer into warning the leader of his pro-Nazi group. Am I supposed, now, to run to the head of the Committee with my alarms? Am I to lead them to him? Her smile broadened.

"But I'm being serious," Paula protested. "When it comes to deciding between living in the country and living in the city, I'm almost driven to schizophrenia. Just as I was talking about Paris, I suddenly remembered how good it was to wake up in the country and see fields and trees all around me. Yet in the country I'll suddenly remember how a city looks with the lights coming on. What do you make of me? I'm not really a fickle kind of person."

"You are certainly devoted to watching that doorway."

Paula flushed. "I was just trying to help." But she smiled, too. "Are you sure you don't have to be worried?" Then she stared at the doorway again.

"I'm sure," Francesca said. That's the Italian in me, she thought. Quickly, she added a touch of Swiss to balance it. "Reasonably sure." How strange was that phrase, that calm phrase, *reasonably sure:* it always awakened equally reasonable doubt. "Don't keep looking at that door, darling."

"But guess who has just arrived—Maxwell Meyer. Imagine! Look, he's coming over here." Paula was delighted with the smallness of the world.

"And who's Maxwell Meyer?"

Paula, who had been about to wave, let the hand she had half-raised in welcome drop back on the table. "He didn't see me," she said. She lowered her voice. "He's sitting just over there to your left."

"You seem to have picked a blind batch of male friends," Francesca said teasingly, remembering Bill Denning.

"Oh, he isn't a friend: just a friend of a friend," Paula said. She was a little hurt, though. Perhaps it wasn't Maxwell Meyer after all, she thought. "What has happened to the singing?" she asked.

"It will start soon," Francesca said, glancing at her watch. "Any minute now." It was almost eleven o'clock.

6: No. 10 Henziplatz

THE ROOM OF "ELIZABETH" WAS SMALL, SQUARE, warmly lighted by a pink-shaded lamp. Heavy red curtains covered the narrow windows, blotting out the rain which slanted through the darkness outside, and silencing the occasional noises of traffic from the Henziplatz. Highly colored pictures of roses and unadorned nymphs were pinned on the wall. A double bed covered with cheap lace and pink silk took more than its share of floor space. A scrap of white fur rug lay before the bed, small cushions and a doll on a narrow red couch. A round table and two chairs waited near the screen which hid a sink and small cooking stove. There was another screen, too, probably hiding the bathroom.

"I'm Keppler," the man said, locking the door as Denning stepped into the room. He shook hands solemnly. He was a businesslike man in a quiet brown suit: quick in word and movement; of medium height and solid build, with close-cropped gray hair above a tanned face, heavy eyebrows over blank blue eyes, a mouth that was pleasant enough, a well-defined nose and a long chin.

He had been studying Denning, too. "You should change

your photographer, Captain Denning. He doesn't flatter you. Have a chair." He waved a hand toward the table.

Denning shook his hat free of the rain and slipped off his sodden coat. Keppler's unobtrusive scrutiny made him still more conscious of his anomalous position here. Suddenly, he stood quite still. A tall thin figure came silently out from behind the bathroom screen.

"Le Brun—Denning," Keppler said, now placing the emphasis on the civilian approach.

"You shouldn't do that," Denning said, smiling at his own tenseness, as he shook hands with the Frenchman. Perhaps Le Brun's nerves weren't too good either, for his melancholy face was not at all amused, and his handshake was brief. Then he sat down on the red couch, pushed aside the doll with a frown, and leaned forward, his long arms resting on his knees, his sad brown eyes watching Denning intently.

"I suppose we'll speak in English?" he asked.

Denning looked at Keppler, but he was choosing a cigar from his case. Americans don't speak French, Denning remembered. "That's all right with me," he said, keeping his voice friendly. I'm the unwanted stepchild, he thought.

"Did you have any trouble in reaching here?" Le Brun asked.

"I had a lot of walking. But no trouble." Denning glanced at Keppler again. Who was in charge, anyway? But Keppler seemed content to let Le Brun lead the discussion. Colonel Le Brun, Denning suddenly remembered. But, as Le Brun asked him some searching questions, about Berlin, his journey to Bern, his connections with Meyer, he became sure that it wasn't only his first joking remark that had nettled a colonel. And it wasn't just the fact that Le Brun's pride was probably hurt: it had every reason to bridle over Charlie-for-Short's preference for the Americans. Nor was it simply a matter of feeling obliged to the Swiss, although there were some people who never felt at ease in the role of guest, preferring to give favors rather than receive them.

Some of these emotions no doubt were mixed up in the basis of Le Brun's growing impatience. But the real clue to his present temper came when he said, suddenly throwing up his hands in despair, "So you know as little as Keppler does about this whole business? As little as I do? Perhaps even less! My God!" Then he let his arms fall and his lips droop. He didn't need to say anything more.

Keppler studied the end of his cigar. He said, "Le Brun is pessimistic about tonight."

"It is too rash, too quick," Le Brun said. "This will probably be a wild duck chase. That is all it will be."

"Then we'll have discovered it was a wild duck we were chasing," Keppler said placidly. "That at least is something to know. What do you think, Denning?"

"Denning," Le Brun cut in, "is as worried as I am. I can see *that*."

But not about the same things, thought Denning.

"I came here yesterday," Le Brun said. "The whole place is placid, quiet. I might have been one of these stupid tourists. Not a single attempt to follow me, to note what I was doing. No interest whatever."

"Are you sure?" Denning asked.

"Of course I am sure. I am not an amateur in this business."

But I am, Denning thought. Is this what is annoying Le Brun? He said, "I gathered you were strictly professional."

Le Brun looked at him quickly. He relaxed a little. "This town is too innocent," he assured Denning. "That worries me very much." He rubbed the long bridge of his nose, slowly. "Tell me," he said suddenly, "you know Colonel Meyer well?" His fine brown eyes were watchful.

"For many years."

"He is not a serious man?"

"He enjoys a joke. But," Denning added quickly, "when it comes to work, then he's more than serious."

"Reliable?"

"Of course."

"But enthusiastic, imaginative?"

"Yes. Why not? Don't you need both enthusiasm and imagination for a difficult job of work?"

"What I am trying to say—it isn't easy, I assure you—but do you believe Meyer's story?"

Denning looked over at the quiet Keppler. "But don't *you?*" He stared at both of them.

Keppler didn't answer. Le Brun shook his head. Le Brun said softly, "So you do believe Meyer."

"If I didn't, do you think I'd be here?" Denning said angrily. "And why are you both taking the trouble to be here, if you think Meyer's story is so fantastic?"

"I had hoped it was true," Le Brun said stiffly. "One must explore every hope."

"Isn't that just what Meyer is doing?"

Keppler intervened tactfully, "Let us consider this truth: even the most fantastic stories have an element of possibility; we cannot ignore that element. That is why we have gathered here. That is why all Swiss officers on duty—may I speak in German? It is quicker for me. More accurate. Yes?"

Le Brun said in French, "Certainly. But what about Denning? Will he understand clearly?"

"I've been in Berlin for the last four years," Denning said in his best German.

Le Brun half-smiled. "My apologies. It does not always follow that an Amer— that a man who works in Germany can speak German."

True, Denning thought, but I can do as well as wild duck chase, I hope. What have I drawn here, anyway? One of those cross-eyed neutralists with their subconscious desire that all Americans may drop dead?

Keppler, the neutral who wasn't neutralist, said in German, "We are not here to display our gift of tongues. It is enough if we understand the essential facts. Now to return to what I was saying so slowly in English—all our customs officers are conducting an intensive search of baggage both arriving and departing. If the Herz diamonds are already in Switzerland, then they will have little chance of getting out. In case they do"—he glanced at Le Brun—"the Italian authorities have been alerted, and Genoa is being strictly watched. Both American and Italian shipping and air lines have been warned. The general alarm has been given, discreetly, of course."

"But isn't it too general at this stage?" Denning asked. "After all, secrecy—"

Le Brun said, "Meyer wanted secrecy. But my government has to make sure that the diamonds do not slip away from us while we sit waiting. We have no choice but to take all precautions possible."

Keppler's face was unreadable. He went on speaking in his even voice. "Well, that's the general situation. Here in Bern, we've gone very cautiously. There are two men watching the street outside. I have placed one man inside the café as a waiter, for tonight. I believe Meyer has a friend of his also inside the Café Henzi."

"Only one man?"

"The same young man, Taylor, who came to see me in Munich," Le Brun said. "It doesn't seem as if Meyer had been given any reinforcements. Perhaps the Americans did not put too much trust in his story?"

"His job, here, is simply to get fuller information," Denning reminded him. "After that, the Swiss will take all the adequate steps." His anger burned into his chest. He turned to Keppler. "Right?"

"That is what we naturally prefer," Keppler said. He added, somewhat wryly, "Switzerland is our country, after all." He rose and went behind the kitchen screen. He returned with a bottle of brandy and three glasses. Le Brun was still sitting on the couch, brooding over his own problems: what would his superiors say when he returned to them with the news that the general alarm had been a false one? Denning was studying the pink fringe of the lamp above the table. By God, he's got a temper, Keppler thought. He may seem cool, confident, detached, but he's got plenty of emotion hidden behind that quiet face. Where did he learn that control? When he first came into the room, I thought, so here's Meyer's friend—a self-contained young man who probably thinks this evening is an amusing interlude in his tour of museums, an intellectual dabbling in a little present-day history and hoping for some vicarious excitement. But I was wrong. He knows what we're up against, he knows what he is doing. He's clever —those eyes don't go with stupidity. Stubborn, too: not easily persuaded against his own judgment. And wary: what problem is he keeping to himself? Doesn't he trust us? Good, very good. Better than I had hoped for. At this moment, he's trying to weigh me up, to feel sure of me, just as I've been measuring him. And I don't believe he's any more interested in the Herz diamonds than I am. I begin to like this young man, thought Keppler.

He placed the bottle and the glasses on the table. "I've washed these thoroughly," he assured Le Brun.

"My dear Keppler, I was only having doubts about the brandy."

"Shall we risk ruining our palate? Denning needs a drink." Keppler almost smiled. "He got chilled by the rain."

"Or something," Denning said. His eyes met Keppler's.

Keppler raised his glass and said in English, "Don't tread on me!"

Denning grinned. "That's as good a toast as any." He watched Keppler for a long moment, still deciding whether or not to trust him.

"Well—" Keppler said, sitting down. It could have been a question.

Denning studied the brandy, glowing even through the tumbler. "I am only a sort of observer in this game. Amateur status, I'm afraid." He restrained himself from glancing at Le Brun.

"But I happen to be partial to amateurs," Keppler said. "What have you sort of observed?"

"There's a chambermaid, who calls herself Eva, at the Aarhof. She distrusts your gardening friend. Profoundly."

"You had proof of that? Definitely?"

"Most definitely."

"We weren't quite sure," Keppler said slowly. "Thank you. Anything else you've observed about Eva?"

"She's curious about me. I'd say she was interested rather than suspicious. So far."

"Interested in *you?*"

"That may only have been the result of the gardener's visit. But she is not the only one who is interested. There's a clerk at the desk in the lobby who sorts the mail. He tried to pass on a bogus message—just to see if I know that Meyer is in Bern."

"Indeed?" Keppler's voice was level, but his eyes were thoughtful.

Encouraged with two small successes, Denning spoke with growing confidence, "And Mr. Charles-Auguste Maartens arrived in Bern this morning with a quantity of excess luggage. He's at the Aarhof."

Keppler was silent for a moment. Was he embarrassed? "I heard he had registered there. Surprising. The Aarhof is a most respectable hotel."

Le Brun said, "We've also heard that Mr. Maartens lunched with two friends who seemed to know him well at the Bellevue-Palace; spent the afternoon in the Bern Historical Museum; had tea at Keppler's—no relation to our Mr. Keppler—" He bowed in the right direction.

"Maartens may have a sense of humor," Keppler suggested.

"That is what I am afraid of," Le Brun replied. "When last heard of, he had gone out to the Kursaal for a leisurely evening in plain view of several hundred people. There, at twenty minutes past ten o'clock tonight, he had gone into the casino, along with another friend, comfortably settling down to a pleasant hour at the tables."

Denning looked at Keppler, who nodded confirmation and pointed to the telephone near the bed. "The report came just before you arrived."

"Perhaps you understand now why you found my enthusiasm slightly cooled," Le Brun said. "Mr. Maartens obviously does not intend to keep his appointment for eleven o'clock. He is still at the casino, or we should have heard. And now," he glanced at his watch, "he couldn't reach here in time."

Denning's lips tightened. "This Maartens could be a fake—a cover for the real one."

"Yet the friend he met tonight greeted him with his name."

"You can hire someone to spend an evening with you, you can pay him to call you by your first name." I should have kept quiet, Denning thought, as he watched the other two exchange glances. The professionals being amused over the amateur's naïve suggestions, no doubt. But Keppler didn't smile.

Keppler said, "Have you ever seen the Maartens who arranged this meeting with Colonel Meyer?"

"No."

"None of us has," broke in Le Brun. "Except Colonel Meyer."

"Then how do you know the man out at the casino is a fake?" Keppler asked Denning.

"My suspicions would seem ridiculous to Colonel Le Brun," Denning said. And what, indeed, would they sound like? This man's clothes are expensive, the kind that the real Charles Maartens—as imitated by Max Meyer—couldn't quite reach. This man's manner is wrong—he gives orders, he doesn't take them: no one could send him as an informant: he'd go of his own accord. This man's German is poor, or out of practice—so Gustav, the boy at the Aarhof, noticed. And there's a schoolgirl called Emily who seems to recognize this man: she may know his real name, and she has certainly placed him on the Riviera. Yes, how would all that sound?

"Now, now, I'm always interested," Le Brun said, but his eyebrows went up, and his voice sounded hurt.

Denning said, "One thing's important—have you no files on Charles A. Maartens?"

"The man exists," Le Brun said. "He evaded arrest in Lyons, two years ago, after a very neat jewel robbery."

"Then it isn't likely he lives in the south of France?"

"That would be improbable, and highly injudicious."

"Where has he been working? Or did he travel around?"

Keppler said, "After the trouble at Lyons, he seems to have kept out of France. He is known to have been living in the Rhineland. He has never been arrested, at least not under the name of Maartens. And there is no photograph in any available police file under that name. As for his passport—the man registered at the Aarhof has the only one we know of. But Maartens was either Dutch or Flemish, so we have checked with the passport people in Holland and in Belgium. We should hear soon. Tonight, I hope." Keppler paused. "Have I said something to make your suspicions less ridiculous?" Or, perhaps, he thought as he noticed the American's tightened lips, perhaps something to make your suspicions more worrying.

"Didn't Max give you any kind of description of Maartens?"

"Yes. And I had a drawing made from Meyer's description. Not a particularly distinguished face—it could pass through a crowd without being noticed very much or remembered at all."

"He was a very frightened little man," Denning said, quoting Max Meyer.

"But that could have been a temporary mood," Le Brun pointed out, accurately enough.

Denning rose abruptly, his chair grating on the wooden floor, and crossed over to the window. "Would you put out that light?"

"And let any watcher in the Square see a suddenly darkened window?" Le Brun asked.

"The lady of this room may like it dark occasionally," Denning said savagely.

Keppler laughed. He reached up, his strong square hand closed over the beaded cord of the pink-shaded lamp, and the light went out. "Don't blame this room on my sense of humor," he said, his voice coming softly through the darkness. "It was the most practical place I could find on such short notice—with the help of my good friends in the police department."

"Careful," Le Brun warned as Denning parted the heavy curtains.

"I'm careful," Denning said grimly.

"You still think Maartens will keep the appointment?"

"The real Maartens will," Denning insisted. Or else, he

thought as he stared across the Square at the Café Henzi, or else Max Meyer would be completely discredited and the story about the smuggling of the diamonds would be considered a silly American scare. Then he thought: was *that* the whole purpose of this impersonation of Charlie-for-Short? Was the story to be smothered, quickly, completely, in Bern? And by whom?

"Anything to be seen?" asked Keppler.

"No."

Down in the Square the rain had stopped. There was nothing except the street lights glimmering coldly over wet cobblestones. The shadows were deep. The street was silent. Most of the restaurants had already closed, and the apartments above them were darkened. Only the Café Henzi was still alive. From its entrance, hidden by the arcade, a warm glow fanned out between the curved arches. Its upper floor blazed with light, turning the boxed geraniums outside its opened windows into stiff pieces of cardboard, stage properties like the motionless sign with its gilded script.

Suddenly a zither began to play. There was the distant sound of voices, joining together in the chorus, and then laughter rising as the song faded away.

"Ah, night life!" Le Brun said. "Did I not say this was an innocent town?"

Down in the Square, a man and a woman walked arm in arm. A dog sniffed at an arch. Two men strolled. A car drove carefully over the wet stones. Another song began, each verse ending with the same refrain.

"It may be the darkness, for it surely isn't this brandy," Le Brun went on, "but I feel a certain envy."

"Momentary, I'm sure," Keppler's quiet voice said. He began to hum the tune to which they listened: ". . . *mein schönes Alpenland.*"

"But simplicity *is* to be envied. You Swiss are essentially a simple people, healthy and moral. Why? Because you are blessed with perpendicular countryside. No invading armies. No wars. No troubles. A world of peace and milk chocolate."

Down in the Square, three young men argued mildly. Two began to laugh as they stepped into the arcade. The third followed them. Hollow footsteps and echoing laughter, retreating into distance, lessening into silence. Then the bells from the clock tower sounded over the pointed roofs.

"Another world," Le Brun said softly, "a world of comfortable burghers falling asleep in feather beds. Eleven o'clock and all is well. The doors are locked, the lights are out, the children safe until morning at least, the wives already dreaming of tomorrow's bargains at the cheese market."

There was drifting laughter from the Café Henzi, silence inside the darkened room.

"You worry me, standing there," Le Brun told Denning. "Either Maartens keeps his appointment, or—" He left the sentence suspended.

"Or the appointment was a hoax and Meyer a fool," said Denning. "Is that what you think?"

"As you wish," Le Brun said wearily. "But could we have some light? If we must wait, then let us wait in comfort." He rose, swore with eloquence and imagination as he bumped heavily against the table, and pulled the light on. "I assure you," he said, blinking under the sudden glare, "I'm as anxious as you are. I *want* Maartens to keep this appointment. I *want* Meyer to get all the information possible." But his voice was heavy with pessimism. He went back to the couch. He picked up the doll and looked at it with disgust. "Where's Meyer been all day, anyway? Even Taylor didn't know where he was."

Keppler frowned. "Did you see Taylor today?"

"With precautions—which proved needless, I may say. I had to know what had developed since he came to see me in Munich. But Meyer? He seems to have other business in Bern besides diamonds."

"That may be of equal importance," Keppler suggested.

Le Brun showed his anger at last. "One thing at a time! We are looking for diamonds. Let us concentrate on them." He rose, throwing the doll back on top of a heart-shaped cushion. "We are not amateurs, plunging from extreme secrecy to wild action. I may say I totally disagree with the way the Americans have handled this entire situation." He looked over at Denning, now. "Logic is what one needs in this kind of work, not a liking for cloaks and daggers and false excitements."

"I know," Denning said with dangerous quietness. "Americans are such an inexperienced people. Another world. A world of peace and popcorn."

Keppler gave an unexpected grin, but his voice was most neutral. "Waiting is always unpleasant. But if it's painful for us, how is it for Colonel Meyer over in the Café Henzi? Or for Captain Taylor, who's watching him from another table?

Or even for my poor waiter? He was to telephone me as soon as Meyer had made contact with Maartens." He glanced again, quietly, at his watch. "But there's no reason to get pessimistic. Maartens may have been delayed. That often happens."

"Or the syndicate," Denning couldn't resist saying, "may have heard that Colonel Le Brun has taken a good deal of quiet action with customs offices and shipping lines. Logically, then, we may expect no more information."

"We know how to take *quiet* action," Le Brun said. He stood looking at Denning for a moment. Then he turned away.

"But can *action* ever be kept quiet?" Denning said. He felt better now. He was even speaking mildly, sympathetically. "The best secrets leak out. For instance, how did the maid and the clerk at the hotel come to be interested in me? Did one of Maartens' friends follow Max Meyer to my apartment in Berlin? Yet Max was careful; he's adept at avoiding people."

"How many Americans are there left in Germany who worked originally with Meyer on Restitution of Property?" Keppler asked. "A handful?"

"Yes."

"Someone could check their whereabouts easily?"

"I suppose so." Denning was disconcerted. Max and I both slipped up there, he thought.

"And you were the only one of the handful to appear in Bern. Of course they'd be curious: was your visit casual, or was it arranged?"

"They must have a damned good intelligence service."

"You are referring to the Nikolaides Syndicate?"

Something in Keppler's voice kept Denning silent. Le Brun stopped pacing between the kitchen and the door, and he looked at Keppler too.

Keppler said, "The maid and the clerk at the Aarhof have no connection with the syndicate at all. They are known to us as political agents, who have been active on behalf of—well, a foreign government." He chose a fresh cigar. "You see, Colonel Le Brun, there is something more than diamonds to worry about. I know that is your immediate concern. It has to be. You have been searching for the Herz collection for years. But, for Colonel Meyer and for me, there may be other considerations. We each have our own countries to protect, too."

"I understand that," Le Brun said. "But you understand my position?"

"Assuredly," Keppler said in French.

"I can see it's difficult," said Denning, and hoped that his apology sounded adequate. It was as far as he could go, anyway. To Keppler he said, "You spoke of a foreign government which has been employing these two agents. Is that foreign government—well, is it in a position to be in control of the Herz Diamonds?"

"Yes," said Keppler. "But then, so far, the two agents have been used only in minor capacities. There is nothing to connect their activities, even today, with the diamonds. The most we can do *so far* is to make an intelligent guess. Would you risk one?"

"Of course he could," Le Brun said. "The Herz diamonds were in East Germany. Therefore it must be the Communists who are to blame. Isn't that the popular fashion with Americans, nowadays? A Communist under every bed?" He was amused, highly.

And that's exactly the reason why I didn't make any kind of guess in front of any damned neutralist, Denning thought. "It could be either the Communists or the ex-Nazis," he said quietly. "They are the only people I know who extend their power by conspiracy."

"You amaze me," Le Brun said. "You actually mention Nazis."

"You aren't the only one who has fought them," Denning said.

Le Brun at least dropped the sarcasm. He actually gave a little bow. His voice became more friendly. "It could very well be the resurgent Nazis who had an interest in selling diamonds for their own benefit. After all, why this trouble in smuggling diamonds, why this secrecy—if Communists are doing it? Wouldn't it be simplier for Russia—I suppose you really mean Russia when you talk so vaguely of Communists —wouldn't it be simpler for her to donate a large sum of money toward any secret fund?"

"Yes," Denning said. "And it would also have been far easier to use a diplomatic pouch for the actual smuggling."

"Doesn't all that point toward ex-Nazis, then? They have neither government money nor a diplomatic pouch—at present, anyway."

"Yes," Denning admitted again. "It could be that. Or it could be—" He hesitated.

Keppler said, "Or it could be what our faceless enemy *wants* us to believe?" He shrugged his shoulders. "Clever, if true. Until now—as far as I'm concerned—this faceless enemy has made only one mistake: he has chosen to smuggle the Herz diamonds through Switzerland. My neutrality is not unlimited when I see a conspiracy directed against other people's innocence."

"But aren't we conspirators, too?" Le Brun said. "Who are we to judge men doing the same kind of work as our own?" He looked at the Swiss and the American, thinking sadly that simple people found simple judgments.

"I must have expressed myself badly," Keppler said very quietly. "But as far as I know, my country is not conspiring to destroy the freedom of any innocent person. My work has never sunk so low as that."

"Now you misunderstand me," Le Brun said quickly. "What I intended to imply was—"

The harsh purr of the telephone cut him short. Le Brun stretched out his hand, then stopped. With grave politeness, he stood aside to let Keppler answer the call. Denning too had risen to his feet.

"I see," Keppler was saying quietly in English, "I see." But there was a look of bewilderment on his face, immediately followed by anxiety. "One moment." He covered the mouthpiece with his hand, turning to the others. "It's Meyer. At the Café Henzi. The informant has not turned up. Neither has Taylor."

Then Meyer's alone over there, alone, Denning thought; and the cold feeling of alarm gripped him. Le Brun was looking shocked—perhaps Meyer's phone call was too unorthodox.

Keppler held out the telephone. "Talk to him about Maartens," he said to Denning. "Find out if your suspicions are ridiculous or not."

Denning looked at Le Brun's startled eyes, then at Keppler's frown. He took the receiver. He said, "Hello, there! So the girl friend didn't turn up? Well, come out to my house and have a drink."

Max laughed. "I'll give her another ten minutes, if the waiters don't sweep me into the streets. You know women." He sounded worried, though, in spite of his amusement.

"Yes, I know Shorty."

There was a pause. "And when did you see Shorty?"

"We arrived together at the Aarhof."

"That's funny," Max said. Then he altered it a little. "That's quite a joke. On me."

"Very smartly turned out," Denning went on.

"*Très snob, très chic* again?"

"And *tout à fait cad* this time. It's the money that does it. I'd say the suit cost at least a couple of hundred dollars. No imitations for Shorty today."

"This gets funnier and funnier," Max said. "Hilarious. Are you sure it was Shorty?"

"Two inches under medium height and twenty pounds overweight. Wrinkles round the eyes, skin too sallow, not a gray hair showing. Pity about the snub nose, but that's your taste, isn't it?"

"That's my Shorty," Meyer said, laughing again.

"What I really admired was the neat little hands," Denning went on. "Neat little hands to match neat little feet."

"Be serious!"

"I don't sound serious?"

"Not to me," Meyer said grimly.

"Okay, okay," said Denning. "I get you. I'll never laugh at Shorty again."

"Don't!" Meyer said warningly. "Have a good vacation." And he hung up.

Denning turned to face Le Brun and Keppler.

"Well?" Keppler asked.

"The man at the Aarhof isn't Maartens. There's one thing that can't be disguised, and that's small hands and feet."

"I think," Keppler said slowly, his face so serious now that Denning's feeling of small triumph turned into something very close to fear, "I think I shall have Mr. Maartens detained for questioning about his passport." He picked up the telephone again.

"I hope," Le Brun said to Denning, his voice more friendly, even a real smile on his lips, "that anyone who listened to your conversation with Colonel Meyer was as baffled as I was."

Denning reached for his coat and pulled it on.

Le Brun's melancholy eyes watched him. "Keppler, look at this idiot," he said quietly.

Keppler, waiting at the telephone, turned his head. "What do you think you're doing?"

"I'm just a tourist, walking back to his hotel." Denning buttoned the coat up to his chin. There was a decisiveness in that last flick of his thumb that ended all argument.

"Stick to that story," said Keppler. His blue eyes no longer looked blankly at Denning. They were not even making any attempt to disguise their worry.

"I'll be all right," Denning said, pulling on his hat.

"Are you armed?"

"No. I'm a tourist, remember? Good night."

And, as the door closed behind Denning, Le Brun said, "Amateurs have their uses, I suppose. But didn't you take a chance letting him go?"

Keppler began making the first of a series of telephone calls. He dealt in turn with the Maartens registered at the Aarhof, with the chambermaid and clerk who worked there, with the American called Taylor who seemed to be missing. "But first, attend to Maartens," he ended his call, and then replaced the receiver. He looked at his watch. Denning ought to have reached the Café Henzi by this time.

Le Brun said restlessly, "And what do we do here? Wait for Meyer to turn up with a report?" A report of failure. Then they'd all argue and talk and argue. What went wrong? That would be the question. God, he thought wearily, how I hate these post-mortems: couldn't we succeed, just once, with those Herz diamonds?

"We'll wait," Keppler said grimly. "That's the major part of our job, isn't it?" Then he thought, perhaps I ought to alert the police. I'd like to have some of them around in the Square. And yet, this wasn't a matter for the police. Not yet. . . . Perhaps it would never be. . . .

Gloomily, he settled down by the telephone.

7: *Assignation*

IN THE CAFÉ HENZI, THE SINGING HAD BEEN GO-
ing on for half an hour, singing and laughter and high soprano
shrieks of enjoyment.

"Had enough?" Francesca asked. "It seems to be more
hilarious tonight than usual." She glanced at the ceiling above
them. "There's nothing like a convention for spoiling other
people's pleasure."

"Oh, it's still quite early," Paula said.

"I thought you were anxious to go. You keep looking at
the door."

"Sorry." Paula laughed. "I was only watching Colonel
Meyer leave. I'm sure that man *is* Maxwell Meyer, even if
he isn't in uniform. What a peculiar thing, though!"

"Why peculiar? Lots of American and English officers
come here in mufti, too."

"I know, I know, but you see," Paula was so honest, so
earnest, "only recently Andy went through to Frankfurt to
call on Colonel Meyer. You know how newspapermen often
come across strange pieces of information. Andy had heard
something or other that kind of worried him. So," Paula took

a deep breath, looked around, lowered her voice to the point
of inaudibility, "so Andy decided to approach Colonel Meyer
on the old-pal level. That's how Americans really like to
work."

Francesca was perplexed.

Paula said patiently, "They like to see someone they know,
or someone who's a friend of a friend, and then they have
a quiet talk. After that, if their problem seems important
enough, they are shown the right door on which to knock.
You see how useful the old-pal level can be? Cuts all kinds
of delays."

"And is Colonel Meyer a friend of Andy's, or—a friend of
a friend?"

"He's a friend of Bill Denning's. Actually, we met him
years ago when he was visiting Bill in Princeton."

"Oh?" Francesca said, properly lost now, yet still trying to
keep contact.

"Well, Andy did get to see Colonel Meyer. And they got
on fine—Maxwell Meyer was interested as all hell's burning.
I'm quoting Andy."

Francesca said, "And so Andy was helped to knock on the
right door?"

"That's all I was told. But Maxwell Meyer never mentioned
he was coming to Bern. That I do know. And that's why it
seems so peculiar."

"Perhaps it was a late decision," Francesca said.

"Perhaps." Then Paula was very still. "Why, he didn't
leave here, after all! He must have been just telephoning, or
something."

This time, Francesca looked. She saw a dark-haired man,
with a prominent nose and chin, sitting down not far from
them, seemingly nonchalant and yet carefully facing the door.
He wore a dark green corduroy jacket, a loose red tweed tie.
She would have taken him for a graduate student or an in-
structor at the University. He had a long glass of light lager
in front of him, and he was making it last. He didn't seem
to be bored, he didn't seem to be waiting. And yet—

"He's looking this way," Paula said. She smiled and bowed
toward Max Meyer. "Well—" she said in some embarrassment.

"He didn't recognize you," Francesca said. What, she wondered worriedly, is so interesting in the Café Henzi to an
American officer?

"He doesn't remember me at all," Paula said. "I feel about six inches high." She looked down at the tablecloth. "I think we should get back to the hotel soon, don't you?"

But Francesca, watching the man in whom Andy had put so much trust, didn't reply. He was only three tables away. He couldn't hear what they were saying, for their voices were low, but he must have marked Paula's American voice. For, without turning his head, he was looking at them. Yes, he was verifying Paula. But he made no move. He took another drink of beer. And then, on the table in front of him, Francesca noticed a pack of cigarettes lying squared off with a box of matches. Yet he didn't touch them. He wasn't even smoking.

Paula had been searching for her gloves. "I think I've got everything now," she said. "Ready?" She looked round for their waiter, and then her eyes widened. "Of all things!"

Bill Denning stood at the doorway, taking off his coat and hat. He shook them before he hung them on a peg, and then made his way to one of the last empty tables on the other side of the room.

"This," said Paula in a faint voice, "this is ridiculous." Look at them, she thought, sitting in the same room: two friends, two Americans in a foreign city, neither knowing the other is here.

Francesca laid a quiet hand on her arm, and Paula's pretty face—round, ingenuous, wide-eyed—looked almost comical in its disbelief. Did Francesca mean that Bill and Maxwell had seen each other?

"Smile," Francesca said. "Smile and tell me all about that apartment you're looking for."

"But I've told you," said Paula. "And look, where did you develop that grip of yours? I bet you were good with a machine gun." She began to laugh.

Francesca, smiling, said, "That's better. I just want you to stop looking like a stuffed Sphinx."

"I don't see how a Sphinx could possibly be stuffed."

"If we say it is, at this moment, then it *is* stuffed. Go on talking. I'd like to stay here just a little longer."

"Why don't you do the talking?" Paula asked.

"Frankly, I can't think of anything to say." And I'm too busy watching the door, Francesca thought.

"The quick brown fox jumps over the lazy dog."

"Original."

"Then you try. Must we talk, anyway?"

"Oh!" said Francesca suddenly. Her handbag seemed to spill open, and she bent quickly to search for its scattered contents. Paula picked up a small comb. Francesca was searching under the table, now, for her compact and cigarettes. And then Paula noticed that a woman had entered and was walking across to their side of the room. She was a middle-aged woman, plainly dressed in a black coat and a black felt hat bulging sideways over the heavy braids wound round her ears. She halted, looking down at Meyer's table. Then she nodded and took a chair beside him.

Paula thought, well, I don't think much of Meyer's taste in women—overweight above, thin hard legs below. She looked across at Bill Denning, but his head was bent over a wine list. "Haven't you found everything yet?" she asked Francesca.

Francesca finished her search. As she raised her head, she was busy draping the scarf she had worn at her throat over her hair. She kept her back to Meyer's table as she knotted it firmly under her chin, covering not only her hair but her brow and the sides of her face.

"Expecting a storm?" Paula asked with a smile, but Francesca only turned up the collar of her coat. She had already started toward the door.

"Where's our waiter?" Paula wanted to know, but she followed Francesca. Francesca's face, turned toward Paula, was white and cold.

"We can pay outside," Francesca said, her voice low, her head still turned away from Meyer's table. The ordinariness of her words was strange when contrasted with the little sigh she gave as they reached the lobby.

Madame, buxom, blithe, and debonair, calculated the price of a bottle of Valais wine. "Poor fellow," she said, pointing to their waiter who was in the telephone booth, "his wife is expecting a baby tonight. He's trying to phone the hospital, and of course its number is engaged. Don't worry, Emil!" she called loudly, "just count to fifty, and then try again." She stared at the money in her hand. "Now, how much did I say that was?"

Hurry, hurry, Francesca thought, hurry and give me back my change before that woman who's talking to Meyer comes out through this lobby. She might recognize me here, even with my head covered: she studied me enough last Tuesday when she followed me.

"Now did I add service? No . . . let me see. . . ." Madame smiled at Paula, listening to the new outburst of song from the upstairs room. "Enjoying themselves," she said cheerfully. She lowered her voice confidentially. "They sound younger than they look, I can tell you." She counted out the change with maddening honesty. "It's stopped raining," she informed them. "It's going to be a fine day tomorrow." Under her white hair, her pink cheeks glowed with her good news. Her blue eyes, her broad smile gleamed with pleasure.

"That's splendid," said Paula, embarrassed at Francesca's silence. But her politeness was ill-advised.

"Have you visited the bear pits, yet?" Madame asked, leaning her arms comfortably on the small counter. "All you visitors should see the bear pits. If you haven't seen them, you haven't seen Bern." Then she spent a full three minutes describing the historical meaning of the bear pits, the simplest way to reach the bear pits, the best time to see the bear pits, and the bear pits. She had even begun (and the waiter in the telephone booth was trying to reach his number for the third time, Francesca noted) to tell them about her favorite bear, Willy she called him, a most comical fellow. Quickly Francesca said, "We must leave this for the waiter," and she handed over a tip to Madame, who thanked her, and, in thanking her, looked at the telephone booth and forgot even Willy. "Don't despair!" she shouted. "Keep trying, Emil!" She turned again to her guests, but they had gone.

Bill Denning had reached the Café Henzi quickly. And safely, he hoped. But in a crisis, speed could be as important as caution. He might not be much of a reinforcement, but at least he was here.

He took off his raincoat at the entrance to the downstairs room, giving himself the necessary minute to make sure that this was the meeting place. Or else he'd have to turn into an Econophilosophist pretty damn quick to get upstairs past Madame's warnings. But this was the room: there sat Max, very much at ease, his arms resting comfortably on a red-checked tablecloth, a glass of beer at his elbow, cigarettes, matches, everything under control. And there, too, was Paula Waysmith with her Nefertiti friend.

He hung up his hat and coat, got the startled look out of his eyes, and made his way to the nearest free table. He became engrossed in lighting a cigarette, in looking at the chess game next door to him. Paula knew Max Meyer; not well, but well enough. She and Andy had met him at Princeton just after Peggy had been killed, when Max had come telling him to get out of the ruins of his private life, to go back to Germany, and to bury himself in a job which carried no memories of Peggy. What shall I do, he wondered now, if Paula comes over here, what the hell shall I do? Damnation, why couldn't Andy keep his Paula chained up in a cellar, a nice pink satin cellar, lace-fringed? The first thing she'd tell him, with those bright blue eyes sparkling, would be Guess who's here! But didn't you see? Poor old Bill, let's buy him new glasses. Come on over, let's join Colonel Meyer, let's all have a party together. *Is*n't this fun?

Yes, isn't it?

Oh, forget Paula, he told himself. Register a few prayers that she didn't see you. Concentrate on Max and his problems.

The waiter brought a lengthy wine list, a beige parchment thing looking appropriately venerable, decorated with curlicues and sixteenth-century pen-twiddles and a pot-bellied monk laughing at a spare old man, skull-headed, with a scythe over his shoulder. The thick black script was teasing to read in the dim light. Denning decided that Max had taken the easiest way out by ordering beer—and, remembering the tall glass on Max's table, he also remembered the pack of cigarettes lying at neat right angles to a box of matches. "Beer," he said to the waiter. "No! Better make that brandy." There wasn't much future in mixing grain and grape. His thoughts flickered back again to that pack of cigarettes. Max didn't smoke. Neatly arranged cigarettes and matches—a signal? an identification?

I'm right, he thought. That's it. Max had arranged with Maartens, on the chance that there might be a delay or an accident, some other means of getting in touch with a substitute for the little jewel thief. That would explain why Max waited so peacefully here while everyone else had given up all hope. Denning thought angrily, I must have been influenced after all by Le Brun's doubts: I was beginning to forget how carefully Max worked out every angle.

"Brandy," he told the waiter again. The man was standing very still, his head inclined politely, but he was watching the woman who had entered and was now walking slowly, almost carefully, along the row of tables on the side of the room where Max Meyer sat. She halted in front of Max, and as she sat down she turned her head to look at the rest of the room. It was all very quietly done, as quietly and naturally as the waiter had walked toward the lobby, leaving Denning with his order unheard.

Denning bent his head over the wine list. He could have been mistaken. He had only risked a brief glimpse of her face. But a cold sweat broke over his forehead, and for a moment his mind was paralyzed.

Yes, the woman was Eva. The messenger from Maartens had arrived. And it was the fat chambermaid with the quick thin legs, the woman who had no connection with anything so civilian as jewel thieves. An agent, Keppler had said. And Meyer, with all his careful planning, how could he know? The woman had recognized the right signals—the cigarettes and matches arranged just so, perhaps the color of Max's jacket, the side of the room where he sat. But who had told her all this? Not Maartens surely, not Charlie-for-Short? She was as much his enemy as she was Meyer's.

Now, Denning thought, what do I do? Telephone Keppler —but I haven't got the number of that pink nightmare of a room, damn it, I haven't got it. . . . But didn't Keppler have one of his men here as a waiter? Where the hell was that God-damned waiter? Then he remembered his own waiter, so quietly vanishing into the lobby. The man would be on the telephone to Keppler by this time, telling him that a contact had been made. Denning relaxed a little, and his language calmed down too. He checked his watch. Barely two minutes had passed since the woman had entered, two minutes that felt like two hours. Abstractedly, he noted that Paula and her friend were leaving. Vaguely, he wondered why the waiter hadn't ended his phone call by this time. But actively, his mind—now recovered from its first blank shock—raced through one plan after another, proposing and rejecting them in turn. How was he to warn Max?

The easy thing would be to walk over to Meyer's table and say, "Hello, Eva! And what are you doing here? Elizabeth won't like it, at all."

That tempted him. But it was dangerous, too. He'd certainly blow his own cover, but, what was more important, he'd probably paralyze what was left of Meyer's mission. And he would arouse interest in "Elizabeth" and give a lead toward Keppler.

Or he could leave when Max left, bump into him in the lobby, say, "*Achtung, Achtung, Achtung!* Look where you're going!" Rude, but effective. Except that, when Max took the warning, there might be someone else within hearing distance who'd report on it. Again, cover blown; mission paralyzed.

Or if that dutiful waiter would only finish telephoning Keppler and come back here, then he could take a note over to Meyer's table. A note? Why not a menu? That was subtle enough to please even Max. A menu, or a wine list.

He looked down at the piece of imitation parchment lying on the table. He found his pencil. With a smile, he studied the skeleton face of Old Father Death. Carefully, he shaded in two heavy coils of hair over each ear. Then he drew a round felt hat lightly over the top of the skull, and was a little proud of the way he made that hat bulge where it rested on the braids. With quick heavy strokes, he fattened the skeleton's body into a squarish mass. He left the skeleton legs exactly as they were.

He looked up to see that Eva was leaving. It was Denning's guess that Max Meyer would follow her quite soon. He looked over at Meyer's table, to try and catch his eye, to give him at least a warning sign, however careful or vague. But Max was studying the pack of cigarettes, holding them in his hands. His face was thoughtful. Then he slipped the cigarettes into the breast pocket of his jacket, leaving the matches on the table, and raised his hand to signal for the check.

Denning rose quickly, taking the wine list, noting the waiter who had made a sign of coming-sir to Meyer. He cut the man out as neatly as a calf, and roped him too. He said quietly, slipping the wine list under the waiter's arm, "Will you take this list to the gentleman in the green jacket who wants his check? It's a joke he will like." And he pressed a two-franc piece into the man's hand, which was ready enough, readier than his wits. "A joke?" the man repeated, and then nodded eventually. "Yes, sir. Certainly." He moved away, still nodding.

Denning reached the row of pegs, and searched for his coat and hat. He pulled on his coat, half-turning to see if the waiter had delivered the wine list. But from the neighboring table to Meyer's, another customer was now signaling, too. The waiter did his best, or perhaps he was color blind. With a bow, he handed the list to the stranger, who was dressed in a bright blue suit. He even explained that it was a joke, for he pointed to Denning at the door and laughed heartily. The customer looked more puzzled than amused. Denning made a bleak attempt to smile. The man in the blue suit smiled back politely, but he looked embarrassed. Then he turned to Max Meyer, his hands and shoulders raised as he expounded on incredible people, senseless jokes.

Denning's smile became real as he entered the lobby, for the man in the bright blue suit was showing Max the wine list, as if he wanted to have his indignation shared. Denning thought, well, that's the first time that a joke against me ever got turned to my account. He could almost feel his heart, descended into his stomach, returning left of center in his breast.

Madame told him, "But you *ought* to have got the check from the waiter." She shook her head over the impatience of customers, over her own stupidity at sending all the waitresses to serve upstairs, tonight: they stuck to the rules and made out the checks properly. "One brandy?" He was probably being accurate, she decided, he hadn't been in the room very long. And she liked his face, she always liked men's faces that were serious and sad if the eyes were not glum. She looked up from her money drawer to see him staring at the waiter in the telephone booth. "Poor Emil," she explained, "he's been trying to telephone the hospital and its line is engaged. Now that's four, five, and ten makes fifteen, and five is twenty. His wife is having a baby."

"He'll pull through, probably," Denning said with a last glance at the waiter. He remembered the telephoning that Keppler had begun as he left the pink room in No. 10 Henziplatz. Keppler was thorough, at least; and he must be taking Max seriously, too. Denning felt better for that. He handed over a tip for Emil. "A little extra," he said quickly. "Good night." He left Madame still talking.

There was a fan of yellow light spreading out from the Café Henzi's doorway, bright and dangerous. But beyond, on either side, the arcade was dimly lit, bleak, its doorways dark, its square pillars casting black bands of shadow over the gutter onto the cobblestones of the little Square. Denning walked along the straight stretch of arcade at a normal pace, with no sign of hurry, no sign of alarm. Then, just before the arcade twisted to the right to form the northwest corner of the Henziplatz, he halted beside one of the pillars as if to light a cigarette. There was no one near him. The doorways he had passed had been empty. A short step took him into the pillar's broad black shadow. He slipped his cigarettes back into his pocket, keeping close to the base of the arch. From here, he could see much. He took a deep breath and examined the Square.

A couple sauntered past the café, their arms linked, the woman's high heels echoing under the arcade. Two men crossed the cobblestones. On the other side of the Square, a man walked briskly. Beyond the café, just south of the lighted doorway, a car was drawn up close to the arch of the arcade. That seemed all. Yet, his uneasiness grew. It was a long minute of waiting.

He heard a car coming from the northern part of the Henzigasse, moving slowly with excessive care. It entered the Henziplatz. He could see it now, gathering speed, bumping over the cobblestones, traveling past him toward the south end of the Square. With satisfaction, he watched its taillights vanishing down the south section of the narrow Henzigasse. And then his relief was wiped out. Why had it traveled so slowly through the northern part of the little street? It had been one of those little German Volkswagen, easy to maneuver. Why had it crawled its way into the Square?

There must be a car parked on that stretch of narrow street, Denning decided: a car parked to the north of the Square, as well as the car parked just south of the Café Henzi. Meaning . . . ? Yet people did park their cars in narrow alleys where—judging by the emptiness of the Henziplatz and the southern part of the street which he could see clearly—parking was not encouraged. Motorists were very much alike in any language.

He straightened his spine as he saw Max Meyer appear at the doorway of the Café Henzi. With him was the man in the bright blue suit, whose sense of humor was now restored for they were laughing together. The man said, "I go this way," and he pointed south. "What about you?" Max must have nodded his agreement, for they turned south, walking away from Denning. Across the Square, a woman stepped out from the shadow of an arch, and signaled.

Max had only taken a few paces along the west arcade. He must have been alert for danger. As two men, tall powerful figures in dark coats, suddenly appeared from the car which was parked so peacefully south of the café, he veered from the sidewalk and started across the Square, leaving his companion to stand and stare after him.

And then a car, empty except for the driver, entered the Square from the northern Henzigasse, its engine roaring with its sudden acceleration. Meyer glanced over his shoulder and began to run. He almost reached the east arcade ahead of him, but the car swerved as it traveled so recklessly through the Square, and it struck him with all the weight of its speed. There was a wild high scream of brakes. The car skidded toward the arcade, swiveling completely round to a sudden halt almost against the arches themselves. And there it stood, motionless, pointing its headlights at the man it had murdered.

In the pink-shaded room of No. 10 Henziplatz, Le Brun started to his feet. "My God, what was that?" he asked, and he raced for the window. Keppler picked up the telephone. I knew it, I knew it, he thought bitterly, his anger rising against himself, as he dialed Detective-Inspector Bohren's private number. I knew it. . . . Why didn't I trust my own instincts, why, why?

That was always the question—afterward.

8: The Running Men

FOR A MOMENT OF HELPLESSNESS, DENNING stood still, his shout of warning frozen in his throat. Then, from the car that pointed toward Meyer's crushed body, the driver slipped out, quickly, quietly, and dashed into the arcade near at hand.

Denning began running. As others were running: the couple who had been sauntering round the Square, the man in the bright blue suit, two or three men from the shadows of the arcades. To run, to see what had happened, to help, that was the first impulse.

From the Café Henzi came Madame, a coat thrown over her shoulders; a waiter with a napkin still folded over his arm; one or two startled patrons, then three or four, then others to group at the doorway and stare across the Square. Upstairs, the singing and laughter had stopped. The only sound in the Square was the clatter of running feet. But from the parked car near the café, Denning heard the gentle sound of an engine being skillfully moved into low gear. The car started quietly forward, creeping slowly along the arcade toward the southern Henzigasse.

In his increasing sense of helplessness, Denning tried to shout a warning to one of Keppler's men who must be somewhere in the Square. But his shout was only a gasp, the cobblestones had turned into a heavy bog sucking down his feet, and for a moment's despair he thought he would never reach the group that had begun to gather round Max Meyer. At least, he thought as he joined them and stood regaining his breath, I have the escaping car's number, for whatever that's worth, I have its number.

But where was the man who had driven into Max? Was he hiding over in that arcade? Yet nothing moved there. Or he could have made for the street which led southward away from the Square—the street where the car that had withdrawn so tactfully could have picked him up. Or, foolhardy as it might seem, he could now be mingling with this little crowd. And yet that hardly seemed credible; except that someone would certainly stay here to verify their success. Who, then? Sharpened by failure, his eyes searched the gathering group.

"But what *happened?*" a woman kept saying. "Didn't he *see* the car?"

"It must have skidded—"

"Out of control—the driver was going too fast."

"Was he drunk?"

"Don't move the poor fellow!" That was Madame protesting.

"That's right," Denning said harshly, and pushed aside a man who was about to bend over the body. "Are you a doctor? Stand back, then. This is my job." His voice was grotesque to his own ears, angry, curt, hoarse with emotion. But it had an effect. The man looked up, startled.

"Let this doctor have a look," Madame said quickly, taking Denning's side—she had pride in her patrons—and she pulled the stranger away from the dead man.

Denning knelt, and raised Meyer's eyelids gently, felt for a pulse that no longer beat, bent his head over a silent heart. Max stared back at him with unseeing eyes, one hand folded purposefully. Denning felt the pulse of that wrist, too. The hand was hiding a pack of cigarettes. Then Denning looked up at the questioning faces around him. Only the man who wanted to be helpful had no question in his eyes: they watched Denning coldly. Denning shook his head. "What about the car?" he demanded, and even the watching man's eyes turned toward the headlights for a moment. Denning rose to his feet, the pack of cigarettes now hidden in his own hand.

He looked down at Max Meyer for a brief last moment—that was all the time Max would have allowed him. And the feeling of the cigarettes in his hand was no comfort at all, even though Max would have approved of it. He restrained the impulse to slip his hands into his pockets at once. Instead, he turned away, his hands by his side for anyone to see.

Someone tugged at his sleeve. "Better take a look at this one, too. The driver looks dead, but you never can tell. Proper smash-up, wasn't it?"

"The driver?" Denning asked, startled for a moment.

Behind him, Madame said crossly, "Oh, can't you leave that poor fellow alone? The doctor said it was hopeless."

Denning looked back to see the same man who had bent over Max now kneeling beside him. "But he didn't feel the heart properly," the man was saying in hard flat German, as he slipped his hand inside Max's jacket.

Denning walked away toward the murder car, grim-faced, his jaw set, his fist clenched. If Max could speak, he'd be saying, with his sardonic smile, "That's right, you ghoul, search all the other pockets too."

He reached the car and stared down at the man who had been pulled into the driver's seat, a little man in a cheap smart suit with an evil gash across his forehead. A cheap gray suit, too tight for him, wrinkled over his heavy body. His shoes were elaborate, with pointed toes dangling from short stiff legs. His satin tie hung loose from a striped silk shirt. Even in death, he was a very frightened little man.

The police had arrived, with three cars and an ambulance. "Weren't they *quick?*" someone said with native pride.

Denning stood aside, listening to the questioning voice of authority. In any language, it sounded the same. And the other voices eager to answer it were the same everywhere—voices explaining, recounting, conscious of taking a small, but fortunately safe, part in a passing tragedy. He was still disguising the pack of cigarettes in his hand. Somehow, at this moment, he distrusted pockets. And he was still watching, from a little distance, the man who liked to feel hearts properly: a tall powerful man with reddish hair closely cut under a dark felt hat. His coat was dark, too, broad in the shoulders with a military look, and long-skirted. The kind of coat worn by the two men who had advanced on Max under the arcade. So one of them had driven away; and the other had come running along with the innocent people. Yes, even from this distance, the silhouette became recognizable.

Denning moved over to the group that was giving information to a tall, solemn man in uniform. A strange little group: the man in the bright blue suit, pink-faced with importance; the woman of the sauntering couple, whose tongue clacked as loudly as her high heels under the arcade; a heavy blonde in a dressing gown, suddenly conscious of her hair curlers; a man with striped pajamas under his raincoat; some of the customers of the Café Henzi. Near them was Madame herself, trying to get back to her cash desk—if the police had any questions to ask, they'd find her there. Facing her stood another obvious policeman, even if he was in ordinary clothes, a man of some authority, trying to pacify Madame. What was he—a detective, an inspector?

Denning said clearly, "This lady did not see the actual accident. I can vouch for that."

"Thank you, doctor," said Madame, and with several bows all around fluttered back to her café.

"Did you see it?" the inspector demanded.

Denning pointed to the northern Henzigasse, as if he were explaining. "I was up there—" he began. Then he dropped his voice, "Get that tall man in the dark coat who's walking south. He went through the dead man's pockets."

The inspector looked southward. "Yes, yes," he said to Denning, then moved away as if to supervise the police photographers.

"I suppose no one can tell very much," the man in pajamas said. "Happened too quickly. Must have been drunk, both of them."

"I feel terrible about it," said the heavy blonde. "Right under my window it was." She giggled nervously. "I do look a fright, don't I?" She covered her curlers with her hands.

"The gentleman who was killed was certainly not drunk," the man in the bright blue suit joined in righteously. "Most certainly not. Let me tell you exactly how it all happened." And so he began his story, for the seventh time at least.

As Denning stood with the listening group, he watched the south end of the Square. The man hurrying through the shadows had almost reached the entrance to the Henzigasse. I've failed, Denning thought, he's vanishing into the darkness.

We'll never find him there. But even as his fear was becoming a certainty, a policeman set out running. Now was the test.

The hurrying man didn't hear the sharp call to halt, seemingly. Yet his pace quickened. And then, abruptly, as he reached the dark street, he broke into a run. A car, standing near the ambulance, switched on its full headlights and shot forward toward the Henzigasse.

He can't escape now, Denning thought, turning away. Strangely, he felt no triumph. Only a sense of chill and emptiness. Only exhaustion.

But the inspector was back again, taking charge, calming new speculations from the curious crowd. There was a look of brisk satisfaction on his face. "Are you the doctor?" he asked Denning. "You're wanted over at the ambulance, right away." And then he turned to the others. "Routine, routine," he said, dispersing them with both his calm tone of voice and his casual wave of the hand.

"Wonder what they want you for?" the heavy blonde said, clattering along behind Denning in her loose slippers. But the inspector caught up with her. "This way, *gnädiges Fräulein*," he said, guiding her toward a policeman with a notebook. "Your name and address as a witness." That scared her homeward. It scared most of the others, too.

People were straggling over the Square as Denning approached the ambulance. It seemed to him as if it were about to leave. He hesitated, wondering what he was supposed to do anyway. "In here!" a voice said from the small blue car he was passing. Its door was open. He saw Keppler lean forward for a moment. "Quick!" He got into the back seat beside Keppler. A man sitting beside the driver closed the door as the car started forward. They moved slowly through the Square, following the ambulance. Keppler's hand pressed gently on his arm, persuading him to sit well back in his corner. He obeyed. He closed his eyes for a moment, trying to shut out even the last glimpse of the Henziplatz.

"I have a lot to tell you," he said, searching his memory. "A lot. . . ."

"Later," said Keppler. "Relax, relax." He had seen this too often: waiting and worrying; sudden action, quick and violent; personal loss and a sense of failure; then—once the strain was all over—the nerves snapped and there was nothing but blankness and despair.

"*Now!*" Denning insisted. "There was a black car parked

near the Henzi Café. It moved away, down here." For they were now traveling through the south part of the Henzigasse. "Its number—" But he couldn't remember the number.

"It was observed," Keppler said soothingly. "The car stopped and picked up a passenger."

"The man who drove the car that killed—that killed—" He couldn't say "Max Meyer." And, fantastically, he now remembered the number of the car.

"You saw him?"

"Yes—as he slipped out of the driver's seat and ran for the south arcade."

Keppler sat quite still for a second. Then he leaned over to the front seat and tapped the shoulder of the man sitting beside the driver. "Did you hear all of that?"

"Yes, sir."

"Keep listening." Keppler turned to Denning. "What else?"

"That red-haired man with the long black coat—he was waiting outside the café near the parked car. He and another man. Together."

"And after the murder, he joined the crowd?"

Denning nodded. "He searched Meyer's pocket. Inside. Over the heart."

"The police caught him," said Keppler with grim satisfaction. "Now, we'll—"

"And there was a woman," Denning went on, his voice flat and unemotional, "who gave the signal when—when Meyer stepped out of the café."

"She could identify Meyer?" Keppler was astounded.

"It was that maid—Eva. Eva. Yes, she made contact with Max in the café. Then she came out. And gave the signal."

"Have you got all that?" Keppler asked the man in the front seat again. "Then we'll drop you off at the police station."

"There's something else," Denning said. He closed his eyes again, he tightened his hands with the effort to remember. The car was stopping. The man in the front seat was leaving them.

"Easy now, take it easy now," Keppler said. "You can tell me all the rest when we reach my place." Then he looked down in surprise at the pack of cigarettes which Denning held out in the palm of his hand.

"Something else," Denning said with sudden bitterness,

and he dropped the cigarettes as though they were burning him.

Keppler stared at the packet in his lap. It was unopened. An ordinary pack of American cigarettes.

"They were in Meyer's hand," Denning told him.

To the driver, Keppler gave quick instructions, seemingly a change in direction, for the car swung suddenly away from the entrance to the Kirchenfeld Bridge and traveled further west to pass the Federal Palace and the wide, open squares that lay around it. "We'll go to my place, later," Keppler was saying. "And there you can tell me everything, exactly as it happened. But now——" and he pocketed the cigarettes, "first things first."

Empty streets, empty squares, Denning was thinking. Quiet squares, without murder or violence. He stared at them blankly. Then he looked quickly back.

"Yes?" asked Keppler, noticing Denning's sudden interest, and he too looked back at the Victoria Hotel. He saw three people walking smartly toward a battered little Renault, which looked somewhat forlorn against such a background of grandeur. Two women, young. A man, tall and bearded.

"Paula Waysmith," Denning said, and he shook his head in wonder. "She was there, in the Café Henzi, tonight, with that other girl. Francesca."

"Who's the man?"

"A stranger to me." A tall powerful man, with a beard. I wish to God Andy would turn up soon and tie that wife of his to a nice hot stove. Or a good soft bed, he thought. Women always had a naïve sense for adventure, a kind of innocent trust that nothing would turn ugly, a kind of schoolgirl approach to—— "Which reminds me," he said, interrupting his thoughts, "I must tell you about Emily. Don't let me forget about Emily." His face relaxed. He almost smiled.

"Of course not." But Keppler looked at him anxiously.

"I'm all right now," Denning said irritably, and he lit a cigarette. "I'm not even asking annoying questions about where we're going," he added, and tried to smile, as the car entered a large courtyard and drew up at one side which lay deep in shadows.

They entered a grubby little room, barely furnished, partitioned off from a larger room.

"I call this my office whenever I visit Bern," Keppler said

as they entered. "But of course you understand that my work as a free-lance reporter keeps me moving around a good deal."

"A reporter?" Denning nodded. It was a cover that was common enough.

"Yes, a crime reporter."

"That's a bit more original."

"Helpful, too. My relations with Inspector Bohren are most amicable. You saw him down at the Henziplatz, I think. A capable man. And a good friend."

"The police are now on the job, then?"

"As far as tonight's car smash is concerned, certainly. It was a clever murder in some ways—no guns, no knives, nothing to alarm the quiet town of Bern. Just a simple accident with a drunken driver. You smelled the gin in that car?"

"Too decidedly."

"Yes. One small splash of spilled gin goes quite far in effect. They forgot that. They forgot several things. Tonight's murder was worse than a crime: it was a blunder." As he talked, Keppler had been clearing the desk, adjusting the lights, producing a sharp knife and a powerful magnifying glass. "Now!" he said, placing the pack of cigarettes on the table, and taking a chair. Then he looked up at Denning. "This is always the moment when I feel sick with nervousness. I always hope for so much. And too often I am disappointed. See how I'm wasting time, talking, talking. . . . Subconsciously, I don't want to open this pack of cigarettes. In case I find nothing."

He picked up the pack and examined it. His powerful hands became light and delicate. "If it isn't too important a message," he was saying, "we'll find something simple, like a piece of paper stuck inside. Perhaps microfilm. Or a message in a special ink." He began easing the folds of the pack open, top and bottom. "You see," he went on, "before I start having some scientific friends awakened at this early hour of the morning, I want to know just what expert help we may need. We'll open the pack—so—" He slit its side gently and the pack became a flat piece of paper. Carefully, he kept the twenty cigarettes still in their triple row of seven, six, seven.

"But there's nothing there," Denning said. "Nothing."

Keppler pursed his lips. "Careful, now," he said, lifting the foil lining and the cigarettes about an inch away from the outside paper cover. "Anything between?"

"Nothing."

Keppler replaced the lining exactly as it had been. He paused, biting his lip. "Then we were too hasty, perhaps. Let us begin all over again." Slowly he folded the pack into its original shape, and pressed the blue stamp back into position over the top folds. Something caught his eye. "This stamp—it's the same size and color as the Swiss tax-stamp used on American cigarettes, but its design is different. It's an American stamp, isn't it?"

Denning looked. He nodded.

"Then Meyer did not buy these cigarettes in Switzerland. Or in Frankfurt?"

"Plenty of Americans arrive in Frankfurt with packs of cigarettes stamped like that."

"Then he prepared this pack in Frankfurt, perhaps. And there, he'd have the necessary equipment to make a really careful message. And the more careful it is, the more important." Keppler's excitement grew. "Now, let us peel off the stamp completely this time. Sometimes you find—" He paused again. "No. No. Here is something else to consider. Look at the stamp to which our attention has been so carefully directed. Isn't it very much to one side? Is that usual?"

"I think it's generally somewhere near the center."

"Then we shan't waste valuable time on peeling off a stamp. Let us take it as an indication showing the side which must be opened first. In an emergency. If, for instance, you had to prevent a message from being found, wouldn't you light the cigarette which contained the message? Now, pretend you have opened that pack of cigarettes. See, the stamp is at this end, slanting. Which cigarette does it point to? Which cigarette would you take?"

"This one."

"Good." Keppler lifted it carefully. "Very, very good," he said. "See?" he pointed to a black dot on the cigarette's paper, no larger than a heavy fleck. "That, I believe, is what we call a micro-dot," he said. "You've heard of such things?"

"Yes, but I've never seen one. Are you sure?"

"I think I'm sure," Keppler said, examining the dot through his magnifying glass. "Yes. It's square, or rather rectangular. Look at that little beauty—just look at her!"

Denning studied it curiously: on a printed page, it could have been a period at the end of a sentence. It could have marked the end of an address on an envelope. It could have been a flaw on a piece of cigarette paper. "And this micro-dot can be enlarged into a full-size page?"

"Provided you have the necessary equipment. And I know where I can find that." Keppler took the cigarette, slipped it into an envelope and placed it in his breast pocket, giving it a couple of affectionate pats. Then he reached for a telephone. "Now I know who has got to be pulled out of bed," he said with a really happy smile. As he waited for his call to be answered, he glanced at his watch. "Either we sit here and wait for this little bit of magic to develop, or I can take you home where we can wait in comfort." He studied Denning's face. The American looked completely exhausted now, drained of energy and decision; and as someone walked along the corridor outside, he looked nervously around, then tried to smile at his foolishness and failed, standing there, not knowing what to do. "An office is a dreary place at one in the morning," Keppler said. And there was still a lot to be discussed. The American's mind had to work clearly. Each small detail he had noticed tonight might have its place in this jigsaw puzzle. Time was precious, yes; but so was accuracy, so was clarity. "My car is still waiting," he said. "We can be at my sister's house in ten minutes. Less."

Then he jiggled the telephone impatiently. "What's wrong with these people?" he demanded angrily. "Never there when you want them. . . ." But someone answered, and he became persuasive, calm, and unrefusable.

9: Paula Is Persuaded

THE DISTANCE FROM THE CAFÉ HENZI TO PAULA'S
hotel was not far, but measured by Francesca's silence it
seemed an endless journey. In all the years she had known
Francesca, Paula had never seen her like this.

"Look," Paula had tried to say, as they left the café and
Francesca suddenly started walking northward, "we're taking
the long way round, it's eas—"

"I know," Francesca had said, "I know." Her low voice
was intense with worry. Or fear. Or both. Her hand on
Paula's arm was tight, urging a quick brisk pace.

It was only when they saw the Hotel Victoria comfortably
near that Francesca's haste slackened. And then she spoke,
too. "Sorry. But I didn't like that car parked just south of
the café."

"Was there one?" Paula felt a little stupid. And then she
felt annoyed. Francesca didn't have to be so dramatic. "I
suppose a car has got to wait some place," she said coldly.
And hadn't they passed other cars, too?

"I'm sorry. I just didn't like it." Or the two men standing
beside it. She shivered. "Don't ask me why. I can give no

reason. You think I'm crazy, don't you? Poor Paula, you look so uncomfortable!"

"I just didn't notice the car," Paula said crossly. "That's all. But I wish you'd stop disliking people without a reason. That woman who sat down at Maxwell Meyer's table, for instance—"

"There, I had a reason. She followed me on Tuesday. Wherever I went, she followed."

"Followed you—actually *followed?*"

Francesca nodded.

"What about today, has she been following us again?"

"No. If she had been, do you think I'd have taken you to the Café Henzi for lunch?"

Paula startled, began revising some judgments: and I thought she took all that business of Schmid the waiter, who was Andrássy the violinist, so coolly. Even the way Francesca had talked about the Committee seemed so matter-of-fact and even casual, underplaying all risk and danger. "I'm sorry," she said suddenly.

At the hotel desk, the clerk handed over the key to her room with the information that a visitor had been waiting to see her for the last three hours. *"Three* hours?" Paula asked.

"Three hours and ten minutes, madame. He's sitting in one of the alcoves over there. Behind the geraniums." The clerk politely nodded in the correct direction.

Francesca pulled gently at Paula's arm and drew her away, across the quietened lobby with its pillars and palms now lonely sentinels, toward the series of deep alcoves, almost small rooms in size, where armchairs and tables and desks were grouped for rest or letter writing or conversation. Now, at this hour, they were practically abandoned: the elderly ladies had left their knitting and listening posts, husbands weren't waiting impatiently for wives who had decided to wear a heavier coat or another hat, wives weren't waiting for bill-querying husbands, children had stopped losing chessmen or silting up inkwells with blotting paper, the post-card scribblers had taken their inspirational phrases to bed with them. There was only a group of four young people entranced in themselves; a white-haired gentleman fast asleep over the London *Times,* a peaceful background to an unhappy couple intense with a private crisis of their own; and, in the last alcove of all, there was a solitary man, bearded, dressed in rough tweeds, who sat with arms folded, his back against the wall, his eyes fixed gloomily on the bank of flowers which shut him away from the rest of the world.

"Ah," Francesca said, pausing for a moment. "When Gregor waits, he waits." She went quickly toward him.

At once he rose, a tall figure with powerful shoulders, dark hair graying at the temples, a heavy beard making him older than he actually was. Or perhaps it was the lines around his solemn gray eyes, the heavy furrows between his broad cheeks and mouth, the permanent wrinkles on his broad forehead, which added twenty years to his age. His was a strong face, with blunt features and a wide mouth. Its grim look vanished as he saw Francesca. Even the wrinkles and furrows changed from heavy despair to overjoyed relief. He hugged Francesca with delight, and then held out a large hand to grasp Paula's.

"I know you well, already," he told her. He had the widest grin that Paula had ever seen, and his accent delighted her, too.

"You had to wait so long," she said apologetically. After all, she was to blame.

"Nothing." He gave an expansive wave of his free arm. "What else I do?" He let Paula's hand go at last. "I come here, Francesca is not here, I wait." His voice was deep, rich with many undertones, a voice normally strong and powerful which he was keeping low. Now, he glanced round the lobby, and then pointed to the wall of the alcove with its screen of geraniums. "We talk here?"

"Why not in my room?" Paula suggested.

He looked a little shocked. "At this hour? Is it—*convenable?*"

Francesca smiled, then. She looked at his tweed jacket with its missing button, at the leather sandals on his feet, at the high-necked gray sweater which he wore because he hated collars and ties. "Perhaps not," she agreed gently. "This is all right, anyway," and she looked around their private alcove and then chose a group of chairs beside a table near the wall. From the other alcoves, only an occasional laugh and the murmur of voices could be heard, but not the words. "So you finished your symphony," she said. "The problem of the chorus in the last movement was solved. I knew it would be."

Gregor shook his head. "They do not matter. Not anything matters." Then he opened his eyes wide. "You think I—you think I celebrate?"

"Well," said Francesca, but now she looked at him worriedly, "it isn't the first time you've suddenly gone driving to Bern at night when you'd finished some work."

"No, no, no!" he said, almost angrily. He glared over his shoulder at the lobby. "We must speak low. Very low. And we must smile. You," he told Paula, "must smile. All the time. We are enjoying. Yes? You speak French?"

"Not very well."

"German?"

"About the same."

"Then I fight with your English." He sighed. "I want you to hear. Your husband—he has a newspaper—he helps us, perhaps? To make public. Yes?"

Francesca sat very still. She had unfastened the knot in her scarf, and pushed the silk square back from her head. "What is wrong?" she asked.

He avoided her eyes. He did not answer.

Was his news so bad? Francesca wondered. "I'm ready, Gregor," she said.

"Schmid did not come today." He was talking to Paula. "*Please* smile," he said.

"Perhaps he decided to stay in Bern for his free afternoon," said Francesca.

Gregor shook his head.

"But he ought to have let you know," Francesca added. She looked down at her slender hands to hide the worry in her face.

Gregor kept talking to Paula in his deep soft voice. "He comes, each Thursday, by motor coach at four o'clock. Four o'clock he arrives. Walks up through village to my house. Little house. In meadows. Behind woods. Two miles perhaps. Half an hour to walk, no more."

Paula, remembering to smile, smiled.

"Good," he said, noting the smile. "When he comes, we have tea, some food. We play chess. We talk music. Until late, very late. We have more food. We talk. Perhaps we sleep. Early, at seven in morning, he goes. Back to Bern."

"He ought to have let you know," Francesca repeated. When Gregor's English became difficult, it was always a sign that he had serious trouble on his mind.

"But he came, he came to Falken today." And now Gregor looked at Francesca again. He said unhappily, "He came. Through village. But not to my house."

"Oh no!" Francesca's face was carved out of white marble.

"Please," Gregor said, "please smile. I am telling you. I wait. I get chessmen all ready. I make tea. He does not come."

"But where—"

"Five o'clock, I go. Perhaps, in village, he talks to Frau Welti. Perhaps he stops to see view. Perhaps there is accident with motor coach. But no, he is not anywhere."

"Did anyone see him arrive?"

"Heinz Gauch. Frau Welti. She waved to him."

"From the inn?"

"Yes. She saw him take road to my house."

"Did you search?"

"But of course. First, alone. It is stupid to worry people. I go to your house. Your aunt says you are in Bern with Paula today. Then I go to some of—" He glanced round, then cupped his face in his hands as he leaned his elbows on the small table, and his voice dropped even lower. "Some others," he ended tactfully.

Some of the Committee? Paula wondered. Her obedient smile was frozen and foolish, as if she were being photographed inexpertly.

"They search, too," said Gregor. "Nothing. I go back to your Aunt Louisa. I am told the American telephoned, you are staying with her tonight. I tell the others to meet at my house. And I drive here."

"What if your friends have found him by this time?" Paula suggested.

"Then there is message for you here. You get no message when you come in?"

Paula shook her head. Her lips were dry with nervousness. She watched Francesca.

"We'll leave now," Francesca told Gregor. Her blue eyes had darkened. Almost to herself, she said, "They've kidnaped him."

"Francesca," Paula said, "*please* don't let yourself think of such—"

"Why shouldn't I? I've seen such things happen before. You haven't."

"But—" Paula looked at Gregor. "This isn't a Communist-dominated little town in a remote part of postwar Italy. This is the capital of Switzerland—with legations and embassies and newspapers and journalists all ready to spread any alarm. And aren't we going too quickly? A man doesn't keep an engagement. What then? Perhaps he changed his mind, or something. Perhaps he wanted a long walk by himself. Perhaps he—oh, there are ten or twenty things that could have happened." Francesca, Paula thought unhappily, lived too much with her bitter memories.

Gregor was looking at her as if she were some strange phenomenon. "Now *you* are being a little stupid," he said.

Paula stared at him. But he wasn't trying to be rude. He was stating a fact. "If you are worried," she asked, "why don't you call the police?"

"Police!" Gregor began to laugh. Then he checked himself. In a voice so low, now, and yet so intense that it was frightening, he said, "What do they understand of political criminals? Pickers of pockets, yes. Murderers of wives, yes. But politicals saying, 'I am noble, look at me how noble!' And then they sell their brothers into slaves. Oh, they are evil, evil, of an evil you do not know. They pick up telephone, like this, easy. They say, 'Two hundred men for Kargopol Camp. At once.' And two hundred men are shipped. Like cattle." He took a deep breath, almost a sob, into his powerful lungs. "I heard them. These men who pick up telephone. The men who are shipped like cattle. I heard them both." Heavy beads of perspiration stood out on his brow. His whole body is crying with pain, Paula thought.

"Come," Francesca said, rising abruptly.

Gregor followed her, and Paula went too. "Let me see you safely out," she said, and returned the cold look given Gregor and Francesca by two smartly dressed women who were entering the lobby.

In the street, Gregor said, "My car is near. This way." Then to Paula, "Your husband comes soon?"

"Tomorrow, I hope." You never could tell, though. Andy might be delayed.

Gregor was speaking in a burst of German to Francesca as he unlocked the door of a shabby little Renault. (My car, he had called it so proudly—was it the first he had ever owned?)

Francesca said, "Gregor thinks Andy can help. He wants the whole story of Schmid made public."

Yes, thought Paula, Gregor is right. Let the story of Peter Andrássy be made known. How many millions throughout the civilized world recognize his name, how many hundreds of thousands listen to his symphonies? They must be told how much he has given up in order to be free—all the special privileges, material rewards, lavish honors which are used to blind a famous man, or to bribe him. Instead, Andrássy has chosen danger—escape, hardship, terror. He has worked as an unknown waiter named Schmid. He is even content to let his name and reputation stay hidden, once he begins his new life in America. He is no longer merely the great man—unapproachable, working apart from ordinary people: he has proved he is a human being with moral courage, a man who has chosen between slavery, however disguised, and freedom, however strange and difficult. Yes, that's how Andy will write about Peter Andrássy: a story of moral courage, without which great men become little.

"And you?" Paula asked Francesca.

"I still don't know. There are others to be thought of." Francesca shook her head. "I don't know what to do," she said miserably.

"We think," Gregor said. "As I drive, we think." He pulled Francesca gently into the car.

"We'll be home before you are in bed," Francesca told Paula. And her hand was as cold as the lips that had brushed Paula's cheek.

"*Please* call me," Paula said. "Let me know—"

But the car slipped away, gathering speed even before it left the Square, and Paula turned back to the hotel. She felt dispirited, troubled, and—in the sanity of the cool night—a little annoyed. Gregor had almost convinced her that he was right, and that she was wrong. He had experienced so much cruelty in his life, so much that was evil, that he had become too quick to judge. And Francesca—she had seen so much that was tragic, that she too accepted the fantastic as possible. What proof, what shred of evidence could either of them produce that something had happened to Andrássy? The tragedy of tragedy was that it could make people too fearful, too credulous, even a little crazed. And there, she thought, I begin to talk, even if I can't think, like Gregor. Is he crazy? Or am I—as he said—just a little stupid? One thing, I admire his courage with English: if I could speak Russian, I know my accent would be funnier than his.

She stopped at the desk to tell the clerk that Miss Vivenzio was not staying, after all.

"Oh dear," the clerk sighed—he was a gentle soul—"then she won't get the flowers."

"Flowers? When did they come?"

"I understood they were being sent tomorrow morning, first thing. A nice surprise for breakfast? The florist telephoned to say he had flowers for Fräulein Vivenzio, and he wanted to verify her room number."

"Are you sure they are for Fräulein Vivenzio?" Paula asked, certain in her own mind that the flowers were for her. Andy often sent flowers when she was alone.

The clerk frowned. "I may have been mistaken," he said, "but I thought they were for—"

"Never mind," Paula said. She was too tired to talk much more. "There will be a card with the flowers. Then we'll know."

She walked slowly toward the elevator. If Andy was sending flowers, then he was apologizing for being delayed in Bonn. That was entirely possible, she thought glumly. She ought to have stayed in Bonn with him, and prevented him from taking on some last-minute job. Then they would both have been on the plane tomorrow. Instead—why, she hadn't even found an apartment.

She felt not only very tired, but very lonely. Heavens, what a night it had been. . . . Next time she was by herself, without Andy, she'd settle for a good book to take to bed.

The corridor leading to her room was peaceful. There was a dim light, but no sound, from the door of the housekeeper's quarters. Everyone was asleep. The thick carpet silenced her steps. She passed only a few pairs of shoes waiting outside their owners' bedrooms to be collected and cleaned. The hotel was still half-empty. In another month it would be bustling with visitors. But now, its quiet emptiness made her feel still more lonely.

The outer door to her bedroom was unfastened as usual, but the inner door opened too easily. Had the maid forgotten to lock it properly? Both beds had been neatly turned down, ash trays had been emptied, glasses cleared. Yes, all was in order. She walked over to the dressing table, unclipping her earrings. "Ridiculous," she said, thinking back to the flowers again, "he got it all mixed up. Why, Francesca—" She laughed. No one knew that Francesca had planned to spend the evening with her, except Aunt Louisa and Gregor. She stared at the looking glass. She was no longer amused. She was troubled. Something was wrong, somewhere.

She began unfastening her watch. It was then, at that moment of dropping it onto a white embroidered mat, that she sensed a movement behind her. She looked at the watch in its nest of carefully stitched daisies, afraid to turn. Abruptly, she swung round.

Two men had stepped out from behind the bathroom door. They seemed as surprised as she was terrified. One was tall, heavy-shouldered in a massive black coat. The other was the quiet little man, with the weak chin and shifting eyes, who had watched Francesca at the Kursaal this evening.

He looked round the room, then back at Paula. "Where is she?" he asked in German.

Paula stared at him. "What?" she asked in English. At this moment she could scarcely think in her own language, far less speak a foreign one.

The little man broke into English. "You were speaking to someone."

"Careful," the large man told him in quick German. "If the girl is not here, then do not mention her."

"I know my job. Do yours! Look in the wardrobe, behind the curtains, look, look!" He turned back to Paula. His shifting eyes flickered like the tongue of a snake. He took a step toward her.

"Nothing, nothing," the tall man said in fury as he searched the room. "You've made a mess of this, a fine mess. Now what?"

The little man advanced another step. His angry mouth was a sign of failure. So were the quick and now unintelligible words of the other as he finished his search.

And suddenly, all Paula's fear had gone and there was only the beginning of a cold rage she had never known before. "Get out! If you take one more step toward me, I'll scream!" She snatched up a bottle of scent from the dressing table. Her heart pounded, but now it was at least steady.

He took another slow step toward her, smiling at her as he brought his hand out of his pocket, slowly, slowly. There was threat in every move.

"I told you!" She opened her mouth wide and gave a piercing scream. Then another. And another.

The man stopped. In amazement, perhaps. And, as his companion made a dash for the corridor, he hesitated. Then he turned and ran, too. But Paula was behind him, the heavy crystal bottle still in her hand. She struck at the back of his neck as he reached the outer door. He staggered forward, and she hit again, and he dropped to the floor. He lay quite still.

I've killed him, she thought, and her anger ended as suddenly as it had begun. She leaned against the wall. Blankly she stared at the figure lying face down over the threshold, and then at the tall man in pajamas and dressing gown who came rushing out of the next bedroom.

"Knocked him out cold," an English voice said, and the man in pajamas looked at her right arm with some respect. "But you could stop screaming, you know."

Paula put a hand to her throat and took a long deep breath.

"That's better."

A lame, elderly porter hobbled from one of the stairways.

"Telephone for the police," the Englishman told him. He looked at Paula. "You agree, don't you?"

"Another man," she said, and pointed along the corridor. But the other man had vanished. "He was tall. A long dark coat. Gray hat."

"There were two men?"

She nodded.

"Get the police," the Englishman said to the porter, who was listening wide-eyed. "Use my phone. Quick." He looked down at the man at his feet. "Do you want me to sit on his head until reinforcements arrive?"

Paula nodded again.

Her new friend sat squarely on the man's back, and searched for cigarettes in his dressing-gown pocket. "Have one?"

She shook her head. At the moment she felt more than slightly sick.

"Nasty little tyke. How did he get in, anyway? Probably sneaked up some back stairs." The Englishman suddenly saw the knife lying under the man's hand. He picked it up. "Did you know about this?"

Paula looked at it in horror. "I thought it was only a gun," she said faintly.

The Englishman searched quickly, now. In one of the man's pockets he found a blackjack, in another a roll of adhesive tape. "Well," he said in amazement, and resumed a firmer seat on the man's back. "Peculiar little arsenal he carries about." Then he sniffed the air. "Good Lord! What did you launch him with?"

Paula looked down at the heavy crystal bottle in her hand. Its stopper had been jerked loose with the blows she had struck, and now it was almost empty. "It was the very best perfume," she said dejectedly.

"Better than the very best butter, for this tea party," said the Englishman consolingly. He had a bald head, an amused smile, and a broadly striped dressing gown. "The crowd gathers," he added warningly, and Paula got control of herself, and tried to ignore the two frightened maids who had come to stare, and the few guests who were approaching hesitantly.

But then, the assistant manager arrived to take charge. The half-dressed guests were calmed and coaxed back into their own rooms with the magic word "safety"; the maids were sent scurrying to find the house detective; the lame porter, whose pride in his telephoning was slightly dashed by the assistant manager's disapproving frown, was given the errand of alerting all the other employees about the missing man. "But it wasn't really necessary to call the police to the hotel. Not to the hotel," the assistant manager kept saying worriedly, unhappily.

The Englishman stared at him. "On the contrary," he said coldly. And so complete silence came to the corridor.

The house detective appeared at last. He was a round-faced, round-bodied man, his round comfortable mind already producing explanations. He had been down in the basement—there had been an alarm—an engineer had seen someone loitering in the boiler room next the laundry. "Probably *him,*" the detective ended, and looked at the man's face. "Why, it's Rauch!—worked here for two months—moved over to the Aarhof last week." He felt better, seemingly, with that discovery.

"Have you handcuffs?" Paula asked anxiously, as Rauch gave a groan and stirred.

The detective looked unhappy again. "In my office—never needed to carry them."

"Of course not," the assistant manager said stiffly. "This hotel has never required—"

"Then I'd better keep a firm seat here," the Englishman said resignedly.

"We can deal with this," the assistant manager said. "Now, if you would—"

Paula said quickly, "I am not leaving until the police arrive." She raised the crystal bottle a little.

"Please don't worry, Frau Waysmith. This is certainly most unusual, but you can rely on us to—"

"But this man is too unusual," she said angrily.

"I beg your pardon?"

"This man is not an ordinary—" Then she bit her lip. Who would listen to her? Or, listening, would believe? Had she believed Francesca and Gregor tonight? She looked quickly to the Englishman for help, but he too was watching her with some amazement—or even embarrassment. "I'm all right," she told him sharply, "all I want is an *intelligent* policeman."

The elevator door rattled open, and the assistant manager said, "The police, thank heaven." But it wasn't the police. It was a tall man with close-cropped fair hair, horn-rimmed glasses, a snap-brim hat tilted slightly to one side, a light-colored tweed coat around his shoulders. He had a load of several newspapers and a tightly packed brief case. Behind him, a night porter carried two cowhide suitcases.

"Andy!" Paula cried, pushing the assistant manager aside, and ran to meet him. "Oh, Andy, make them get me an intelligent policeman." She threw her arms around him.

"Of course," Andrew Waysmith said with a grin and kissed her.

"How wonderful! You caught an early plane," Paula said, suddenly welcoming him properly. "Oh, Andy—" But she didn't have time to explain. Andy had seen the group at the opened door, and his wide smile vanished. He looked at Rauch, feebly stirring, then he verified the number of the room. His face, deceptively mild behind his thin horn-rimmed glasses, tightened to show a jaw that could be aggressive and a mouth that could close like a steel trap. Too quietly for anyone's comfort, he asked, "And just what is going on here, anyway?" He dropped the brief case, newspapers, and coat. "What's been happening to my wife?"

"Exhibit One," the Englishman said, rising from Rauch's shoulders, and stepping back as Waysmith reached down to take a firm grip of the man's arms and jerk him to his feet. "Exhibit Two," the Englishman added, handing over the knife and blackjack and adhesive tape to the assistant manager, who flinched but took them awkwardly. "Exhibit Three." He pointed to the bottle in Paula's right hand. "That's all we really know," he added suavely. "There was another man, your wife says. He was gone before I reached here. But this specimen overstayed his welcome."

"He ran. And I hit him," Paula said. "Oh, Andy, I'm so

glad you're here." Then she noticed the Englishman moving discreetly toward his room. "And that gentleman—"

"Not at all," he said, turning, half-pausing, to give a small bow. "Any time you need help, just—well, scream, perhaps?"

"Thank you," said Paula with an answering smile.

Andy glanced after the broad-striped dressing gown. "And what was that last crack?"

"He's a friend indeed. He answers screams most efficiently," Paula said. But the elevator door rattled again, and this time two policemen stepped into the corridor.

"Intelligent enough?" Andy asked his wife grimly, as he watched the handcuffs being quickly produced, and listened to the assistant manager's brief explanation. "Now just come into our room and tell me exactly what happened and how and why." To the assistant manager, he said, "Do you think you could arrange for some peace? And some Scotch and ice, and a sandwich?"

"Certainly, Herr Waysmith." The assistant manager was grateful for such a request. Peace was all he wanted, too. He frowned nervously along the corridor, quiet now; the bedroom doors had closed. But tomorrow—what explanations, what calmings of fears, what diplomacy he'd need. He frowned now at Paula, transferring some of his worry into annoyance. These pretty young women always caused trouble: if only hotel guests could all be old and plain, how simple life would be. Even now Frau Waysmith was creating more complications. She didn't want the man to be handcuffed to one of the policemen—not yet. She wanted, no less, both policemen to go into the bedroom to hear her story. As if he hadn't given them all the necessary particulars. She was suggesting that this pitiful little clerk should be handcuffed, meanwhile, to the house detective, who would "make quite a good anchor." What phrases Americans used. . . .

"And of course you'll keep watch, won't you?" Paula ended, turning to the assistant manager who was now completely speechless.

Andy Waysmith looked at his wife. Then he said, with the philosophic air of the happily married man, "All right, all right. Let's get this over with. And then we can *all* go to bed."

"Now then—" the senior policeman began in German, with a quick glance round the white and gold bedroom, and he opened his notebook. "The lady wishes to make a statement?"

"I want your help," Paula said. She was feeling better with every passing minute. The two neat blue-gray uniforms with sane reliable faces above their stiff collars were very comforting. But most comforting of all was Andy, sitting quietly in the background, watching her. Oh, Andy, she thought, what a difference you make to everything. She gave him a special smile.

"This is your husband?" the policeman asked, looking at Andy. "American?"

"Both American." Andy handed a card to the younger policeman, who passed it over. "That's how we spell our name."

"I understand you arrived after Rauch had entered this room?"

"Yes."

"Your wife spent the evening by herself?"

"Look," Paula said quickly. "This is *so* urgent. We'll give you all details about ourselves tomorrow, or whenever it suits you. But now I need help. I really do."

The three men turned to look at her.

She rushed on, "Have you got a police captain, or an inspector, someone important who can take quick action, someone who is also very clever?"

Andy sat up and stared at her with almost horror on his normally placid face. The policemen stared at each other.

"Someone," Paula went on, feeling now that she could have expressed herself more tactfully, "who knows about political criminals?"

The policeman with the notebook—he was a gray-haired serious man—stopped writing.

"Andy, do you understand me? I'm so anxious I can't remember my German."

Andy looked as if he understood nothing at all, either. But he said, "You're doing fine. If you get stuck, speak English and I'll translate."

Paula went on. "That man you've arrested—he came here to find Fräulein Francesca Vivenzio. He thought she was spending the night with me."

Now, the policeman was writing. "Fräulein Vivenzio is Italian? And this man, is he a friend of Fräulein Vivenzio?"

"She doesn't know him, at all. He was watching her tonight —out at the Kursaal."

"He is infatuated, perhaps?"

"No, no, no! This is something *political.*"

Andy was sitting forward on the edge of his chair: his eyes watched her worriedly.

"Believe me," said Paula, as the policeman's pencil hesitated and he exchanged glances with his younger colleague, "Fräulein Vivenzio is in danger."

"What kind of danger, *gnädige Frau?*"

Paula took a deep breath. She flushed slightly. "It's political," she said. "It's all because of politics." She began to feel incoherent. The policeman was looking at her curiously. She thought of Andrássy now. "Doesn't anyone ever disappear? Because of politics?"

"Paula—" Andy began.

"Look," she rushed on, "the man had a knife. He wasn't a murderer or he would have killed me. He was just trying to scare me. He wanted Francesca. And the other man who was here with him—" She broke off to ask, "You are searching for him?"

The policeman nodded. "He was reported to be tall, wearing a dark coat and hat."

"A *gray* hat. And a *long* dark coat." Suddenly, she felt it was all useless. The man must have escaped completely by this time. And if Rauch denied there had been any other man—if Rauch insisted he was only a thief, who would believe her? She said, despairingly, "They both came here to get Francesca. She *is* in danger."

"Then," the policeman said reassuringly, "we shall warn her. Her address?"

"She lives with her aunt, Fräulein Louisa Lüthi—"

"Swiss?" He was, at least, taking notes once more.

"—who lives in Falken," Paula said. "Falken." She began spelling it.

"I have heard of it," the policeman said with a polite smile. "I go skiing there each winter. A quiet little village."

"Falken," Andy repeated. Suddenly he was on his feet, moving toward the door. "Better make your report as quickly as possible, gentlemen. And as quietly as possible, too. If this is political lawbreaking, then you will have to alert the proper authorities."

The two policemen looked at each other. Until this minute, there had been a feeling of alliance in this room—three men trying to calm a pretty young woman who had been through a frightening experience and was best soothed by being humored. But now, Herr Waysmith had suddenly been persuaded there was some truth in this vaguely defined danger. At least he was standing near the door, trying to hurry them away. The policeman looked down at his notebook.

"*Please,*" Paula said. "I'll give you all the other details tomorrow. But now—*please*—"

"This is all very unusual," he told her severely. "Yes?" he added, watching her face. "The lady has forgotten something important?"

"It's just—that if they came to force Francesca to go with them—wouldn't they have needed a car?" She looked at Andy for help. "Near the hotel?"

"All cars are being searched, tonight," the policeman said. He didn't explain further. But he rose at last. Frau Waysmith really believed her own story, he decided. No questioning would alter it.

"If I were you, I'd keep a firm eye on that man Rauch," Andy said. "Just in case he knew he had friends waiting for him in a car."

The policeman shook his head as he walked to the door. "He doesn't have much courage in him, that one." Anyone who ran away from a screaming girl wasn't much of a problem.

But Andy wasn't listening to him. He had opened the inner door. Now he could hear the sound of quiet scuffling from the corridor. He flung open the outside door, and he broke into a run. So did the two policemen.

Paula followed slowly. He's escaped, she was thinking.

But Rauch had not escaped. Not quite. He had almost reached the flight of stairs just beyond the Englishman's room, but Andy and the two policemen had him in a firm grip. The remains of the silent battle were strewn along the corridor. The assistant manager was picking himself slowly up from the floor. The lame porter was still sitting there, one arm over his brow. And at Rauch's feet the house detective was stretched flat on the ground, one hand (with the handcuffs still secure about his own wrist) grasping the man's ankle.

Now he let go, and tried to rise. As Andy bent down to help him, he held up the useless handcuffs on his wrist. "He slipped out of these," he began in a breathless whisper. He wiped away some blood from a gash over his eye. He gained some more breath. "Jujitsu," he warned the two policemen in a whisper that had strengthened to hoarseness. "He was so quiet. Wanted a cigarette. Then—" He snapped his fingers. "Like that. So quick. One, two, three. But I tackled his leg. I held on." Pride raised his voice to normal. "He dragged me all the way." He felt his shoulder and wiped away more blood from his brow. "He kicked."

"Sh!" the assistant manager said, gesturing toward the closed bedroom doors. "Quiet, everyone!" he added in a whisper.

"Good man," Andy said to the house detective in a normal voice. "Good man."

"A most dangerous criminal," the assistant manager told the policeman, as they started to lead a thoroughly subdued Rauch downstairs, "see that he doesn't escape."

"He won't," the older policeman said grimly. "Come on, you! Quick!" He tightened his grip on Rauch.

Thank heaven for that, Paula thought. She had liked the way the policeman had meant "Quick!" too.

To Paula, the assistant manager gave a bow as he pressed a handkerchief to his swelling jaw. "My apologies, Frau Waysmith."

"Why the hell didn't you give a shout?" Andy asked.

"Sh! Please! The other guests, Herr Waysmith," he murmured unhappily. "Besides, we held him, didn't we?"

Andy gave him a look. Then he put his arm around Paula and turned back toward their room.

The Englishman's outside door opened as they passed. "Thought I heard voices—"

"Round two," said Andy. "All over."

The Englishman looked astonished. "But I heard nothing alarming."

"I wasn't there," Paula said. "Men don't scream, seemingly. But I must say a scream in time saves—"

"Good night," Andy said quickly and hurried her along the corridor. As they entered their bedroom, he said, "Come on, Paula. Tell me all about it." He led her over to an armchair.

Paula didn't answer. She was looking at the half-opened wardrobe door. The man in the long dark coat had touched that handle. And I forgot to tell the police, she thought now. What else did I forget?

Andy was saying, "If you can stand out in the corridor and chitchat to that aging Sir Walter Raleigh, you can damn well sit on your husband's knee and tell him how you happened to get into this—this mess."

"I wasn't chitchatting. I was only being polite. He did help when I—" Then she saw Andy's face, worried, drawn. She sat down on his knees and slid an arm round his shoulders. She kissed him. "That's for believing my story so quickly. No one else did, very much. Not until Rauch tried to escape." Her lips drooped suddenly. "Oh, Andy, it is terrible to give a true warning, and have everyone look at you as if—" All the emotions she had felt in the last hour suddenly culminated in frank tears.

"Now that's all right, all right," Andy kept saying as he found a handkerchief for her.

"But it isn't—that wall of unbelief. . . . And everyone listening is your friend, everyone is really on your side, only they just can't believe. What makes us all so *slow?* So slow and stupid? Gregor said I was stupid. He was right."

"Darling, let me get you to bed."

"But I have so much to tell you—"

"Later, later," Andy said worriedly. "I'll get you to bed." And next time, he was thinking, you'll damned well stay beside me, and travel with me. No more of this. If Francesca had been here, if they had kidnaped Francesca, what would they have done to Paula to silence her? He bit his lip.

The telephone rang. Andy groaned. But Paula, suddenly alert, was saying, "Is that Francesca?" He watched his wife in amazement as she slipped off his knee and ran across the room to answer the call, all her exhaustion gone, her tears vanished. How long did you have to live with a woman to know what to expect next? He studied her as she listened; then as she spoke. It must have been Francesca on the other end of the wire, because Paula ended with "Take care . . . *please* take care." She came away from the telephone, slowly. I've come to Bern, he thought, and found a different kind of Paula: or had we all these unsuspected resources which we called upon when we needed them? Were the hidden possibilities within each of us our true character, the essential core of a human being which surface manners and normal behavior only veneered?

"Andy, I'm afraid," Paula was saying, and her face was white and haggard. "I'm afraid, terribly afraid." She covered her eyes with her hands. She sat down on the bed.

"I'm here," Andy said, and he rose and crossed the room

to sit down beside her. He took her cold hand and kissed its palm. "You ought to get some rest," he added gently.

"It's Schmid I'm afraid for," she said. "And Francesca."

He unbuttoned her jacket and began drawing it off her shoulders.

"Schmid is gone. He hasn't been found. They've been searching all evening, all night."

"Who?"

"The Falken Committee."

Andy folded her jacket and placed it carefully on a chair. "What do you know about that Committee?" he asked quietly.

"You remember when I helped find a job in California for Andrássy, and had to keep it all so quiet?"

"Andrássy, the composer? Was he being helped by the Falken group?"

Paula nodded. "And while he waited to leave for America, he was called Schmid. He worked as a waiter at the Café Henzi. And now he has vanished. This afternoon. In Falken."

"You never told me that Andrássy had any connection with Falken."

"I didn't know. Until Francesca told me today—"

"She's on this Committee?"

"Yes." Then Paula looked at him quickly. "What do *you* know about Falken?"

He didn't answer for a second or two. "Remember when I went to see Meyer in Frankfurt recently? Well, what bothered me was a story connected with Falken—"

"Maxwell Meyer? But he's here!"

"In Bern?"

"I saw him tonight."

"By God, that's something. Where can I reach him?"

"Bill Denning could tell us. He's in Bern, too. At the Aarhof."

"By God—" Andy said again. He bent down and kissed her shoulder. "Either get into bed, or put something warm around you," he told her as he lifted the telephone.

But there was no answer from Denning's room at the Aarhof. "Then I'll have to keep bothering you every fifteen minutes until I do get an answer," Andy warned the operator. He turned to see his wife carefully pushing the wardrobe door further open with the side of her arm.

"We must get the police back here, first thing in the morning," she told him. "The tall man opened this door, and he didn't wear gloves, so it's got his fingerprints. That's better than any description I can give of him."

Andy stared at her. She was too busy tying the red silk sash of a lace dressing gown around her, to notice his amazement. He suddenly smiled. "Is that your idea of something warm?" But there was a discreet knocking at the bedroom door, and Paula retreated modestly into the bathroom while a table was wheeled into the room.

"What a waste of a perfectly good supper," Paula said, when it was safe for her to come back into the bedroom. And what a waste of a perfectly charming negligee, she thought. "I'd feel properly Edwardian if only I wasn't so—so angry."

"Angry?" Andy looked down at the assistant manager's excellent apology: chicken in aspic, asparagus, *cœur de crème,* wild strawberries, and a bottle of Piper Heidsieck 1947. It seemed ungrateful to say that all he had indeed wanted was a plain ham sandwich and a good Scotch and soda.

"Yes, angry," Paula said, slipping her feet into red satin slippers. And she was angry, now. "What do these men think they are, anyway?" She lifted a roll and broke open the hard crust. "I'll have a glass," she added, pointing to the champagne. "Yes," she went on, her lips tight, her eyes hard, "these men who think they can take away people's freedom. By lifting a telephone, as Gregor said. By having a secret conference. By deciding, in cold blood, that a man like Andrássy has no choice in where he is going to live. By hunting down a girl who was only trying to help him and all the others who wanted freedom to choose. Mind you—" she watched Andy pour carefully—"if Andrássy had stayed in Hungary and actually plotted against the government, then they would have a case against him. But all he wants is to leave a country against which he has neither conspired nor fought. His only crime is that he wants to go and work in another country. But *they* don't want that. *They* won't allow any innocent man to have freedom of choice." She lifted her glass of champagne. "Gregor was right. Freedom of choice! Now *there's* an editorial for you, Andy!"

"Who is this Gregor?"

"If you'll have some supper, I'll tell you all that happened today." Paula's eyes softened as she looked at her husband. "When did you eat last?"

"This afternoon. Two o'clock." He waved that away as unimportant now, but she began serving him some food.

"At least," he agreed as he took her advice, "this will keep us awake until Bill Denning gets back to his hotel."

But by four o'clock, they gave up even that idea.

10: Keppler

"NO ONE FOLLOWED US," KEPPLER SAID REASSUR-
ingly, as the car barely stopped to let them out on a quiet
street, tree-shaded, near a narrow gate in a garden wall.
Denning watched the car disappear round the corner into a
broad avenue. They had driven quickly from Keppler's dingy
office, crossing the River Aare by the Kirchenfeld Bridge.
That much he knew. But apart from the fact that this house
belonged to Keppler's sister, that Keppler stayed here when
he visited Bern, he knew little else. He had the feeling,
though, that the route they had followed, however quick,
had been circuitous once they had crossed the bridge, that
Keppler had been taking precautions, that now they were
entering a house which did not lie so far from the river.
Perhaps it was only his nerves, but he felt an irritation that
he had been told so little. Yet Keppler must trust him enough,
or he wouldn't have been brought here. But he was uneasy.

Keppler noticed it. "No one followed us," he repeated as
he unlocked the heavy front door of the stolid house, encircled by its compact garden, shielded from neighboring
houses by small trees and flowering shrubs. He stood aside

politely to let Denning enter the dark hall. "A crime reporter keeps strange hours. The neighbors pity me, but they aren't curious. My sister only says that there must be easier ways to make an honest living." He switched on a dim light. His manner, like his voice, was calm and matter-of-fact. Now, he led the way from the narrow hall—a gleamingly clean hall, smelling of beeswax and turpentine, of spices from the kitchen, with a woman's gardening hat, old raincoats, a dog's leash hanging against one pine-paneled wall, a bowl of flowers on a polished table—and they climbed a steep staircase which led up through this seemingly normal house.

On the first landing, they passed a room where someone snored. "My sister," Keppler said. "But my rooms are on the top floor. She won't disturb us."

Denning felt a wild fit of laughter about to seize him. He gripped the railing hard, tensing all his muscles to control himself, and fought the laughter down. The joke wasn't as funny as all that, he realized. And he gritted his teeth in anger against himself when he started nervously at the appearance of a large dog on the landing above them.

"That's all right, that's all right," Keppler said reassuringly, patting the silent dog. But Denning felt the words were meant for him too. The dog, a massive German shepherd, gave a panting smile and lay down again on the landing. "He has a habit of barking at every visitor when he is kept in the garden," Keppler explained. "At night, it is less disturbing for the neighbors to have him here." So much that Keppler said seemed so simple, on the surface.

"I'm out of training," Denning said, as he looked back down the staircase and saw, now, an innocent house. Keppler caught his true meaning. "You can relax here," he said. "I always do. This sort of place is my safeguard. For in my kind of work, the greatest danger is to become abnormal." He shook his head. He looked at this moment like a grocer who had worked late making out his monthly bills, or a schoolteacher who had spent the evening grading exam papers.

They entered a most private apartment, small but simply arranged for work, eating, and sleeping. Plainly furnished, but comfortable. Quiet, too; secure. The strong door had an elaborate lock. And on one side wall there was another heavy door, barred. ("That leads to an outside stairway down that side of the house," Keppler explained and smiled as he added, "with four steps which creak abominably.") The windows were narrow and short. ("And no balcony," Keppler said, his eyes following Denning's glance. "Ever since an unfortunate experience in Geneva five years ago, I don't like a balcony outside my windows.")

Denning looked round the room again, and then chose a chair. Yes, this room was so normal in spite of its quiet precautions, that tensions were loosened, nerve ends stopped vibrating, and the mind slipped from worry into calm. Near his chair was a phonograph, a pile of records, a stack of foreign magazines. Wooden shelves fixed against the wall held some dictionaries, books on psychology, on wood carving, on folklore, a mixed stretch of poetry—Browning, Heine, Pushkin, Rilke, Spitteler—and a large box of cigars. This was Keppler's own particular corner, but Denning was too exhausted to move. He watched Keppler, busy with a small electric cooker which stood conveniently, if inelegantly, near his desk and typewriter. "It's quiet here," Denning said. Quiet and secure. He began to relax.

Keppler brought over two cups of hot chocolate. "The gourmet would lift his eyebrows," he said, "but the sad truth is that neither good food nor excellent wine ever solved any real problems, only pleasant speculations. And tonight our problems are very real, our speculations far from pleasant."

The hot chocolate was too sweet for Denning's taste, but the extra lump of sugar was probably part of Keppler's cure, too. He drank it, anyway, and in spite of his doubt he felt better. More confident, for one thing. And his brain was beginning to function properly, again: it had stopped jumping from Eva to Charlie-for-Short, from the bogus Maartens to the missing Taylor, from why and what to how and when, so that nothing had been clear except an oppression of worry and urgency.

"Now," Keppler said, laying aside his own emptied cup and leaning back in the chair opposite, "how do you feel?" His voice, like his actions, was leisurely. Don't worry, don't rush, he seemed to be saying.

"Better." Denning almost smiled. "Thanks," he added. "I've a lot to tell you, but it's hard to know where to begin."

"At the very beginning. When you arrived in Bern. Tell me about everyone you met, everything you saw and heard, suspicious and unsuspicious. Even the smallest thing can be of the greatest importance. And don't forget Emily."

Denning's smile was natural, at last. He began his account

of what he had seen, what he had noticed, what had puzzled him, ever since he had met the man who called himself Charles-Auguste Maartens in a corridor of the Aarhof.

There was no interruption from Keppler, except an occasional sound like "Uh-huh!" or "Mm-mm" as he registered either interest or foreboding. But, almost at three o'clock, as Denning was reaching the last phase of his story, the telephone bell rang. Keppler said, "Hold it! Don't forget a thing!" and he hurried over to his desk.

He listened to the call with obvious excitement. "Good, good," he said briefly. "You know the arrangements." He put his finger on the telephone cradle, to end that conversation, but he didn't leave the desk. He began making a call of his own. As he waited for the connection, he grinned widely to Denning. "Meyer's message is all there, clear as a dry Sunday. Another hour or so, and we'll have it."

Then he began speaking into the telephone again, now using one of the numerous dialects you could find in Switzerland. To Denning's ears it sounded like one of the impossible Romansch group; there wasn't a word that he could begin to understand—if you were Swiss, he thought, small wonder that you weren't afraid of languages—but he did notice that Keppler was giving instructions for the first half-minute, then he was listening for the next four minutes, and whatever he heard was, first of all, good, and then bad.

He came away, fuming. Something troubled him. But he said nothing, sat down opposite Denning again, and cut a cigar with great attention.

"Yes?" he said at last to Denning, after he had lit his cigar. "And so the woman Eva came into the Café Henzi. She didn't know Meyer at first—you're sure?"

"She learned his identity only by recognizing the pattern formed by the cigarettes and matches. That drew her attention, I noticed."

"And how did she know that? Who told her?"

"It could have been Charlie-for-Short—they could have questioned him before they killed him."

"They . . ." Keppler said. "Well, it won't be long before we see their faces clearly. They've hidden themselves well, but not everything went right for them tonight. They may be forced to act too quickly, to reveal themselves. . . . Sorry. Go on."

Denning went on with his story. Keppler remained silent.

Even after the story was ended, he remained silent. He studied the ash forming on his cigar. He seemed completely relaxed, almost too casual, sitting there with his head resting easily against the back of his chair. Then his blue eyes, blank of expression, turned toward Denning. "And what are your plans, now?"

"Plans?"

"You aren't here under any military orders?"

"No."

"Then you are free to go on with your holiday in Switzerland?"

Denning looked at him in amazement. "Just what do you take me for?" he asked.

Keppler ignored that. He continued, evenly, "Meyer's death will be investigated, of course. Other Americans will come to Bern. They may not care to have—well—" Keppler hesitated in sudden embarrassment. Or was this his way of being tactful?

"An amateur complicating their investigations?" Denning suggested. "They needn't worry. Nor need you. I'll keep as far away from them as they will keep from me."

"But what do you intend to do? That's the question."

Indeed it was. "I—I don't know." Wasn't Keppler going to suggest something?

"That is what worries me. I can understand why you want to stay here. But I—" Keppler shrugged his shoulders.

"But you don't approve of it?" What was this anyway, Denning wondered angrily—a cool dismissal?

"As a human being, yes. As a security officer, no. That's being frank."

"You sound like Le Brun."

Keppler shrugged his shoulders.

"Where is he, anyway? Still talking about a hoax?" Denning asked, his bitterness no longer disguised.

"Meyer's death ended all arguments about that," Keppler said quietly.

"That's just fine," Denning said savagely. "A man has to die in order to be heard."

"I too didn't altogether believe Meyer's story," Keppler said. "Not at first, not until it was too late. In that sense, I—" He paused, his voice sharpened. "I didn't do enough to protect him."

Denning thought, And if I hadn't been a friend of Max

Meyer, would I have trusted his story completely? Would I have gone over to the Café Henzi, or waited in the Square, or noticed that pack of cigarettes? "I suppose Le Brun was only acting according to his book of rules," he conceded at last.

"We all have our rules," Keppler said. "And in addition, Le Brun suffers from an acute case of a nagging superior officer. Results, results! That explains much. Including the fact that Le Brun has left for Genoa."

"Genoa?"

"His theory is that this outburst of violence is only to distract our attention from the diamonds. He believes they must already be out of Switzerland. He may be right."

Denning rose. He looked at Keppler. Then he turned away. "How far is it to my hotel on foot?" he asked. "Twenty minutes?"

"So you've stopped trusting me." Keppler shook his head sadly.

Denning said, "I trust, when I am trusted. No more, no less."

"You think I don't trust you? Because I won't tell you the latest reports I got over that telephone?"

"Why don't you?"

Keppler said, "And if you were I, how would you act?"

"Warily, I suppose. I can see your point of view too, you know."

"Can you?"

"I was only Max Meyer's friend. Isn't that your problem?"

"Now, come," said Keppler with some annoyance. "I'm not quite so—so haphazard as all that. I did learn what I could about you, before I even would write a note signed Elizabeth." He thought of the report from Meyer, and of the files he had studied. "I know a little," he said slowly. "September, 1941, you were a student at Princeton, specializing in French and German. By February, 1942, you were in the army. Then North Africa—as an interpreter. Then London, in OSS, under Max Meyer's command. April, 1944, you parachuted into northern France. In 1945, you were in Germany, transferring along with Meyer to the section that was searching for missing property. In 1946, you left the army, went back to Princeton, and studied for a Fine Arts degree. In January, 1949, you were married. June, 1949, you graduated. August, 1949, you were interviewed for a job in the Metropolitan Museum in New York. You got it." Keppler paused. Then he said, "But you refused it, and returned to further service in Germany. Now, that service is over. You are going back to New York again. Am I right?"

There was a silence. Yes, Denning was thinking, August, 1949. . . . The night I came back from New York with the job I had wanted—the night Peggy was coming to meet me at Princeton station, and never came. The car smashed up on the Trenton highway, and Peggy dead. And the empty little apartment with the celebration dinner all prepared: the candles on the table, waiting to be lit. . . .

"Yes," Denning said at last. The life and hard times of Bill Denning, he thought. He looked at Keppler. "Little enough, I grant you. I get your point of view, all right." He moved toward the door.

"But you don't!" Keppler said angrily. "Do you think I want to add you to my conscience? It's bad enough to worry over Meyer, over Taylor. . . ."

Denning halted. He looked round at Keppler.

"Yes, Taylor," Keppler said. He threw his cigar down into the ash tray, and tightened his lips. "If I thought you'd go back to the Aarhof, pack your bag, and clear out of Bern, I'd let you walk right out of that door. But you won't. So I won't. Instead, I'll break one of my rules." He pointed to a chair. "Sit down!" he said angrily, but his anger wasn't against himself or Denning: it was against the men who had killed Taylor.

"What happened to Taylor?"

"He was found in the Aare tonight, just below the Nydeck Bridge."

"Accident by drowning?" Denning's voice was sarcastic.

"A very willful accident," Keppler said bitterly. "Did you know Taylor?"

Denning shook his head.

"You never met him? Then that's lucky—for you."

"What other news?"

"I've given you the worst. The rest is mostly disappointments. Eva has vanished. And so has the man who pretended he was Maartens. Just before midnight, he interrupted his mild gambling at the Kursaal for a walk on the terrace. He strolled down to a private car which must have been waiting for him. When last seen, the car had taken the road to Thun and was traveling fast, too fast for my men to keep up with.

The car never reached Thun. It must have branched off on one of the many side roads. In the darkness, that is easy."

"His luggage at the Aarhof?"

"Picked up by arrangement earlier this evening. His bill was paid then, too."

"While he was out at the Kursaal?"

Keppler nodded. "Expertly planned. But not well foreseen. He didn't expect any murder to happen. Or why leave the place where he had been establishing an alibi so carefully, just in time to have his movements become unknown about midnight? That is when he needed his cloak of innocence most of all."

"Then you don't think this gang of jewel thieves were responsible for Meyer's death?"

"An interesting footnote," Keppler said, "is the fact that Nikolaides and his syndicate always stopped short of murder. They believe that expert thieving and killing don't mix."

"Well, they're mixed up in murder this time," Denning said, with grim satisfaction. "Let them get what they've earned." Then he thought for a moment or two. "I'm sorry for the real Charles Maartens, though. He was only the errand boy. Why did he have to be killed?"

"You've already suggested the reason for that," Keppler said quietly. "If some men forced information about Meyer out of Maartens, then Maartens—if he stayed alive—could name the murderers of Meyer."

"How carefully they are covering themselves," Denning said slowly. He frowned.

"Tantalizing," Keppler agreed. "We have, perhaps, as much evidence as we can ever gather. All the pieces of information are probably now in our hands. Yet to scramble them around until they fit into a recognizable pattern—that's what's so tantalizing. . . . For the last hour I have only been able to think how stupid I must be."

"I haven't got all the pieces of information," Denning reminded him. "Or do you think you've told me enough?"

Keppler smiled. "The rest of the news is good. We have captured the man Rauch—the clerk who gave you the false message at the Aarhof. He was arrested early this morning at the hotel Victoria for unlawful entry, carrying weapons, and resisting arrest. It was your friend, Mrs. Waysmith, who caught him. I didn't get all the details, but Inspector Bohren took charge and now two of my own men are interrogating

Herr Rauch." Keppler nodded with considerable satisfaction.

"Paula Waysmith?" Denning was incredulous. Paula was the girl all men thought they had to protect. "And what had Rauch to do with Paula?"

"He entered her room."

"But he isn't a thief."

"Not a jewel thief," Keppler said. "But I shouldn't trust any valuable information near Herr Rauch's nervous fingers."

"But Paula—"

"She is a friend of a young woman called Francesca Vivenzio. Do you know anything about her?"

"No I just met her today."

"You have never heard of Falken?"

"No."

Keppler studied the toe of his shoe. Then he said, "So we have Rauch. And we have the man who searched Meyer's pocket."

Falken, Denning wondered, Falken. . . . He said politely, "What did he take?"

"Why do you think he took anything?"

"Why else did he run when he was challenged?"

Keppler smiled. "You are back to normal, my friend. You weren't so much out of training after all. Yes, he took a wallet with money and a few scraps of paper. He threw away the wallet and money before the police car reached him, so he can't plead he is an ordinary thief."

"He's denying everything?"

"He was—for the scraps of paper weren't traceable. Only, he couldn't wear gloves when he picked Meyer's pocket, so we have fingerprints on the wallet. We can't prove the wallet was Meyer's, but we can prove the man is lying when he says he never saw it in his life. And when Inspector Bohren suggested his fingerprints might be in the murder car too, he was obviously nervous."

"But he wasn't the driver of that car."

"No. But he could have traveled in it on his way to Bern."

"From Berlin? He spoke with flat hard vowels and slurred consonants."

"From East Berlin. That we did find out."

"His politics?"

"He keeps saying he was a Nazi."

"He *says* that?" Denning shook his head. "Then he is the first Nazi I've ever heard of who admitted it freely." But this suits Le Brun's theory, he was thinking. Had Le Brun been right, was I wrong? "Perhaps I'm wrong," he said slowly. "Perhaps the ex-Nazis are behind all this."

"Once he was a Nazi—and that information he volunteers; now he is a Communist, which is more evident than he realizes with his limited brains. Bohren has quite an ear for their phrases. That's the trouble about regulated ideas: the phrases are never original, the same words keep recurring. But basically he's a thug pure and simple, a man who can be bought to do any ugly work."

"Clever of them," Denning said. "An ex-Nazi who's now a Communist." Then he looked sharply at Keppler. "And was that why you were so noncommittal before Le Brun, when we were discussing the two agents, Eva and Rauch? Did they too once work for the Nazis?"

Keppler nodded.

"And now for Soviet Russia?"

Keppler nodded again. "Not for military intelligence, however. We've always considered them minor agents, interesting to watch. We could have arrested them anytime, under Article 272. But the small fish can pilot you to the big fish, you know."

Denning was silent. The small fish . . . Charles-Auguste Maartens, a frightened little man, a very small fish . . .

"Well," Keppler said, "there are all the pieces. What kind of picture do they make?"

Denning half-closed his eyes. He was beginning to see the first vague shape. First, Nikolaides needed help when he sent Charles Maartens to Max Meyer in Frankfurt. Then, in Bern, Nikolaides didn't need help: he needed it so little that he tried to end any interest he had aroused. He discredited Max Meyer. Ah . . . he did not only want to discredit, he also wanted to discourage Max himself. Was that the explanation for the totally unnecessary piece of acting by the fake Maartens? Max was not only to look like a fool—that would not have discouraged him, not Max—he was to feel he had been fooled.

Denning looked at Keppler.

"No guesses, at least?" Keppler asked.

"Guesses, yes. And probably stupid."

"Such as?" Keppler was smiling. He liked that quick look in Denning's eyes.

Denning said, "Nikolaides wanted Bern to himself. He

wanted Max Meyer to leave, completely discouraged. Why? Because the diamonds are in Bern. What's more—they must be stealable."

"Then they've been sold. They've been sold to a private individual—" Keppler snapped his fingers.

"—on whom Nikolaides can safely go to work in his usual way," Denning added.

"But what about Genoa? Was that only an addition by Nikolaides to make sure that the Americans would take action?"

They looked at each other. "It could be," Denning said slowly. "At least, Nikolaides seemed to have his own ideas about Americans and their motives. I remember Meyer told me—yes, Genoa could have been Nikolaides' idea of a sure bait."

"Come," Keppler said, his excitement growing, "keep throwing your ideas to me; I'll throw mine to you; between us, we'll catch some truth. Forget Genoa at the moment. Back to Bern. Nikolaides must have been very sure that the diamonds were here, easy to steal, before he canceled Maartens' meeting with Meyer. He must have been very sure."

"He made a deal with them," Denning said slowly.

"With the political agents of the power that was smuggling the diamonds?" Keppler grinned. "Don't you admire my restraint?" He waved away his aside. "A deal . . ." he said thoughtfully. "Nikolaides was to end our interest in the diamonds; in return, Nikolaides was told the name of the buyer. Yes . . . that would be sufficient for Nikolaides. Only the diamonds, themselves, would be a big enough bribe. Who was this poor foolish buyer, anyway?"

"No interest," Denning said. "But what is important is *how* his money will be used." Max had talked in Berlin of a secret fund for political purposes. Was it already set up?

"Nikolaides won't let that trouble his conscience."

"But Max would have. *That's* why he was killed."

"Perhaps," Keppler said slowly, "he had even discovered how the money was to be used." He glanced at his watch. The message in Meyer's pack of cigarettes should have reached them by this time. He rose. He tried to conceal his sudden worry. "Certainly Nikolaides didn't know he was being drawn into murder when he made the deal. That's the trouble when you start doing business with political gangsters. Their plans always go far beyond yours."

"My heart bleeds for him," Denning said grimly. "No doubt he'll start thinking he's in danger, too. Well, I hope he sweats it out." Then, thinking of danger, he thought of Le Brun who had made contact with Taylor today. "Le Brun—will he be all right?" he asked anxiously. He looked at Keppler, who was walking round the room restlessly. "Le Brun," he said again, "shouldn't you warn him?"

Keppler stared at Denning for a second, as if he were making a long journey back to cope with that question. "Yes," he said, "yes." He passed a hand wearily over his eyes. And Denning, watching him, wondered what further guesses Keppler had been making by himself. They had upset him.

"Of course," Denning said, "all these guesses of ours may be wrong."

"Guesses they may have been," Keppler said grimly, "or suppositions, or inferences, or deductions. But there's enough truth to—"

On a wall above his desk a bell rang, then rang three times more in short quick jabs. Keppler glanced up as Denning had. He took a deep breath. He relaxed. A smile came back to his face as he crossed the room with his light step. "I switch the front bell to ring up here at night," he explained as he unlocked the door. "Doesn't alarm my sister." The dog outside had risen and was growling in a deep bass rumble. "I heard the bell, Fafner. I heard it," he said, and the door closed.

Denning looked round the room, then at the books and records near his comfortable chair. He felt a touch of envy, a warm sympathetic envy, more a recognition of what he would like than a hunger for something he could not possess. Here I am, he thought, a stranger in another's armchair: yet not a stranger. His friends are my friends. There is the Brahms Fourth, asking to be played. There, on the shelf above, is Rainer Maria Rilke, waiting to be read.

A corner of one's own, like this: it wasn't so much to ask, it wasn't so difficult to obtain—except for the jobs that had to be done, the business of life pulling you away, pushing you out from your own thoughts or from the ideas that others could offer you. Jobs to be done, the business of living. Were they the things that unsettled you? Or were they merely an excuse?

He reached over to the bookshelf and pulled out the thin book of Rainer Maria Rilke's poems. It fell open easily at

"Day in Autumn." So Keppler liked to read this too. *Wer jetzt kein Haus hat, baut sich nimmermehr. . . .*

> The homeless man finds it too late to build.
> The lonely man will keep his loneliness,
> Will lie awake, will read, will write long letters,
> Will wander to and fro under the trees
> Restlessly, while the leaves run from the wind.

Keppler was back in the room, a strange mixture of excitement and triumph. "Made any more guesses?" he asked when he had regained his breath.

"Only about the shape of my own life." Denning pushed the book of poems back into place on the shelf. He tried not to look too curiously at the envelope in Keppler's hand.

Keppler smiled suddenly. "Here," he said, "read this and see if it makes any sense." He held out the envelope. "I looked at it, down in the hall. Couldn't resist it," he admitted.

"Doesn't it make sense?"

"In its own field, yes. Of considerable importance, I'd say. But as you'll see, there isn't a thing in this report about the Herz diamonds. Or about Charles Maartens." Keppler shook his head. "Yet there must be some connection." Why else should Meyer have held that pack of cigarettes in his hand when he saw he was a marked man? Why underline its importance in just that way? He laid the envelope on Denning's knee. Yes, he thought as he moved over to his desk, Meyer himself was the connection, Meyer and whatever he had verified in Bern today. That was the connection between this report and the Herz diamonds.

Denning opened the envelope, an ordinary-sized envelope able to be slipped safely inside a man's pocket. Inside, there was a stiff sheet of cream paper, glossy, hard, cracking where it had been folded carefully between the paragraph spacings. The typewritten text was clear, perhaps even heavier, more intense than the original had been. And this, thought Denning as he unfolded the page, this had been a small black dot—no more than a period at the end of a sentence or of an address on an envelope, no more than a flaw on a piece of cigarette paper. And this, he thought as he began reading, was Max speaking. Max had written this just before he left Frankfurt. Less than a week ago. Five days ago, to be exact.

For a moment, he saw Max quite clearly. Too clearly. Max

with a smile in his intelligent brown eyes as he stood among the piles of books, the open trunk, the discarded magazines in a Berlin room. Max saying, "—when we meet in Bern, I'll be able to fill in a lot of gaps for you."

Denning passed a hand wearily over his eyes. For a moment, the heavy black type blurred and shifted. For a minute, he sat quite still, not reading.

"Interesting, isn't it?" Keppler's voice asked from across the room.

Denning nodded. He began reading.

11: Max Meyer's Last Word

THE PAGE WAS CLOSELY TYPED, SINGLE-SPACED. There were three major paragraphs—three case histories, seemingly—followed by a small separate note. Concise, factual, written with abbreviations and ellipses so that as much information as possible could be packed into one page. Max Meyer had worked carefully over this composition.

Denning read the case histories quickly through, then—letting his mind enlarge the cryptic phrases into fuller sentences and a richer context—he began to read again. The three case histories became alive: they became three men.

Alexander Burkhart was the first. He was a neurologist of established reputation who had worked in Vienna until 1938, in Zurich until 1945, and then (apparently he had trusted the Communists more than the Nazis) had returned to his clinic in the Russian sector of Vienna. He had no political affiliations, his sole interest was research. In 1949, he was "invited" to Leningrad. From then until July, 1952, he was consistently praised in the Soviet press. In that month he escaped to Falken, Switzerland. His appearance, there, was given no publicity. In March, 1953, Alexander Burkart arrived legally, quietly, in the United States. Since then he had been living and working, again without any publicity, in Baltimore.

But on the 2nd of May, 1953, Burkart had left Baltimore, taking a few clothes and books. And all that could explain this sudden departure was a typewritten sheet of paper, a brusque letter, which stated that, as Burkart could not live or work in America, "a fascist country filled with hysteria and warmongering," he was returning to his clinic in Vienna. The signature was identified as Burkart's. And only the fact that two scientists, with whom he was working at Johns Hopkins, happened to call on Burkart that Saturday evening, and had found the letter before his landlady discovered it, enabled the disappearance to be kept as quiet as his arrival in the U.S.A.

The two colleagues could not believe the letter: Burkart had begun a series of experiments for whose success he held the highest hopes; he was keenly excited about his research and had often praised the freedom of his working conditions; the books which he had seemingly taken were replaceable anywhere, but the notes and important material on which he had been working had been left in his laboratory safe. His colleagues immediately relayed their suspicions to the authorities at Johns Hopkins, who at once communicated with the Immigration Service, the F.B.I., and the C.I.A. The Immigration Service reported that only three weeks previously, Burkart had taken out his first papers for citizenship, and had also made inquiries about the possible immigration of his sole surviving relatives—his daughter and son-in-law, who had been living in Munich since 1946. Within two days of the disappearance, the search was on. It was important to handle the whole matter with the greatest secrecy: Burkart's life could be at stake. While the F.B.I. followed a lead to a foreign freighter, ultimate destination Hong Kong, which had fueled at Baltimore on May 2nd for its leisurely journey down the eastern seacoast of America, the C.I.A. arm of the search reached Munich. Burkart's daughter was tactfully questioned, but knew nothing. The search spread further through Western Germany. Meyer's office was alerted.

"In this way," he wrote, "I first heard of Falken." That was on the 6th of May.

(On May 8th, the freighter had reached Havana, where it was searched by Cuban police despite heavy protests of the captain. A seaman, "seriously ill," was found in a locked cabin: he was identified, by accompanying U. S. agents, as Alexander Burkart. He was "heavily drugged and in a pitiful condition." But he was safe. The search was called off.)

The name of Falken, however, was not allowed to be forgotten. Only three days later, on the 9th of May, Meyer was to stumble across it once more, this time in connection with a man of considerable fame, called Heinrich Kahn.

Dr. Heinrich Kahn was a nuclear physicist who had returned from exile, in 1945, to his home in East Germany. By 1949, he was reported to be working in Russia. Some time early in 1953, he had escaped. First news of this came from a small town in the Rhineland, which reported with considerable pride in its weekly paper that Heinrich Kahn, the famous scientist about whom the world had been speculating for eight years, was spending a few days with relatives in Erzbaden before leaving for America. The editor of the Erzbaden *Anzeiger* welcomed Kahn, congratulated him on his dramatic escape, and offered all good wishes for his future in the United States. There, in that gesture of good will, in that editorial written with so much polish and care, was Heinrich Kahn's death sentence.

The editorial paragraph came to Meyer's attention on May the 9th, when Kahn disappeared on the road to Stuttgart, from where he had intended to fly to America. Some quick research among Immigration Service files showed that Kahn had arrived, five months ago, in Switzerland; that he had lived in Falken under an assumed name and identity, and then in Bern, where he had worked as a janitor. (The files were closed permanently when a man—trying to escape from a car which had been halted on the outskirts of Bayreuth by a flat tire— was shot as, crying for help, he almost reached a group of workmen. The man was Heinrich Kahn. His two murderers, who had been changing the tire, escaped.)

Meyer grimly noted: "Careless operation—insufficient drugs. Murderers—described by witnesses— Storm-trooper types. Car traveling toward E. Germany."

The third case history dealt with Karel Hálek, teacher, writer, university president, a Nobel Prize candidate who had escaped from Czechoslovakia late in 1952. Traveling to London in May, 1953, where he was to lecture at University College, he had broken his journey at Bonn, to meet several of his old colleagues and pupils, now exiles like himself. He had been prevailed upon by his friends to give a talk on "The Perversions of Teaching." Hálek's reputation was too great to have the lecture kept the secret it was intended to be. An American journalist—the European editor of *Policy*—Andrew Waysmith, was interested in Hálek's work and reappearance. He attended the lecture. Waysmith noted that there were several outsiders besides himself; that after the lecture was over, Hálek had been embarrassed, even disturbed by one questioner who—in the most gentle and friendly way—referred vaguely to Hálek's "stay in Falken." Hálek evaded that question and left the lecture hall quickly. Waysmith followed to ask him for an interview on Czechoslovakia, which would be published in *Policy* whenever Hálek considered it safe to appear in print. Hálek agreed, and arranged for a meeting with Waysmith on the following day.

But on the next day, the 15th of May, Waysmith learned that Hálek had received a telegram asking him to leave as soon as possible for London, and that he had already taken an early plane. Waysmith wired his magazine's representative in London to make contact with Hálek and arrange for the interview. Having no reply, Waysmith telephoned London. His representative was away for the week end. By Monday, May 18th, he was reached. He assured Waysmith that Hálek was not expected until May 20th—why this fuss and bother? With a few well-chosen phrases, Waysmith got him to fuss and bother too. He reported back that Hálek had not arrived, and still was not expected until May 20th.

Waysmith then checked with Hálek's friends in Bonn: two of them had accompanied him to the airport, but hadn't actually seen him enter the plane for London; the telegram had seemed authentic—it had contained certain references which Hálek had accepted as positive identification; no one was alarmed. Waysmith decided to risk looking foolish. He drove to Frankfurt and sought out Meyer for advice.

These were the three men. Burkart; Kahn; Hálek. May 2nd; May 9th; May 15th.

Near the foot of the page, Meyer had added his own observations. *First,* there was a pattern to these acts of violence: all the men had escaped with great secrecy; all had some connection with Falken; all had considerable reputations— "propaganda value," as Meyer wrote; their abduction back to

Communist countries was to be kept secret, too—so that few people would know they had rebelled. *Secondly,* abduction on this scale cost money: hired thugs had to be paid, and paid anonymously. Nothing was to be traced to the source that ordered these abductions. *Thirdly,* Hálek had not been found. By this time, all information about Falken must have been forced out of him. ("They're playing rough," was Meyer's guess.) The next move would be against the escape committee at Falken—their files or records would give the present addresses of the exiles who were still free. And soon, they wouldn't be. The move against them would be quick, complete.

Meyer's last entry was unexpected. "In April, a sum of $3,000,000 was lifted from the account of Richard van Meeren Broach with the National City Bank of New York, and transferred to Switzerland. Broach has renounced (see *New York Times,* March 14, 1953) his United States citizenship. He is now living in Falken."

Denning lifted his eyes and found Keppler studying him.

"Yes?" Keppler asked, coming forward to take Meyer's report.

"Who is this Broach?"

"Obviously a man who likes a dramatic gesture. He has applied for Swiss citizenship, but that isn't how he phrases his action: the renunciation is what he wants emphasized. Meanwhile—he is still using his American passport."

Denning said thoughtfully, "Any connection with *the* Broach family?" They came from New York, a decent enough family on the whole: they had performed some public service and a lot of good works as well as having collected overmuch money.

"He's the only surviving son. The other was killed in the last war. This one is around forty. He dabbled in Communism twenty years or so ago. Then he seemed to have lost interest."

"Seemed?"

"That's the story he has established in the mind of the public. He's still openly leftist in sympathies, but many of us are."

"Then what interests you in him?"

"He has visited Switzerland before. Last year, we discovered that he used us for rather a secretive entry into Czechoslovakia to attend a Cultural Congress in Prague."

"But I've noticed some honest men attending Communist-run Congresses. Out of curiosity or hope, I suppose."

"Honest men don't hide their attendance. They don't travel under a false name, or stay secretly with organizers of the congress, or meet *only* with highly placed officials. To do all that, you have to have influential friends."

"The Communists kept his visit secret?"

"Completely, although all other foreign visitors were publicized. He came back to Geneva at the end of a week, talking about his walking trip through the Engadine."

"And then he went back to America?"

"By way of Guatemala."

"Has no one suspected that he may have been a 'sleeper' all these years?"

"One of your United States agencies had several suspicions. And sometimes I have wondered if Broach didn't want them to act against him, so that he could become a political martyr. You know the line: why am I being crucified for opinions I held in my youth? I grant you," Keppler said quickly, noticing the expression on Denning's face, "that honest men have every right to ask that question. But a man who has taken action has no right to disguise it as opinion. That is only misleading the public."

"And now he has come to live in Switzerland?"

"After making an appeal that any honest man could have made. He refuses to live any longer in America—as a protest against political conditions. And I assure you that most Europeans don't question his statement: they take it as another proof of all the stories they've been hearing about America."

Denning looked angrily at Keppler.

"Don't blame the Europeans entirely for believing that propaganda. How many well-meaning men in the United States have made speeches or written articles that added weight to the neutralists' myth?" Keppler shook his head gloomily. "Hell is paved with overstatements." He looked down now at Meyer's report. "We had thought Broach was a kind of unhappy joke—he has plenty of money, but his father made it; he has some brains, but he's a mental pygmy compared to men like Burkart or Kahn or Hálek; he has a distinguished name, but other men earned that for him." His voice lost all amusement and turned bitter. "Well now—

there's a lot of work to be done. And quickly. The pattern, as Meyer gives it, is clear; but the danger to decent people is great, because it is so urgent."

"At least, the enemy is no longer faceless."

"Not to us. But with all this purposeful secrecy, how would your country—or France—have any clear evidence to bring before the United Nations? A public protest, a public challenge could cancel other abductions. The Communists are quick to change tactics when they become a liability. But where is our clear evidence for the United Nations? My God, if so many people disbelieve a proved charge against spies and traitors, where would we stand with *this?*" He held up Meyer's report. Then, turning to the desk, he said, "I'd better start that work."

Denning sat still for a moment. Then he rose. "And I'd better get back to the hotel."

"You're welcome to use my bed." Keppler gestured to the adjoining room. "I won't need it for the next two hours."

"If I have been having a night on the town, it will seem more natural if I get back by the dawn's early light to catch up on my sleep."

Keppler considered that. Then he reached for the telephone. "I've told a taxi to come out here and get you."

Denning stared at him in amazement.

"One of *our* taxis," Keppler said patiently. Then he went back to the notes he was making, a man working out problems, arranging his course of action, mapping out his tactics. Soon, it was Denning's guess, there would be considerable telephoning.

Denning tried not to watch the man in the brown suit working so intently at his desk. When the blue eyes looked up at him for a moment, and the heavy eyebrows frowned, he knew that Keppler wasn't even seeing him. And he suddenly thought, what did Keppler get out of all this, anyway? The answer was: nothing; nothing at all in a material sense. Neither money, nor fame, nor even public thanks. And there he was, beginning a job which could last days if not weeks and bring its share of danger, a job which canceled all other work and private plans. Max Meyer, too, hadn't calculated the cost to himself; nor had anyone at Falken who had aided some unfortunate human beings. What was it, then, that awakened such determination? Something in addition to patriotism—neither Switzerland nor America was directly threatened; the evil was aimed against powerless men, political exiles, foreigners to both Meyer and Keppler. Something far above political or religious considerations: who knew what opinions on politics or religion had been held by Burkart, Kahn, Hálek—or who cared? And there was the answer, perhaps. Neither Richard Broach nor Nikolaides would ever understand it. Keppler's "danger to decent people" was not one of the steps in their thinking. Both of them, each in his different way, saw men and women not as human beings but as instruments.

The bell rang above Keppler's desk, again in a peculiar rhythm. "Fafner and I shall see you safely downstairs," Keppler said, rising quickly. "And don't be alarmed if your journey back to the hotel seems overlong. You may even change taxis halfway."

As they reached the hall, he added, "One thing I ask of you. Do as little as possible."

"I'll take it easy," Denning said to reassure him.

Keppler looked at him, and then grunted.

"How can I reach you," Denning asked, "in case I need— advice?"

"Tourists mislay passports. Naturally they complain to the police."

"To Inspector Bohren?"

"In your case, yes," Keppler said. He glanced through a narrow slit of heavy glass, inserted at eye level in the massive front door, before he released the lock and the bolt. "But try not to mislay anything," he added, as he swung the door open. "We're taking action enough. In your own words— relax." He smiled suddenly, gripped Denning's shoulder for a moment, and nodded his good-by.

Another day had begun. Denning shivered at its cold touch as he followed his escort down the tree-shaded path to the narrow front gate. Behind him, the house, like all the other houses, seemed plunged in that last precious hour of deep sleep.

12: *The Gaps Are Filled In*

IT WAS ALMOST SIX O'CLOCK WHEN DENNING
came to the Aarhof—a morning of pale gold promising a
day of sun and blue sky. In the lobby there were a few early
travelers, shivering from shortened sleep or the cool air which
streamed through wide-opened doors and windows, while a
small army of cleaners discreetly mopped and swept and
polished. The night porter handed over the room key with a
brief smile: he had his own worries this morning. Denning,
in spite of his exhaustion, could sense the same subdued
feeling of mixed excitement and concern from the clerks and
the elevator boy. Had the news of Rauch's arrest reached
them? Probably. They all were too preoccupied with a shared
problem to pay any attention to Denning. Not that he cared
at this moment. Physically, emotionally, he was too tired.

His room was cool and quiet. He drew the curtains, hung
a DON'T DISTURB sign on the outer door, and then pulled his
clothes off. He was suddenly so listless that he could scarcely
set his alarm clock. Three hours he'd give himself. Three
hours. . . . He fell into bed, already half-asleep.

He was awakened by the telephone. (It must have been ringing for some time, for it stopped before he had gathered enough wits to reach for the receiver.) He didn't feel too bad. He had a headache, a slight headache, but that was all. He could have felt worse. At least, the need for sleep was over.

He looked at the clock on his way to the bathroom. It was eleven. He must have slept right through the alarm. Or had he set it badly? No, it was set fully. For nine o'clock. He cursed himself for an idiot.

But after a shave and a bath, and then a breakfast tray which the boy Gustav brought up with a cheerful smile and a general air of suppressed excitement, he began to feel he hadn't been too much of an idiot after all. Five hours of deep sleep had cleared his mind. The second cup of coffee had wakened him thoroughly, set his brain to working briskly. And somewhere, somehow, in those five hours of complete unconsciousness, a few ideas had been born. They gave their first small sign of life when he was reading the morning paper which Gustav left beside the coffeepot.

"Who was this poor foolish buyer, anyway?" Keppler had asked when they were discussing the possible sale of the diamonds. And I said, "No interest," Denning remembered; but now I am interested. Last night—or early this morning—before I read Max's report, the buyer was unidentifiable, beyond having a few certain characteristics. Anyone who bought the Herz diamonds must have promised to keep them secret for a considerable time—months certainly, perhaps even a year or two: he must have been someone who trusted the Communists completely. He probably was someone who thought it an honor to pay a fortune, without question, without haggling, to a fund started by his Communist friends.

But did he know the purpose of this fund?

I hope not, Denning thought. Let's give him the benefit of the doubt. So there was his picture—a sympathizer with Communist causes, eager to serve, easily duped, wealthy. . . . That's all I had last night, until I read Max's report.

But Max had never done anything without a purpose. His reference to Richard Broach—the transfer of three million dollars from America, the new home in Falken—was not just some fantastic guess, a rumor dragged in to complete a page. It was there because Max must have had a strong suspicion. And when had Max's suspicion become a certainty?

Yesterday. . . .

He had found something yesterday to confirm suspicion and make it provable fact. He had found it too late for any addition to the report contained in that minute piece of film called a micro-dot. But the sign that he had found it and recognized its truth was in the way he had taken the pack of cigarettes out of his pocket—perhaps as he tried to run across the Square—and held it in his hand. "This is what is important," he had been trying to say, "this I have verified, this I hand over to you."

Johann Keppler, of course, would have his own questions about Richard Broach; no doubt he had already started investigating the reasons behind Broach's appearance at Falken. But any thorough investigation took time. And we have little time, Denning thought. I knew Max and how he worked. I was Max's friend. There I have an edge over Keppler. If Max hadn't found the evidence connecting Broach with the sale of the Herz diamonds, he would have ripped that pack of cigarettes open as he sat at his table in the Café Henzi. He would have burned the micro-dot with a match. Max never made a challenge without real proof. I know that Max was pointing a finger at Broach.

If I'm right, Denning thought with growing excitement, then one thing follows quite naturally. Wherever Broach is, there will we find some of Nikolaides' single-minded men, discreetly waiting, their fingers itching. That's definite. If I'm right.

I feel I'm right, but how do I prove it?

The quickest, and most final, proof could come from Nikolaides himself. But would he admit he knows who is the buyer of the diamonds? Or rather, why should he admit it?

For Nikolaides and the men who work for him don't suffer from a sense of moral obligation; they are purely self-interested characters: doing nothing, saying nothing, which doesn't benefit them. Strictly *quid pro quo* types, with a loyalty applicable only to their own small group. Honor among thieves is definitely limited. Give evidence against someone in order to benefit the majority of citizens? Not they. For the laws are made by the majority, and Nikolaides is the lawbreaker. The citizens are his social enemy. He, and all the other professional thieves, never forget that, even if sometimes the ordinary innocent citizen does.

That's our mistake as well as our virtue: we, the ordinary citizens trying to live an honest life, like to think that all people—simply because we share the same ways of swallowing and digesting food, of taking air into our lungs, of propagating, of being born, of dying—must feel as we feel, must mean what we mean, must act as we would act.

It's all a very charming belief, does us credit. But it isn't going to help us pin Nikolaides down; or the men who have murdered Max or abducted Burkart, Kahn, and Hálek. Hálek, poor devil . . . what haven't they put him through by this time?

Denning rose abruptly. He could feel the hot blood rushing into his cheeks. He opened the windows wide. Anger, raging anger, wasn't the way to deal with kidnapers and torturers. Cold, determined purpose; calculations as in a chess game. That was the way. And how did you calculate, forestall each move of the enemy, and win? By making your own thought follow the patterns in which your opponent's mind worked. That was the lesson to learn, that was the way to checkmate.

I'll start with Nikolaides, Denning decided. He turned back to the table, picked up the newspaper, and studied once more the paragraph about the murders in the Henziplatz last night. It was skillfully written (was Keppler really a part-time journalist?), and although Max was not identified, the frightened little man was named quite clearly: Charles-Auguste Maartens. Nikolaides wouldn't like that paragraph at all.

Denning opened the bureau drawers to begin packing. But Gustav entered to clear away the breakfast tray.

"You saw the newspaper?" he asked, with an excitement he couldn't conceal in spite of all his efforts.

"Yes." Denning lit a cigarette and tried not to look impatiently at his watch.

"It's caused a lot of trouble down at the desk," Gustav said. "Of course, the Victoria is trying to hush it all up. And we, too, aren't supposed to talk about it. But there have been policemen everywhere. Did you see the detectives in the lobby when you came in?"

"I didn't pay much attention," Denning said, but he reached for the newspaper again. It was another small paragraph, almost crushed out of its column by a description of the resistance of Chinese prisoners of war to interrogation by Communist officers in Korea. *Feodor Rauch, a hotel clerk presently employed by Aarhof, was arrested last night for illegal entry and disorderly conduct in the Hotel Victoria.* That was all.

"He wasn't much liked," Gustav said, "but it does seem unfair that he was arrested. After all, it wasn't such a fault."

"What wasn't?"

"He just went to see a friend of his, and she suddenly got angry and yelled. Of course," Gustav added sagely, "he shouldn't have made friends with any guest. That's against all rules. No wonder the Hotel Victoria is hushing it all up." He suddenly realized that Denning was staring at him. He reddened.

"I've annoyed you, *gnädiger Herr?*"

Denning restrained himself. He even smiled. "Where on earth did you get all that information?"

"Downstairs. We're all talking about the disgrace of it."

"But who spread the story about Rauch's visit to a woman friend? Who is responsible for that?"

Gustav looked uncomfortable. "Everyone's saying it."

"But who said it first? The rest of you are just repeating the story. Don't you see?"

Gustav picked up the tray. He didn't look happy: his mind was divided between what his friends were saying, what the police had done, and the amused disbelief on the American's face.

Denning relented. He said seriously, reassuringly, "Rauch would be free now if the police didn't think he was a suspicious character. He isn't being unjustly—"

"He wasn't a thief," Gustav said quickly. "We are sure of that."

"He wouldn't announce his plans to you, would he?" How easy it would have been to prove to Gustav that the whole story was definitely a lie, that Paula Waysmith had only arrived in Bern, that Rauch couldn't have been in the habit of visiting her. How simple it would have been to pass on Keppler's information: "Rauch has tricked all of you. His job here was simply a cover. He is an agent working for a foreign government." But the truth couldn't be told, and the story-spreader had relied on that. "Where's the maid, by the way?"

"She's gone," Gustav said. "She was Rauch's wife, so of course she couldn't face all this disgrace."

"I thought you didn't like her."

"Not much."

"But now you're sorry for her?" Denning smiled. "You've got the right impulses, Gustav," he said quietly, sincerely.

The boy looked happier.

"But," Denning added, "don't let anyone abuse your impulses."

"Please?"

"Had Rauch any special friend here?"

Gustav shook his head.

"Had his wife?"

Gustav glanced at him sharply. Then he moved hurriedly toward the door. These questions bothered him.

"Now I wonder if that friend made up the story about Rauch visiting a lady?"

"I didn't mean to trouble you with all this," Gustav said, almost with annoyance. "Excuse me, sir."

Anyone criticizing a member of the staff was criticizing Gustav—was that it? Denning shook his head in wonder. Nowadays, hell was also paved with justifications.

"It's a small matter," Gustav added, and all his natural politeness surged back to rout his annoyance.

"I guess so. Except to the lady at the Victoria who is being falsely accused."

"Accused?"

"By Frau Rauch's helpful friend."

It was obvious that Gustav hadn't got around to that stage of deduction as yet. He looked back at Denning, now with alarm, as he went out.

But Denning, seeing a stiff-starched blue uniform passing along the corridor, said quickly, "Is that the helpful friend?"

Gustav, in spite of his slow thought processes, found the phrase amusing, for he grinned and nodded.

"And she's going to look after my room?" Denning asked. Now that really was being helpful. He took the DON'T DISTURB card and hung it outside once again. "I'm tired," he told Gustav with a broad smile.

He locked the inner door, and began packing. What was the best way to get to Falken?

The telephone rang. It was Andrew Waysmith.

"And where the hell have you been?" was the first question.

"Now that's what I call the real friendly approach," Denning answered. "How are you, Andy? When did you arrive?"

"Around one o'clock this morning. Just in time for a pretty picnic. Can I see you?"

"Any time."

"I'll be right over."

"Wait a minute—I'll come over and see you. That's better."

"But—"

"It's *much* better," Denning insisted.

"All right. Meanwhile, give me Meyer's address. I phoned you half of the night, and then again this morning."

"At eleven? Yes, you wakened me."

"Where can I reach Meyer?"

"He isn't here."

"He has left?" There was a short pause. Then Waysmith said, "This is urgent, you know."

"I know."

There was another pause from Waysmith. "When will I see you?"

"As soon as I can make it."

"No sooner?"

"Andy, calm down. I shan't waste time getting my shoes polished."

"Well, don't be too late. I've rented a car, and we're driving into the country early this afternoon."

"I'll see you before you leave," Denning said reassuringly, and hung up.

At the desk in the lobby, Denning asked for his bill.

"Immediately, sir," said the clerk politely. It was the clerk who knew so much about geraniums. Denning waited, looked round the lobby. It was almost twelve o'clock, but there wasn't a sign of a uniformed schoolgirl. Where was Emily? Didn't schoolgirls eat lunch? Outside the dining room, some thrifty visitors were already gathering. Surely Emily's teacher believed in the little economy of board combined with lodging? The three pink-cheeked clergymen were loitering quietly. So were the English businessman and his wife. So were the young French couple, and several Swiss visitors. But where was Emily?

Denning saw Michel, the gardening expert, doing one of his transplanting jobs on the central table of geraniums. "By the way," he said, "you'd better tell the gardener that one of the geraniums in my window box looks pretty ill. He might want to change it before a new guest arrives."

"Thank you, sir, that's very helpful of you." The clerk was delighted at such appreciation of his flowers. He beckoned to Michel; then began to explain the bill. "We're only charging you for one day. It would," he added sadly, "have been much cheaper for you if you had stayed three days. Pension terms, you see. So: room with bath—sixteen francs. Two breakfasts—five francs. Conveyance from the station to the hotel, transport of luggage, heating last night (that was one-and-a-half francs) and tips—for a one-day stay, that is fifteen per cent. Then there's the tax—"

"Yes, yes," Denning said. "It's all clear." He counted out the money quickly as Michel approached. Then he leaned over to the porter's desk and dropped his key. "Checking out," he said clearly as Michel passed by. "Have someone meet me at the station with my luggage at half-past one."

"He isn't allowed on the platform, I'm afraid."

So much the better. "Then I'll meet him at the entrance," Denning said. He turned away, reasonably sure that Michel had heard enough, and strolled toward the door. He paused there, lighting a cigarette, and looked along the arcade with its handsome shops. This was a very different kind of arcade from the one which edged the Henziplatz. Here, at night, there would be few shadows from these bright lamps overhead. Here, the trolley cars— And then he saw the platoon of schoolgirls, walking two by two, with Mademoiselle Dupré leading them at a brisk trot. Run, ma'mselle, run: luncheon, pension-price, waits for no man, not even for a harassed lady with fourteen hungry mouths to fill.

She stood at the side of the doorway, urging her charges to hurry and wash their hands and be downstairs in the dining room in five minutes. "Five minutes," she kept saying in her beautiful French (did she come from Tours?), and she gently pushed the girls through the door. (Perhaps she was counting them.) She gave Denning a quick look, in between two polite pushes. He bowed and raised his hat.

"Quite a responsibility, Mademoiselle Dupré. May I congratulate you?"

Mademoiselle looked at him in astonishment, and forgot to count. And there was Emily, the last of all, quickening her dragging pace as she saw Denning.

"Emily!" he said, taking hold of her hand and shaking it violently. "I've been looking everywhere for you. Your mother would have been so disappointed if I hadn't seen you. And how are you? Mademoiselle Dupré, may Emily come to lunch with me?"

Mademoiselle first shoved the flock of curious girls inside. "Five minutes," she warned them, and sent them scattering.

A gaggle of geese, a giggle of girls. Denning said to the

wide-eyed Emily, "Well, it's good to see you. And how's your sister?"

Mademoiselle pushed a stray wisp of her straight bobbed hair under her gray cloche hat, pulled down her neatly tailored gray flannel jacket, and said, "Who is this gentleman, Emily?"

"He's Bill. My cousin. My American cousin." In her delight, Emily flashed a smile which she forgot to cover with her hand.

"In French, Emily, if you please."

In French, even in Emily's French, it sounded more authentic.

"Yes," Denning said quickly, "Emily's sister married my brother officer. You see?"

"You do not speak French, monsieur?"

"Denning. Bill Denning. I'd be frightened to speak French in front of you. You come from Tours?"

"How did you know?"

Denning smiled (and when he smiled like that, naturally, with all wariness gone from his eyes, his face relaxed, then— as Paula Waysmith had often remarked to Andy—he could charm a gatepost into putting forth green shoots) and he shrugged his shoulders with his best Paris accent. "I heard Emily's sister speak of you—the family is so delighted that Emily is being taught the very best French. I hope Emily is learning it as thoroughly as you teach her?" And Mademoiselle let herself smile.

"May I go to lunch?" Emily asked.

"I don't think so." Mademoiselle's thin white face was worried again.

Denning looked at his watch. "I've an appointment for one o'clock. So I'm afraid it would be a very quick lunch."

"I can eat lunch in twenty minutes," said Emily.

"Emily! I'm afraid we must go in, Monsieur Denning. But perhaps you could arrange a visit next week end at school. Sunday afternoon, for tea?"

"I'm leaving this district quite soon. I'm making a tour of museums, you see. My interest is Renaissance art."

"Oh?" Mademoiselle was disbelieving.

"I've looked at the Nicolas Manuel altarpiece in the museum, and of course the choir stalls in the Minster. But now I'd like to see the influences of the Italian Renaissance at Lugano."

"Ah yes—San Lorenzo," Mademoiselle Dupré murmured,

with a flash of interest approaching the point of friendliness. Besides, anyone who studied museums and churches was definitely in a trustworthy class. But she still hesitated.

"Why don't you lunch with us, Mademoiselle?" he asked.

"Impossible, I'm afraid," she said, sweeping an arm toward the hotel lobby and the rest of the schoolgirls who stood watching.

"Then perhaps some other time?"

"If we don't go now," Emily said, "then I shan't even have twenty minutes to eat *anything*. Oh, please, Mademoiselle Dupré—I shall be back, in the lobby, by one o'clock. I promise."

"I'll see she keeps her promise," Denning said. He raised his hat and bowed.

It may have been his politeness, or the museums and churches, or Emily's promise (one reliable thing about Emily —when she contemplated mischief, she never gave any promises), or the fact that Mademoiselle Dupré was tired, hungry, and saw the rest of her schoolgirls already losing all discipline in the lobby, for suddenly she said, "Please don't be late, Emily. You know how I worry."

She looked at Denning, and he smiled, and she seemed reassured. For she hurried indoors to gather her scattered brood.

"Poor Mademoiselle," Denning said.

"Oh, now—" Emily said in dismay—"you can't be taking her side!"

"For a moment, I was."

Emily considered that. "Are we so awful?"

"I don't think you're so awful. Or I shouldn't have asked you to lunch. But where?"

Emily took off her Panama hat. She made a conscious effort to turn out her toes. "Yes, where?" she asked, suddenly languid.

"And keep your toes straight—just as they were," he told her. "That's the way dancers and athletes walk. Besides, I loathe splayfooted women."

"Do you?" She let herself walk naturally, easily. Her voice became natural, too. "Then you wouldn't mind if we had an ice-cream soda for lunch?"

"Would you like that?" He hoped he hadn't flinched.

"I'd adore it. Besides, it's very nourishing, isn't it?"

"Sustaining," he admitted. "But I—"

"There's a little shop just around this corner—they have all kinds of American things as well as the most smashing cream horns and apple tarts with pink speckles all over the baked meringue. Do you mind?"

He looked into eyes suddenly anxious, as if they felt a mistake had been made. "That sounds fine," he said, and the large brown eyes were sparkling again.

"Bliss," Emily said. "What bliss!" She pushed aside her second ice-cream soda. "Except I really can't eat anything more. How odd. Every time I've passed this shop, I've always wanted to come in and taste so many things. And now, I can't. I can't possibly." She looked sadly at a half-eaten cream puff. "Perhaps it was a mistake to have two éclairs."

"That's one of the strange things about growing up," Denning said. Then he bit his lip. He hadn't meant to let that phrase slip out: the young were always so vulnerable about their youth. Was no one ever satisfied with the age he had?

"What is?"

"When I was a kid—"

"*My* age?" Emily asked coldly.

"Oh, heavens, years younger than you are. How old are you, anyway?"

"I'm sixteen. Almost. Fifteen years and ten months. And four days."

He stared at her.

"Yes," Emily said dejectedly. "And I wear black stockings, and my hair like this, and this kind of dress and hat, and no powder or lipstick. Why, this is the first ice-cream soda I've ever tasted!" She sighed. "I can't even smile properly." She clicked a forefinger angrily against the silver bands over her teeth.

"I bet that hurt."

"More than I expected," she admitted. She began to laugh, then covered her mouth with her hand.

"In a year or so, you'll be darned glad you suffered," he told her. "But I didn't know our British cousins had adopted that dentist's version of the Iron Maiden."

"They haven't. Not unless they've got an American relative with helpful ideas."

"Ah, so the general suggested this?"

"Yes. But you can't blame Pimmy, really. Priscilla, that's my sister, was *always* talking about my teeth. I suppose

Pimmy just had to quieten her, somehow." She looked down at the marble-topped table.

"He could have braces put on *her* teeth."

Emily imagined that picture. "Thank you," she said at last. "Thank you for that vision of judgment. Priscilla with braces—" She began to laugh again. Then she looked at him, her brown eyes merry, no longer earnest at being important. "Why," she asked, and she was very honest and very young, "why did you want to see me? Did you have a question to ask?"

Denning, who had been preparing a few remarks about the Riviera, a side approach to the monster who looked so hairy when he went bathing, returned her frank look. "Yes," he admitted.

"The same question as the policemen asked this morning?"

"Policemen?"

"Two policemen. In plain clothes, of course." She giggled. "They were so serious. And Mademoiselle Dupré was so flustered. And all the rest of the girls were rather impressed."

"I think you've had a most successful visit to Bern."

"Don't you want to know what the policemen asked me?"

"Yes," he admitted again.

"They asked all about the monster."

"And you told them." Well, that angle was taken care of. Keppler and Inspector Bohren must have had the same ideas he had had, only several hours earlier.

She frowned, pushed aside a lock of red hair, and then studied the table top again.

"You didn't tell them," Denning said. "Why?"

She flushed. "They treated me like a child. So I gave them childish answers." She raised her large dark brown eyes. "Yes, I'm afraid I behaved badly. They were really quite nice men."

"You didn't tell them the monster's name?"

"I couldn't remember it. I suppose," she added dejectedly, "I didn't try, really. They were *so* off-putting."

"You've forgotten his name?"

"Is it important?"

"Yes."

Emily smiled. "I've remembered it. You see, you gave his name to Mademoiselle Dupré. Then I remembered everything."

"You're way ahead of me. I gave his name?"

"When you were talking about an altarpiece."

"Manuel?"

"No. The other bit of that name."

"His name is Nicolas?"

"You look so astounded," Emily said with a giggle.

"I am." He stared at her. "Are you sure, Emily?"

"Of course I'm sure." She was hurt. "One does not mislead one's friends." And she was suddenly stiltedly grown-up, voice thinning coldly, eyes looking with distaste at some invisible object above his right shoulder. "After all, he was so *unlike* Father Christmas. That's how I'm quite sure of his name."

"Of course," he said quickly, not even wasting time to struggle with that one.

"It always amused us," Emily went on, everything quite clear in her mind. "I'm sure he'd steal the presents out of the children's shoes."

He looked at his watch. "We've a promise to keep," he said.

"But you haven't told me why you wanted to know about him."

"He went off very quickly and borrowed my car. Without my permission."

"Aren't you a detective?"

"No. Not at all. I'm just a man who is looking for his car."

"And I thought he'd done something really—really—" Words and expression failed her.

"Really monstrous? Oh, I don't think so. He's just absent-minded, I guess."

Emily shook her head violently. "He's a complete toad."

"How do you know?" He smiled as he watched her honest protest.

"He looks like one. Even his neck swells out at the side like a croaking toad."

"Perhaps he suffers from sideways goiter."

Emily's brown eyes widened. "Is there such a—" she began. Then, saying "Oh!" indignantly, she rose. "Do you always tease people?"

"Only if they have a sense of humor," he assured her.

She gave him a slow, measuring look. Then she smiled and said, "I suppose Mademoiselle is now throwing a pink and purple fit."

"We've still got five minutes," he reassured her.

In the distance, at the door of the Aarhof, Mademoiselle was waiting.

"She's seen us," Denning said. "So now we can all relax. No need to hurry."

"Where do you come from?" Emily asked, suddenly anxious as she watched Mademoiselle Dupré's still figure, an ominous sentinel, an impatient Charon waiting to sweep her away from this world. Emily remembered to stick her hated hat back in place on her head. "This awful elastic," she said angrily.

"New York." He watched Emily's face. "Mademoiselle will ask questions?"

"Indubitably." Emily was nonchalant, profile-showing; her voice was fluting into its Oscar Wilde notes again.

He whistled.

"Yes?" the grand duchess asked, with an upraised eyebrow.

"Wish I could do that," he said. "Indubitably. . . ."

"It's my special word," Emily said, "meanwhile. I use it only for the most formidable occasions." She smiled suddenly, giving him a side glance. "New York . . ." she added thoughtfully. "Is that really quite enough?"

"My address is the Princeton Club. Got that? Princeton."

"Because you travel so much?" Emily's answers to Mademoiselle's questions were already being born behind those large dark eyes. "Are you really interested in churches and things?"

"Yes."

Emily sighed. That was hard to take, seemingly. "I have a cousin who does rubbings," she said, trying her best.

"What's your address?" he asked quickly. Mademoiselle Dupré was looming larger and larger.

"The school is called 'The Hermitage.' Near Moosegg." Then as he looked at her, she repeated, "Moosegg. That's near Moosbad. Can you remember?"

"I'm afraid it's going to haunt me."

"Then at home, my address is Upper Slaughter, Gloucestershire. That's all. And I'm Emily White Hyphen Cooper, spelled Cowper."

"And I suppose Upper Slaughter is near Lower Slaughter?" he asked, with a smile he couldn't repress.

"Actually, it is." Her eyes looked at him reproachfully. "No one *ever* believes me. Sometimes, I think I don't even exist."

"All right," he said hastily. "I believe you. And what's the name of the place on the Riviera?"

"Oh, I shan't be there again until next Easter," she assured him.

"I may be there some Easter, too."

"It's Cap d'Hercule." She looked at him, and she began to smile. "And the house of Monsieur Nicholas is called *Le Nid*," she added softly.

"Oh," he said, and he looked embarrassed.

Mademoiselle Dupré fluttered forward, excessively polite, now that all her forebodings were proved so base.

"Four minutes late, Mademoiselle," he said quickly. "My deepest apologies. Family affairs, you know." He shook hands with Emily. "And thank you. Thank you for having lunch with me. I'm very grateful." He was. She had made him laugh on a day when laughter had seemed impossible. For that, one would always be grateful.

"I hope you find your car," Emily said. "And I think I like vanilla better than chocolate after all."

"Less of an aftermath," he agreed. "My love to Priscilla. *And* to Pimmy, bless his three stars."

"And you won't forget to send me postcards for my collection?"

"Emily!" said Mademoiselle Dupré. "You must not ask—"

"But I always send postcards," Denning assured her, "the most hideous postcards I can find—of sunsets having pink and purple fits."

Emily giggled. And Mademoiselle Dupré, finding everything unintelligible, was completely reassured: such good-bys were normal among the unfortunate English-speakers, an uncouth language, it affected their minds; or perhaps, poor people, it was not given to all languages to perform with the precision, the clarity, the grace of a French epigram.

Denning bowed and watched Emily being led away. He began walking slowly along the arcade. Nicolas, he was thinking. Or was it Nicholas? Saint Nicholas with his presents on Christmas Eve? Had that been Emily's conversational swirl? Talking to Emily made him understand Laocoön's problems much more vividly. Nicholas . . . that was something, anyway.

Suddenly he thought, Nicholas . . . Nikolaides. . . . It was odd how people could be superstitious about the sound of their names, or about their initials: so often when a man adopted a false name, it had the echo of other names he had used, a resemblance that seemed childish when the truth was discovered. But the truth was not discovered by a resemblance. All that he had found out, thanks to Emily, was that the fake Maartens lived at Cap d'Hercule, in a house call *Le Nid,* and was known as Monsieur Nicholas.

He looked at his watch: twelve minutes past one. He'd better turn tourist who had lost his passport. He searched for a telephone kiosk, and then called the police station.

But his luck did not hold. Inspector Bohren was not available; he was out of town. Inspector Bohren was not expected back at any definite time. Denning left his name as an indication that he needed contact. He stepped out into the sunny street, a man with a piece of information which he couldn't get rid of, a man who felt useless because his usefulness couldn't be used.

He found a taxi and drove to the station. He was punctual, at least, although the rest of his schedule was all in pieces: he'd have to telephone the Waysmiths again, and apologize. When will you learn, he asked himself, to stop planning time so optimistically? How often have you arranged things so neatly, then found you only have one pair of feet?

At the entrance to the station, among a small group of four hotel porters, he saw an Aarhof-banded cap. The porter —a tall man, lugubrious-faced under the hard black peak of his hat, thin-shouldered under his dark green jacket—was vaguely familiar. Yes, he was the man who had met Denning at the station yesterday morning. He had also been the man who had taken charge of Denning's luggage, and then mislaid the smaller bag just long enough for it to be opened and have Denning's credentials quietly verified. Was this Keppler's man? Or not?

He was brusque, clear-voiced. "I checked everything in the baggage room. Was that all right, sir?" He held out the tickets. Now, lips scarcely moving, in quite a different tone, "Michel notified Elizabeth you were leaving. She sent you this message." And as he passed over the baggage checks, the small slip of paper was neatly hidden among them. "Any reply?" A lip reader would have had no success with him.

Denning looked down at the checks, as if making sure of them. Was this Keppler's man? The note was scrawled in pencil, in strange writing he hadn't seen before, even if it was signed "Elizabeth." He stared at the tickets. "Darling," the note said, "Have a good trip, but *please* let me know your address.—Devotedly, Elizabeth."

The man sensed his caution, perhaps even the blackness of his indecision. He said, "Elizabeth telephoned the message. I couldn't imitate the signature. Normally, two curls and a dash." It was an accurate description of Elizabeth's final flourish.

"Good," Denning said in a normal voice, "and where is this baggage room?" As the man pointed, he added quietly, "Memorize this: the Riviera address is *Le Nid,* Cap d'Hercule. The name is Nicholas. Nicholas, Cap d'Hercule."

The porter, still pointing, nodded as he explained it was advisable to be there fifteen minutes before the gentleman's train was due to leave.

"My address," Denning added, "will be Falken." Then he raised his voice to normal. "How much do I owe you?" He became busy with his wallet, putting away the checks, finding the money.

The man touched his cap, plodded away, and was already out of sight before Denning found a cab to take him to the Waysmiths' hotel.

Where did he vanish so quickly? Denning wondered. Into one of those telephone booths round the corner? Was he now calling Keppler?

You worry too much, he told himself. And yet, in this kind of work, one small mistake, and there was no chance to say you were sorry: one small mistake, and you were dead, and so were several other people, too.

13: Journey to Falken

THIS, THOUGHT DENNING AS HE ENTERED THE Hotel Victoria and asked for the Waysmiths' room, might be called an unnecessary delay in his journey to Falken. (Le Brun would certainly disapprove of it.) Yet he was worried about Paula. Somehow, in spite of all his precautions yesterday, he had drawn her into this circle of danger. Why else would Rauch, the temporary mail clerk at the Aarhof who had startled him yesterday with that bogus message from Max, enter Paula's room to search it that night? In his own mind he felt that he was responsible for that. Now, he had to warn Waysmith to keep Paula out of Bern until all trouble with Rauch and his friends was settled. One way or another, he added grimly.

But he managed to look cheerful, even confident, when Andy welcomed him into the Waysmiths' white and gold bedroom. Their suitcases were packed and locked, Paula was wearing her hat, their coats were lying on a bed, the remains of lunch were on a small table drawn up at the French windows.

"Hello," Andy said. He was in a bad temper. He shook hands, and gave Denning a careful look.

"Hello, Bill!" Paula came forward, her smile wide and gentle. "We had almost given up hope. But I'm so glad you could manage." She held out her hand, and looked over at Andy pleadingly.

Denning said, "I owe you two apologies." He took her by the shoulders and kissed each cheek. "There they are. For yesterday, Paula." He smiled into her blue eyes.

"But for what?" It was a sweet pretense, telling him he was forgiven.

"Brushing you off at lunchtime and cutting you dead at supper." He looked at Andy and grinned. "It takes really good friends to be able to endure that treatment. Sorry for being late today, Andy. I had some business to clear up before I could see you."

Waysmith had softened a bit. "Well, you don't have to kiss me to prove it." He was smiling more naturally now.

"Don't I?" Denning dropped his hat on the bed. He looked at Andy. He put out his hand again. This time, they shook hands warmly.

"Have you had lunch?" Paula asked. "We were too hungry to wait. But I left some sandwiches for you." She pointed to the table.

Denning looked embarrassed. "To tell the truth, I've just had a couple of ice-cream sodas. Couldn't face food for the next ten hours."

"What on earth have you been doing?" Waysmith asked. "Entering your second childhood? Have a seat, anyway."

"I think I'll walk around and try to digest."

"Did you really give the little schoolgirl a lunch of ice-cream sodas?" Paula asked delightedly.

Denning's walk was cut short for a moment. "Where did you see her?"

"With you. I was hurrying back here after interviewing all the house agents in Bern. You seemed to be concentrating hard, so I didn't stop."

"She's English," Denning said briefly. "In addition, she has a turn of phrase all her own. You have to concentrate with Emily."

"Titian-red hair and the largest dark eyes in town," Paula told her husband.

"Carrot head and braced teeth," said Denning.

"In three years, no man will even remember having thought that," Paula predicted.

Andy glanced at his watch. "Cut it out, both of you. We have to leave here within the next fifteen minutes." He looked at his wife. "*If* you mean to keep your promise to Francesca." Then he turned to Denning. "We had a bit of an upset here last night. A man broke in, two men to be precise—"

"Two?"

"The newspapers were very poor about it," Paula said. "Not that *I* wanted publicity. But the whole report of last night's incident was played down almost to nothing."

"Perhaps the newspapers were very good," Denning said quietly. "As they were in the report of Max's death." They stared at him, then at each other. Waysmith reached quickly for a newspaper. Denning told him, "Page three, column five."

"In the Henziplatz?" Waysmith asked.

Denning nodded.

"Was it that car smash?" Paula asked, crossing quickly over to her husband. She read the brief paragraph again. "Oh, Bill . . ." she said. And why, oh why, had she used the words "car smash"? Must she always remind Bill of Peggy's death? He never talked about it, never even mentioned Peggy. But his silence keeps her alive, Paula thought, and I wish—for Bill's own sake—that wasn't so.

"It wasn't an accident," Denning said. "It was murder. But keep that quiet meanwhile. Will you, Andy?"

Waysmith looked at him. "Why tell me at all?"

"So that you'll listen to me."

"I'm listening."

"Will you get Paula out of Bern? Not just for a week end. Keep her away from here until Rauch's friends lose interest. They aren't gentle people."

"We're just leaving Bern," Paula said, too quickly. She glanced nervously at Andy.

"We're going to Falken." Waysmith's voice was sharp again, with the anger which springs from concealed worry.

Denning stood very still. "Take Paula to Interlaken, Grindelwald, Zurich—plenty of places to choose from." He moved around the room, glanced out of the window, kept his expression as casual as his voice.

"I'm supposed to be working in Bern," Waysmith reminded him. "And—" He halted and shrugged his shoulders.

Quickly, Paula said, "And Falken is so near. . . . We are

going to take a house there, and Andy can commute."

Denning pulled out his pack of cigarettes. Even a small gesture like that reminded him of Max. "I'd leave Falken alone, Andy," he said.

"No," said Paula. "We've decided all that. Bill, I'm in no danger from people like Rauch. It's Francesca. That's why we're going to Falken. She lives there. Perhaps we can help her. Perhaps we can't. But we're going." She looked at Andy, defying him to change her mind.

"Sure," Andy said, "we're going there, armed with a pea-shooter and a slingshot. Paula——"

"No," Paula said again. "We've argued enough, Andy. We're going. You want to go, anyway. You know that."

Andy shrugged his shoulders. "You see?" he said to Denning.

"Not altogether. What danger is Francesca in?"

Paula looked a little uncomfortable. She glanced over at Andy, but he was pulling on his coat and gathering some magazines and newspapers together. Paula said, "She tried to help some people. And that started some complications."

Andy said, "Complications? Is that what you call having our lives twisted, knotted, and thrown around?" He began opening and closing drawers, giving a last checkup to the room as he talked. "I've had one hell of a day, Bill. Kept phoning you until four in the morning. Then I didn't sleep till nearly six, and was wakened at eight. Called you again. No answer. Argued with Paula all through breakfast. Got the police to come round and take fingerprints off that wardrobe-door handle, and made the mistake of telling them we were leaving for Falken. So we got a summons to the police station, and had a nice friendly talk with an Inspector Bohren. Then I rented a car while Paula went house-hunting. Called you again and got through at last. Packed. Waited. Did some business by telephone. Waited. Waited for Paula. Waited for you. Well—now I'm going. The bill is paid, the car's parked outside. Can we give you a lift back to your hotel?"

"You can give me a lift to Falken."

Waysmith closed the last drawer with a bang. "Is this a sudden whim?"

"No."

"Why are you going?"

"I've told you as much as I can. At the moment. Later, I'll——"

"All I want to know is this: are you on a mission?"

"Nothing official."

"Just what do you mean by that?"

"Well—you're on a mission of your own, aren't you?"

"We're just helping a friend."

"So am I." Max might be dead, but now he needed help more than ever.

Waysmith had been watching him closely. "Sorry if I sounded too suspicious. But when I'm giving a lift to anyone, with my wife in the car, I'm damned if he's going to be a professional agent on a mission."

"And you'd be right," Denning answered. He meant that, too.

"Let's get the bags downstairs," said Waysmith. "We're wasting time here." He moved to the telephone and called for a porter.

Denning was just as quick. He lifted his hat on his way to the door. "I'll taxi to the station and pick up my things from the checkroom. Meet me there. Main entrance. A quarter past two?"

"You're all packed?" Paula asked in amazement. You see, her eyes said to Andy: Falken wasn't such a sudden whim after all.

Denning looked at them both. "It's good to see you again," he said unexpectedly, almost with a touch of emotion. Then he was gone.

Paula began packing the sandwiches in some spare Kleenex. "He'll be hungry before we even reach Falken. Ice-cream sodas are only lethal in the first hour." She laughed softly. "Bill— with an ice-cream soda! He always loathed them. And how did his English Emily come into the picture, anyway? For that matter, how did Bill?"

"*You* ask me that?" Andy wanted to know, as he finished counting the suitcases in spite of distractions.

"And what about you?" she countered. "Weren't you the man who rushed off to Frankfurt to see Max Meyer?"

He was silent for a moment, thinking of Max Meyer. His lips tightened. Then he looked down at her. "Paula—" He put an arm round her shoulders.

"We're going, darling," she said gently.

"Now's the time to change your mind." If I had only known about Max, he thought, I'd have made twice the resistance about going to Falken.

"Could you change yours? Could you turn your back and walk away?" She smiled and shook her head. "Darling, you're the hardest man to persuade to do what you really want to do."

"Paula," he said, tightening his grip on her shoulder. He kissed her, long and hard, a tense kiss telling her all his worries and fears.

Then a discreet knock sounded on the door, a porter entered, Paula straightened her hat, Waysmith wiped the lipstick from his chin, and all became businesslike once more.

And everything went so smoothly at the station—no delays, no difficulties—that their spirits began to lighten, as if they felt that this easy departure from Bern was a good omen. They sat packed together in the front seat of the inconspicuous Citroën which Waysmith had rented, a car similar to many they passed, even to its Bern license plate. Waysmith was driving, relaxing little by little as he became sure that no car was following them. Paula had a map ready for reference if necessary, but her eyes were quick with memories: this was the same, that had altered, here were new houses, over there was a village she had always wanted to visit. And Denning, still pessimistic, still concealing it, began to feel at least a new sense of reassurance: the basic worries still remained, but the unnecessary fears were vanishing. Dangers, if you could see them clearly, were not unbeatable; if you could see them without blurring them in a mist of worry increasing worries, of fears compounding fear, of doubts adding to hesitations, you had a chance of winning. And even if the chance was small, it was still a chance.

"Feeling better?" Paula asked suddenly.

"Better enough to be hungry."

"Didn't I tell you?" she asked Andy, and produced the wrapped sandwiches from her outsize handbag.

"Peggy used to have a bag like that," Denning said, "a kind of magician's catchall."

Paula looked at him quickly, before she could control her sudden amazement. But he was talking on, quite naturally, about Peggy, dipping into the past which they had all shared. Paula relaxed. Conversation, she thought, was like learning to ride a bicycle: when you worried about hitting a telephone pole you rode straight into it; but take away that fear, and you never even noticed the telephone pole. The four years' gap in their friendship no longer was a wide gulf: it closed over, gently, quietly, and gave the sure footing they needed to step into the present. They could talk freely about themselves and the new shapes their lives had taken.

They followed the road to Thun for less than sixteen miles. "A piece of cake," said Waysmith, as he turned the car at Paula's direction into a narrower southbound road. "How on earth does it take forty-five minutes to reach Falken?"

"Villages keep passing at eleven miles an hour," Paula reminded him. "Here's another one. Slow down, Andy, or we'll all be arrested." She didn't add that this mountain road had more twists and turns than the easy first half of the journey. Andy would find that out soon enough.

"There isn't a policeman within sight," Waysmith said. Then he thought, I wish there were, though; I wish there was a whole garrison of policemen strung along this peaceful road. They met no cars, either. But there were other hazards: horse-drawn carts, stacked with timber; a farmer's wagon; several cyclists; three hikers; escaped chickens; a herd of surprised goats; the constant houses, with their balconies and broad red eaves, which would suddenly appear, among a clump of trees, around a curve of a hill; and children who ran out to look or a woman who interrupted her work to wave at the passing car.

"What's going on, anyway?" Denning asked suddenly after they had seen four houses with uniforms hanging to air over the balconies, and two front doors where men sat on wooden benches and cleaned their rifles. "General mobilization?"

"Reservists," Paula said. "They are all in the army until they are sixty."

Waysmith looked at his wife.

"But it's true," she insisted. "Francesca was talking about it yesterday. After basic training, all men spend three weeks each year in the army until they are thirty-six. After that, two weeks each year in the army until they are forty-eight. And then, they still keep their rifles and uniforms until they are sixty. General inspection once a year. Shooting practice once a week. What's more," Paula added, watching her husband's face with sudden amusement, "they pay for the bullets they use each week. So they're all expert shots."

That's comforting, Waysmith thought. "I'm glad I married a native, almost," he said. "So helpful on safari." His confidence began to rise. So did the speed of the car.

"Eleven miles an hour," Paula reminded him. "There's a village just around this corner."

They passed seven houses and a small white church with a narrow spire. "That was Gurgli," Paula told them.

"No comment," Denning observed.

"In about three minutes, we'll go through Gurgli-Bad," Paula went on. "And don't ask me if that makes Gurgli good. I was a schoolgirl here, myself."

They approached five houses and a miniature castle.

"Still no comment," Waysmith said, and changed down from second into first. But if Paula thought he was going to travel this route each day, just to have the pleasure of passing Gurgli-Bad or better, then— He stopped thinking in order to concentrate on the twisting road with its steep drop, on one side, toward a rush of blue-white water.

Paula gave a last wave to the small castle. "That was where I went to school. And Francesca too."

"Paolo and Francesca," Denning said with a grin. "Or was that a standing joke?"

"Of course—what else would you expect?" She half-smiled, as she looked back at the school and watched the hills changing into mountains, the steep sloping meadows bright with blue and white flowers, the scattered houses sheltering under their wide-spreading roofs. And how I hated it, she thought: all I wanted was a city street and noise and people, a sense that I was alive and a part of the world. "When we were young, how unsure of ourselves we were," she said. "Always afraid we were missing something. But now—I'd like to live a few months each year deep in the country like this, where I could catch my breath and take stock of myself."

"Without Andy?" Denning asked.

She looked at him quickly, but he was smiling. She smiled too, and shook her head.

"I'm all in favor of that kind of place for my wife's school," Waysmith said, looking back too for a moment as the road stopped climbing and straightened to run through a stretch of pine and birch trees.

"Nothing to do but pipe her woodnotes wild," Denning agreed.

"Like an oboe player on an off-night," Paula suggested.

"Can you tell me," the unmusical Waysmith asked, once the joke was made even worse by having to be explained to him, "can you tell me why we should all be so damned hilarious?" And that reminder sobered all of them. Or perhaps it was the first sign of Falken, no more than a mile ahead of them.

The road had brought them through the small forest, and as the trees began to thin out, they could see the beginnings of a broad valley, where the mountains had stepped back and Falken's toy houses were scattered, like a handful of confetti, over the sloping meadows. It was a smiling village, lying open to the sun among green fields and tongues of forest, a place of innocence and peace. Even the torrent, which had rushed in cold fury to meet them for the last five miles, had become a placid stream flowing calmly through the meadows, a straight band of pale blue crystal, to form the spine of the valley.

"Stop here, Andy," Denning said as they reached the last fringe of trees. The road ahead followed the stream, and then bridged over it. There it divided, one branch continuing over the hills and far away, the other leading into the village of Falken itself. A cluster of white and brown houses. A church. Then more woods creeping down from the hillsides. Meadows interlaced with trees, sprinkled with more houses. And curving around, cupping the gentle valley, forming the background in depths, were rock-capped ridges, then white-crested peaks.

Waysmith drew the car to the side of the road, and cut off the engine. He watched Denning's worried frown. "Yes?" he asked.

"It's bigger than I imagined. Scattered." A good place to hide in, a difficult place to search.

"Does *no one* like the view except me?" Paula asked.

"At the moment," Denning said wryly, "I don't like it one bit. Far too many houses."

"But they aren't close together—except in the village itself."

"That's the trouble. Where does Francesca live?"

"With her aunt, Fräulein Louisa Lüthi."

"Yes, darling," Waysmith asked, "but where?"

"I'm trying to tell you, if you'll just let me." She turned to Bill. "Don't you want the complete picture? Briefly?"

"Might be an idea," Denning admitted.

"Briefly," Waysmith agreed, with emphasis. Perhaps to make sure of that, he began a quick account of the Falken Committee, of Francesca's connection with it, of the real threat behind Rauch's attempt last night, of Andrássy's disappearance.

Denning sat very still, even after Waysmith had ended.

I told him something new, Waysmith thought with pleased surprise. He began to feel better, personally, about this whole visit to Falken. But it was Denning's turn, now, to hand over any information he knew. "Anything to add to that?" Waysmith asked.

"It's new to me," Denning admitted. But not new to Kepler, he realized. Last night, when Francesca had been mentioned, "Do you know anything about her?" Keppler had asked. So innocently, casually. And then, with the same simple curiosity, "Have you ever heard of Falken?" One thing I do know, Denning thought as he looked at the village in the valley: there, we'll find Keppler waiting for us. He's probably been there since eight o'clock this morning, and that's why he had to telephone "Elizabeth's" message. In which case the porter was trustworthy. You can stop worrying about him at least. And my message about Nicholas of Cap d'Hercule—that's probably in Keppler's hands too.

"Francesca—" began Paula.

"Why doesn't she leave?" Denning asked irritably. "There's enough trouble in Falken without having to worry over Francesca." Yet, he knew it was a foolish question the moment it slipped out. There were others on the Committee, too: how could they all leave? And for where? And for how long? Wherever they went, there would be danger from hired men like Rauch. The only end to the danger would be to find the man who did the hiring.

"I asked her that question when I phoned this morning," Paula said. "She said, 'And keep on running? Where do I stop? And when?' That silenced me, I must admit."

Denning looked at Paula. It silenced him, too, to hear his own thoughts put into words by a girl he didn't even know. Suddenly he felt his deep pessimism about this new trouble in Falken begin to lift. Where there was courage, there was a chance. "There's a point of no retreat for all of us," he said at last. When you reached that, you turned, and fought back.

Waysmith nodded. "Had enough view?" he asked. He looked at the wide valley of flowering meadows, at the stream which came running to meet them. In the still air, the sound of children's voices carried over the fields from a farm; there was an echo of a woodsman's ax from a forested hillside, the gentle murmur of bells as the cows moved slowly through the deep pasture. "Let's move," he said, "or else I'll find myself promising to come and live here." He grinned and ruffled Paula's hair. "And how do we find Francesca?"

"Over the bridge, through the village, first turning on the right after we reach the church, keep on going for about half a mile," Paula said abstractedly as she searched in her handbag.

"Brief enough?" Denning asked, with a smile for Waysmith's astonished face.

Paula had pulled a small map, page-size, from the bag. "Yes," she said with some satisfaction, "I thought that was *Waldesruhe*." She pointed to a red roof, some distance to their left, that was almost hidden by the trees on its small hill. "The man was right: it is sheltered from the road. But it is said to have a perfect view."

"What man?" Waysmith asked.

"The real-estate man. In Bern." She held out the map, and they could see it was a diagram of the valley with all the houses marked by black squares. The square just at this point on the road was circled with red pencil. Another red circle was drawn around a house near the village itself. "There are only two houses for rent," Paula explained. "This one, here, and—"

"For heaven's sake, Paula," Andy said, "we aren't—"

"I didn't say we were looking at houses *now*. All I wanted to do was to save time. Here's the view you get from *Waldesrueh*. Do you like it? Shall we even bother to come back and look at the house? That's all."

Waysmith started the engine. Women, he was thinking. . . . What a genius they had for picking prize moments.

But Denning was saying, "Paula, when you have finished with that map, I could use it." He smiled. "Just to keep me from losing my way."

"Have it," Paula said. "I've found *Waldesruhe*. That's all I—" She halted. "Someone from the house is coming down to see who is admiring their view so much."

It was true. Two men were walking slowly through the trees, down toward the road.

Denning stared at them. "Then admire it," he said quickly. "Paula, Andy, get out and admire it."

Afterward, Waysmith wondered why they had obeyed Bill so quickly. The urgency in his voice? The note of warning?

Whatever it was, Waysmith was standing on the road beside the car, and Paula was beside him, pointing a hand toward the valley, saying very clearly, "It is lovely, isn't it?"

One of the men came forward, away from the trees, almost to the edge of the road, his city shoes slipping on the sloping grass, and paused there, one hand outstretched to rest against the silver bark of a solitary birch tree and balance him more securely on the green bank. He stood there above them, silent for a minute, studying the car, his thin long feet buried in a thick cluster of blue harebells. From behind him, from the last group of trees, his hidden companion spoke to him urgently. He replied in the same language, still watching the two Americans standing beside their car. Then, in German, he asked loudly, "Having trouble?"

"No," Waysmith answered. "Just admiring the view." He waved a hand toward the village. "Very fine view." It was a word which lost its charm rapidly.

"Wonderful," Paula said, with her brightest smile.

There was a pause. Again the foreign words came from the last group of trees, and the man nodded.

"To be sure," he said unconvincingly to Paula, and turned abruptly away. He slipped on the grass, and slipped again. His companion stepped out from the trees to catch him by his wrist and pull him onto the earthy ground where his footing was surer.

"Come on," Waysmith said. "Let's go and take some photographs of the village." He helped Paula into the car, had a last defiant look at the view, and then followed her.

The car started toward Falken. "Take it slowly," Denning advised. "We are being watched."

"Not exactly country folks," Waysmith said. Who were they? he wondered. Denning seemed to know. He waited. But Denning only looked back at the house. "Handsome cuff links, if your taste runs to glittering stones," Waysmith tried. "Did you see them flash when he put out a hand to grab the tree?"

Denning nodded. He was looking now at the rough driveway to *Waldesruhe*, which twisted down through hilly ground between scattered boulders and trees. It entered the road ahead of them, just beyond a high bank formed by the abrupt drop of *Waldesruhe*'s hill.

Paula said, "What language was that, anyway? Russian?"

"Not quite," Denning said. He was remembering the few Bulgarian refugees he had interviewed back in Berlin.

"Sounded like Bulgarian." Bulgarian . . . with an overlay of travel. It had been many years since those men had spoken Bulgarian in Bulgaria. "Stop again, Andy," he said. "Just under the shelter of this bank."

"I refuse to look at any more views," Waysmith said. But he halted the car. "What do you think you're doing?" he asked suddenly, as Denning reached into the back seat for one of the newspapers lying on top of the piled luggage, and then opened the car door.

"I'm going house-hunting," Denning said with a smile.

"Just a moment—" Waysmith's voice had sharpened, as it always did when he was worried. "Who were those two men?"

"That's what I want to know."

"Friends of Rauch?"

"No."

"Then, why—"

"I thought I recognized one of them."

"Look," Waysmith said angrily, "have I got to drag every piece of information—"

"You've got to get Paula into Falken," Denning reminded him. "Drop my things at the inn. And if you see your friend Inspector Bohren, let him know I'm around here, will you?"

"There's a bus," Paula reported, "leaving the bridge." She had been sitting very still, unhappily watching the road ahead of them. She had sensed Andy's battle with himself: he wanted to go with Denning, he had to stay with her. "I want to see the house," she said in a low voice. I wish I were in Falken, she thought miserably, I wish I were in Falken and all this trouble over and Francesca safe and no more threats and nothing to do but enjoy ourselves.

"I'll wait until the bus passes," Denning said, ignoring Paula's last remark, but he gripped her wrist for a moment as he got out of the car. "You're my witness," he said lightly. "Get to the village as soon as you can."

"We'll take you up to *Waldesruhe*," Andrew Waysmith said. "We can at least drop you at the front door."

"You take Paula to the village and leave her there. Then if you've any surplus energy left, you can come to *Waldesruhe* and collect me. I never did like walking back. See you soon then?" He stepped quickly onto the roadway. He heard Waysmith say something which sounded very much like "stubborn bastard." "Same to you," he called after the moving car. Then he began walking to the entrance to *Waldesruhe's* private road.

He paused there to light a cigarette and wave to the bus as it passed him. Plenty of witnesses, he thought as he noticed the curious faces looking out at him. He glanced at his watch. When last seen, William Denning was walking smartly toward the house known as *Waldesruhe.* . . . He smiled at his self-dramatization. If he used the right approach, the next hour—although tricky—could be harmless enough. And the right approach was certainly this, walking quite openly, by the front driveway, straight up to *Waldesruhe* itself. The right approach was simple-minded stupidity, naïve trust, a state of mind which a man like Nikolaides always confused with innocence.

14: The Quiet Inn

PAULA WAYSMITH GLANCED WORRIEDLY AT HER
husband as he drove toward the Falken bridge. She restrained
herself, with a considerable effort, from looking back toward
Waldesruhe, from talking about Bill Denning or speculating
about the two men who had aroused his interest. For Andy
was wearing what she privately called his near-mutiny look.
When he set his brows and jaw that way, it meant he was
doing something completely opposite to what he wanted to do.

Beyond the bridge, on the road that branched up into
Falken itself, there was a group of men. "An accident, or
something?" Paula asked, glad of a distraction. Waysmith
said nothing; he eased the car over the narrow stone bridge,
avoiding some children who were more interested in the
working men than in traffic, and brought it to a halt. "What
now?" he asked angrily. For the road into Falken was being
torn up and resurfaced. "It's a fine time to dig up the pavement."

"Reminds me of New York."

"Where do we go from here?" He waited impatiently for
one of the men, who was walking slowly toward them, his

heavy boots slipping on the pile of debris he had been helping to create, his face and arms red from a day's work in the sun. "If it isn't one damned thing, it's another," Waysmith said, reconciling himself to more trouble.

The man had almost reached them. "Going into Falken?" he called.

"That was the idea."

"You can't go this way."

"So I see."

The man was standing by the car window now. He pointed along the other road. "Follow that route until you reach the trees. There's a back road there that will take you into Falken. It's rough. Go slowly."

"The first group of trees to the left of that road?" Waysmith verified. But he was studying the man's face. I've seen him somewhere, he thought.

"That's right." The man ran a crumpled red cotton handkerchief round the back of his neck. He was young, fresh-complexioned, fair-haired. He lowered his voice. "Go to the inn," he said. Then he turned away with a wave of his hand, and climbed back over the fragments of road.

"Thanks," Waysmith called after him, and turned the car's nose along the valley road.

"That was our young policeman," Paula said. "Last night. Remember?" This small excitement and Andy's relaxed face sent her spirits soaring again.

"A nice natural roadblock," Waysmith commented. "Someone's in charge here, after all." He felt better, too.

He felt still better when they had entered a rough road shielded by trees, and started climbing a short hill into the back of Falken. For there, too, was a little trouble. A long, low-slung lumber cart had tilted over toward a ditch, its side wheels embedded dangerously in the narrow road's soft shoulder. Its load of logs was being lightened. Not very neatly. It took considerable care to ease the Citroën past the precariously balanced cart, the two nervous horses which had been unharnessed, and the four foresters who were working so slowly. Again, one of the men came up to give Waysmith advice. Again, appearances were noted and the contents of the car quietly examined in the time-space of a helpful sentence, with that same impersonal trained eye.

"Are they *all* policemen?" Paula asked, as they skirted the last log lying askew on the road.

Waysmith shook his head. "I doubt that. Bohren can't have a whole army up here. He must have recruited some allies." He smiled, then. "I begin to like Falken," he said with some surprise. Then he put out a hand and gripped Paula's arm gently. "Sorry. I just hate being treated like a twelve-year-old mind."

"But Bill would have told you more if I hadn't been there. Blame it on me. If you had been alone with Bill, you'd have been driving up to *Waldesruhe* right now."

"I doubt that." But his smile had broadened. "Paula, why the hell do you love a bad-tempered bastard like me?"

"Because you ask such a disarming question, darling. Careful, Andy, careful! Two hands are needed for this road."

That was true enough. The road was narrow and rough, and it twisted between the houses which were set down on broad meadows with complete independence, brown wood houses on firm stone foundations, white plastered houses with fretted balconies, red-brown roofs spreading wide, windows climbing up the broad gables to hide under the eaves themselves. Wood smoke drifted from the chimneys. Somewhere a cock mistimed the day, and crowed triumphantly. There was the steady sound of rushing water from the stream that wandered down the hill, a soft perpetual background to the intermittent tinkling from off-tone bells.

"What's that?" Waysmith asked, listening.

"Cows, darling."

"Do these houses all have farms in their back yards?" He took a deep breath of air. "Yes," he said, answering his own question, "I guess they do." Peace, and plenty of it. Even here, on the street which they had suddenly entered, there was nothing but peace. And there was the inn with *Gasthof zu d. Hirschen* painted in spiky black lettering across one white wall, and a stiff wooden sign (a picture of two stags gazing off, in complete harmony, toward the upper windows) suspended over its entrance.

"Now, that's what I like," Waysmith said, as he halted the car against a two-foot-broad sidewalk opposite the inn. He looked at the name and the sign. "Grammatical accuracy, economy, and idealism," and he nodded with approval. "What more does a journalist need?" Then he noticed the wooden bench at the side of the inn's doorway. There sat two red-faced elderly men, with black waistcoats opened comfortably over white shirts, pipes cupped in their hands, their white heads gravely nodding as they listened to a tall man who looked more like a schoolteacher with a passion for climbing than a policeman. But it was Inspector Bohren, all right.

Paula hadn't noticed. She was too busy looking up at the inn's name and its sign. "I don't get it," she said frankly. "Accuracy and economy—that's in the name, yes. But idealism?"

"You can think that one out while you're waiting. Give me two minutes. I'll just leave these"—he reached energetically for Denning's two bags, golf clubs, hat, and coat—"and then we can get to Francesca's house."

She looked at him, both amused and relieved at his sudden enthusiasm. "You do like Falken, then?"

"Quaint as all get-out. But it looks real enough. No fancy dress among the inhabitants, at least." He shook his head over three visitors, beplumed and caparisoned for at least an eighty-mile walk, who were looking hungrily into the window of a pastry shop next door to a small display of postcards and climbing tackle. But the concessions to tourists had been kept to a minimum. The end of the wedge was still very thin; apart from the short-trousered hikers and a couple of wild dirndls loose on this narrow street—and a regrettable tall white box of a café-restaurant with three striped umbrellas on its side patch of field—the rest of Falken concentrated on itself. A horse-drawn cart rumbled, without benefit of axle, across the street from one side lane to another; three bright-faced women carried their bundles of wet wash back from the stream; a deeply tanned man cycled to a job with a saw over his shoulders; towheaded children, busy or curious, stopped to stare at the car. No policemen anywhere—except for some special visitors like Bohren. Not even a possible police station in sight. Nor a locksmith's shop. Falken probably never even bolted its doors at night, and if windows were closed tight it was against night air and not marauders.

"I'll give you a tip," he said, pointing up at the two amiable stags over the doorway. "A woman painted that."

He crossed the street. The two elderly men and school teacher Bohren only interrupted their serious discussion long enough to give him a nod and a civil good day. "And another thing," Bohren was saying, as Waysmith stepped over the threshold, "all that early rain . . ."

At least I've been checked in, Waysmith thought, even if I'll never learn what the early rain did or did not do. Then he became aware of the sudden silence which had fallen over the room he had entered.

It was a low-ceilinged room, smelling not unpleasantly of good beer and spiced sausage, a room dimly lighted from a row of four close-packed windows where stiff-starched lace was drawn above precise geraniums on a broad stone sill. A shaft of sunlight from the bright street struck obliquely toward the scrubbed wood floor, cutting through the room's stillness with its beam of dancing motes. They were the only movements in the room. The ticking of a clock against a pine wall was the only sound. For that moment. Seemingly long. Yet brief. And so intense that Waysmith felt he and the eight people, who sat at the long dark tables round the room's edge, were frozen into a still life, inanimate objects arranged in a painter's pattern.

Then, just as suddenly, everything clicked back into normal sound and movement as a white-haired woman put down her knitting needles, pushed back her chair, made an apology to the two men who were sitting at her table, and came toward Waysmith. A third man, sitting by himself, smoking a placid cigar, was scanning the pages of a newspaper. Two more men were at another table—walkers, by their rucksacks and sticks. In a far corner, a bearded man faced a fair-haired girl, whose back was once more turned to the room. Waysmith gave that well-shaped head, with its smoothly knotted blonde hair, a second look. But it couldn't be Francesca. Not here, sitting so casually as if she had nothing to do but pass a pleasant hour. And certainly she would have recognized him and come running across to meet him. He laid Denning's belongings neatly at the foot of the staircase beside him—not much privacy here, the steep stairs climbed quite openly up one side of the room—and then faced the inn's owner.

"I am Frau Welti," she said, and waited. Her smile was strained. Her pale gray eyes were worried. There was a little nervous frown drawing her brow into a polite question. She smoothed down the embroidered apron over her black dress, and touched the tight braids of her hair as she waited.

"Good afternoon. My name is Waysmith. I've brought—"

"Waysmith," she repeated carefully. Her smile became real, now. "We have your room all ready. This way—" She took a step toward the staircase.

"But I—"

"Andrew Waysmith?" The fair-haired girl had risen from

her table, and was walking toward him, slowly, a little hesitantly. "Is this Mr. Waysmith?" she asked, quite seriously.

You know damn well it is, he thought as he put out his hand. He could play along with a joke any time, even with a variation on that old Stanley-Livingstone theme. But before he could make his reply, she was saying gravely, "I am Francesca." It was the first time she had ever given him a limp two-finger handshake.

"Francesca," he repeated, staring at her. Was everything then solved? Was all the danger over, to let Francesca walk around her village without one worry showing? Certainly, there was no feeling that she was being guarded—unless you counted the tall bearded man who had risen and then hesitated and now was walking over to the newspaper rack near the door.

"Yes," she was saying, "Francesca Vivenzio. I went to school with your wife." She wasn't even smiling.

"Oh! *That* Francesca." And this joke has gone far enough, he thought.

"Gregor!" she called in the direction of the newspaper rack. "Won't you come and meet Mr. Waysmith?" He came slowly, politely, but with no enthusiasm—indeed, there was no emotion at all—on his strong broad face, furrowed, heavily bearded. He had a large hand with a strong quick grasp, and intelligent gray eyes. But his smile was brief. He seemed a taciturn individual.

"Gregor is gloomy today—it's his birthday," Francesca explained. "But where is Paula?" The use of the first name was only an old school habit, obviously: her voice was casually polite, no more, no less.

"In the car. Waiting." Waysmith had become stilted. He felt unreal and strangely uncomfortable. He glanced over at the three men who sat at the window table. The two who were friends, apparently, had reached a lull in their desultory conversation. One lit a cigarette—he was dark-haired, prematurely balding, with a thin, worried face that was a little too pale (compared to Gregor, he was almost ghostlike), a little too set in perpetual earnestness; his friend was small and plump, a quiet round-faced man whose lips smiled gently at the glass of beer in front of him. The third man, at the other end of the long table, seemed engrossed by his newspaper; his round head, with its close-cropped gray hair, was slightly tilted, one heavily rounded eyebrow was lifted with interest in what he read; he had a long chin, a determined-looking nose, tanned skin, and a steady hand, for the ash on his cigar was unbroken. Across the room, the two men on a walking tour were now discussing a map spread before them.

Francesca was saying, "Then I'd better go out and welcome her back to Falken. I suppose she's anxious to see it again after all those years."

"Your room, Herr Waysmith—" Frau Welti said impatiently, one foot already on the bottom step of the staircase.

"But what I wanted was a room—"

"There really isn't much choice," Francesca interrupted him. She looked down at Denning's suitcase with its neatly printed label clearly visible from where she stood. Then she smiled brightly at Waysmith. "While you take your luggage upstairs, I'll show Mrs. Waysmith where to leave the car. Our street is too narrow for parking." Her blue eyes were serious, almost pleading, and her smile became only a pathetic piece of play acting. She wasn't enjoying it, but she was obeying orders even if she felt they were unnecessary. He could see that by the way she turned and walked toward the door.

Frau Welti began protesting. He didn't have to carry up the bags. Emil would soon be on duty again—this was his afternoon off. And Willy was sick. And Minna was at a christening. Such complications, with the week end beginning, such complications.

"That's all right," Waysmith said, picking up Denning's belongings, cutting short the protests. He followed Frau Welti up the scrubbed wooden stairs.

Down in the room, Gregor walked slowly over to the door. The gray-haired man laid aside his newspaper and studied the end of his cigar. "Americans are discovering Falken, it seems." he said genially to the two men at the other end of his table.

"I hope not," one of them answered, speaking German with an American accent. "After all, I came here to forget about them." He laughed, pleasantly enough. His voice was pleasant enough, too, except for an odd touch of defiance. Not defiance exactly, Waysmith decided as he glanced down from the top of the stairs, more a defensiveness, a kind of and-what-do-you-think-of-that? The silent friend was still smiling politely. Or was it obediently?

"Who is the man with the dark hair?" Waysmith asked quietly as he followed Frau Welti's majestic stride down the narrow passage which ran the full length of the inn's upper floor.

"Herr Broach. He lives in Falken now. Very rich. Very pleasant, too." But she spoke without much enthusiasm.

Broach. It had a sound he recognized. Where had he heard the name?

Frau Welti went on, "And with him is his secretary."

"He looks well tamed."

"Please?"

"And the man with the cigar?"

"A visitor. He comes to climb the mountains." She stopped at the last door in the corridor. But as she opened it, she pointed across the passage to a narrow back staircase. "Emergency," she said with a proud little nod of the head.

"Useful," Waysmith conceded. "For fires?"

"Yes," she said, smiling. "For fires." And as he stepped over the threshold, she closed him quietly into the room.

"Well!" Waysmith said, facing Inspector Bohren. "That's a useful staircase, indeed." He laid down Denning's bags and clubs, dropped the hat and coat near them, and rubbed his reddening palms. He looked round the room: it was clean and bright, with plenty of view. "Well . . ." he said again, this time smiling.

"We have to be quick," Bohren said, as crisp and business-like as ever in spite of his holiday clothes. "First, you are staying here. Second, your wife is only a casual school friend of Francesca Vivenzio; you yourself have never met her before."

"I gathered that."

"Just making sure," Bohren said equably. "Third point is this: your wife met Miss Vivenzio by chance yesterday in Bern. So they dined together. That's all."

"In other words, we know nothing about anything?"

"Precisely. Your wife is simply revisiting a village she knew well when she was a girl. Possible?"

"Yes. But our idea in coming here—"

"—was to show that Miss Vivenzio has friends?"

"I thought a show of solidarity might be discouraging to her enemies."

"Discouraging. Yes. But for how long? Until you had to move away. Then what?"

"By that time, I had hoped you'd have this trouble settled."

"We cannot settle it until it starts." The quiet emphasis on

Bohren's last three words, so gravely spoken, made them all the more ominous.

"You're enticing them into their next move against Francesca?"

"As quickly as possible."

Waysmith said worriedly, "She's taking a chance."

"She knows that."

"And meanwhile she's walking around with only Gregor as watchdog? And what about her aunt, Fräulein Lüthi? Are these two women to be left in a lonely house?"

Suddenly Bohren was worried. "Was he too obvious?"

"Gregor? Far from it. I thought he and Francesca had been quarreling."

"Good." Bohren relaxed. "Don't worry so much," he said. "We have made many arrangements."

"So I noticed as we entered Falken. Getting some co-operation from the village?"

"The Lüthi family have lived here for more than three hundred years," Bohren reminded him.

"Can you give me an idea of the arrangements you have made? I was never good at walking blindfolded."

Bohren looked at him for a moment. Then, talking quickly in his hushed voice, "Roughly, we have at least three problems to face: Andrássy's disappearance; the protection of Francesca Vivenzio; the elimination of the threat to the Committee. Three separate problems, needing three separate teams of searchers and helpers. We've enlisted aid from all the men we consider most reliable. We need plenty of help, I assure you."

And Bohren is linking the three separate problems into one over-all plan, Waysmith thought. "Suppose I have to get in touch with you?"

"Not directly. If you need me, then you'll find the journalist downstairs a reliable sort of man. He has volunteered to be a kind of errand boy. His name is Keppler. A crime reporter, normally."

"And what's my role?" Waysmith asked with a smile. "Do I join the play-acting team downstairs, or do I start searching the woods?"

"Neither the woods, nor the houses, nor the alpine huts," Bohren said. "I want you to interview someone. For your magazine. He's a man called Broach."

Broach. . . . And now Waysmith remembered. "Richard

van Meeren Broach, who's just given up his American citizenship?"

"That Broach and no other." Bohren stepped around the suitcase to reach the door. He stopped, looking down at the labels, and then glanced up questioningly at Waysmith.

"They belong to a friend of mine. We gave him a lift from Bern."

"Where is he now?"

"At a house called *Waldesruhe*."

Bohren said quickly, "Why?"

"We stopped for a view. Two men from *Waldesruhe* seemed interested in our car. Bill got interested in them."

"Who were they?"

"City boys. From Bulgaria, I gathered."

Bohren stood very still. "Start work on that interview," he said. "We want it soon."

"It won't be easy."

There was a brief smile. "Your problem, Mr. Waysmith." And he was gone, leaving the door open, to reveal Frau Welti still outside in the corridor. Considering his height and solid substance, he was a quiet descender of stairs.

"Useful staircase," Waysmith said to Frau Welti. "For fires."

It seemed to be the kind of simple joke that appealed to her—perhaps because she had helped to create it—for she began to laugh in brief little bursts of high-pitched giggles which were just as surprising as her sense of humor. They sounded like a soprano machine gun, muted, all the way along the corridor. Waysmith thought of the men downstairs as, worriedly, he followed her swift footsteps. A disastrous joke, he decided, in every way. Yet it wasn't the joke alone that was responsible for this sudden merriment: probably it was Frau Welti's sense of relief. It was only now he realized the nervous strain which must have racked her all that afternoon as she had sat knitting, waiting, talking, waiting for Paula and him to arrive.

Downstairs, against all his hopes, the three men still sat at the table, although the hikers had left. They had been talking, and now they looked at the cheerful Frau Welti. The man with the close-cut gray hair smiled, stroked his long chin, and said, "That reminds me of the old days, Anna."

"Ah . . ." Frau Welti said. She was in control of herself again.

"Come and have some beer," the gray-haired man suggested to Waysmith. "My name is Keppler. And these gentlemen—" He smiled benignly on the two gentlemen who were studying Waysmith with a considerable display of negligence, and left them to introduce themselves. They hesitated, exchanged a brief glance.

"Broach," the dark-haired man said. "My secretary, Mr. Walters."

Mr. Walters had half-risen. He looked at his watch. "The afternoon mail must have arrived by this time," he told Broach. He wasn't American. Or English, although he spoke the language with a carefully cultivated accent.

"Must you run away?" Keppler asked with his simpleminded politeness. "There's still plenty of time before the mail is sorted. Sit down, sit down. Anna, we'll all have some more beer." He watched her hurry away, and shook his head. "Once, Anna Welti had the merriest laugh between here and Bern. That was before her husband was killed trying to get a couple of stranded climbers off the face of the Fernhorn. He ran the inn then. Never worried about complaints." He smiled over at Waysmith. "If guests didn't like their rooms, they could go and sleep with the cows, for all he cared."

"You know Falken well?" Broach asked, settling back in his chair. He at least wasn't going to give the appearance of running away.

"In the old days, yes. Used to come here each spring. Then Fritz got killed—he was one of the best guides around here, climbed with me a lot. So I stopped coming. This year, I suddenly wanted to see it again. Perhaps try an easy climb or two. Getting old in my joints." He shook his head sadly. "And are you here for the climbing, too?"

"I live here." Broach glanced over at Waysmith.

"You do? And here I am, thinking you are an American."

"I *was* an American." Broach now looked Waysmith full in the face. The defensive note had crept back into his voice. But the effect was lost, for Waysmith's attention switched to the door, where Paula and Francesca had entered, and he went forward to meet them.

That was the comfortable thing about Paula, he thought, as she interpreted the question in his eyes and gave him a nod and a smile. Yes, she was saying silently, I've been told what to do; I don't like this, but I'll try it anyway. "I couldn't get the car started," she said cheerfully enough, although she was holding on to his hand with too tight a grasp as he brought her and Francesca over to the table. "But that nice man with the beard came and took charge. Gregor?" She looked at Francesca for confirmation.

Francesca nodded. She barely acknowledged the introductions, and chose a chair furthest from Broach, quietly, unnoticeably, but definitely. Broach knew that too. He looked at her, kept looking at her, as if her coldness, her elusiveness fascinated him, attracted him against his will. That, at least, was Waysmith's guess, and he was sure that Paula had noticed the tension too. Interesting, he thought. . . . Then he had to say, "Beg pardon?" for Francesca was concentrating on talking to him.

"How was the room? No complaints?" she was asking.

"On the contrary," Keppler said, "Mr. Waysmith seems to have delighted Frau Welti. We could hear her laughing all the way down here."

"It was my German that delighted her, I'm afraid." Waysmith shook his head. Mr. Walters, he noted, had interested eyes above that gentle smile. "What's the word for 'nice,' anyway? *Gemütlich*, isn't it?"

Francesca nodded.

"Well, that's all I said. I looked at the bathroom, and said *gemütlich*. What's so funny about that?"

Even Mr. Walters thought that was at least amusing. Broach thought it was hilarious. And his next question showed why. "Are you the Andrew Waysmith who is European editor of *Policy?*" he asked.

"That's right," said Waysmith, and rose to help Frau Welti with her tray of beer glasses.

"I read your editorials occasionally for the pleasure of disagreeing with them," Broach said.

"There's nothing like a good argument," Waysmith said evenly, "to keep the blood circulating. Prevents atrophy of the brain." He pulled out a chair for Frau Welti.

"You're against conformity?" Broach's voice was mocking.

"Why," said Paula indignantly, "Andy argues with everyone—even with himself in his sleep."

But Waysmith was staring at Broach. "Richard van Meeren Broach?" he asked with sudden interest.

Broach nodded. "Do you still want to have a glass of beer with me?" It almost seemed as though he hoped for a snub.

"Why not? In fact, I'd like to hear your point of view."

"Don't you know it?"

"Roughly, I know what you're against. But I've never read any explanation why."

"Do you expect it would be published?"

"Why not?" Waysmith asked again.

"*You'd* publish my story?"

Waysmith considered that carefully. "If it dealt with facts," he said at last.

Broach stared as if he hadn't heard correctly. Then he smiled, that peculiar smile which was a mixture of so many things, yet with the principal ingredient lacking. "Careful," he said in his humorless way, "or you'll lose Miss Vivenzio's friendship. She doesn't approve of me at all. Do you, Miss Vivenzio?"

Francesca's eyes were on her hands. Then she looked at Broach. For a moment, she said nothing. And then she rose. "Why must you have other people's approval? Are you so uncertain in your own heart?" She walked to the door.

"You see?" Broach said. His smile had a bitter twist, but his eyes followed Francesca.

"What—what's wrong?" Paula asked her husband. She rose, hesitating. "Shall I go and bring her back?" Frau Welti's knitting needles had stopped.

"She wouldn't come," said Broach. "Do you know, these are the first words she has actually ever spoken to me?" He glanced at his watch. "Time for the mail," he added, and rose. He gave everyone a genial good day. With a small bow, Mr. Walters followed him.

"I'll find Francesca," Paula said, but she still hesitated. Broach and Walters had reached the door. They were standing there, looking out into the street, watching the afternoon sunlight and the people who walked there. Watching Francesca? Paula, uncertain of what she was expected to do now, glanced for a cue in the direction of her husband.

He was sitting quite still, studying his long glass of beer. At this moment he could have shaken Francesca until her pretty white teeth rattled.

Keppler stood up, and looked through the window. "I never pretended to understand women," he said with a laugh. "I think I'll go and collect my letters, too. Are you staying here long, Mr. Waysmith?" His voice was clear. It carried easily to the doorway.

"Just snatching a quick holiday before I start work in Bern."

"Are you doing any climbing?"

"Not if I can find a good excuse to stay where my feet belong."

"I couldn't persuade you to join me tomorrow? I'm trying one of the easier saddles. Fine views from there. . . . Ah well, too bad. I'm sorry. I'll have to find someone else." He walked over to the door. Broach and Walters moved away before he reached them. But then, people always fled from someone who bored them: their curiosity was stillborn in the effort to disentangle, to evade, to stay free.

Waysmith rose. "Let's get unpacked," he told Paula. Then he remembered he hadn't brought in their bags. "Oh hell, where's that damned car?"

"Let's just get upstairs anyway. Francesca can find us there." For once, unpacking seemed of little importance to Paula.

"Francesca—" he began angrily.

"This wasn't quite my idea of Falken, either," she reminded him.

So they climbed the stairs, each with a private load of disappointments and worries.

"Women," Waysmith said as they reached the bedroom, "women should be—"

"Yes, darling," Paula agreed, slipping her arm round his waist, laughing as he suddenly smiled and kissed her neck, "women should be."

He opened the door of their room. It wasn't only Paula's answering kiss that cheered him. For their bags stood against one wall in a neat row, and Denning's luggage had been just as quietly removed. Some things, at least, were well under control.

15: Nikolaides

IT WAS A PLEASANT WALK TO *WALDESRUHE*, A
gentle climb over a green slope cleared of trees to give the
house, from its front windows at least, a view of the valley.
Here and there, saplings, miniature Christmas trees, pushed
their way through the long grass, as if the surrounding woods
had not yet given up their battle to recapture the wide meadow. The road was narrow and rough, marked by grass ridges
between graveled earth furrows, and occasional patches of
mud showed where last night's heavy rain retreated so slowly
before today's bright sun. Around these dark pools, small
butterflies gathered, fluttering up in a blue cloud as Bill Denning approached, then settling again at the edge of the cool
wet earth as he passed by.

It was a pleasant walk, with the gentle breeze bringing a
scent of pine trees out of the woods, with the sun warming
his shoulders, and the soft grass laced with flowers under hi
feet. Some day I'll come back and enjoy this place, he promised himself. And smiled at himself, knowing only too wel
that life had a way of never giving you the time to come back
How many places had he seen in the last ten years which he

186

had meant to revisit, to enjoy? Some day. The most hopeful phrase in man's language, the most promising in his thoughts, the most unfulfilled.

But now—the harsh word of reality—now he must notice the tire tracks still soft in the damp earth but firmly molded in the drier stretches of this road. A car had driven up here, just after the last rainstorm had ended. Late last night, it had driven here. The tracks led him all the way to the house, to be lost there in grass, in overgrown garden.

Waldesruhe seemed deserted. The windows were closed, the door was locked, the house was as silent as the thick woods which surrounded it on three sides. No one answered the clanging bell.

Yet they are in there, Denning thought. I saw them stand on these very steps, watching the car as we drove toward Falken: they watched us, then they turned—as if reassured—and went into the house. He rang again.

And I'm being watched right now, he suddenly thought. He didn't glance at any window. His throat was dry, the palms of his hands were moist.

"Mr. Maartens," he said clearly, "Mr. Charles-Auguste Maartens."

The door half opened. A small thin man stood there, one hand behind his back, one foot against the door. "What is it you want? This is private property," he said, all in one breath, his voice thin and high.

He's as nervous as I am, Denning told himself, and took some comfort from that. "I've brought urgent news for Mr. Maartens."

"You make a mistake. Go away."

"Maartens is in danger. Doesn't that interest you?"

"Go away," the thin little man repeated angrily. He moved uneasily, and then quickly raised his hidden arm.

Denning caught the man's wrist and twisted it a little. He kicked aside the heavy stick which dropped to the floor with a clatter. "That was stupid of you. Losing your head as well as your grip? What excuse were you going to give my friends when they arrived in twenty minutes?"

"Jean," said a voice from the doorway of a room, "let the man go." That was rather a euphemism, Denning thought, as he tightened his grip on Jean's arm and then released it completely. Then he looked at the speaker, knowing by the peremptory voice whom to expect. It was Mr. Nicholas, Emily's monster: Nikolaides himself? Only, Denning reminded himself, Nikolaides is one piece of information you had better not let slip: Nikolaides guarded that name too well to allow it to be identified. Nicholas, he told himself firmly now, use only Nicholas, think only of the name Nicholas. Nicholas.

"Jean," explained Nicholas, "distrusts stray callers in such a wild and lonely countryside." He was studying Denning as he talked. "I've seen you before." His face was polite, expressionless.

"Outside my room at the Aarhof."

"Ah, yes," Nicholas said, as if he hadn't remembered that and had been waiting for an evasion or a downright lie, "Come in."

"I've brought you this," Denning said, stepping forward and taking the newspaper out of his pocket. "Thought you probably hadn't been visiting the village to buy any—"

Nicholas made a sign and a powerful grasp from behind Denning pinned his arms back against his shoulder blades. Jean, snickering with delight, danced excitedly in front of him. Denning didn't resist. "This is extremely civil of you, Mr. Nicholas. But you'll find I am unarmed."

Jean, at a gesture from Nicholas, began his search. His fingers were light and quick, his sharp white face expectant. His long thin red hair, brushed over a bald spot on his head, hung loose in stray wisps. "Nothing," he said to the man who held Denning's arms. "Nothing," he repeated in disappointment.

"What is that in his right pocket?" Nicholas asked.

"A book." The little man plastered his hair back into position. He held the volume up in disgust. "In English."

"There are books in English," Denning told him.

"That will do, Georges," Nicholas said. "And we don't need any sarcasm from you, Mr.—?"

"Denning." He stretched his shoulders as the man behind him released his grip, and glanced round at Georges. Yes, this was the man who had watched the Waysmiths' car along with Nicholas. Another white face. Three white faces staring at him blankly in this half-lighted hall. He lifted his book out of Jean's hands, and put it back into his pocket. Then he walked toward the door where Nicholas stood. "In here?" he asked, and entered.

Nicholas followed him, frowning. "I am a patient man," he began, "but—"

"—but too suspicious," said Denning, rubbing his shoulder.

"First, you call me Maartens; then you call me Nicholas, and now you make me follow you into my own room." The little man was angry.

At least I've ended some of that suave control, Denning thought. "The light in the hall was bad. You wouldn't be able to read this." He handed over the newspaper. And I wanted to be able to see your face when you read it, he thought. "If you hadn't left Bern so quickly, you'd have had this news for breakfast. There it is." He pointed to the paragraph about the death of Charles-Auguste Maartens in the Henziplatz. Then he glanced at the hard uncomfortable room with its hard uncomfortable chairs circled round a central table littered with cans of food, bottles of wine, a torn loaf of bread, a round of Brie half demolished and turning liquid. He passed the table, dragging one of its chairs quickly to the wall. There, with his back protected by the yellow pine paneling, with the table separating him from the men who watched him so intently, he sat facing them. "That," he said, as he smiled at the table with its *pâté*, caviar, mushrooms in wine, "that is what I call pigging it in style."

Nicholas studied him. Then, at last, he looked at the newspaper. His heavy eyelids drooped over the blank brown eyes, and his head with its gleaming black hair bent forward. He read, it seemed, for an endless minute. Denning saw the neat small hands which held the paper tighten. That was all. Unless it was the greenish light, filtering through the trees outside, which made Nicholas' sallow skin turn more sickly. But apart from that, his control was perfect. Only his stillness gave him away. He must have read the paragraph twice, three times, even four.

Denning lit a cigarette and studied the room.

"You may leave, now," Nicholas said harshly, looking at Denning.

"Better tell them to leave," Denning said. Jean and Georges had sensed something was wrong. They had lost all interest in him. "I have other news to give you, too."

Nicholas wavered for a moment. He gestured to the two men and they went, slowly. He took the chair opposite Denning, his short legs barely reaching the wooden floor, his hands clasped over the front of his tight gray suit which bulged from the heavy woolen sweater he wore, incongruously, underneath its precisely cut jacket. He was tieless, his collar was unbuttoned, perhaps as a concession to country life. He looked, at this moment, a very simple man who waited patiently and politely. He was smiling gently, his eyes seemed half asleep. But his neck—even as Emily had said—had swollen sideways as if its strong muscles were knotted, as if he had teeth tightly clenched in anger behind that quiet smile. A man, Denning decided, of violent passions, of terrifying control, a man dangerous to thwart, terrible to deceive.

Denning said, "I am not a policeman, nor a detective. Nor am I connected with any organization, political or criminal I am here simply because I am interested in one thing."

Nicholas leaned slightly forward. Was he waiting for the mention of diamonds?

"I want the name of the man who bargained with you."

"With me?"

"The man you trusted.. The man who gave the orders to kill Charles-Auguste Maartens."

Nicholas' eyes had opened a little more, his smile had faded.

"I'm assuming," Denning went on, "that you didn't know about the plan to kill Maartens."

"I—kill?" He was horrified.

"I don't believe so, although the police have other ideas. After all, you destroyed your own alibi last night. You will naturally be suspected."

"I—of murder? Ridiculous."

"Who was the man who arranged with you to impersonate Charles Maartens? Who was the man who got you to cancel out Max Meyer's story?"

"Why are you so interested in all this?"

"The man who was killed by the car, last night, was Max Meyer. He was my friend."

Nicholas leaned back. He was studying Denning once more. "He was your friend. So you come up here alone, and face—" He smiled broadly. "No, no, no. We could have treated you very violently. Perhaps we might even have killed you. And all that for a friend who is dead? Courage won't bring him back, Mr. Denning."

"I'm not as brave as you make me out. I came up here believing you didn't use violence—at least, not too much." Denning grinned. This was a little easier now. Suspicion was slowly vanishing. "And I don't believe that you're inclined to murder, either. I think that you've too much pride in your particular profession to lower it to thuggery."

Nicholas was both listening and approving. "What is my profession?" he asked blandly.

"Shall we say speculation in fine jewels?"

"What kind of jewels?" The suspicion was returning, suspicion springing from greed.

"No interest. You can have all the jewels in the world for all I care. What I want is the name of the man who bargained with you."

"Why that man particularly? He couldn't have killed either Charles or your friend. Believe me."

"Because he wasn't in Bern last night?"

Nicholas looked down at his fingers. A hangnail caught his attention. He frowned. "You are less naïve than you seem, Mr. Denning."

"You haven't told me anything new. Thugs, hired murderers, did the actual killing. The police will catch them. But more thugs can be hired. What we want is the man who hires them, plans, gives the orders."

"We?" He was stalling now. Suspicion, greed, caution, all were holding him back from frankness.

"You and I," Denning said firmly.

"Why should I worry?"

I've made a mistake, Denning thought: I assumed he would want to see Maartens' murderers exposed. But all he wants is those diamonds. "You've been thoroughly double-crossed," Denning said. "Isn't that information worth something from you in return?" He paused, but Nicholas only dropped his eyelids. Denning's voice became cold, sarcastic, filled with a distaste he could barely control. "Apart from the fact that Maartens was your friend, or at least a—a business associate, you are now in danger yourself."

"You mean I may be killed?" He was a little surprised, but mostly amused. And then, gradually, his amusement ebbed away. The surprise went, too.

Denning waited. "You can answer that question better than I can." He rose. "I've given you the warning. It was more than you did for Max Meyer. Or for Charles Maartens."

There was a long silence. Then came the surprising question. Softly, "Who told you my name is Nicholas?"

"The police heard that."

"The police?"

"From a telephone call, I believe."

"An informer?"

Denning walked slowly round the central table. He picked up a jar of *pâté* and studied its label. "It looks," he said slowly, replacing the jar, "as if you had been twice tricked in the last twenty-four hours." He looked now at cans of mushrooms, anchovies, a crock of caviar. "And you sit there and take it?"

"But this man you want—he may not have been the informer."

"Did he know you were Nicholas? And who else could know?"

Nicholas was silent.

"There's your answer," Denning said. He glanced at his watch. "If you don't hurry and give me my answer, my friends will be arriving from the village."

Nicholas rose, too. He moved over to the door with his quick, light step. "The arrival of your friends," he said, "is as likely as all the rest of your story." He opened the door and the two men came in. "Our young friend has a taste for diamonds," he told them. "*And* a most vivid imagination. I think we should see that he stays here until we leave, when neither his taste for diamonds nor his imagination can trouble us." He turned to Denning. "I don't like violence, but if you resist, we shall tie you up very unpleasantly. However, you can always console yourself that it is only for a few hours. After we leave here, *and* complete our business in this neighborhood, I shall try to remember to telephone from Bern and warn the police where you can be found. With luck, you will be free by midnight. Will you kindly walk upstairs?" He was smiling, now. "You almost persuaded me," he admitted. "Would you care to know your mistake?" He began to laugh. "My friends will be arriving from the village," he mimicked, "my friends will be—"

"When they do arrive," Denning said, deliberately and clearly, "will that prove the rest of my story? Or do you prefer to wait until you've been murdered like Charles Maartens?"

Georges and Jean stared at him.

"Are you as expendable as Charles Maartens?" Denning asked them. "Will your boss let you be killed too, as long as he gets the Herz diamonds?"

Suddenly, Nicholas was screaming, screaming in high piercing anger like a frenzied woman, his mouth wide open in

Picasso-like fear, as he rushed at Denning with his fists clenched, upraised, beating the air as if it were Denning's face.

Denning caught up a bottle of wine from the table. "Now, now," he said, as Nicholas halted out of reach and the screaming ended as abruptly as it had begun, "keep those pretty little fingers to yourself. You wouldn't want them permanently scarred, would you?" He knocked the bottom of the bottle against a hard-backed chair, and dashed the spilling wine in Nicholas' face. To Georges, who was no fool, he said, "You'll see Maartens' death in that paper. Page three." And even Jean, edging round by the window in a flanking attack, stopped and waited, staring now at Georges, who had picked up the newspaper. Then something else caught his attention, the sound of a car, faint as yet. He looked quickly through the window.

"Someone *is* coming," Denning said very quietly. And I hope it's Waysmith, he thought, but he wasn't too sure of that.

Jean said, "The car is down on the road."

"It may pass," Nicholas said. He wiped his face with a white silk handkerchief. The look in his eyes was an ugly one.

"The car has stopped," said Denning. Stopped? Or had it passed out of earshot?

"See what it is," Nicholas said to Jean with a quick gesture toward the door. Now, he was in control of his emotions. His eyes, heavy-lidded again, looked expressionlessly at Denning. "You disappoint me," he said with a cool smile, pointing to the jagged bottle which Denning still held ready. "I did not think you were the type of man who'd descend to such violence."

"That isn't the first time you've guessed wrong today," Denning reminded him. "Or yesterday."

Jean's lightly pattering steps came running through the hall. "There's a car on the road. Men, too. They're climbing up the bank."

"Quick!" Nicholas said as he moved to the door.

"Taking to the hills?" Denning asked with a smile. "For it certainly won't be any use driving away in your own car. Have a look." He pointed to the window and stepped back against the wall, the bottle still held ready in his hand. Slowly, carefully, over the rough track which he had followed to the house, moved a second car.

Nicholas stood quite still. Almost politely, he said, "You have many friends, Mr. Denning."

"More than I thought."

"You lied to me," Nicholas said sadly. "You said you were not a policeman."

"I'm still telling the truth. I am not a policeman."

At the window, Jean cried out, his voice cracking with high alarm, "The car has stopped. They're waiting—they're waiting!"

It was strange that a car, halted quietly only fifty yards from the front of the house, should raise such sudden panic in the room. Denning stared in amazement at the three men, now speaking in the quickest burst of French he had ever heard. Impossible to understand them. Did they even understand each other or was the bitter recrimination in their voices enough? Nicholas won the contest, seemingly. The others fell silent, watching him, as if they waited for him to speak. Quickly now, he turned to Denning. "I make a bargain with you. You tell nothing—about me. Yes?"

"That depends on what you tell me."

"I met the man in Bern, two days ago. He called himself Mr. James. You understand—such a name may be false?"

Denning nodded. "Nationality?"

"Eastern European." Nicholas shrugged his shoulders. "Perhaps," he added. "The plan was made as you said. But no talk of murder. No mention of killing." Again he looked pleadingly at Denning.

"His appearance?"

"Not very tall. Quiet. A gentle smile. He seemed a gentle man. Not one to kill. Businesslike, yes. But not a murd—"

"Yes," said Denning quickly, "and what color of hair?"

"Nothing."

"Nondescript?"

"Like yours."

"Where is he now?" Footsteps were approaching the house from the wood.

"In Falken. He—" Nicholas stopped, staring at the men who passed the window now, men in ordinary country clothes, men with tanned faces and hair bleached by the sun. "They aren't policemen," he said, and drew in his breath.

"He told you where to find the Herz diamonds? And the time to take them—when it would be safe for you? How did he know? Nicholas—keep your bargain!"

Nicholas shook his head. He smiled. "They aren't police. And I don't think they are your friends. Now perhaps I can make quite another bargain." His eyelids drooped. "With them," he added quietly. He hurried into the hall to meet the men who had entered.

He was pushed back into the room. Four men followed him.

For a moment, Denning did not recognize the tallest of the newcomers. But it was Bohren, all right, Inspector Bohren dressed to look as if he spent all his life climbing up through steep woods. Denning lowered the jagged bottle, and then laid it awkwardly on the table. Somehow, he felt foolish with four pairs of grave eyes watching him. The bottle rolled off the table and smashed on the floor. "It keeps doing that," Denning said.

Bohren almost smiled. "You live here?" he asked.

"No. Just visiting." Denning sat down on the nearest chair. The back of his collar was soaked with perspiration. He loosened his tie.

"What is this, what is this?" Nicholas demanded. "And who are you? How dare—"

"Police," said Bohren. He pulled an identification badge out of his pocket for a brief moment.

Nicholas spread his small hands wide. "Police? But why? What have I done? You have no right to enter my house."

"We've not only entered, but we intend to search it."

"Impossible."

"We are searching every house in this district."

"Why?"

"A man has disappeared. He's ill, loss of memory. He may be hiding."

"Insane?" Nicholas blinked his eyes with appropriate nervousness. "But, I assure you, no one could have entered here without my—"

"I've got a report to file," Bohren said. "Sorry, but I must search, Mr.—?"

"Nicholas."

"Of Cap d'Hercule?"

Nicholas forgot to control his stare.

Bohren turned to one of the men with him—husky, open-air types all of them—and said briskly, "Heinz, give the Frenchmen the signal."

"Frenchmen?" Nicholas asked. He glanced at Georges and Jean, but they were standing away from him, moodily, with a kind of fatalism, as if they expected worse to come and could only evade it if they did nothing to attract attention.

Perhaps Georges was remembering Maartens—the newspaper was still clutched in his hand; and Jean may have started to think, now that his excitement had suddenly ended, and he faced the cold hard realism of Inspector Bohren.

For an answer, they all heard the waiting car move toward the house.

"Yes," Bohren said, "two of your fellow citizens who have some questions to ask."

"Policemen? I tell them nothing, I tell you nothing." Nicholas spoke contemptuously. "Nothing, nothing at all." He drew himself erect. "Because I know nothing," he added as a safeguard.

Denning said wearily, "But he will make a bargain with you. He has a passion for making bargains. Which he won't keep, I may add."

Bohren moved into the hall as the car stopped outside.

Nicholas seemed to measure the two stolid men who stood watchfully near the door. Then he turned to Denning. "I keep my bargain," he said quickly. "The man works in the house. *The* house." He glanced nervously at his audience. "Many work there. Well-guarded. Tonight, no guards. You understand?"

"Why no guards?"

Bohren had stepped back into the room again. Perhaps he hadn't gone far beyond the door. He looked interested, certainly.

"Business. Big business," said Nicholas, and laughed, delighted now with his caution in referring to the house so vaguely.

Bohren came forward with an anger which may have been pretended, but sounded real enough. "What are you two sending each other? Telegrams? What's your name, anyway?" He glanced at Denning. Jean shrank against a wall.

"William Denning."

"Identification?"

Denning produced his passport. Nicholas looked worried for the first time.

"What's your purpose, here?" Bohren asked.

"Traveling for pleasure. I'm staying in Falken. I was told this house was for rent. So I came to see it." He pulled Paula's map from his pocket. "That's the name of the house agent in Bern, stamped there. But his files weren't up to date, apparently. I find the house has already been leased to these gentlemen."

Nicholas was visibly relaxing. He nodded his approval. Jean took some comfort, and smiled anxiously all around. Georges was still frowning at some invisible blot on the wooden floor: his process of thought, if slow, was certainly interesting. "I'm so sorry," Nicholas said to Denning. "We thought you might be—well, a burglar." He smiled, fluttered his little hands, disposed of all the unpleasantness with a shrug of his shoulders. "So sorry we seemed so rude."

"I think I'll wander back to the village," Denning said. "Is that all right with you, officer?" He pocketed his passport securely.

Bohren gave him a peculiar look. "I place you now," he said slowly. "You've rented a room at the café-restaurant."

Have I, indeed? Denning thought.

"I'll find you there when I need you," Bohren warned him. Then he turned to the doorway, to welcome Heinz and the two Frenchmen.

Nicholas took two side steps toward Denning. His voice was barely audible. "You keep the bargain?"

"Haven't I?"

"I like you, Mr. Denning. A man I can trust. If ever you need a job—" He paused significantly, tactfully.

"You'd take me on?"

"Why not? You have a certain style."

"You flatter me, Monsieur Nicholas." Denning moved toward the door.

"But not at all, Mr. Denning."

Denning resisted an impulse to sweep an eighteenth-century bow. But why mock a man's pride when it was going to be so thoroughly deflated within the next two minutes? For the tall, thin Frenchman with the amused dark eyes and the long intelligent face was Colonel Le Brun, back from Genoa. He came forward, now. "What kind of job?" he asked, with a narrow smile.

"In my business of importing and exporting," Nicholas began with dignity, "there are many openings for intelligent young men."

"So, Nikolaides—you have become a businessman?"

The hooded eyes looked blankly at Le Brun. "My name is Nicholas."

"It was Nikolaides, twenty years ago, when you calmly lost

such a fantastic fortune at Monte Carlo, and I happened to be sitting—most admiringly—opposite you. It was a night I've often remembered. That was before you developed other talents, of course, and other names. Now, I hear you are much too busy for the uncertain joys of gambling, except on useful occasions such as last night's performance at the Kursaal in Bern." Suddenly the light, amused voice changed to cold contempt. "You have become a naturalized citizen of France?"

"I am a good citizen. I have done France no wrong."

"In that case, you will wish to give her every possible help."

"But of course."

"Then you will give us all information you possess about the present location of certain stolen property which belongs to the French government."

"Stolen? What is stolen?" The protests of ignorance and innocence were beginning.

A tactful moment to leave, Denning thought.

So did Bohren. For as Denning moved toward the door, he said, "We'll search the house meanwhile. Shall I post a man here, or can you manage?"

Le Brun's companion, his sharp brown eyes watchful, nodded as he produced a neat little gun from his pocket. He released the safety catch. Two of Bohren's men clattered upstairs, the third started toward the back of the house. But Bohren himself walked silently through the hall, following Denning. Behind them, the act of innocence had begun.

"Let me refresh your memory," Le Brun was saying. "The stolen property I mentioned is the Herz collection of diamonds."

"I've never seen it in my life. I haven't got it, I assure you—"

"You know where those diamonds are. Legally, they belong to the French government. Anyone refusing to give information leading toward their recovery will automatically be aiding and abetting . . ."

Bohren closed the front door quietly behind him. For a moment, he stood looking at Denning. "All right?" he asked. He drew Denning round to the side of the house, away from the room where Nikolaides was being questioned.

"Reviving rapidly." This was good clean air. He took a deep breath.

"I'll have to stay here until Nikolaides starts talking to policemen. Any news?"

"I made a bargain," said Denning with a smile.

Bohren was not amused.

Denning said, "Actually you know more about Nikolaides than I do. But find the house where the Herz collection is hidden, and you'll find the man who planned, and is directing, the attack upon the Falken Committee."

"The top Communist agent?"

"For this particular operation, yes."

"He stayed close to the diamonds? Isn't that a little foolish?" Bohren was skeptical.

"Yes. But who could guess that any dangerous man would be so foolish?" Denning asked softly. "Or that he would be a servant, pretending to take orders?"

"He's got the right technique," Bohren admitted. "He will interest Keppler, I think. If he is the top agent, that explains one puzzle—" He looked at Denning, hesitated for a moment, then momentarily discarded his habitual caution. "Now I understand why Nikolaides, himself, came to Bern. He is not the kind of man to take direct action. He likes to plan from a comfortable distance."

"I didn't think he was enjoying this trip to Switzerland, particularly. He must have been pretty sure it was worth his while before he started it." Certainly, Nikolaides wouldn't have come to Bern to talk to a minor agent. Nor would he have acted on any information unless he was sure he had obtained it from an authoritative source.

"And tonight, big business?" Bohren glanced worriedly at his watch. "Or else," he looked frankly at Denning, "that is just another of Nikolaides' elaborations. Like Genoa."

"I'd take it as the truth, this time. He meant to leave me, trussed and gagged, in a locked room. I was to be released around midnight, by a phone call from Bern. Which means he planned to complete his msision and be in Bern by midnight, on his way out of the country. You can work out his Falken schedule from that."

"Indeed we can," Bohren said, and his smile was suddenly benevolent. He had got the information he had wanted. "Better get to the village. Take that footpath, up there to your left. It's quick." It was also out of sight from the window of the room where Nikolaides and his friends were protesting.

"Good luck," said Denning. "And if you need any extra

arguments, there are some excellent tread marks on that road. They were made just after the rain stopped last night."

"The best argument of all will be his false passport," Bohren said. And Denning remembered the strange expression in Nikolaides' eyes when Denning had handed over his passport to be examined. "I'll send Heinz Gauch after you, just to make sure you reach Falken," Bohren added as he turned away.

"I don't need to be convoyed."

"Don't you?" Bohren's grin was wide. "But thanks for leading us back to *Waldesruhe*. It was searched for Andrássy yesterday evening and found empty. No one knew it had been rented, either." Quietly he opened the door. Quietly closed it.

16: Trouble on the Blümlisalp

THE NARROW FOOTPATH, ALMOST UNNOTICEABLE
until Bohren had pointed it out, led Denning over high mead-
owland along the lower edge of a fairly dense wood. At
first it seemed to draw him away from Falken in its wide
curve over the sloping hill; but, as he approached higher
ground, he saw that the path was beginning to cut down to
the village, a short direct route, a backward approach to
Falken's single street and the main cluster of houses.

Once, he heard a dog bark, powerfully, angrily, somewhere
up there in the woods to his left, as if another house was hidden back among the trees. But he kept on, at an even pace,
to prove to himself as much as to Bohren that he didn't need
Heinz Gauch to see him safely into Falken. He allowed himself one last glance at *Waldesruhe,* however, already out of
sight except for a match-box chimney on a spread-eagled roof.
What on earth had made him go there alone? Would he do
it all over again, knowing Nikolaides as he did now? I must
have been crazy, he thought. And now he must be sane, for
he felt a cold shiver run down his back.

Yet, it wasn't altogether useless what he had done. Another

thing, he had saved time; and, judging by Nikolaides' planning, time was running out. Stop finding justifications, he told himself as he quickened his pace: you were a damned fool, and luckier than most. That's what Bohren thinks, and he's right. In his way, he's right. In a way. But sometimes it's useful to be a damned fool, even if it chills your spine when you think about it afterward.

The dog barked again, nearer now. Suddenly he heard hurrying footsteps coming down through the trees, a clatter of heavy boots slipping on rock, dull steady thuds on soft pine needles, and then a crackle of dry branches as a man stepped onto the path ahead of him. It was Heinz Gauch, red-faced, his jacket slung over his shoulders, his sleeves rolled up. He was looking back at the wood, his hands on his hips, his feet widespread as he waited for Denning.

"Hello," said Denning. "And where did you come from?"

"Short cut." He still watched the woods, his blue eyes hard, his lips tight with anger.

Then the dog appeared, straining at the end of a leash held by a tall, powerfully built man dressed in a chauffeur's uniform. He halted, smiling, as he pulled back against the dog's forward leaps.

Heinz yelled, "Next time I go for a walk, I take my gun. That isn't a dog, it's a wolf. And the land's free. Do you hear? It's free!"

The uniformed man laughed, enjoying his sense of power; then he gave a violent tug to the leash, a sharp command, and walked away slowly into the maze of trees, the dog obediently following. They disappeared from sight.

"All right," Heinz Gauch said, now ready to leave, and he and Denning continued together on the path. He was silent for at least three minutes. Then, in his slow solemn voice, he said, "That's a good path through the woods. We've always used it. These foreigners—they come here and think they've bought the land!" His lips tightened for a moment. He was a man, almost forty perhaps, muscular, lean, who spent most of his time in the open air, for his face was weather-tanned, and fine wrinkles crinkled away from the outside corners of his frank blue eyes. His light hair, sun-bleached, receded from his high broad brow, and his smile—even with two broken front teeth—was pleasant to see. Now, he was giving it generously to Denning, as if to show that the reference to foreigners wasn't directed against him. "You're on our side?"

The question, so direct, so simple, was heart-warming. Denning nodded. "Yes," he said. "I'm on your side."

"There are two other Americans here too. A man and his wife. Came this afternoon. Staying at the inn."

"At the inn?" The question had escaped him. He hoped it would be taken for polite interest rather than surprise.

"Bad days," said Heinz Gauch, and brooded over that. "Falken's a quiet place, usually," he added angrily. "We live and let live." Then he jerked his thumb over his shoulder in the direction of *Waldesruhe*. "Who were those?"

"More foreigners."

Heinz Gauch thought over that too. "They're the kind we can do without."

"Like the man with the dog? Where did he come from?"

"Up there. That house on top of the hill. See?" He pointed. His forearm was thick and strong, the muscles prominent and hard.

"Does its property stretch to the edge of the woods?" Denning asked in surprise. The house must have been half a mile away.

"We never knew where its property began or ended until these men came. The trails are free." Gauch swept his arm around the valley where paths, narrow and broad, straight and twisting, wound through green meadows, interlacing the village with the woods and the hills. "Herr Broach is all right. So is his secretary. It's the men who work up at the house that cause the trouble."

"Broach? He lives in that house up on the hill?"

Gauch nodded. "He's all right. Quiet. Pleasant. Buys in the village."

"How big is his staff?"

"Now he has four men."

"Now? You mean some are recent additions?"

"Three came last week."

"What do they find to do?" A chalet might run to eight rooms, perhaps even less.

Gauch shrugged his shoulders. "Each man spends his money in his own way. If I were rich—" he grinned, "I'd have seven pairs of climbing boots, one for each day of the week. Herr Broach likes to have servants."

"A cozy establishment. Do all people who live here keep such a private army?"

Gauch looked at him. "That's what the Inspector was asking too. Are you a policeman?"

"No. Are you?"

"I'm a guide. Today—well, I'm just kind of helping out."

"That's my status exactly," Denning said.

"I thought you were a friend of the Inspector's."

"Why?"

Gauch grinned. "He came running out the back door of the inn, got hold of us, and all the way to *Waldesruhe* he kept cussing you."

"I guessed that, somehow," said Denning, not too amused. "Tell me, has Broach made any friends in the—" But Gauch caught his arm, silencing him. From a high alp across the valley, on the other side of Falken, there drifted down through the clear air a long-drawn-out call.

"Yodeling?" Denning asked with a smile. A pretty effect. But the village lying before him didn't need any additional local color. He already felt he was stepping onto the front page of a Swiss calendar, with a carpet of blue gentians rolled out in front to welcome him toward the dreaming houses. Yodeling and its silver echoes were too much. Falken was the kind of place you had to take little by little.

"Sh!" Gauch held up his hand impatiently.

Again the high call. And then, again.

"Three," said Gauch. "That means the Blümlisalp."

Then came a series of shorter calls, ringing down over the mountainside, running so close to each other that they formed little circles of sound, falling, falling into the valley. Heinz Gauch stared at Denning. "Trouble," he said. "They've found trouble up there," and he began to run. Denning started after him. In a nearby field, a man dropped his hoe and ran toward his house.

In the village street, there were others who ran. And those who didn't run had stopped to look up at the mountains which lay westward. At open doors, people stood. There was nothing to hear but the steady running pace, even, sure, that echoed over the stones.

Denning halted and regained his breath. Gauch had disappeared into a house. The other runners were disappearing into their houses, too.

"What's wrong?" he asked a white-haired woman standing at the door of the inn. She didn't seem to hear him.

"Someone needs help, up there," a very quiet voice said be-

side him. It was Keppler. "But the guides will take care of it."
He stared up at a green patch, high on a wooded mountainside, sheltering under the ragged rims of gray precipices.

The white-haired woman said, "The hut on the Blümlisalp
was only opened up for the summer this very day."

"Yes, yes, Anna," said Keppler quickly, silencing her, and
moved on his way along the street, stopping to talk to someone here, pass a remark there.

The woman called Anna put her hand quickly to her mouth.
She had made a mistake, there. Another amateur like myself,
Denning thought. He smiled and said, "I'm looking for the
café-restaurant."

"Cross the street. Follow that little road." Her hand had
dropped to her heart; her blue eyes were worried as they
looked, not at him, but over his shoulder. He turned as the
approaching footsteps reached him: two men, visitors probably, judging from their clothes.

"What's wrong?" one of the men asked, halting beside the
doorway. He was young, strongly built, with a breadth of
shoulder and length of arm which would be formidable in a
fight. His companion was a husky specimen too.

"I'm trying to find out," Denning said. He didn't quite like
the way their eyes were examining him.

But now Heinz Gauch came out of his house, heavily
booted, a rope neatly coiled over his shoulders. He began
running again, with that steady lope, along the street toward
the woods beyond the church. From another house, one of the
other men joined him, then another and another, one with a
rope, another with a sheet wound round wooden poles; and
the sound of the heavy boots, keeping their running pace,
echoed through the little street.

"Whenever I hear that—" Anna turned abruptly and went
indoors.

Denning thought, that's the kind of excuse I could use too.
But he said, "It looks as if a climber had got stuck on a
mountain face."

"Where?"

"Up there. Somewhere." Denning looked vaguely at the
backdrop of mountains.

The curious young man was more interested, suddenly, in
the file of six steadily running men, now past the church,
entering the trail which seemingly began in the woods. "That's
the Blümlisalp trail," he said to his friend quickly, as if the

remark had been surprised out of him. Then he noticed that Denning was listening. "Isn't it?" he asked, too casually.

"A lot of trails begin there and then branch off." That was a safe enough answer. You could always depend on trails branching off.

"I wonder if the guides need any help." The man took a step away.

Was this an offer, or an excuse to follow? Denning said, beginning to move away too, "It's a team, obviously. Like a fire brigade or a lifeboat crew. If they needed volunteers, I guess they'd have asked for them."

"They can't keep up that pace," the one who did the talking said, as if he resented such efficiency. Then he walked on, his silent friend keeping step with him. They stopped a woman and asked her a question, for she shook her head. "No, no," she said in her loud innocent voice, "it can't be trouble on the Blümlisalp. Why, a child could climb up there and down again." She laughed merrily at such ignorance, and it seemed to Denning that the men were more than a little taken aback, perhaps because of her unfortunately clear voice, perhaps because her estimation of climbing the Blümlisalp didn't please them.

He crossed the street slowly, as if there were no need for haste, and entered the narrow road which led away from the center of the village. There he could begin to hurry. Keppler must have reached the café-restaurant by this time.

But Keppler wasn't there. Not immediately.

Instead, there was a note, short and glowing, from Elizabeth. Nothing seemed to dampen that girl's enthusiasm. "Darling," she began, "at last you're in Falken. We'll have a wonderful week end. Wait here for me until I get rid of the family. And keep this evening free for a party at the inn. But tomorrow we'll have to ourselves, I promise! All love, as always. . . ."

Tomorrow, he thought, sounds wonderful: a day for oneself, a day to stretch out on a soft piece of green grass under a birch tree—the kind that had invited him today as he walked toward Falken, with its delicate leaves showing blue sky between them; a book to read, sleep to come softly; no one talking, questioning; no one to worry about, whether friend or enemy. A day to be kept for oneself.

It was too good a promise. He looked round his room, a

small white box inside a large white box, a ground-floor room tucked away near a back entrance to a café-restaurant which didn't even sell beer. Keppler's humor was peculiar. Or practical.

He felt cheered, oddly enough. For there was his luggage, waiting to welcome him: it was another sign, however small, that someone was organizing something around here, and efficiently too. Or perhaps Elizabeth's optimism was having its effect. Had Keppler intended that? Wily old bird, Keppler—what assumed name had he chosen to match his new identity? He had looked so completely at home in this mountain village, a visitor who had every right to be strolling around its quiet roads.

Denning didn't bother to unpack. But he took off his shoes and jacket, slipped his tie loose, and stretched his spine out on the narrow white bed.

And then suddenly he knew why he was encouraged. Until now, what had depressed him most was the feeling that against him, against Heinz Gauch and the white-haired Anna at the inn and Francesca and the Waysmiths, were a few men tightly organized, completely ruthless, relentless, with one single purpose and a plan long made. But somehow, within this last half-hour, the balance had shifted. "You're on our side?" Heinz Gauch had asked. And the "Yes" he had given as an answer had come surging back onto his tongue, as he stood at the inn door and watched the six men set off to the Blümlisalp. Heinz Gauch, and Bohren, and Le Brun, each with his own pattern of action, each part of the same general plan. The Waysmiths, himself—how many more? Their particular problems had merged—the village's concern for the missing Andrássy, the Waysmiths' worry over Francesca's safety, Le Brun's search for the Herz diamonds, Bohren's tracking down of murderers, his own preoccupation with Max Meyer's death. They had merged, and Keppler had done it.

Suddenly he rose and crossed over to the window. It faced west. Yes, up there, slightly to his left, he could see a small green patch on the shoulder of the mountain. The Blümlisalp —the high meadow of little flowers. It haunted him, somehow.

A soft step, a careful closing of his room door made him swing round.

"If I had been a murderer," Keppler said quietly as he

locked the door behind him, "you wouldn't have had much chance."

"Interesting," Keppler said, "interesting. And let me compliment you on the way you present a report." He glanced at his watch with approval. Five minutes since he had come into the room; and Denning hadn't wasted one word.

"I've been writing reports for the last four years," Denning said with a smile. There, he could claim to be a professional.

"Ah—that explains it: no wonder you accept action so readily. Four years of report-writing. . . ." Keppler shook his head in commiseration. "It's always been one of my theories that the most effective men are intellectuals in action. But they also cause a few palpitations, a good deal of annoyance, *and* sometimes a lot of unnecessary trouble. Still, who doesn't?"

Denning wasn't quite sure whether that was praise or censure.

"The intellectual in action," Keppler said again, enjoying the phrase as though it were a mouthful of wine worth rolling around his tongue.

"Look—if you want to cuss me out, do it in Bohren's way. That's easier to take."

"Ah—Bohren. He's stopped cussing you out. In fact, he's now at the stage of wanting to pin a decoration on your chest."

"You've seen him?"

"He telephoned ten minutes ago. That's what delayed me getting here."

"Any success with Nikolaides?"

"At first—no. Flat denials. And then, suddenly, he crumpled. One little thing did it.

"The passport?"

"No. The tire marks left by his car late last night. They could have led to a murder charge. That's what he thought, seemingly. Had you prepared him for that idea?"

"A little."

"Then you saved us at least a couple of hours. Thank you."

Denning's face flushed slightly. "And what did Bohren discover?"

"Let me see, now," Keppler said with tantalizing deliberation, "if I can remember how to put a report together. We've learned a lot of things from Nikolaides."

Denning's smile was back. Keppler, the diplomat, was

amusing in his own way: what could he tell, what would he leave out? That was his problem.

"First, the diamonds. The man who bought them is indeed Mr. Broach. They are in his house. So is the man who is in charge of the whole operation against the Committee. To-night, the final move—in Falken, at least—is to be made. Broach will be alone then, in his house on the hill. It seems he knows very little. He certainly is taking no active part."

"Except furnishing the money for kidnaping, torture, and murder," Denning said bitterly.

"Which brings us to my second piece of news. The threat against the Committee is centered on the girl Francesca. She alone knows the present addresses of the exiles whom the Committee helped. She keeps no files. Everything is in her memory. Dangerous, yes. But also wise. However, my department has known about this Committe and its purpose since its beginning, and we insisted—naturally enough—that all names and addresses must be registered with us. A matter of simple precaution. We have the only existing file, and it's kept safe. I see to that. So the danger here is around Francesca. She is, in fact, the file that the Communists want. If they can abduct her, question her, they'll have all the information they need. Within a few days of extracting it, there won't be one of the Committee's exiles who will be left in freedom. Re-member, the Communists have had much practice in secret assassination and political kidnaping. Since 1930, they have developed their techniques. Did you ever hear of Eugene Mil-lar, Navachine, Klement, Krivitsky, Koutiepov? All murdered secretly, or abducted. Last year, in Berlin, there was Linse. Since 1948, more than one hundred Germans have been kid-naped for political reasons. So the problem we face here, in Falken, is not a fantasy."

"Tell that to Richard van Meeren Broach."

"I hope I have that pleasure," said Keppler, with equal grimness.

"What about Andrássy?"

"That is my third piece of news. We think he is being held here, until Francesca Vivenzio can be taken out with him."

"How would they be taken out?"

"Quite simply. A specially chartered plane leaves the Bern airport. Foreign diplomats traveling to Czechoslovakia or Hungary or Poland. Two of the passengers seem listless, dazed. But they've got diplomatic passports and identities. And immunity like all the others on the plane. We may try to question the passengers. Difficult. Impossible, if Andrássy and Francesca have been so drugged that they can't give their names, can't help us. Without actually forcing them off the plane, getting a doctor to examine them, bringing them out of their drugged condition—what can we do? Diplomatic immunity is what beats us."

"Is there any chartered plane leaving Bern late tonight?"

"There are three, with diplomatic missions on board. Bern has all the embassies, remember."

"Three," repeated Denning blankly. "And two could be genuine?"

"Yes. That's one of our problems."

"Seems to me we'd better solve it right here in Falken— never let them get near any airport."

"I agree. So this is our plan. We have created the impression that everything is normal, that Francesca is alone with a sick aunt at her house. Actually, her aunt is staying quietly out of the way—at Schlossfalken-Bad. And Francesca, once tonight's party is over at the inn, will seem to walk back to her house. Gregor will accompany her. At the church there begins a good stretch of trees. You will be waiting there, in the first shadows, with a very charming young policewoman who will be dressed like Francesca. She walks on with Gregor. Francesca, you, and three policemen will make your way through barns and fields—we've planned the route carefully—to the back door of Heinz Gauch's house. That's where Francesca will spend the night, with you and the three policemen to guard her. We'll have other guards round the house. And it stands right in the center of the village street. All clear?"

Denning nodded. "Sounds good to me. Even the party at the inn—that's one way of keeping her in public view for all of the evening." But the dangerous moment would be in the shadows of the trees, when the exchange of Francesca and a policewoman would be made. "Thank heaven, they've only got five men—if you count the secretary."

"I do count him. And they have two men staying in the village—making seven in all."

"Those two at the inn door?"

"Yes."

"They were interested in the Blümlisalp."

"As they very well might be."

"You think they took Andrássy up there last night?"

Keppler began to smile. "I've been waiting for that question ever since I stepped into the room." Then he was serious. "Yes, he must be up there. That's what the signals told us. But whether he's alive or dead, we shan't know until Heinz Gauch and the other guides bring him down."

"How long will Gauch take?"

"At his pace—two hours up, three hours down. With good luck they may have Andrássy back in the village before the party is over. And then—" Keppler took a deep breath. "Then *we* can take some action. In fact, Bohren has ordered up some extra policemen to make the arrests. They'll be arriving in Falken shortly."

Denning was studying the white scrubbed planks of the floor. The small square rug had roses embroidered with loving care.

"Yes?" Keppler asked. "You think we are too confident?"

"Andrássy worries me, frankly. If they plan to ship him out tonight, then they'll send a couple of men to bring him down from the Blümlisalp. That could be happening right now. I hope Gauch is ready for trouble."

"Did you count the number of men he took with him?" Keppler answered. "And that stretcher they carried hid two rifles. Gauch is one of our crack shots."

Denning half-smiled as an apology. And Gauch was the kind of man who needed only one warning. If there might be trouble ahead, he'd expect trouble.

"You're still worried," Keppler said reprovingly.

"Not worried. Puzzled. About Broach and the Herz diamonds."

"We'll give him a chance to explain where he stands. Fair enough? And I think Waysmith may be the right contact to use there. A man like Broach is always impressed by an interview—self-justification, all that."

"But how did this business of 'liberated' diamonds ever get mixed up with hard politics? A secret conspiracy like this one must have plenty of funds."

"For clandestine operations, yes," Keppler agreed sadly. "They always have plenty of money."

"Then why all this trouble they've taken over three million dollars? That's nothing, in their terms."

"In their terms, three millions mean Broach. With the Herz diamonds, they've got him. Right there." Keppler cupped the palm of his large strong hand. "Right there," he repeated softly. "He's their prize exhibit—the American millionaire who denounces the myth of America. And now he's their puppet for the rest of his life, to nod, to shake his head, to open and shut his mouth, as the strings are pulled. One sign of revolt, and he will be threatened with exposure—a receiver of stolen diamonds, a financier of kidnaping. They've got him completely."

Denning said slowly, "Yes, they've got him all right. Every way."

"You sound less happy about it than I had expected."

Denning said nothing.

Keppler looked at his watch. "Almost six o'clock. Why don't you slip over to the inn and get invited to the party? I'll follow you. Remember, you know only the Waysmiths—no one else. Just let things play along. Waysmith may want your help, by the way. He's been told to interview Broach. He made a good try, this afternoon, but Francesca spoiled it." Keppler frowned slightly. "How much do you know about women?" he asked suddenly.

"The more I know them, the less I understand."

Keppler nodded. "They're as unpredictable as a horse. Ever tried riding? Don't. Unless you can keep your ears, eyes, and all your senses constantly on the alert. The minute you take a horse for granted, you can end up in a ditch with your back broken."

"Francesca? What's wrong?"

"Nothing's wrong," Keppler said, almost angrily. "The girl's completely honest. What's more, she knows all the political facts of life."

"And yet—?"

"Just keep an eye on her tonight, will you? Talk to her. She may need a lot of—"

"Oh, hell, no!" Denning cut in with disgust. "I wondered why you were sticking me into Gauch's house when you've got all these policemen round. But as nursemaid? No, thanks."

"You didn't do so badly with Emily."

"Emily? I happen to like Emily."

"So." Keppler looked amused.

Denning said abruptly, "I'm going to wash and change," and he moved toward his suitcase.

"Wash, but don't waste time changing. You're pretty enough."

Denning laughed, then. And as Keppler moved quietly

toward the door, he asked, "By the way, what name are you using?"

Keppler's heavy eyebrows rose politely.

"Aren't you using an assumed name in Falken?" Denning asked in amazement.

"But of course." Keppler's blue eyes were politely blank. He paused at the door, listening.

"Then what is it?"

There was a fleeting smile, a gleam of amusement on the solemn face. "Keppler," he said. He half-opened the door, waited for a moment, and then he slipped out into the empty corridor.

17: Francesca

IT WAS FANTASTIC THAT FRANCESCA SHOULD come into the inn looking so radiant. She had changed her blouse and skirt for a pretty dress of cool sprigged cotton, she had brushed and dressed her lovely hair, she had even discarded her sensible moccasins for red shoes with saucy heels.

"Don't tell me you walked from your house on these things," Waysmith said, looking at the shoes with amusement and some speculation. "Where's the party?"

"Here." Francesca pulled Gregor forward to join the Waysmiths at the window table. Frau Welti was with them, in presence if not in mind: her anxious eyes would flicker over the other guests, note that a glass needed refilling, and give a silent signal to Minna, happily and tearfully returned from her new nephew's christening. But Emil and Willy were still on the Blümlisalp: that was Emil's call which had sent Heinz Gauch and his rescue team up to that steep slope. And because Frau Welti was worried about Willy and Emil, worried about what they had discovered in the alpine hut on the high meadow to set them calling for help, she frowned now at

Francesca's dress and her cool, carefree smile. Besides, she owed Fräulein Francesca a frown for that lie she had inspired: imagine Herr Broach, quiet pleasant gentleman that he was, saying that Francesca had never spoken to him before, nor he to her. As if Frau Welti hadn't seen them talking. Briefly, yes. A word here, a word there. But still talking when they had been here and thought they had the place to themselves. He was in love with Francesca, and only a fool wouldn't see it, including himself. And Francesca? She was a strange one: you could know her for years and yet not know her at all.

"Gregor gave me a lift in his cart, he and his woodcutting friends," Francesca was explaining gaily. "So I'm here earlier than I thought. Sorry for rushing away this afternoon, Paula. I had some shopping to take home for Aunt Louisa. She's in bed with a cold, but she hopes to be better tomorrow. And will you come to tea then?"

"Delighted," said Paula, but she wished she were as light-hearted as Francesca. And the apology was a politeness accepted between friends because truth was sometimes more embarrassing than necessary. She could guess Andy's thoughts, too: he enjoyed the casual, but there was a certain point beyond which the charm of casualness ended very abruptly. We're all pretending like mad, Paula reminded herself, so Francesca's brittle gaiety is only her way of covering her real emotions. She's worried, Paula thought, and she's nervous and excited: that, I would expect; but what has she got to be happy about, at this moment? "And when *is* this party?" Paula asked, noting that Gregor was carrying Francesca's coat as though they were expecting to stay here until evening came. "Now, or later?"

"Later. Around eight. It's for Gregor's birthday. I decided he simply had to have some celebration." Francesca gave the silent Gregor a smile to encourage him to sit down and enjoy himself. He did sit down. "But," Francesca went on, watching him anxiously, "there's no reason why we shouldn't start celebrating now. Gregor never thinks a party is real unless it lasts at least seven hours."

Gregor was watching her as he might have looked at a favorite child, performing before company, whose pretty little ways were going to mean a couple of well-earned slaps once the visitors had gone.

"Well, I hope we're invited," said Waysmith, conscious of

his heavy humor and annoyed that it had been forced out of him. But someone had to say something. So far, Gregor's small talk had amounted to a few noncommittal grunts, hardly a type of conversation to contribute much to the general gaiety.

"But of course!" Francesca said. "Everyone's invited."

What eyes she has, Waysmith thought: blue sea, blue sky, a sunlit pool, idiot.

"Even these amiable gentlemen who are just leaving?" Paula wanted to know, watching the heavy stride of two men —visitors, certainly—who had become bored with the room after studying its occupants for the last half-hour.

"Why not?" Gregor said angrily. "She asks everyone. Even the man Broach."

"What?" Paula and her husband exchanged quick glances.

Francesca said, "We met in the post office. He said he was sorry if he had annoyed me. What could I say? I was the one who had been rude."

"So you invited him, to show you were sorry," Waysmith said, shaking his head.

"No," Francesca said indignantly. "I invited him because he said everyone avoided him. I told him he never gave people a chance to know him. Why didn't he come down some evening to the inn when we were all there?"

"And so she invites him," Gregor said gloomily. "A man I contempt. She invites him. To my party."

"I'm sorry for him," said Francesca. "He's so—so terribly unhappy."

"Oh, not that!" Paula said involuntarily.

Waysmith, who had been watching the door, suddenly looked relieved. "Hello, Bill. Good to see you. When did you get here?"

"Earlier in the day," Denning said, crossing over to the window table. "I've been out for a walk."

"Just a country-lover at heart?"

"That's right. Have you had time to see the blue butterflies yet?"

Waysmith stared.

"The size of your thumbnail. Look like a bed of gentians until you walk through them."

"Introductions." Paula reminded her husband anxiously, but Bill Denning was bowing gravely to Francesca as if he had never heard of her. He didn't even show surprise when

Andy introduced him as a specialist in birds, bees, and flowers. The only problem on his mind seemed to be a glass of beer. "We're discussing a party," Paula told him as he sat down beside her. He lit a cigarette, relaxed. His easy smile seemed to include all of them. But his eyes were studying Francesca. And why not? Paula thought: Francesca's face is worth looking at.

But Francesca was still engrossed with her own problem. "I don't see why we shouldn't invite Richard Broach," she said defensively. "Look, Gregor, you believe people should be free to live where they want to live."

"Honest people," Gregor emended, quickly coming to life as an argument lifted its Janus head. "A man must earn the right to choose. Yes?"

"But Richard Broach isn't a criminal. He just doesn't want to live in America any more. What's wrong with that?" She looked at Denning suddenly. "And you disapprove."

"Why should I?"

"You are an American."

Denning laughed. "To be quite frank, I agree with Gregor: people should have freedom of choice."

Gregor leaned forward. He nodded slowly. His serious eyes watched Denning intently. But the frown on his broad brow was no longer sullen. "Freedom of choice," he repeated. "That is the whole question." He smiled, and now his face was filled with new interest, almost delighted expectation, as though he had suddenly recognized a friend.

Is he so lonely? Paula wondered. Do most of us, when he meets us, seem just polite shadows?

Francesca was saying, "You grant Broach freedom of choice, yes. But you disapprove of that choice."

"Broach can live at the South Pole for all I care."

"You dislike him," Francesca insisted.

Denning looked round the table. "Persevering girl, isn't she?" His tone was amused, friendly, but his eyes were hard. "I've never even met the man," he told Francesca.

Oh, Francesca, Paula thought in dismay, why do you antagonize Bill and hurt Gregor, all for a weak unimportant man like Broach? She said aloud in disgust, "I give up."

But Francesca didn't. "Yet," she said softly to Denning, "you recognized his name when you heard it, and you reacted just like Gregor. You haven't given him a chance, either of you."

He sat still. "My mistake," he said at last. And he looked at Francesca in a new way, polite, guarded.

"You see, I am an exile too. I always feel sorry for exiles." She spoke pleadingly.

Gregor said, "Feel sorry? I feel happy for them. Because they are free. They escape. They are free. That is what matters. Not money, clothes——" He broke off, looking down at his worn jacket. He began to laugh with honest amusement.

Denning said quietly, still watching Francesca, "You still feel an exile here, where you have so many friends?"

Her cheeks colored, and the pink flush spread down her slender white neck. Her eyes widened for a moment, and then she looked away.

"Now we're all even," Waysmith said. "What's the next contest? Hair-pulling or eye-gouging?" He glanced at his watch. Six o'clock. If Keppler didn't appear in the next five minutes, then the interview with Broach was off. Inspector Bohren could have picked a more businesslike errand boy, Waysmith thought: Keppler was pleasant enough, transparently honest, no doubt a solid reliable sort, but thickheaded. Recalling Keppler's visit to the Waysmiths' room only an hour ago, he could only worry now whether the man had forgotten his own message.

"I'm sorry," Francesca said. She spoke to Denning again, gently. "But you know I don't really think you understand my point of view. I wasn't good at putting it into words, I'm afraid."

"That," said Paula, "is what women always say when they don't convince anyone. Not even themselves. Why," she added with relief, "here's Mr. Keppler!"

Waysmith rose to his feet. "Care to join us, sir? And here's a possible mountain climber." He introduced Denning, but he didn't sit down again even when Keppler had taken a chair. "By the way, did Broach accept your invitation to the party?" he asked Francesca. Would Keppler catch on, he wondered, or would he have to underline this piece of news?

"Yes," said Francesca. "I think he was touched by it." She looked sideways at Denning.

"Perhaps you've touched him into giving an interview," Waysmith said, watching Keppler's benign smile. He glanced openly at his watch. "I've just got time before all the festivities begin. Like to come along, Bill?"

"Sure."

Keppler said to Paula, "And you'll keep me company here? It isn't often that I have such a pleasant hour given to me. Two delightful young ladies."

Francesca was troubled. "Now?" she asked Waysmith. "Are you sure this is a good time for an interview?"

"Don't worry," Denning said, "I shan't spoil it. I'll give your friend every chance." He saw Keppler's eyes gleam.

"He isn't my friend," Francesca said indignantly, "he's just—"

But Denning was moving away.

"Bill," Paula called after him, "look at the sign outside over the door, will you? And tell me what amuses Andy so much."

Frau Welti's knitting needles slowed down.

"Did you ever see two stags without their antlers locked?" Denning asked with a grin.

Waysmith waited impatiently for the moment it took Denning to lift a stick from the stand beside the door. In the room behind them, the knitting needles had stopped completely. Paula was laughing, and then Francesca.

"Is that yours?" he asked, eyeing the heavy cane in Denning's hand as they left the inn.

"For the next hour, it is."

"If you think we're going to walk—"

"There's a dog around the place."

"Have you been doing some scouting?"

"Vaguely."

"How was *Waldesruhe?*"

"God awful. Tell Paula not to bother even looking at it. You'd never live there."

"Look," Waysmith said patiently, "I'm not a moron. You don't have to clam up."

"What do you think of Broach?"

"Is that a test question? If I side with you or Gregor, then you'll start telling me your news? Actually, I agree more with Francesca. He's got a set of opinions I don't like, but that doesn't mean he's untouchable."

"If it were only a matter of opinions—" Denning said. He shook his head. "That was Francesca's mistake: she thought I disliked him instinctively, like Gregor."

"You've got reasons?"

"Facts," Denning said briefly.

Waysmith looked at him.

"Our job right now is to find out just what shade of gray his guilt is."

"It couldn't be slightly off-white?"

Denning shook his head. "At best, he's an accessory to kidnaping. The law isn't going to excuse even that."

They had come into the narrow field, its grass close-cut, which served as the inn's back yard and parking space. "Over there," Waysmith said, leading the way toward a clump of birches where his car stood near the rough track that would lead them back to the street. Across the field, a battered jeep stood in solitary state under another cluster of trees; a wagon settled back on a white mass of daisies with its arms stretching to the sky; a small brewery truck was drawn up near the back door of the inn; two tethered goats turned their gentle eyes and thin Manchu beards toward the strangers. Beyond the scattered groups of trees, the other houses showed their sides and backs as if to manifest their independence, their white walls glowing pink, their red roofs bronzed by the warm light of the evening sun.

Denning looked toward the west. The slopes of the nearest mountains were in shadow, their peaks black silhouettes against the sun which had already traveled over them. The Blümlisalp could scarcely be seen: it had lost all its bright color and was only a gray streak amid dark gray forests. In these woods, dusk had already begun, cold and still.

"I forgot that," Denning said, half to himself, "I forgot how these mountains would cut out the sun. Come on, let's hurry."

But he paused at the car's door to look now at the brewery truck. It had a Bern license plate, with its unmistakable emblem of a small black bear climbing a yellow ramp on a background of red.

"Is this your idea of hurrying?" Waysmith asked. So Denning got into the car.

They circled round the field, drove past the side of the inn, and halted carefully before they made the sharp right turn into the narrow street.

"See that car?" Waysmith asked, after they had slowed down once more to let a black Lagonda ease past them. "It's Broach's little runabout."

"Who was the man in it?"

"The secretary. Walters. Want to turn back?"

"I'd just as soon see Broach by himself." Denning looked back along the street. The Lagonda had stopped at the post office. "The quicker, the better. Take the first cut-off to the right."

"Seems to me as if there are more tourists around than when I entered the village," Waysmith observed. "I hope they are friends of Inspector Bohren, that's all." But this was one time he was in no danger of being stopped for speeding. He pressed his foot on the accelerator, and waved to three tourists who had nothing better to do than study the premature sunset.

In sharp contrast to the west side of the valley, the eastern slopes were bathed in warm light. At the top of this gentle hill, its green meadows now golden, its woods still alive with the evening song of birds, the house waited with flaming windows blazing back the sun's brilliance as if they were diamonds. A radiance of diamonds.

Broach's secretary halted the Lagonda in front of the post office. He stepped out in his neat quiet way, closed the door carefully, and walked briskly down the street for twenty yards or so before he crossed toward the inn. He held an envelope in his hand.

He nodded pleasantly to a small group gathered round the bench at the front door. Inside, the room was half-filled, placid, with quiet people resting after a day of work or pleasure. He hesitated, glancing around the room in his shortsighted way. Frau Welti, he saw, was not in her office: she was sitting at the window table, listening to the mountaineering bore. The Russian was talking to the American woman. Vivenzio was daydreaming.

Gregor had begun talking in his confidential tone, a low hoarse whisper shielded by his cupped hand. "I take care of Francesca," he had said as if to answer Paula's unspoken worries. Watching the affection in his eyes, the softening of his face, Paula wondered if she hadn't found the reason why he stayed in Falken. She glanced at Francesca, who seemed lost in a world of her own ever since Andy and Bill had marched out of the room.

"But you're in danger here, Gregor," Paula answered in a lowered voice. In greater danger than Francesca, she thought.

He almost smiled. "If I am famous, I am in danger. However important I believe I am, I cannot say I am famous. Me—" his whisper became almost inaudible—"they do not kidnap. I have no value. Thousands like me escape. But only twenty, thirty like—" He wouldn't say Andrássy's name.

Paula nodded to show she understood.

"But thank you. Your worry is a—" he searched for the word—"compliment." He studied her face. *"Simpatichny,"* he said with great gentleness.

"Yes," Francesca said unexpectedly. "That's Paula." Then she relapsed into silence again, thinking now—as she had thought during every space of peace in the last eighteen hours —of Andrássy. How did they find out about him? she wondered for the thousandth time. Had they an informer in the village, who had recognized the humble waiter called Schmid? But who in this village could recognize a composer? And no one here in the village would inform against Gregor's friend —and that was all they knew about Schmid. Even Anna Welti only thought of Schmid as someone who was once in a German prison camp with Gregor. The people in Bern with whom he had stayed, or who had employed him, knew only his false name, his false history. That was the rule the Committee had always followed. We've been so careful, almost ludicrously careful, Francesca thought. How did the Communists find out about Andrássy?

Was it my fault?

She took a deep breath. From the very beginning, ever since the idea of the Committee had been formed, she had retreated from normal relationships. The cold, reserved Francesca. The only real friend she had allowed herself for all these months was Gregor. And even Gregor couldn't share all she knew about the Committee's work. Couldn't, because he wouldn't: he had always believed that when the Communists learned about the Committee, they would guess that he was its leader. "The less I know, the less they force out of me," he had said. They had certainly forced information out of Andrássy about her. But who had told, or been forced to give information, about Andrássy? Hálek? He had known Andrássy, and they had met in Bern before Hálek left. Hálek? But he was safe in England, about to begin his lectures in London. Dear Hálek, she thought with gratitude, the gentlest man she had ever met. The work for the Committee had been hard, even grim; but its reward was learning to know such men as Hálek.

Keppler's quiet voice said, "And here's Mr. Walters coming to pay us a visit."

Francesca looked up. Indeed it was the little secretary. He walked across the room with his short-paced step, halted with a polite little bow, gave his timid smile. He held out an envelope to her. She took it.

"We tried to reach you by telephone," Walters said. "But we couldn't."

"My aunt is in bed. Ill." Francesca opened the envelope.

"I'm sorry," Mr. Walters said in distress. "I hope the telephone bell didn't annoy her."

It was a friendly little note inside the envelope:

Dear Miss Vivenzio,

What will you think of me? When I got back here, I found I couldn't postpone another engagement I had already made for tonight. I've been trying to reach you by phone. Believe me, I am disappointed. If Walters can find you with this note, will you telephone me at 8-14-57? I'd like to talk to you for a moment about the Italian lessons I need before I leave in July to visit Italy. Could they begin on Monday? Afternoons are best for me.

Thank you for tonight's invitation. It pleased me more than you can guess.

Sincerely,
Richard van Meeren Broach

Francesca smoothed the note out on the table and frowned down at its questions. It was impossible for her to give any lessons on Monday. Tuesday afternoons were already booked each week for English lessons with the French doctor at Schlossfalken-Bad. In fact, afternoons weren't good at all for the next few weeks. *If I am alive to teach,* she added to that.

Mr. Walters was still waiting, as if he expected a reply.

"Tell Mr. Broach—" she began, then stopped. It was all too involved. She rose. "May I use your telephone, Frau Welti?"

"What's wrong?" Paula asked.

"Nothing that two sentences won't straighten out." As she moved toward the passageway that led to the back of the inn where Frau Welti's little office served as a useful telephone booth, she smiled and said to Gregor, "He can't come to your party. Do we start un-arguing ourselves again?"

Mr. Walters still waited beside the table.

"Perhaps Mr. Walters will come to the party?" Keppler

asked, propping his elbow on the note in his bumbling way so that Mr. Walters, about to pick it up, decided not to make the attempt. Mr. Walters smiled, bulged his eyes with his earnest politeness: no, indeed, it was impossible, but how disappointing for him as well as for Mr. Broach. He talked on. And on. There was no end to the stream of affability once it had been tapped.

Keppler listened with a smile. But he was thinking of Frau Welti's small room where two of Bohren's men, acting as communications officer and special messenger, had been in charge of the telephone all day. No further calls had come in from Bohren: he must be on his way back from *Waldesruhe* now, bringing Nikolaides for a tender recognition scene with his Mr. James who worked at Broach's place. That's one meeting I hope I don't miss, Keppler said to himself.

Gregor had his own troubles. He half rose as if to follow Francesca. And then he sat down again, remembering that he couldn't interrupt a telephone call between Francesca and Broach without looking as though he were curious, spiteful, jealous. So he stared balefully at the hapless secretary who didn't seem to know how to disentangle himself politely from this unenthusiastic company. Perhaps Frau Welti's clicking needles had mesmerized him.

This, thought Paula, is really tedious. She closed her ears. She tried not to worry about the way Francesca had sat at the table, lost in thoughts of Broach and herself. Francesca must like Broach a good deal more than she had admitted yesterday; perhaps even more than she was admitting to herself now. Who was he, anyway? An ex-American who obviously didn't approve of his own country. If Francesca had been an American, she might have wondered why. But Francesca was a European, and knew as little about America as Paula knew about Italy. There were plenty of Europeans who liked individual Americans, but criticized the America they had never seen. Broach wouldn't seem strange to them. They would accept him at his own face value. I wish I could, Paula thought, and half sighed.

Suddenly, Gregor rose. He looked toward the silent passage that led to Frau Welti's room. "I think I go." He hesitated, though. His face was a study in divided emotions: the instinct to go; the dislike of interfering, of being the friend who was turning jailer.

At that moment, Mr. Walters' hand discovered several

letters in his jacket pocket. "Why, I nearly forgot! I must post these. And my car is waiting in the street, blocking all traffic. I shall be arrested!" He laughed, bowed to each and every one, and walked unhurriedly toward the inn's front door.

Keppler's amusement had faded. Quickly, he glanced out of the window. The Lagonda was parked in front of the post office, surrounded by curious children, obviously empty, seemingly innocent. Yet his sudden suspicion increased. Walters, now stopping to speak to a couple of villagers, was a man who had established an alibi.

He rose, pocketing Francesca's note, and hurried toward Frau Welti's room. Gregor followed him. In the passageway, they began to run.

The back door to the inn stood open. The office itself was empty, except for one policeman stretched out unconscious on the floor.

18: *The House on the Hill*

THE BRILLIANT WINDOWS HAD LOST THEIR FIRE. They had become blank squares, flanked by green shutters, underlined with petunias in white window boxes, as empty and unresponsive as the house itself on its lonely hill.

"Four and a half minutes," Waysmith said, timing the Citroën's climb from the village. "Not bad."

Denning nodded, as he stepped out onto the sharp gravel bed of the driveway. So this is where Broach lives, he thought. He looked around him.

The trees, beginning so abruptly at the edge of the cleared land, seemed to reach across the circle of well-kept grass and pull the house itself into their deep silence. The driveway had brought them to the flight of wooden steps which led up to the wide balcony that encircled the house, but it didn't end there now. Recently, judging from the newly graveled surface, it had been continued, in a curve away from the front door, to disappear among the trees on some private business of its own.

"Where's that dog?" Waysmith asked with a smile.

"Everything's too quiet," Denning admitted.

"Peaceful is evening in the shrine garden."

Denning took a deep breath of the resin-scented air which came in warm waves from the pine trees. You could hear a needle drop, he thought. "Too quiet," he repeated. And then, sharply, "Is anyone here?" Where had they gone, anyway?

"We can find out." But Waysmith didn't take any step toward the placid house. He stood by the car, searched for a cigarette, and looked at Falken down in the valley. "Or shall we just go back?"

"Lost interest in the interview?"

"Lost my enthusiasm when I failed the first time." Or perhaps, Waysmith thought moodily, I lost it when I heard that Broach might not be what he seems: how badly would this report hurt Francesca? It was about time that girl found some real happiness in life.

Denning said, "Don't let a woman discourage you."

Waysmith lit his cigarette. "Francesca?" he asked, as if he hadn't been thinking about her. "I must say she picked a fine time to be sorry for people. Hasn't she enough to worry about?"

"That may be the trouble. Too much pressure, too much strain."

"Perhaps she's become a professional champion of the underdog."

"If this is being an underdog," Denning looked at the house and its quiet display of wealth, "then I'll join the ranks any day. Come on, Andy. Let's get this over with." He took a step toward the balcony and waited.

"Of course, she could be flattered. Who is there to pay attention to her around Falken? He couldn't keep his eyes off her. You didn't see—"

"I can imagine," Denning said dryly. "She's easy to look at."

"How deep, do you think, is she in—"

"Once it was families, Capulets and Montagues, who kept people apart. Now it's politics. Romantic enough for you? For God's sake, Andy, if you don't stop brooding, we'll never get this job done."

Waysmith ground out the half-smoked cigarette under his heel. "Nice sunset," he said, turning away from the view of Falken with its background of mountains. He wished it was as easy to turn away from his worries about Francesca.

The door on the balcony opened.

Is this Broach? Denning wondered. He saw a dark-haired man, fairly tall, thin, with a pale set face, a rigid jaw that could mean nervousness. Then the man spoke, and his voice was recognizably American. "Hello," he was saying, in surprise, perhaps even with relief. "I heard a car stop and wondered—" He looked down at the rifle in his hands. "Just cleaning one of my guns," he reassured them.

"Thought you had joined the reservists," Waysmith said, climbing the steps. "This is Bill Denning, by the way. Another newspaperman. May we come in?"

"Why?"

"I thought you might like to discuss that interview."

"I have no interest in any interview, frankly."

"What about an article, then? Giving your point of view?"

"Am I so important?" Broach smiled then.

Denning said quietly, "You became important yesterday."

Broach looked at him quickly.

Denning sat down on the top step. "This will do," he said to Waysmith. "We can talk here. Suits me."

"Not a bad place for an exchange of ideas," Waysmith agreed. "Nice sunsets you keep around here, Broach."

But Broach was looking toward that part of the driveway which circled into the woods. "It's all right!" he called out. "It's all right. Go back!" And the man who held the dog on its leash turned and went back.

There must be a house in the woods, Denning thought, a house or a shack, a cabin, something.

Then Broach looked toward the empty road that led from Falken to the house. "Come in," he said suddenly. He held open the door. "Come in."

"It's all right out here," Denning assured him. He liked this fresh air. He could almost forget the smell of Brie cheese and Nikolaides' hair pomade in *Waldesruhe's* airless room. He had become allergic, perhaps, to closed spaces in strange houses whose owners just happened to be cleaning rifles.

"Come in!"

Waysmith grinned and said, "Sure. Can't stay long, though. We've a party tonight. You're coming, aren't you?" He followed Broach. Denning followed him. Waysmith's grin widened as he saw that Denning still carried the stick with him. But Broach didn't even seem to notice. Was he worried about something? The word "yesterday," for example?

The house was the opposite of *Waldesruhe*. And the large

airy room into which Broach led them hêld only the scent of roses from the smoke crystal bowl on the walnut coffee table. "My secretary's work," Broach said with his quick, sad smile, pointing to the flowers. "Have a comfortable seat," and he gestured to the low couch of silver-gray tweed. He laid down the rifle on a table of Carrara marble near his own high-backed armchair of dark red velvet. "We've had prowlers around here," he said as he went toward a portable bar with its crystal decanters and silver ice bowl. "What will you have?"

"Nothing, thanks," Denning said. Waysmith merely shook his head. "Strange. . . ." Denning glanced around the room. Silk tweed curtains, rich carpeting, no books worth mentioning, no pictures, an oversized radio, filed magazines, a phonograph and a few records.

"What is strange?"

"This room. It's the kind of place Nikolaides would like." Silver and silk, softness to sit and walk on.

But the name of Nikolaides had no effect at all. "Do I know him?" Broach poured himself a drink.

"Perhaps not. This is his room, though."

"I don't care about rooms, frankly."

"Is this Mr. Walters' work, too?" Waysmith asked, looking around with interest.

"Yes. His taste is excellent, as you see." Broach came back to his armchair. "Well?"

Waysmith said, "Would you write an article for *Policy*— a testament of faith, as it were?"

"I like that idea. But—" Broach looked a little embarrassed, "I don't really know whether I'll write it or not."

"Will you think over it, seriously? Tell me your answer tonight."

"Tonight, I'm afraid, I can't be at the inn I had promised the staff that they could go over to Interlaken for a dance there. And Walters has to meet his cousin in Bern and help her through the customs and give her supper and that sort of thing. I've sent him down to the inn with my apologies to Miss Vivenzio. In fact, I'm expecting a phone call from her at any minute."

"When can you give me your answer?"

"By Monday?"

"I may not be in Falken then. Look, here's my office in Bern." Waysmith scribbled its address and telephone number on a page from his small notebook. "Leave word there."

"Such efficiency," Broach said, and smiled. Then he looked at Denning. "What newspaper do you represent?"

"I work for a news-gathering syndicate."

"And your syndicate thinks I'm important? Since yesterday?"

Waysmith thought, so that's the word that fetched him. That's the reason we're sitting inside this room, even if he can't make up his mind about an article for *Policy* until secretary Walters gives him some more advice. Waysmith settled back in the couch. Denning could take over from there.

"Since yesterday," Denning repeated.

"What do you mean by that?"

"We've had two pieces of information. I'm here to verify them."

"Why?"

"They're unpleasant."

"The newspapers have always been unpleasant about me," Broach said with a laugh. "I gave up worrying about their wild exaggerations, long ago."

"The facts we have are sober enough."

"Such as?"

"First, the Herz diamonds."

Broach sat very still. "What about them?"

"They are the property of the French government. They have been missing for—"

"That's the first lie," Broach said angrily. "They were Nazi property, now belonging to the government which—" He stopped short. "What happens to Goering's jewels is nothing to weep over."

"They were owned by Josef Herz," Denning said patiently, "who died, along with his family, in a Nazi gas chamber. He left his collection to the French government. They have been smuggled illegally into Switzerland by the Communists."

"Always the Communists," said Broach angrily, "that's right, blame everything on them. It's a fashion I—"

"Not everything. But certainly this: three million dollars have been paid by some rich dupe toward a hidden fund."

"A dupe?" Broach had caught control of himself. He even laughed. "Of course, that's what you would think."

"He's a dupe because he's paid out money for diamonds that he can never own. Or what else would you call him? An accessory to a crime?"

There was a long silence. "And what has this got to do with me?" Broach asked.

"Would you pay three million dollars for diamonds?"

"For honest diamonds? Certainly. If I felt like it."

"For the Herz diamonds?"

"Why argue about this? Your facts are all wrong. And I'm not interested in hypothetical questions."

"You've never heard of the Herz collection?"

"I know nothing about any stolen property. I never have. I never will." He rose. "Clear out, both of you."

"Certainly," Denning said and got to his feet along with Waysmith. Andy's face was a study in worry and horror, both directed against his crazy friend: to come here and insult a man like that—you might as well throw a pot of scalding water over him.

But Broach suddenly sat down again. "You said you had a second piece of information. Two laughs are better than one, I'm told."

My God, thought Waysmith, he's going to make sure of thumping damages in the biggest slander suit in history, and I'll have to be a witness. He started for the door, and waited there. But Denning didn't follow him. He didn't sit down either. He walked over to the small pile of records.

"You like music?"

"Isn't that evident?"

"I see you have one of my favorite composers here."

"Do we have something in common, then?" Broach asked with mock seriousness.

"You must have met him last year when you attended the Cultural Congress in Prague. Andrássy was especially produced, wasn't he, to conduct one of his own compositions?"

"I have met him," Broach said carefully, ignoring the Cultural Congress. "And extremely disappointing he was to meet."

"Was he still disappointing to meet in Falken?"

Broach hesitated. "In Falken?" His voice was stilted.

"Yes. He is in the same situation as you are."

"As I am?"

"He decided he wanted to live abroad."

"Now," Broach said with amusement, "surely you aren't comparing me with Andrássy?"

"Not man for man." Denning almost smiled. "He's only one

of the great musicians. But your situations are similar—according to Francesca. She believes that each individual should be free to choose where he wants to live. Do you agree with that?"

Broach said, "Andrássy may have been a good composer. At one time. But he has become a traitor. Our circumstances are completely different."

"They certainly are. You are free to talk like this. And he has been abducted. Possibly tortured. Doesn't that turn your stomach, even a few degrees?"

"If I let myself believe all the fantastic stories spread around—"

"All right, all right," Denning said curtly. What was the score, anyway? The diamonds: Broach hadn't known the full story on them; there he could be graded as an ignorant dupe, who hadn't bothered to check on the facts. Andrássy: Broach had known about him, and twisted the record to justify his actions; there he was more than a dupe; there, he could be graded as willing to tolerate evil, willing even to take a small part in it. Compared to Broach, Nikolaides was a petty offender: theft of property was nothing, nothing at all, compared to the theft of a man's life.

Still watching Broach, Denning took a step away from him.

The gesture was not missed. Broach said, his voice rising, "You really believe all these lies that the capitalist press invents? You believe them? An intelligent man like you—how can you believe them?"

The telephone bell rang.

"Ask Francesca," said Denning. "Ask her if these facts are lies. Why don't you answer her call?"

Waysmith took a deep breath. First, the pot of scalding water; now, the bucket of ice: shock treatment, if ever he had seen it. He went instinctively toward the telephone. Broach hadn't moved at all. Perhaps he scarcely heard the steadily ringing bell. Waysmith said, "I can't bear to leave a telephone unanswered," and he picked up the receiver. Denning turned his back on Broach, and looked out of the window.

Waysmith answered in surprise. "Speaking," he said. Then, sharply, he called, "Bill!" And Denning, glancing quickly round, saw Waysmith's hand now raised warningly for silence as he listened intently.

The sound of a car's engine, making a last burst of speed

up the hill toward the house, broke into the stillness of the room. Broach came to life. A look of surprise, of sudden worry, of consternation appeared on his face. He looked at his watch.

Is the car unexpected, or too early? Denning wondered. He glanced back at the driveway. But it wasn't a car that had appeared, and swerved across the grass to avoid Waysmith's Citroën at the door. It was a small brewery truck, running lightly now down the curve of driveway to enter the woods.

Broach said, "Get out of here! Both of you." He advanced on Waysmith. "Give me that call. It's mine."

"Just a moment," Waysmith told the man at the other end of the telephone. He held onto the receiver with both hands, as he faced Broach. "They've got Francesca," he said. "She went to telephone you in Frau Welti's office. And that's where they snatched her. Got away through the back door. One policeman with his skull smashed—his helper was out, delivering a false message. Who sent that false mesage to the inn? You—you?" He raised the telephone as if he'd strike Broach with it.

Broach yelled back, "You're wrong, you're wrong. This has nothing to do with Francesca. Nothing!"

Denning shoved him aside as he reached Waysmith. He took the telephone. Keppler's voice was saying angrily, "Where's Denning? Where's—"

"Here," said Denning quickly. "For what it's worth, there was a Bern brewery truck at the inn's back door. Gray in color, small. It has just arrived here. Seems to be delivering beer right into the woods, northwest of the house. And you'll find a hut there. Certainly there are a man and a dog, besides the two men on the truck."

Broach made a lunge toward Denning, but Waysmith caught hold of him. Broach shouted, "The truck was never near the inn. You're lying, you're lying!"

"Did you hear that?" Denning asked Keppler quietly.

"Yes," said Keppler's voice. "It sounds as if there were another truck around."

"Same model, color, and license plate?"

"For Andrássy. . . . So that's how they were going to do it. Who would notice two trucks if they looked identical?"

"Who would notice even one brewery truck in Falken?"

"I'll have a search made of the road near the foot of the

Blümlisalp trail. You stay where you are. Who's with you and Waysmith?"

"Broach."

"The secretary hasn't arrived back yet?"

"Not yet."

"He left the village just a few minutes ago. Alone. With an iron-fast alibi established."

"Do we wait for him, or start searching the woods?"

"Wait for us. Ten minutes, and we'll be there. Bohren and his men will attend to the woods. Can you manage? Good luck." The connection switched off.

Broach had now recovered his dignity. He was hard-eyed, tense-lipped. "Take your hands off me," he told Waysmith coldly. "And get out, both of you. Contemptible, contemptible lies. Now I know how you build up your cases against innocent people. You see a truck delivering some beer to the inn, you see it delivering a barrel here. So you fabricate a story from that, invent a crime to link me with—"

"With what?" Denning asked. "With Francesca's disappearance?"

"That's a lie."

"Everything you don't want to hear is a lie," Waysmith said wearily. "Come on, Bill. There's just so much of this that I can take."

"We'll stay here, Andy."

"We're wasting time," Waysmith said sharply.

We've almost ten minutes to waste, thought Denning. He didn't move. And Waysmith, watching his face, stopped protesting. Broach picked up the rifle. "You are now trespassing. Do I have to call the police?"

Denning laughed.

Waysmith said, "Sure, this guy just about kills me, too. But I'll do my laughing afterward. If Francesca is still alive."

That stopped Broach, and held him.

Denning's voice was suddenly grim. "There's a chance she is still alive. They'll have to transport her out of Bern before they can really go to work on her. She won't give out information easily, not Francesca."

Broach stared at him. His nostrils were rigid, white-edged. There was a strange gleam over the surface of his pale face.

"When I worked with the French underground," Denning went on, "I met two girls like Francesca. They outlasted our best men when they were caught and tortured. One held on for three weeks in Ravensbrück."

"This," Broach burst out, "is a despicable act. You think you'll blackmail me with lies to—"

"I've given you up," Denning told him contemptuously. "You can believe what you like." He turned back to Waysmith. He went on talking, ignoring the rifle, ignoring Broach.

And Waysmith, quick to follow Denning's lead, wondered for one wry moment if Denning was conscious as he was of Broach's strained face, of the rifle's dangerous tilt, of the taut hand that gripped it and ungripped it with savage nervousness. "Funny thing about this fellow," Waysmith said, "he argues when he could go and see for himself. All he has to do is to walk into the woods and have a look at a truck."

"He won't find Andrássy, either. Perhaps he knows that. Perhaps he prefers to stay here and act pure."

"Like the people who saw the trainloads of political prisoners being carted off to labor camps and never objected."

"Perhaps he's waiting," said Denning. "For instructions."

"That's it. He's waiting for his secretary to give him permission to—" Waysmith broke off. "Say, Bill, have I stumbled on something?"

"I'd call that a pretty good stumble," Denning said slowly.

But tactfully it wasn't good. For Broach, standing so still, regained his assurance. "I'm waiting for no one," he said. "Walters has gone on to Bern." He raised the rifle. "I'll count up to ten. Get out."

"There is Walters arriving in Bern right now," Denning said. "Hear him?" The strong drone of a powerful engine climbing the hill to the house came steadily nearer.

Broach forgot both of them for that minute, at least. He crossed swiftly to the window. Then he turned and stared at them.

Denning took out a cigarette and lit it slowly. How many of the ten minutes had gone? Only half of them? Surely more.

Waysmith took off his glasses and polished them with his handkerchief. He cursed them as he did every day. He didn't like a fight with his glasses on; yet, without them, he'd misjudge distances. But there was one thing to be thankful for at this minute: the rifle was no longer pointed at his head. One false move, there, and Paula would never have recognized his face again. Stop thinking of Paula, he warned himself: no weakness, Danton! He counted the steps of Mr. Walters, coming briskly into the house.

The little man halted at the door. He looked at the rifle, at the stick lying beside the couch where Denning stood, at the glasses in Waysmith's hand. He frowned, puzzled and annoyed. Then he came forward with a smile.

"I got your message, sir," he said to Broach. "So I came back here."

"But I sent no message."

Mr. Walters blinked. "Then it must have been from Haase."

Waysmith felt a sense of disappointment. His guess about Walters hadn't been so good after all: there was still another who gave orders around here. But Denning saw the quick look of warning which Broach received, and Keppler's peculiar phrase jumped into his mind: "iron-fast alibi." Mr. Walters was always quick to establish his minor role, it seemed.

"Oh," said Broach, recovering himself, "Haase. Of course, Haase."

"I'm sorry if I interrupted you and your guests, sir." Walters eyed Denning's stick again, as he backed toward the door with a polite bow.

Denning said, lifting the stick and leaning on it. "This is only for my bad knee, Mr. Walters. No need to be alarmed. We came to interview Mr. Broach."

Walters' alarm was apparent only for one moment. "No doubt you had an interesting conversation." He was still edging toward the door.

Waysmith put on his glasses, and crossed the room quickly to reach the door before Walters. "Don't go," he said. "In fact, perhaps you could settle some of the arguments we got into."

"Arguments?" Walters looked at Broach, almost sadly.

"Don't worry," Broach said. "I think I handled their arguments all right. They are fairly clever propagandists, these two. I shouldn't be surprised to find that the State Department bribed them to come and persuade me back to America. Just look at their faces—I've hit on the truth."

Waysmith shook his head in wonder. "You really do believe you're an important kind of fellow, don't you?" He leaned against the doorway, his feet outstretched, blocking Walters' exit. "What's that?" he added quickly. "*Another* car coming up your little hill?"

Walters crossed quickly to the window. He looked incredulous, worried. He stood beside Broach and waited for the car to come into the driveway.

Denning called softly, "Mr. James—"

Walters turned round.

Then he realized what he had done. "What did you say?" he asked coldly.

But Broach had taken a step away from the window. "It's a truck," he said unbelievingly.

Walters glanced back at the driveway quickly. For a moment his control slipped.

"An earlier delivery than you expected?" Denning asked. But there was a hollow feeling in the pit of his stomach: Heinz Gauch had failed, Keppler had failed. Here was the brewery truck with Andrássy, and not one policeman, not one security agent in sight. And how many of Walters' men were in that truck? Certainly two, perhaps three. "Andy," he said quietly, and gestured toward the door.

"Then there were two trucks. Two," said Broach. His voice rose. "Who was in the first one?"

Walters paid no attention: he had his own problems. "Fools. Idiots." He turned angrily away from the window, wrenching himself free from Broach's hand, and ran toward the door. "Where do you think you're going?" he shouted at Waysmith and Denning. "Broach! Cover them with that rifle!" And he ran into the hall, toward the front door, yelling another set of commands to the men outside. "Don't stop there, you fools! Drive on!"

Broach stared at Denning for a long moment. Then his mouth twisted. He caught the rifle by its barrel and swung it high over his head as he took a step forward, smashing the butt down into the bowl of roses, sideways at a vase, down into a porcelain lamp, down, up, sideways, down, swinging, smashing blindly with each slow step. His face was livid, rigid. And then, suddenly, he stopped. He threw the rifle at the door. And he stood there, staring at Denning again, his breath coming in gulping sobs, his eyes hard with rage against the whole world.

But never against himself, Denning thought. Broach dropped onto the couch and covered his face with his hands.

Waysmith picked up the rifle. "It wasn't loaded after all," he said, shaking his head, his voice mild with wonder as he remembered his fear. Now it seemed ludicrous. Yet Denning's face was still tense. What next? Waysmith wondered. Then he heard the heavy footsteps mounting the wooden steps to the front balcony.

Denning took a firm grip of the end of his stick, as if it were a club. He faced the door, backing away from it. He said, "There's a window over there, just behind us. Go on, Andy. You first. And keep that rifle pointed. It looks real enough."

But Walters had returned. Alone. Swiftly he looked around the destruction, swiftly he crossed over to the couch. "Broach! Broach!"

And Denning, halfway to the window, halted; for there was desperation and fear as well as anger in Walters' hushed voice as his hand caught Broach's lapel and shook him.

Walters was saying with quiet intensity, "That girl was the leader of the conspiracy against us. Her smiles were lies to catch you, catch me. She was head of the Committee. D'you hear? Head of the Committee. Of the Committee."

Broach looked up at Walters, blankly at first, and then as the word "Committee" was hammered into his consciousness, his face lost the slack look of complete disbelief. He turned his head to look at Denning accusingly. "Was she?" he asked, his voice still hoarse.

Mr. Walters stepped back. He was satisfied. He turned to face the men who had entered the room. "Gentlemen, I must protest against this armed invasion. We have our rights. This is an outrage." He blinked his eyes, he fluttered his hands.

"A terrible outrage," Keppler said quietly, making his way into the room behind the three policemen and the two men in tourist dress who had grouped themselves at the door. There was Le Brun, too, with his sardonic smile and quick eyes already searching for his diamonds.

"Look at the damage these criminals have done!" Walters swept his arm around him. He finished with a dramatic gesture toward Denning and Waysmith. "Just see what they've done! Arrest them!" As he spoke, he retreated over to the back of the room.

But Denning was already there. "I also had that window picked out for a quick exit, Mr. James." And he caught the secretary's shoulders, and swung him round. The blandly innocent face, indignant, contemptuous, sparked Denning's anger. He hit hard.

"Was that necessary?" Keppler asked, but he was smiling as he signaled urgently toward the hall.

"Yes," Denning said briefly. He rubbed his knuckles, as he stared down at the man now sitting at his feet, nursing a bruised jaw. I didn't hit hard enough, he thought.

There was a stir near the door. A small dark man, firmly attached to Le Brun's assistant, was brought into the room. He hesitated, nodded nervously, then looked bleakly at Le Brun.

"Look around you," Le Brun told him abruptly. "Anyone here whom you know?"

Nikolaides looked at Broach, at Waysmith. He shook his head over each of them. Then he looked at Denning. "Yes. I've met Mr. Denning." His eyes dropped to Walters, now. He raised his free hand to point. "Mr. James," he said, his voice rising, "the man who called himself James!" And he broke into a stream of French, detailing briefly but fluently James's ancestry, his appearance, his antecedents, his future. "I spit on you," he ended, and suited his action to his words. "Murderer and liar, I spit."

"Now, now," said Keppler with distaste, signaling Nikolaides away. There was nothing so bitter as injured complicity.

Le Brun addressed Keppler. "If I may start interrogating?" He nodded in the direction of Broach.

"Certainly. I've got all I want," Keppler said grimly. He was watching the policemen as they encircled James.

"Don't touch me!" James said in fury. "I have immunity. I insist. I have diplomatic immunity."

One of the policemen hesitated, looked at Keppler.

"He will have to prove that," Keppler told him. "Meanwhile, arrest him."

And the policeman produced his handcuffs as he began his brief recital. Waysmith felt a shudder down his spine as the earnest voice droned on: ". . . for the murders of Charles-Auguste Maartens . . . of Benjamin Taylor, Captain . . . of Maxwell Meyer, Lieutenant-Colonel . . . in the City of Bern on the night of Thursday, the twenty-eighth day of May, 1953." Then he stared over at Denning.

But Denning was leaving the room.

Waysmith caught up with him at the front door. Together, they stood facing the quiet woods for a moment.

"Bohren ought to be there," said Denning. But his voice was worried. They looked at each other. Then they set out at a run, cutting across the grass, avoiding the harsh clatter of the graveled driveway. As they reached the first trees, there came the crack of rifle fire, its echo slapping sharply against the wooded hillside.

19: The Silent Woods

AFTER THAT BRIEF BURST OF SHOTS, THERE WAS only silence in the woods. Denning, now at a quick walk, led the way through the trees, keeping to the needle-covered ground, still avoiding the surface of the narrow road which guided them obliquely down a gentle slope. He halted suddenly.

"Did you hear something, too?" Waysmith asked in a low voice.

Denning nodded. There had been a clear snap of a dried branch, the dull sound of a fall smothered by the carpet of pine needles. And these noises had not come from the direction of the shots, but from somewhere up there, to Denning's right, on higher ground. It could be some of Bohren's men, circling around. Yet had there been enough time to let them climb the eastern heights of the wood? Judging from the shots, they had entered the wood at its western boundary bordering on the meadows through which Denning and Gauch had walked that afternoon, and then filtered through the trees to find the road and the truck and Francesca.

But had they found Francesca? Denning pointed ahead.

There, lying on the sparse fine grass that led as a green trail, away from the road, up through the trees, was a small vivid blot of red. Ten more paces, and the blot took shape: it was a red shoe.

Waysmith, who had advanced further than Denning in order to see clearly, turned and waited. But Denning wasn't going to follow the grass trail. He signaled for Waysmith to come back, and gave a full-arm sweep toward the slope under which they had stood when they heard the cracking branch. Waysmith gripped the rifle he carried, wished again for some bullets, and decided that he was at least better off than Denning: a walking stick didn't even look impressive as a weapon. He retraced his steps quickly. Then, together, keeping a distance between them, they began to climb up through the wood. Here, the grass was smothered by the withered pine needles. Remembering the cracking branch, they picked their way carefully, avoiding any fallen twig or an occasional dead arm of the close-crowding trunks. The last deep yellow sunlight gave a golden cast to the stiff green pine trees. The air was still, warm, heavily scented. The silence of the sleeping wood pressed in from every side.

Suddenly, below them, from the direction of the road which they had left, they heard a man's voice and the quick rush of boots over the gravel. That could be Inspector Bohren's men, Denning thought. He hoped so. They had discovered the red shoe which Francesca had been able to kick off as she was carried up the hill. He hoped so, again. But he knew one thing: if Francesca had been able to do that, then there could only have been one man who had carried her. The others must have stayed near the truck to hold off Bohren, to give that one man time. Time to escape—with dusk, this wood offered many hiding places. And if escape seemed a failure? Then the man would kill. They had killed Kahn when he had almost got free of them. The trained kidnaper was a trained assassin, too.

One man up there. . . . Denning stood still, listening to the returned silence, as oppressive as the warm breathless air. Yes, again the silence was broken near the road. More heavy boots crossed the gravel. Then silence again.

Waysmith looked inquiringly at Denning. Bohren? he seemed to be asking.

Denning shrugged his shoulders, gave a wry smile. I hope so, he seemed to answer.

Waysmith pointed through the trees in the direction that the grass trail must follow.

Denning nodded. The newcomers were using that trail.

Waysmith made a circling sign with his arm. Do we climb up that way? Outflank?

Denning nodded again. And let's hope, he thought, that the man hiding up there with Francesca is watching the grass trail.

Waysmith may have been thinking along the same lines. For he grinned suddenly and gave the old cavalry sign to advance.

Now, they walked half-crouching, ready to take cover, ready to drop on their faces. The yellow light was fading. A gray-green shadow was spreading coldly over the ground, rising upward gradually. Soon the trees would be in darkness, only their pointing crowns still lit by the setting sun.

One moment there had been nothing except the trees; and then, all at once, Denning and Waysmith saw the dog. It rose to its feet, rigid, its coat bristling over its powerful shoulders as they stepped quickly behind sheltering branches. Near the dog, lay Francesca. Her legs and arms were bound; a white cloth was tied around her lips. She lay quite still where she had been thrown, helpless, unseeing, hopeless.

The dog's low growl of warning reached the ears of the man who knelt, his back to Denning and Waysmith, only twenty paces away. He had been so intent, watching the trail from behind his thick screen of small fir trees, that he hadn't seen Denning or Waysmith—just as they didn't see him until he gestured angrily back to the dog.

The gesture meant silence. For the dog's growl died away into an unhappy complaint. Its impulse to search conflicted with its orders to guard the girl, its instinct to give warning was thwarted by its obedience to a gesture. It whimpered miserably.

"Quiet," the man whispered, turning his angry face toward the dog. "I've heard them. It's all right. Quiet!" Again he made the signal—a downbeat of an arm, abrupt, imperative.

For a moment the dog was silenced. Then it whimpered again, uneasily.

Has it seen us? Denning wondered. He stood as unmoving as the tree trunk beside him. Waysmith had clenched his teeth over his bottom lip as if he were trying to silence his breathing. A trickle of perspiration ran down the side of his forehead. Denning's eyes flickered watchfully from the dog to the waiting man, signaling violently again for silence, no longer risking even a whispered command. Were Bohren and his men climbing up through the wood by the green trail, so near him now?

Denning saw the man's arm stop signaling, saw his body go tense. Yes, Bohren must be on that trail within sight. But the man would never have chosen this small patch of trees as a stopping place if it were noticeable from the trail. At this moment, Bohren could be passing by, eyeing the trees carefully on either side, but still keeping quietly to the path where he had found a red shoe to direct him.

Carefully, Denning slid his hand into his pocket for his cigarette lighter. He felt its familiar weight in his hand, then with a quick flip of his wrist he threw it sideways. It hit a tree and laced its way through the branches to the ground. But the crackle of its fall was hidden by the sudden deep growl of the dog. The kneeling man turned in horror, and as he turned the dog barked anxiously, warningly.

From the trail came the sound of a quick command.

The man rose from his knees, came running toward the dog, cursing with a violence that matched his movements. As he ran he pulled a revolver free from its shoulder holster.

Denning saw the dog, facing its master in desperation, its haunches tense, its coat still bristling, its head jerking with each sharp warning from its powerful throat. He saw the man raise his gun, his face distorted with fury. And he sprang forward toward the man and the dog and the helpless girl, even before the quick crack of a bullet ricocheted from tree to tree.

The dog dropped with one last whimper, a brief protest of innocence and pain, a lament that died away into complete and permanent silence. As the revolver turned on Francesca, Denning's stick struck savagely upwards at the man's rigid forearm. That bullet hit the tapering point of the tree overhead, and now Denning had dropped the stick and gripped the man's wrist with both hands. For one bleak moment, he realized the man was heavier, taller, more powerful than he was. But he held on, trying to pull him away from Francesca, trying to avoid the menacing mouth of the revolver.

He heard Waysmith's yell behind him, and—further away —other voices, running footsteps. Waysmith was shouting, "Stand clear, Bill, stand clear!" Then he heard the crack of a bullet, and the man beside him staggered, fell. Denning could pull the revolver free from his hand.

Denning stared down at him. The man was holding his left shoulder, his face grimacing in pain. Denning gulped for breath. Waysmith was mopping the sweat from his brow. And Inspector Bohren, with Gregor, and a policeman, and a man still holding his rifle at the ready, came forward at a run.

"That was pretty good shooting," Waysmith told the man with the rifle. "Thought you'd probably hit my friend here." He looked down at the gun he held in his own hands. "No bullets," he explained, and felt as foolish as he must have looked. But the man gave a friendly smile and clapped him on the back.

Bohren had pulled off the bandage across Francesca's mouth. Waysmith was kneeling beside her. So was Gregor.

Denning heard her say, her voice weak, uncertain, yet happy, "Andrássy is alive. He's alive!"

She's all right, he thought. In every way, she's all right.

Then, he thought, that's all over now. All over. He took a last steadying breath, gave the revolver to the policeman, said, "Thanks a lot" to the man with the rifle, and began to walk slowly away.

Keppler was waiting anxiously on the balcony. Then he ran down the steps as he saw Denning come out of the wood, and hurried to meet him.

"Everything all right?" he asked, looking at the solitary figure with some amazement.

Denning nodded. "The others will soon be here."

"Francesca?"

"Alive."

Keppler took a deep breath. But he asked no more questions. Denning's face was grim.

Then Denning said, "I suppose Broach is standing firmly by James?"

"Yes. But I hadn't hoped for a conversion. Not so quickly. Habits of thought aren't easily discarded."

"He almost rebelled. Then James got hold of him again."

"How?"

"By using the word 'Committee.' Broach reacted as if it were vitriol. The name Francesca now means something evil to him."

"Pavlov's dog," Keppler said and shook his head.

"They shoot dogs, even dogs that are doing their best for their masters." Denning's face had that grim look again. "As soon as their will has been crossed, they shoot."

Keppler raised an eyebrow speculatively. I'll have a talk with Waysmith about all this, he decided. Denning's the type who saves a child from drowning and then walks away without even leaving his name and address.

For a moment, Keppler laid a hand on Denning's shoulder. Then he began talking about the Herz diamonds which Le Brun had found in the safe, hidden behind the radio's cabinet. "The greatest pile of stones you ever saw," he said. "But they are only fit for a locked case in a museum. Tiara, dog-collar and necklace with loops hanging in every direction, rings to weigh down any hand, bracelets broad enough for a Ubangi woman, earrings. . . . There was a thirty-carat yellow diamond which Le Brun said was worth two hundred thousand Swiss francs alone. That's fifty thousand dollars, for one stone. And there were blue, pink, and even green diamonds. Ever heard of that? And some had radiance, and others had definite cast." He shook his head, but more in amazement than in admiration.

"A definite cast of blood," Denning said.

Keppler nodded. Then his eyes caught sight of the slow-moving group which was coming out of the graying wood. "There they are," he said with a relief he no longer disguised.

Denning watched the little procession. Francesca was walking—had she insisted on that? Gregor had one of her arms, Waysmith the other. Her dress was ripped at the hem, her hair had fallen loosely over her shoulders. She was talking too much, and there would be bruises where the ropes had bound her legs and arms, but even if she walked slowly, a little painfully, she could smile. Denning thought, then no one has yet told her that those woods or this house belong to Broach.

Bohren gave a wide wave of his arms when he saw Keppler. "Three!" he called and pointed back to the brewery truck now lumbering slowly out of the woods. A policeman stood on its running board, another policeman was at its wheel, and two more men followed it along the gravel driveway. It was a procession of exhaustion, of exhaustion and triumph.

"I wish," Denning said quietly, "I wish Max could have seen this." He turned and went over to Waysmith's car.

Bohren broke into a run. "So you got a truck, too?" he said as he reached Keppler. "How many men?"

"We're even. Three men: one man waiting with the truck near the Blümlisalp trail; two inside the house."

"Then two are still missing."

"They've gone up the trail to get Andrássy. Gauch and his party will deal with them."

"I've left a couple of our men back in the woods, keeping an eye on a hut that's built there. Strange thing—we found two stretchers inside it. Looks as though they were preparing to receive Andrássy and then carry him and the girl over the hill trail down to the Interlaken road. Our blocking of Falken bridge wouldn't have been worth much to us, then."

"It's paid full dividends. Do you think they'd have rushed this operation, changed its tactics, if they hadn't seen they couldn't leave Falken even by a truck?" Keppler looked at Francesca, walking so surely toward him. "She'd have been in Bern by this time if you hadn't blocked the road. And I give you two guesses where she'd have been taken." He jerked a thumb over his shoulder. "Mr. James is inside. He's claiming diplomatic immunity."

"What?" All the broad smile disappeared from Bohren's face. His eyes narrowed. "We'll see about that," he said grimly, but there was a look of frustration around his lips. He moved quickly into the house.

"Andrássy must be alive," Francesca said excitedly as she halted in front of Keppler. She was laughing now. Laughing, and still talking too much. Next would come tears, Keppler thought: better get her to a doctor as soon as possible. "He's alive," she repeated, "he *must* be. Or they'd never have had two stretchers ready. Would they? He's alive, isn't he?"

"There's a chance, a good chance," Keppler said gravely. He took her arm to lead her to Waysmith's car.

She calmed down a little. She looked around her. "So this is where they brought me," she said in wonder. "And it's such a pretty house."

Then suddenly she looked at the house again, she looked at its view of the village as if to make sure, she looked back at the house. She had recognized it at last.

Gregor said quickly, "Come. We go to the village now. This car?"

Keppler nodded.

Francesca was staring at the house. She shivered. "It's cold," she said.

Gregor put his jacket round her shoulders and helped her into the car. She stumbled. Denning put out an arm and steadied her. She looked at him, hardly seeing him. Then she recognized him. "You came, too?"

That was all she said.

"I'm going back to the village with you," Keppler told Waysmith, pushing Gregor into the car, following him. "We'll leave this house in charge of the experts."

Waysmith looked at him thoughtfully for a moment. Then he started the engine.

20: Waiting for Andrássy

IT WAS TEN O'CLOCK, A CLEAR CALM NIGHT WITH rich dark blue sky and brilliant stars. The evening breeze had fallen. Now the shadowy trees stood motionless, waiting like black sentinels, waiting like the quiet village. People were astir, but they moved with soft footsteps, stood together at lighted doorways, spoke with low voices. Only Falken's rushing stream chattered and clattered with noisy confidence over its rough course of boulders and pebbles.

They're waiting for Heinz Gauch, Denning thought as he walked slowly up the village street and noted the lighted windows. They would have been in bed and asleep, these people, if it weren't for Gauch. What was delaying him? Some trouble that Keppler hadn't thought of? Stop worrying, he told himself, Heinz Gauch could take care of Nikolaides and Mr. James and a couple more besides.

He kept his steady pace, slow as it was. Tired? Yes. He was tired, suddenly old, with a longing for sleep and sleep and sleep. He had taken a bath, changed his clothes; eaten— his first decent meal since when? But he couldn't sleep. Not like Waysmith, who had stretched himself luxuriously after the enormous dinner at the inn, and said, "Now what about bed and some well-earned rest?" But Andy had his Paula. It's good to see someone happy in this twisted world, thought Denning.

He stopped at the window of the tourist shop, still lit, still open. You're on vacation, he told himself, remember? . . . Edelweiss. Carved clocks that popped out voluble cuckoos. Music boxes. Handkerchiefs. Picture postcards. . . .

The woman standing at the door said in surprise, "Of course you may buy a postcard." She led the way into the little shop. "I'm waiting for my husband. He's gone up to the Blümlisalp. I've had his supper ready for the last hour." She nodded toward the back room.

"It smells good."

She tried to smile. "It will be spoiled if he doesn't come soon. Do you think there's danger up on the Blümlisalp trail?"

"Don't worry. The trouble is over now."

"I hope so. It's been bad, hasn't it? No one knows exactly. But we feel—" She broke off, almost in tears. "All these policemen. We never need one policeman. Excuse me." She rushed into the back room, and a pot lid clanged on a stove's hard top.

"I'm taking this one. And have you a stamp I could buy?" Denning asked when she returned.

"We have prettier views on that rack over there," she suggested as she looked at the card he had selected.

"I'm sending it to a friend who collects this kind," he told her reassuringly.

"I suppose some people like them," she said politely.

Denning nodded with approval as he smiled down at the sunset having pink and purple fits. Then he turned the card over and began to write: "The monster was tracked to his inevitable lair. Your description fits—he was a croaking toad. Thank you from everyone at Falken. Yours to the last ice-cream soda, William." He addressed it to Miss Emily White Hyphen Cowper, The Hermitage, Moosegg. He was smiling as he fixed the stamp.

The woman seemed to find his smile encouraging. "Good night," she told him, almost optimistically.

He slipped the card into his pocket as he walked up the street. When Gauch and Andrássy got back, he'd have the card ready to mail. Thanks to Emily should go off at once, he felt. And tomorrow he would spend sleeping. But the smile still lingered on his face, and his step was brisker.

He reached the church. There were several men waiting near there, grouped together at the entrance to the Blümlisalp trail. But he didn't go over to join them. He sat on the wall circling the little graveyard. The trees were a black mass of shadow, the mountain slope above them was formless, lost in the night.

A man left the group, and walked over to Denning. It was Keppler. "Why aren't you having some of Waysmith's well-earned rest?" he asked.

"How about you?"

Keppler laughed softly. "Lonely men don't sleep so readily."

"You enjoy it?"

"Being alone? A case of necessity. My kind of life is too hard for most women to share. Perhaps some day I'll retire. Some day I'll go back to schoolteaching. And then, a house of my own, a garden, a stream to fish."

"You were a schoolteacher?"

"With a passion for chess."

"I can believe that."

"I heard you were offered a job today."

For a moment, Denning couldn't follow. "Oh yes," he said, remembering. "Nikolaides. I didn't take it as a compliment."

"I should. He's completely amoral. All he is interested in is brain power."

"Thank you," Denning said dryly. "I guess he could use some new talent in his firm."

"What are you going to do, anyway?"

"I think I'll start aiming toward that house of my own."

"I was afraid so. Too bad. And yet—" Keppler sighed gently. *"Wer jetzt kein Haus hat, baut sich nimmermehr."*

There was a silence. Denning was remembering the rest of the poem. Last night—was it only last night?—he had read it in Keppler's room. Waiting for Max's message.

The lonely man will keep his loneliness,
Will lie awake, will read, will write long letters,
Will wander to and fro under the trees
Restlessly, while the leaves run from the wind.

"Yes," he said at last, "that's just about it."

"I'll give you another quotation to balance it," Keppler said. "Do you know Juvenal?"

"Vaguely. I had only three years of Latin. Above my standard, I'm afraid."

"Then I'll translate for you. Let me see, now." Keppler paused. He began in his quiet voice:

Pray for a brave heart, which does not fear death,
which places a long life last among the gifts
of nature, which has the power to endure any trials,
rejects anger, discards desire. . . .
If we have common sense, Chance, you are not divine:
it is we who make you a goddess, yes, and place you in heaven.

This time the silence was long. He has translated his own epitaph, Denning thought. His own and Meyer's too. He found he could not speak.

Keppler rose from the wall. "Did you hear that?" he asked excitedly. Denning pulled himself back into the scene that stirred suddenly into life around him. There was a movement from the shadowy mass of waiting men, as the call came circling down through the darkness.

"Give them one back," Keppler shouted. "Tell them all is well here. Tell them to come in." Then he put a hand on Denning's shoulder. "I'm going up to meet them—they're near enough now. Coming?"

"I doubt if I can make it," Denning admitted. But he stood up.

"Then better wait here. Dark trails aren't comfortable places. Sit down, man. I never did like conscious heroes."

Denning half-smiled. "To tell the truth, I'm not much of any kind of hero. I'm all worn out through being scared stiff for a couple of days." And he sat down again.

"I'll see you some time," said Keppler. "I'll come and visit you in that house of yours."

"One more of my guesses—you won't be called Keppler." Keppler laughed softly. He gave a firm handshake. He moved away.

Was that really a good-by? Denning wondered. I suppose it was, he thought in amazement. Where was Keppler going now, after he found Andrássy? Back to Bern? Or Geneva? And then, another job?

The group of men, Keppler among them and Gregor, too,

had lit torches and lanterns. Slowly the dancing lights flickered away from the church, disappearing, reappearing, climbing slowly up through the woods.

"I thought it was you," Francesca's voice said behind him. "What on earth are you doing here?"

"I had to come. Like you." She drew her heavy coat more closely around her throat.

"But you were supposed to be—"

"I know. They put me to bed. They gave me pills to make me sleep. But I spat them out when Paula wasn't looking."

"Look—I don't think you should be—"

"Of course, I should. I'm all right. They found nothing wrong with me. The doctor was very disappointed. And Mr. Keppler was cross because I didn't cry. I just kept asking questions. You see, there was so much I didn't know."

"You know enough."

"No. Or I wouldn't have treated you as I did. I've come to say I'm sorry."

"For what?"

"For not trusting you."

"Me?"

"You see, I didn't trust your friend. I saw him last night at the Café Henzi. The woman who talked to him there—"

"Eva?"

"She was an enemy."

"So Max could have been your enemy?"

"He could have been." She sensed his amazement and annoyance. "I'm sorry," she said again.

He looked at her face, now. "You're a strange girl, Francesca."

"Yes. Too strange. Too uncomfortable for most people."

The bitter sadness in her voice startled him. "But you aren't alone. You have Gregor."

She smiled. "Yes," she said softly, "I have Gregor."

"And Paula and all your other friends."

"Paula is only really at home with me when we start remembering schooldays together, and make jokes, and—" Her voice trailed away. "The fault is in me," she said. "I know that, now. I hurt my friends. I smile for those who would hurt me. I—" She began to cry. She turned her face aside from him. And as she spoke she wiped away her tears with the back of her hand, and as she wiped them away they fell again. Her voice became incoherent, telling cruel things against herself. She giggled to make herself clear. She broke into sobs.

"Look—" he said gently, catching her shoulders, "we've all our bad moments, but you've no need to feel as unhappy as this."

She bent her head to hide her face. The tears wouldn't stop.

"Let them flow," he said. "Just to please Keppler."

She gave a half-choking laugh.

They stood there, waiting for Andrássy. She didn't even notice that his arm was around her. And as for Denning—he only wondered why she, the cold and self-sufficient Francesca, should have broken down before him.

"Why did you say all these things to me?" he asked at last.

"Because you dislike me, because—"

"Of all reasons—" he began.

"Because you see me clearly. Gregor would never have listened to me. And then," she was able to smile now, "I had such a sense of guilt about you, I suppose. You see, I know now what you have done." ·

"I don't," he said abruptly. He became embarrassed. He looked at the fireflies coming down through the woods. Would the men never arrive?

"I told you I asked Mr. Keppler a lot of questions," Francesca said. "Andy had to answer me too." She thought, I wouldn't be standing here now, if it weren't for this man. "I couldn't give any honest meaning to my thanks until I had said, first of all, I was sorry."

"Which meant tearing yourself to pieces?" He tried to laugh.

"I always had too much pride," she said. She suddenly started forward, then waited for him with outstretched hand. "There they come—see?"

As they began to hurry toward the edge of the woods, where the first men had stepped onto the roadway, he said, "You're wrong about some things, though."

She looked at him.

"I don't dislike you," he said.

She still looked at him. "We can be friends?"

"Why not?"

She said, "There's Andrássy—but they're carrying him on a stretcher. Oh, Bill!—" Hand in hand, they began to run.

Keppler had gone. He had vanished. Denning kept searching for him among the group that still lingered in front of the church or walked slowly to their houses, talking over the strange happenings on the Blümlisalp. But Keppler must have slipped away as soon as the two doctors from the neighboring Schlossfalken-Bad had taken charge of Andrássy.

"Will he live?" Francesca asked.

Gregor said, "He is among friends. He will live. Surely." Then he looked severely at Francesca. "Why are you here?"

"That's right, Gregor," said Denning. "You tell her to get right back into bed and sleep until Sunday."

"Perhaps I shall." Francesca held out her hand. "Good night, Bill. Thank you." Then she hesitated. "When are you leaving?"

"I don't know."

"Why don't you stay here for a few days? Falken can be a happy village."

"Ah—" Gregor said quickly, "you like it now?"

She smiled a little. "Yes, Gregor. I know my friends." She looked at Denning. She half-raised her arm, shyly, to signal good night. Or perhaps she thought it was good-by. Then she turned and walked away with Gregor.

"Well," Heinz Gauch said, "that is over." With some pleasure, he watched the two men he had brought down under armed guard from the Blümlisalp trail, now being transferred to the custody of Inspector Bohren and three policemen.

"That is over," Denning said.

"We surprised them."

"We certainly did."

"Now home—for some food, some talk, and much sleep. Good?"

"Nothing better. I'll walk part way with you."

They fell into step, Heinz Gauch's heavy boots scraping against the rough stones.

"You had a bad time?" Denning asked.

"So so. The two men were ugly to deal with. But we surprised them." Gauch paused. "We were angry then. We saw what they had done to poor Schmid before they left him up there, coiled with ropes, strapped down, in a cold empty hut; you wouldn't treat a dog that way."

Denning looked at him. Poor Schmid. . . . Heinz Gauch and his friends had gone out to help a waiter called Schmid.

"This is my house," Gauch said, halting suddenly. "Come in and eat."

"Not tonight. Some other time."

"You're staying here for a bit?"

"Yes."

"I'll take you up to the Blümlisalp." Gauch put out his broad hand. "Good night," he said. And then to a man passing down the street, "Good night, Peter. We surprised them, didn't we?"

"Good night," said Peter. "That we did."

"Good night," said someone else, laughing too. "Good night."

Denning heard the friendly echoes of good nights follow him along the street. He stopped at the post office and slipped the postcard for Emily through the slot in the door. For a moment he looked back at the church, glimmering white against dark shadows. The houses were silent now, lights were lessening, doors were closing, the heavy footsteps had left the street, the echoes of voices had died away.

I should feel lonely, he thought.

But he wasn't. It had been a long time since he had felt such peace as this.